Margaret Oliphant

Memoir of the Life of Laurence Oliphant

and of Alice Oliphant, his wife

Margaret Oliphant

Memoir of the Life of Laurence Oliphant
and of Alice Oliphant, his wife

ISBN/EAN: 9783337334116

Printed in Europe, USA, Canada, Australia, Japan

Cover: Foto ©Andreas Hilbeck / pixelio.de

More available books at **www.hansebooks.com**

MEMOIR

OF THE

LIFE OF LAURENCE OLIPHANT

AND OF

ALICE OLIPHANT, HIS WIFE

BY

MARGARET OLIPHANT W. OLIPHANT

AUTHOR OF 'LIFE OF EDWARD IRVING,' 'LIFE OF
PRINCIPAL TULLOCH,' ETC.

NEW EDITION

WILLIAM BLACKWOOD AND SONS
EDINBURGH AND LONDON
MDCCCXCII

PREFACE TO THE NEW EDITION.

IT has been suggested that the publication of this new edition of the Memoirs of Laurence and Alice Oliphant would be a fitting opportunity to take some notice of the much discussion and the many revelations and explanations made on the subject of Mr Thomas Lake Harris since the first edition was published. Up to that time the world in general knew very little of the prophet of Brocton, now the autocrat, teacher, and proprietor of Fountain Grove, Santa Rosa, California, and all the souls appertaining thereto. I have been accused of making no attempt to obtain information about him, and of neglecting opportunities thrown in my way. This, however, is so completely a mistake, that my efforts to obtain information concerning the antecedents and personality of a man whose influence upon the subjects of my work was so remarkable, were many, but were mere gropings in the dark until the publication of that work attracted general attention and lighted up lanterns everywhere. I am not sure, after all, that this new flood of information has thrown very much light on the subject; for to know that Mr Harris was born

in England, instead of being a native American, and that
for a period he was a well-known preacher in New York,
gives very little aid in solving the problem of his extraordinary power and tyranny. I have fully stated my
impressions of his evident great personal ability, and I do
not know that I have ever asserted him to be an impostor,
which is a character in which I have only a very faint
belief. The explanation of such a man is beyond my
power; but Mr Harris is not even a unique specimen of
the class. Particulars have been sent to me since the
publication of the book, of the histories of at least two
others professing to possess the same incomprehensible
power, with results which would be equally remarkable if
it had happened to them to secure any followers belonging
to the class of the immortals. People who were, unlike
Laurence Oliphant, unknown to and unlikely to arrest
the attention of the world, have gone unnoticed through a
similar martyrdom to his, at the hands of one spiritual
tyrant or another, and in England as well as America. It
is a chapter in the history of religious delusion which
would afford many extraordinary revelations, should any
one undertake the task of making it known.

Since this book was first published, the reign of Mr
Harris has been expounded and interpreted on all sides:
some of these explanations have come from his remaining disciples, whose argument is simply that all things
he has done are right, that all his motives are pure, that
Laurence Oliphant having been in the later part of his
life rebellious to the Master's authority, was righteously,
he and his wife, swept out of his path, and given over
to destruction, — arguments to which, as I conceive it,

there is no answer, since those who can put them forth
are beyond the limits of reason, as ordinarily understood;—and some from other quarters adding detail upon
detail to the story of his spiritual despotism. My table is
covered with American papers in which these details have
been worked into sensational articles, thrilling with descriptions of the luxurious seclusion of Fountain Grove,
where a man who cannot err, and will never die, lives surrounded with every luxury, while his dependants, who have
furnished all his revenues, live and toil in a subdued
humility, working his vineyards, accumulating wealth
which is not for them, and giving up heart and soul to his
service.   It is not for me to attempt to penetrate that
retirement.   Mr Harris himself has recently spoken from
it, announcing his discovery, after many researches, of the
method by which eternal youth and power is attained, and
by which he, a man of seventy, has been re-endowed with
all the forces of his prime, and enabled to enter afresh,
with increased strength, upon the Propaganda which for
many years he would seem to have practically given up.
He does not deny, he allows with calmness, that the Oliphants having rebelled against him, he warned them of
the fatal consequences that must follow, and if he did not
absolutely execute his own vengeance, permitted it, by the
unseen powers, to be carried out.   That Mr Harris should
say, and permit his champions to say, such things as these,
carries the question far beyond anything to which I can
reply.   The elixir of life, the command of death, the right
of one individual to rule for time and eternity the destinies
of others—these are the questions of a fairy tale, not of
human argument.   My indictment was far more modest

than his own assertion. I did not mention in my record of Laurence Oliphant's concluding years the letter in which Harris's last warning and sentence were conveyed, desiring myself, as I had not seen it, to believe that the report of it might have been exaggerated. Mr Harris himself, however, not only admits but asserts that he gave that warning, uttered the threat, and that his verdict—a sentence of death—was righteously executed. The statement seems sufficient for all purposes. If it is true, the Magician in California is the most wonderful of human beings: but at all events he thus meets every charge brought against him boldly, by allowing it, on the ground of his own unique and irresistible power.

February 15, 1892.

PREFACE TO THE FIRST EDITION.

I HAVE, in concluding this book, to thank almost all the persons most closely connected with Laurence Oliphant for their kind confidence in intrusting me with the numerous letters which reveal his character so much more clearly than anything else can,—especially those which show the formation of that character, addressed to his mother in the early part of his life, which I owe to the courtesy of Mrs Rosamond Oliphant, now Mrs James Murray Templeton : a courtesy all the more marked that I believe she herself intended, or still intends, to make some record, though probably from a different point of view, of her late husband's life. I have also to render my best thanks to Mrs Wynne Finch, the mother of the late Mrs Laurence Oliphant; to Mrs Waller, her sister, and to Hamon Le Strange, Esq., her brother, for much most interesting information and a number of important letters. Other letters have come to me through Mrs Wynne Finch and other channels—from Lady Guendolen Ramsden, the Hon. F. Leveson Gower, Major Goldsmid, and others, to whom my best thanks are also due. I have also most grateful thanks to give to Mr and Mrs J. D. Walker, formerly of San Rafael, California, for an account of many incidents of great value in the record of the two lives; to Mrs Hankin, of Malvern, for the use of her notes of intercourse, both by letter and personally; to Arthur Oliphant, Esq.; and to Lady Grant Duff, in whose house Mr Oliphant died.

I have one other acknowledgment to make, which in happier circumstances would have been said only to the private ear of him to whom it is due. A great part of the letters quoted here were selected, arranged, and connected for me by my dear son, Cyril Francis Oliphant, whom it pleased God to take to Himself just as the book was ended, the last work he did on earth being included in these pages. It can never bear to me any other memorial and inscription than his beloved name.

December 8, 1890.

CONTENTS.

CHAPTER I.

HIS PARENTAGE AND CHILDHOOD.

CHAPTER II.

BEGINNING LIFE.

CHAPTER III.

THE BAR—THE EXPEDITION TO RUSSIA.

CHAPTER IV.

AMERICA AND CANADA.

CHAPTER V.

THE CRIMEA.

CHAPTER VI.

THE MISSION TO CHINA.

CHAPTER VII.

POLITICAL ADVENTURE—SOCIAL LIFE.

CHAPTER VIII.

THE NEW LIFE.

CHAPTER XII.

THE POSTSCRIPT OF LIFE.

ILLUSTRATIONS.

MEMOIR

OF THE

LIFE OF LAURENCE OLIPHANT.

CHAPTER I.

HIS PARENTAGE AND CHILDHOOD.

THE subject of this memoir, Laurence Oliphant, was a man
so unique in himself, so entirely individual and distinct in
his generation, that it is more than ordinarily unnecessary
to distinguish him by the mild and modest honours of the
family of Scotch country gentlemen from which he sprang.
I may be permitted, however, the natural weakness of some
brief notice of the race of which he has proved one of the
most distinguished members, and to which I also belong,
both by birth on the mother's side and by marriage. The
fond superstition of ancient race, to which the Scot in all
his developments is prone, may be accepted as an excuse
for this unfortunately somewhat vague and not very brilliant passage of history. We have not, I fear, been very
remarkable as a race. After the first somewhat misty
heroes of the past, the house appears only in the occasional mention of a name here and there,—when a Lord
Oliphant witnessed a royal charter, or lent his silent support to a protest or revolt of the Scots nobility of his time.
There is a page in a manuscript of the seventeenth century,
preserved in the Heralds' College, which sums up their dis-

A

positions in words very quaint and graphic, and very satisfactory in the point of view of the domestic virtues, but
not, perhaps, indicative of much greatness. "The Lord
Oliphant.—This baron," says that anonymous authority,
"is not of great renown, but yet he hath good landes and
profitable; a house very loyal to the Kings of Scotland;
accounted no orators in theyr wordes nor yet foolish in
theyr deedes. They do not surmount in theyr alliances,
but are content with theyr worshipful neighbours." "As
for the antiquity of the family and sirname," says Nisbet
in his 'System of Heraldry,' in the chapter which treats
of "Celestial Figures; the Sun, Moon, and Stars," to
which the bearings of the family belong, "there was an
eminent baron of that name who accompanied King
David I. to the siege of Winchester in England in the
year 1142, named David de Oliphard; and the same man
or another of that name is to be found frequently a witness to that king's charters; and particularly (says Mr
Crawfurd, in his 'Peerage') in that to the Priory of Cold-
ingham, whereto his seal is appended, which has thereupon three crescents, which clearly prove him to be the
ancestor of the noble family of Oliphant, who still bear
the same figures in their ensign armorial."
    In the Scottish War of Independence, Sir William Oli-
phant of Aberdalgy, in Forfarshire, the acknowledged head
of the house, held Stirling Castle against the English; but
was not, I fear, quite free of the intrigues of the time, and
those occasional changes of side which even the great
Bruce himself, before he settled into his noble career, was
sometimes betrayed into. His son was, however, rewarded
for their exertions in the cause of their country by the
hand of Elizabeth Bruce, the king's daughter, who was not
indeed a legitimate princess—but the distinction counted
for little in those days. A generation or two later, the
heir of the house acquired some portion of the estate of
Kellie in Fifeshire, upon which he settled his second son,
Walter Oliphant, my own ancestor, and the founder, it is
believed, of the picturesque old house called Kellie Castle,
in the rural parish of Carnbee, still standing in perfect
repair, and most admirably restored by its late inmate,

Professor Lorimer of Edinburgh. The barony was conferred afterwards upon the head of the house in 1467. It
was renewed on failure of the direct male line by Charles I.
in 1657, and became extinct in 1751. In the meantime
the family threw off many branches, one of the latest of
which was that of Condie, which bears the three crescents,
"within a bordure counter compony gules and argent,"
and changed the original crest of a Unicorn's head to that
of "a Falcon volant," and the old thrifty motto *A Tout
pourvoir*, which, I am proud to say, was retained by the
Kellie branch, into the newer fashion of a Latin proverb,
Altiora Peto, of which, the reader will remember, the most
brilliant descendant of the house of Condie made in after
days a whimsical use.

I am grieved to say that none of the many branches of
the house have done anything very remarkable in life.
The Jacobite Lairds of Gask have supplied an interesting
volume to Scots family history by means of their present
representative, Mr Kington Oliphant, whose own achieve-
ments in philology and cognate subjects are not small;
and Caroline Oliphant, afterwards Lady Nairne, of the
same family, was one of the band of women-poets, full of
the native music and delightful natural sentiment of their
country, who have left so pleasant and so bright a tradition
behind them. Perhaps no work of genius ever gained a
more universal or delightful fame for its author than the
song, "The Land o' the Leal," written by this accomplished
woman, has done. Otherwise the record of the name is
like the shield of Sir Torr—void of achievement. The
house of Condie was no exception to this law: country
gentlemen, Scots lawyers, a soldier brother now and then,
have maintained the worthy tradition of one of those plain
Scotch families, in whose absence of distinction so much
modest service to their country is implied. Anthony
Oliphant, a second son of the house, went farther afield
than to the Parliament House of Edinburgh, and found his
fortune in the colonies, where he held various dignified
posts. Sixty years ago he was Attorney-General at the
Cape, where he married Miss Maria Campbell, the daughter
of Colonel Campbell of the 72d Highlanders, and his wife,

a member of the large and important family of Cloete; and there, at Cape Town, in the year 1829, Laurence was born. He was the only child of a pair both of whom were notable in their way: she, full of the vivacity and character which descended to her son; he also a man of much individual power and originality, an excellent lawyer and trusted official. Both were deeply stamped with the form of religious feeling which was most general among pious minds at the time. There is no scorn of religion implied in the fact that it too has its fashions, which shape in successive waves the generations as they go. This couple were evangelical in their sentiments, after the strictest fashion of that devout and much-abused form of faith. The constant self-examination, the minute and scrupulous record of every little backsliding, the horror of those gaieties and seductions of the world (much modified, in fact, by that considerable share in them which their position made necessary), which were but too agreeable to the social instincts of both, is characteristically evident in a letter which Sir Anthony, then Chief-Justice of Ceylon, addressed to his little son Laurence, ten years old, at that time in England with his mother, and whose tender mind the parents were so anxious to train into the ways of godliness. The glimpse this letter gives of the natural man, a little warm of temper, a little rash in ejaculation, underneath the cloak of the conscientious Christian, who felt that for every idle word he would be called to judgment, is, if I may dare to say it, amusing as well as attractive, though the intention of the writer is far removed from any such thought. It is addressed to his dear little boy, who had been very ill, and had just recovered. and written his first letter, "very well written and spelt," to his papa. This loving and tender papa had been transferred from the Cape to Ceylon in the absence of his wife and child in England, and describes to his little son his extreme loneliness in arriving at his new post.

"COLOMBO, *May* 31, 1839.

"After mamma and you went away from the Cape to England for mamma's health, mamma asked the

great people in England to remove me from being
Attorney-General at the Cape, and to make me Chief-
Justice at Ceylon, and they consented, and I went to
Ceylon after mamma had been a year away; and when
I arrived at Ceylon I heard that my son had been almost
dead, and that mamma was so ill that it was not likely
she would ever come out to me, and I became very
sorry: and I did not see anybody that I have ever
known before.   There was no John Bell, nor Lady
Catherine, nor General Napier, nor Cecilia, nor John-
stone, nor Janet, nor the Butlers, nor any other body
to comfort me or speak about mamma with, nor anybody
except Mr Selby and George that cared about me.   I
felt very low-spirited and lonely, and like a tree standing
by itself that has lost all its leaves, and I looked about
for somebody that I thought would not think it tiresome
to hear about mamma and you, and as I did not know
anybody, or what sort of dispositions they had, I was
obliged to guess by their faces.   I saw an officer, who
was tall and thin like Robert Baillie of the 72d, and
I thought that he looked of an affectionate mild disposition, like dear Jimmy Erskine, and Cousin Day,
and Carolus Graham, who are so fond of us, and that
he would let me speak to him about my wife and child
without thinking it tiresome, and that he would let
me love him and be kind to him like Jimmy and the
other cousins, although he was no relation.   So one
day I took him a drive into the country with me.   I
had been so long living by myself without having prayers
every morning at breakfast-time and on Sunday evenings,
that I had fallen away a great deal from the love
and fear of God, and God had left me to myself in
a great measure, because I had neglected His Word
and become careless.   But God had not turned away
His face altogether, but only hid it, neither had He
forgotten or forsaken me, because you know it is written,
'A woman may forget her sucking child, yet will I
not forget thee, saith the Lord'; and also, 'I will never
leave thee nor forsake thee.'   So I had become careless
in my speech, and used bad words thoughtlessly, that I

had got into the habit of using when I was a young man and frequented gay company, and I spoke foolish things for want of something to say."

This picture, drawn by his own hand, of so important a member of society in the busy and prosperous colony, the chief law officer of the Crown, casting his eyes about with a remnant of the shyness of his Scotch youth, to see what face among the new society around looked kind enough to be made a confidant of, and who there was who would listen to his anxious talk about his wife and child without finding it tiresome, is most engaging and attractive. All did not go well, however, in this first drive. One wonders what the Chief-Justice said, with that grave young officer sitting by,—whether he launched too vigorous an epithet at an unwilling horse, or held in a too impetuous one with an objurgation, and what were the foolish things to which he gave utterance, before he ventured to open his heart as he desired, about his pretty young wife, who was far away, and little Laurence, who was the light of their eyes. The Officer — one feels it necessary to put his name with a capital, as if he had been in 'Sandford and Merton'—made no remark upon his eminent companion's freedom of speech; but when the Chief-Justice asked him to dinner some time later, declined, on the score that "by mixing in society I am acting inconsistently with my religious principles." This excuse awoke the slumbering conscience of Sir Anthony, who wrote again to the young soldier, asking if it was anything in him, in his conduct or conversation, which had occasioned the refusal, or if it was merely on general principles— in which latter case he hoped that they might still meet, as people of similar minds, in their evening rides or drives, and that if the absent wife was ever able to join him, she as well as he might have the advantage of the pious youth's society. This elicited a letter full of feeling from the young soldier, and a warm friendship was formed.

The whole narrative breathes of a time gone by. I

fear we should be disposed to think the Officer sancti-
monious and a religious prig in these changed days. But
the genuine humility and moral sensitiveness of the
middle-aged lawyer, judge and autocrat in his own sphere,
is exceedingly touching and beautiful. These are not
exactly the qualities we look for in a Chief-Justice,
any more than the shy outlook for a sympathetic face.
He was so much impressed by the incident altogether
that he reported it thus at great length to his child, in
the hope that when his Lowry was as big as the Officer in
question "he will do exactly as he did." "When I am
better acquainted with him I shall ask him, that in case
I should die soon, and he is ever near my son, to go to
him, and ask him if he ever associates with people from
whom he can learn anything bad, and to ask him to show
him this letter, and if he acts upon it. And my Lowry
must keep this letter which I now write, and read it
always on his birthday; and if he is able to draw all the
morals from it that it contains, and to act as Mr B. did,
if he never meets Mr B. on earth, he will be happy with
him in heaven. And I write this for my son's welfare,
and that mamma may know that there is somebody here
who will love and take care of papa when she is far
away." The Chief-Justice of Ceylon is a little confused
in style, though that arose no doubt from writing down to
his correspondent of ten; and his appearance here is not
what we should expect from his imposing position and
authority: but how delightful is the glimpse of him thus
afforded! Chief-justices, after all, are but men; they
yearn for wife and child like the humblest individual,
and are subject to the influence of human approbation or
disapproval. But few, very few, are those who would
admit or yield to the tacit reproof of a stranger with such
a tender conscience and so much humility. I fear his son
would have been disposed to laugh at the Officer and his
grave young face.

The mother and child, thus so far separated from the
tender and longing head of the house, spent some part of
their time coming and going at Condie, the ancestral home
—"sweet Condie," as little Lowry called it—the old

Scotch mansion-house of which he spoke in after and
graver years. There is a pretty anecdote of his childhood
here, which seems to point at even an earlier age than that
mature ten years which he possessed when his father wrote
the letter above quoted. Certain ladies of the neighbourhood, coming to call upon the laird's sister-in-law, young
Mrs Anthony from the Cape, were introduced into the
drawing-room, where there seemed to be nobody, but where
the small boy was playing with his box of bricks in a
corner. Perhaps the visitors did not perceive him; perhaps
thought him too young to note what they were saying,
which was an imprudent confidence. At all events, they
began to talk of the lady they were waiting to see—what
a pretty young woman she was, and what a pity the child
should be so plain. At this point they were startled by
the sudden uplifting of a small voice from the corner.
"Ah," said the boy, moved, yet philosophically, impartially,
by the criticism upon himself, "but I have very expressive eyes." The sense of humour, which never deserted
him, must thus have shown itself at a very early period.

There is not very much appearance of it, however, in
the schoolboy letters which he wrote from Mr Parr's school
at Durnford Manor, near Salisbury, where he began his
education. They are amusing sometimes, as every child's
letters are, with their jumble of subjects and transparent
innocent self-absorption; but it is happily evident that
little Lowry, though something of a hothouse plant,
brought up at his mother's feet, had none of the precocious development common to children accustomed to the
constant society of their elders. The little letters are
often accompanied by a note from the lady of the house,
apologetic of poor Lowry's carelessness, or his handwriting,
or the difficulty there was in getting him to write. On
one occasion he loses his mother's letter before he has
finished reading it, and begs her in the next to put down
"some of the most importinate facts" of the lost epistle.
His style certainly lacks clearness. "All together," he
says, "I am third in my class. Græme, Alfred Montague,
a queer little beggar, who sends his complemences to you,
but a nice little chap upon the whole, he was sitting next

and rubbed it all out, till Mr Waring told him to go away."
On another occasion he begs his dear mamma to let him
send his letter on Tuesday, because it is more convenient,
and because Alfred Montague sends his on Tuesday. He
counts the weeks till the holidays, yet thinks on the whole
the time passes very quickly. "We generally have what
we call larks at night," says the candid little boy. "There
are two boys that are very passionate, and we like, of
course, to tease them. We shut them up in the fives-
court, and they got in such what the boys call a wax,
which means a rage." "Do excuse my both bad writing,
and am not inclined for writing," he adds. In another
Lowry falls a little into the vein of religious retrospection
in which he has been trained. "You asked me to speak
to you as I used to do," he says; "I should tell you some
more of my besetting sins. One of them is my not saying
my prayers as I ought, hurrying over them to get up in
the morning because I am late, and at night because it is
cold; another is my hiding what I do naughty and keeping it from Mr Parr's eyes, not thinking the eye of God
is upon me, a greater eye than man's; and another my
cribing things from other boys, which is another word for
stealing—not exactly stealing, but leads to it." After
this calm discrimination of morals, he goes on to other
matters. "I am such a horrid sumer" (sum-er—*i.e*, arith-
metician), he says, with felicitous vexation; "it is that
that gets me down in my class so much. I was perfectly
beaten last week, for they brought me down from top to
bottom." There are many people who will feel the deepest sympathy with Lowry in his tribulations as a "horrid
sumer." "Excuse the blots," he adds; " but I put it in my
shelf, and when I came to get it to finish it, and it was out
on the table—but I must now finish, for I am impatient."
It cannot be said that the writing is much to Lowry's
credit, and the anxious excuses of his master's wife are
not without justification. But it is very touching to find
these little letters so carefully preserved after fifty long
years, so living in their childish freedom and confusion of
over-active thought. The little fellow was not clever, so
far as appeared; but he was the light of his mother's eyes,

and already a favourite everywhere,—the brightest restless child, always doing, forming already his succinct little
opinions upon things and men.

In 1841, Lady Oliphant—who during this interval had
been spending her time partly in England, partly in Scotland: at the paternal house of Condie, which was paradise
to Lowry in the holidays; at Wimbledon, in the house of
Major Oliphant,[1] another brother of her husband, where
the boy found comrades and companions of an age similar
to his own; and for a considerable period in Edinburgh—
joined Sir Anthony in Ceylon. But it soon became apparent that to be separated thus from her only child was too
great a strain upon the happiness and health of the tender
mother; and she had not been long settled in the island
before imperative orders were sent home for the return of
Lowry, accompanied by a tutor who could carry on his
education. "Send out the kid at once" was, I have
been told, the telegraphic summons; but this must be a
fond invention of later days, for there was then no telegraph, nor was Sir Anthony at all likely to use such an
expression. This decision was simplified by the fact that
there were two boys, the sons of Mr Moydart, a neighbour
at Colombo, of an age to share his lessons, and afford boyish company for the Chief-Justice's only child. Laurence,
who had followed his schoolmaster, Mr Parr, to Preston,
in Lancashire, where that gentleman had accepted a living,
was summoned from school in all haste, and the much-
trusted Uncle James at Wimbledon was charged with the
choice of the tutor. The gentleman selected by Major
Oliphant was Mr Gepp, now vicar of Higher Easton, near
Chelmsford, a very young man just from Oxford, to whom,
as to his pupil, the long journey overland, then a new
route, and captivating to the imagination, was a great
frolic and delight.

By this time Lowry had developed out of the early stage
of childhood into an active and lively boy, eager for new
experiences, and all the novelty and movement that were
to be had. One bustling delightful visit he had at Condie

---

[1] Afterwards Lieutenant-Colonel James Oliphant, for many years a
director of the East India Company, and chairman of that body in 1854.

to celebrate the marriage of his uncle, where there were
tenants' dinners and outdoor dances, at which Lowry
"kissed the lassies" with whom he danced, in delightful
emulation of another young and gay uncle. He was between twelve and thirteen, with all his faculties awake,
and his whole being agog for novelty and incident, when
he set out to join his parents in the late winter of 1841.
He has himself given an account of this, the first great
journey which he made independently, the first he could
fully recollect. It is astonishing to note the enormous
difference between the means of travelling then and now,
although the modern age of rapid movement had set in,
and the English world was already exceedingly proud of
itself for its first steps towards speed and ease in that long
journey, the most important and momentous of all to
Englishmen. From Boulogne, "where we arrived in a
steamer direct from London Bridge"—to Marseilles occupied eight days and five nights of incessant diligence travel,
varied by the incident of sticking in the snow at Chalons,
from which they had to be dug out. The mail-train rattles
across the Continent from Calais to Brindisi now in three
days. Yet I suspect Laurence and his companion had the
best of it. Packed up in the *banquette* of the old-fashioned
diligence, they saw and enjoyed everything,—the new un-
familiar landscape, the quaint villages, the old towns, the
winterly brightness of France, newer and more original to
them than anything is now to eyes so accustomed to dis-
count every novelty as ours are. And the jolting, dirt,
and wretchedness of the most highly organised *train de
luxe*, with its sleeping-carriages and dining-saloons, one
more odious than the other, yet the last word of luxurious
organisation and supposed comfort in travelling—are a
poor exchange for the more leisurely progress, which at
least permitted a tranquil meal now and then, and unfolded
the country through which he passed, and many amusing
and agreeable incidents to the traveller.

"Adventures," somebody says, "come to the adventurous," and this first voyage of the boy who had so many
before him was signalised by a visit, made necessary by an
accident, to Mocha, a place very little visited either then

or now by the Giaour, and where the Shereef was exceedingly civil to the English travellers—a civility, I believe,
explained by the fact that an English gunboat lay not far
off, though the strangers were unaware of this strong inducement to politeness on the part of their entertainers.
The voyage altogether, with the repeated breakdowns of
the ship and pauses for repairs (there was then no P. & O.),
lasted about three months. We are not told to what pitch
of despairing anxiety the parents in Ceylon had been driven
by all this delay. But at last it came to an end, and Lowry
settled down in the new brilliant Eastern world, where
everything was a wonder, to his lessons with Mr Gepp and
the Moydart boys, and to that close companionship with
his mother which occupied so large a portion of his life.
She was still a young woman—" there were but eighteen
years between us," he used to say; and though Lady Oliphant loved to be obeyed, yet she had from his infancy
placed the boy—the "Darling," as his father invariably
calls him, with a little affectionate mockery—in a position
of influence and equality not perhaps very safe for a child,
but always delightful between these two; for the quick-
witted and sharp-sighted boy had always a chivalrous
tenderness for his mother, even when, as happened sometimes, he found it necessary to keep her in her proper place.
I have been told an amusing little illustration of this in
an incident that happened one morning when, the tutor's
scheme of work appearing unsatisfactory to Lady Oliphant,
she came into the schoolroom to announce her desire that
it should be altered. To do this before the open-eyed and
all-observant boys was; perhaps, not very judicious, and
the young preceptor was wounded and vexed. There was
probably a sirocco, or its equivalent, blowing—that universal excuse for every fault of temper in warm latitudes
—and a quarrel was imminent, when Lowry rose from his
books and came to the rescue. "Mamma, this is not the
right place for you," said the heaven-born *diplomat*, offering her his arm, with the fine manners which no doubt she
had been at such pains to teach him, and leading her away
—no doubt half amused, half pleased, although half angry,
with the social skill of the boy.

An education thus conducted, and subject to all the social interruptions of the lively colonial life, where visitors were continually coming and going, and the house of the Chief-Justice a centre of entertainment and pleasant friendliness, must have had its drawbacks. But except for the short period at Salisbury and Preston when he was a little boy, Laurence never was subjected to educational discipline of a severe kind. He was one of the pupils of Life, educated mainly by what his keen eyes saw and his quick ears heard, and his clear understanding and lively wit picked up, amid human intercourse of all kinds. He was in no way the creation of school or college. When, as happens now and then, an education so desultory, so little consecutive or steady as his, produces a brilliant man or woman, we are apt to think that the accidental system must be on the whole the best, and education a delusion, like so many other cherished things; but the conclusion is a rash one, and it is perhaps safest in this, as in so many other directions, to follow the beaten way. I do not think he himself ever regretted it, and he had little or none of the traditionary respect for university training which is so general. He had a most cheerful delightful life, between the gay little capital Colombo—where he knew everybody, and saw everything that occurred, and took his share in entertaining great officials, governors and suchlike, on their way to and from India, as well as less important crowds, civil and military—and that home of health, Newera Ellia, among the hills, which the Oliphants were among the first to make popular. In after days a continual flight of letters, daily recording everything that happened, went up to that green and wholesome spot from the young man of much business in the court at Colombo and elsewhere, to his mother; but in the meantime Lowry accompanied her in all her moves, and the strong bond of united life, so possible, so perfect, between an intelligent child and a woman full of simplicity, notwithstanding her intelligence and maturity, grew stronger day by day.

CHAPTER II.

BEGINNING LIFE.

I⊤ was not, however, so much the intention of his parents, who were fully purposed to complete their son's education in the usual way, as accident, which secured to Laurence the exemption from ordinary studies and restraints, which conduced so much to make him what he was. He had been sent home again to the care of a tutor in England, about whom I have not been able to obtain any information, and was being prepared for the university and the ordinary course of a young Englishman's training, when his father returned to England from Ceylon with a two years' leave of absence—the first real holiday which probably the hardworking Judge had ever had. "I was on the point of going up to Cambridge at the time," says Laurence, in his 'Episodes from a Life of Adventure'; "but when he announced that he intended to travel for a couple of years with my mother on the Continent, I represented so strongly the superior advantages, from an educational point of view, of European travel over ordinary scholastic training, and my arguments were so urgently backed by my mother, that I found myself, to my great delight, transferred from the quiet of a Warwickshire vicarage to the Champs Elysées in Paris; and, after passing the winter there, spent the following year roaming over Germany, Switzerland, and the Tyrol." It was in the year 1846 that this transformation was effected, and the boy turned once for all into the "rolling stone" which he continued to be for all the rest of his life. There could be no more exciting period for a plunge into the Continent, which was so entirely new to the little party of travellers—as novel and strange as if they had been rustics newly setting out from their fields—notwithstanding their acquaintance with the Eastern world and places far away. "I often wondered, while thus engaged," he continues, "whether I was not more usefully and instructively employed than labouring painfully over the differential calculus; and whether the execrable *patois* of the peasants in the Italian valleys, which I took great pains in acquiring, was not likely to be of quite as much use to me in after-life as ancient Greek." This is a question which it is never very easy to answer. If it were put in another form, and we were to ask whether the brilliant and remarkable individuality of Laurence Oliphant were not worth a host of ordinary university men trimmed to one pattern, it would be simple enough; yet we may be permitted to believe that the ancient Greek and the profounder culture might have saved him and the world from some wild dreams of after-life, without diminishing the originality and force of his being. These, however, are speculations without use; for no doubt the manner of development is all involved in the product, and no man can contradict his nature. However, this free life and acquaintance in the dawn of individual intelligence with the ways of thinking and life of other nations, had doubtless much to do in determining his career.

In 1847, the family party, ensconced in the comfortable ark used in old days by such leisurely travellers, with its varying team of four or six horses, according as it climbed or descended the mountain road, passed across the Alps to Italy, then seething with a universal fever of revolution. There never was such ideal travelling as in this lurching, heavy, altogether delightful vehicle, packed in a hundred pockets with everything one could want, pausing wherever it seemed good to the voyager, and with a long rest in the heat of the day at some delightful old town or picturesque village. The travellers thus gained a knowledge of the country in detail—its endless stores of beauty, its ever-friendly people, its humble shrines and fortresses, its overflowing life, such as no hurried railway can afford. One can travel all over Italy now without hearing a word of anything but formal Italian, the language of the books; no need to puzzle what the peasants say, though it is often so quaint and witty. But it was otherwise in those days. No doubt Lowry occupied the covered *banquette* in front, from which he could give notice of every new *castello* or change in the prospect. He was seventeen, at the age when enjoyment of this kind is unalloyed, and the air and movement and constant change are a pure delight. And at such a crisis there was much for an intelligent boy to see and do. The enthusiasm which was growing and swelling through the entire country went to his young head, easily touched at all times by the contagion of popular excitement. He recounts the "salient features" of this wonderful journey as "indelibly stamped upon my memory."

"I shall never forget joining a roaring mob one evening, bent I knew not upon what errand, and getting forced by the pressure of the crowd, and my own eagerness, into the front rank, just as we reached the Austrian Legation, and seeing the ladders passed to the front, and placed against the wall, and the arms torn down: then I remember, rather from love of excitement than any strong political sympathy, taking hold, with hundreds of others, of the ropes which were attached to them, and dragging them in triumph to the Piazza del Popolo, where a certain Cicero-acchio, who was a great tribune of the people in those days, and a wood-merchant, had a couple of carts loaded with wood standing ready; and I remember their contents being tumultuously upset, and heaped into a pile, and the Austrian arms being dragged on the top of them, and a lady—I think the Princess Pamphili Doria, who was passing in a carriage at the time—being compelled to descend, and being handed a flaming torch, with which she was requested to light the bonfire, which blazed up amid the frantic demonstrations of delight of a yelling crowd, who formed round it a huge ring, joining hands, dancing and capering like demons,—in all of which I took an active part, getting home utterly exhausted, and feeling that somehow or other I had deserved well of my country.

"And I remember upon another occasion being roused from my sleep, about one or two in the morning, by the murmur of many voices, and looking out of my window and seeing a dense crowd moving beneath, and rushing into my clothes and joining it—for even in those early days I had a certain moss-gathering instinct—and being borne along I knew not whither, and finding myself at last one of a shrieking, howling mob, at the doors of the Propaganda, against which heavy blows were being directed by improvised battering-rams; and I remember the doors crashing in, and the mob crashing after them, to find empty cells and deserted corridors, for the monks had sought safety in flight. And I remember standing on the steps of St Peter's while Pope Pio Nono gave his blessing to the volunteers that were leaving for Lombardy to fight against the Austrians, and seeing the tears roll down his cheeks—as I supposed, because he hated so much to have to do it. These are events which are calculated to leave a lasting impression on the youthful imagination."

One wonders rather how the excellent judge felt when he found his son thus rushing in where full-grown diplomatists feared to tread, compromising himself—if anybody had as yet minded which side Lowry took—even perhaps compromising England, had it been known that the young abettor of revolution was the son of a distinguished British official; or whether the mother did not suffer agonies of anxiety while the crowd rushed by with her boy, as she must have known, in the thick of the mischief, whatever it was. However, no harm would seem to have come of it, unless indeed this first taste of the sweetness of excitement and the fire of the multitude in motion awakened the latent spark in the mind of one destined to see so much of such movement in after-life.

At the end of this extraordinary "education by contact," the remarkable substitute for Cambridge which commended itself to the Oliphant family, Laurence returned with his father to Ceylon, where he seems to have been considered old enough at nineteen to enter into a quasi-public life as the Judge's secretary, and where he very soon advanced to the position of a barrister, pleading in the supreme courts, and conducting a great deal of very serious business. He had been engaged in "twenty-three murder cases," he himself tells us, before he had attained as many years of age. We find a rapid outline of his life at this period in the little notes which he dashed off daily from Colombo and other places to his mother at Newera

Ellia, the hill-station which is to Ceylon what Simla is to India: sometimes written from court while the fate of some of his murderers hung in the balance, and he cries out indignant that had they been but tried by papa or before an English jury they would have been safe; sometimes in the moment before dinner, when he is preparing to entertain, in his mother's place, papa's dinner-party of serious officials or distinguished strangers; sometimes from the cricket - ground; sometimes after a ball. Lowry was everywhere, in the centre of everything, affectionately contemptuous of papa's powers of taking care of himself, and laying down the law, in delightful ease of love and unquestioned supremacy, to his mother. There is not a sentence in those little letters to quote, but they place the position before us with the most vivid yet playful clearness. Papa, we may infer, smiled a little sardonically, with that sense of amusement in the precautions taken for him, which is one of the privileges of a parent; but the mother accepted it all, with pride and confidence unbounded in her boy, to whom it is evident, though he took such care of everybody, a great deal of freedom was permitted. His shooting expeditions, in which he sometimes ran considerable risk, for the game in Ceylon is big and dangerous, were reproduced long afterwards in sketches so brilliant and lifelike that it is easy to see how he must have thrown himself into those exciting moments of life in the jungle—though papa was left to take care of himself at such periods in the distant assizes in different parts of the island, whence his son had escaped to more exciting experiences. One does not know whether any recollection of this bright-faced lad, with his boundless high spirits and energy, still lingers in Ceylon; but the whole island comes to view in his letters, in rapid life-giving touches, a sort of dissolving panorama of a busy society in colonial completeness, great and small, with its eager interests and the buzz of a hundred little intrigues, arrangements, disagreements, all of such absorbing interest, all so entirely dead and gone. The Governor's house at Newera Ellia still bears the name, we believe, of the Oliphants, and the island is governed from the spot where Laurence's mother waited for her daily courier, and saw through Lowry's letters, as in a camera, everything that was being done.

This period of home-dwelling, however, did not last very long. In the end of the year 1850, Laurence being then twenty-one, an unusual and interesting visitor touched at Ceylon on his way from England back to India. He was one of the first native envoys ever sent from the unknown East, and his appearance had been hailed in England with a warmth of curiosity and interest which was fresh in these days, when public curiosity had not degenerated into the foolish and selfish society fever over a novelty, which makes social success nowadays so little of a compliment. Jung Bahadour was a revelation to the country, which jumped at the idea, not unnatural in the then ignorance of Eastern affairs, and always delightful, that India was about to accept with enthusiasm the culture and sentiments of the West, and that this enlightened and splendid native prince, with his blazing diamonds and his advanced views, was but the first of a noble harvest of liberal minds and civilising measures to come. It is to be supposed that he must have produced a similar impression at Ceylon, notwithstanding the more complete knowledge and the small public faith in "natives" with which a colonial community is endowed. At all events, the romance about him, the distance and novelty of his unknown country far away, and the instinct of the traveller and adventurer which was so strong in young Laurence, combined to surround the envoy with a halo of attraction. It seems wonderful that an only child, so cherished and adored, should have been able to persuade his parents to consent to such a wild expedition. But they would seem at all times to have had the most unbounded confidence in him, and conviction that his impulses were not to be restrained, nor his conduct made the subject of parental dictation.

It is very probable that their friends condemned Sir Anthony and his wife for their fond submission and concurrence in all Lowry's vagaries, as no doubt they censured his want of formal education and the irregularity of

his training. On this particular occasion one of them at
least seems to have spoken out. "My approval of your
retaining Lowry in Ceylon was never meant to extend to
such an excursion as that which he has undertaken to
Nepaul, which can hardly improve his legal prospects,
financially or professionally," says one of the most trusted
counsellors of the family. Another friend, however, highly
disapproves Lady Oliphant's desire to retain him by her
side, and especially that she should tell him his father approves while she does not, thus raising a feeling of conflict
in his mind. "Let him alone," this lady says. Thus it
was evident that there were debates on the question. But
the young man's wishes carried the day. He left Ceylon
with his new friend in December 1851. The result of the
expedition was a book, the first of many vivid sketches of
adventure, in which, as happened to him in his general
good luck on more than one occasion, he had an entirely
new field to explore. What is more important, however,
for our present purpose, is that it brings us his own account
of himself in a series of letters, carefully marked by his
mother's hand No. 1, 2, &c., in which the story of his first
adventure by himself in the world is told. The little narrative begins with a sketch of a fellow-passenger in the
steamer in which he leaves Ceylon, whose character he
conceives to be something like his own, for which idea it
is worth while to quote it.

"He is a pleasant enough fellow as a companion, but
abominably selfish and a thorough charlatan. His faults
in the latter respect are something like mine—in fact, I
saw that I might well take warning from him. His interest was the first thing which he considered, and he was
rather unscrupulous in making everything subservient to it.
He toadied me like fun, and thinks I don't see through
him. But I must not be so dreadfully uncharitable,
though I could not but be struck by the almost providential
neighbourhood of a man who seemed myself exaggerated."

Laurence must have corrected early these faults, like
the "besetting sin" of "cribing," of which he accuses him-

self on an earlier occasion. Certainly, self-interest was the
last thing that his worst enemy could lay to his charge.

"The Minister" [Jung Bahadour], he adds, "is a glorious
fellow, and we are great friends. He amused himself all
day shooting at bottles. I have seen him hit three running
fastened to the yard-arm; first hitting the bottle with right
barrel, and then the neck, which was still hanging, with the
left. He knows a little English, but his stock is confined
to making love—'Give me a kiss,' and a few other phrases
equally short and sweet. We had great fun jumping, but
I beat his head off, whereat he was much disquieted; but
being determined not to be done, he immediately com-
menced hanging by his heels in ropes in the most fantastic
way, which I found impossible, not having been, like him,
shampooed from earliest infancy. Oliphant Sahib being
considered unpronounceable, I am Lowry Sahib, in return
for which I call the young colonel (brother of Jung) Fe-fi-
fo-fum Sahib, that being the nearest approach I can make
to his name."

Calcutta the young man found worth coming to see, even
if he were to go no farther, and was much amused to find
himself the fashion, and sought after everywhere. "The
idea of going up to Nepaul with Jung Bahadour on a
shooting expedition is my passport everywhere, and constitutes me a lion at once. Mrs Gordon takes a delight in
introducing me to all the big-wigs. She certainly has a
great knack of making one feel satisfied with one's self,
and would spoil the most modest young man. So you
must not mind my giving myself airs when I come back,
unless somebody takes me down a peg in Nepaul. If I
were going to live in Calcutta," he adds, "I should not
devote myself to seeing and being seen in the way I do
now; but for a week I think I ought to see as much of
men and manners here as possible. I hope you are not
afraid of the gaiety: it is but for a short time and of no
very serious nature, and I make a point of being alone a
good deal in the morning. I hope you will write me a
letter of good advice as I want it now, and certainly shall

by the time I shall get it; and never mind boring me—it won't at all." Thus it will be seen the boy was still a dutiful boy, thinking of his mother's anxieties, and how much she feared that balls and other vanities and perpetual society would be against his spiritual advantage, notwithstanding the independence and freedom of his twenty-one years.

The mode of travelling, when at last he started up country, was peculiar, but it seems to have been comfortable enough. He and his companion went from Calcutta to Benares in "a large coach which only holds two, but in which two very good beds can be made up. In this, which is very comfortable, Cavanagh and I have been living for the last two days, and shall have to do so for four more, making it our home both by day and night. Ten coolies drag us along a very good road. In the mornings and evenings we walk alongside or sit on the coach-box, and if we have a lazy team, drive them along in a most barbarous way. Papa would be amused at this specimen of Indian backwardness, being dragged for nearly five hundred miles along a magnificent road in a four-horse coach by men instead of horses the whole way. It would have delighted you, however," he adds, "for the coolies never shy, stumble, nor run away, or misbehave in any other way but being lazy and importunate."

On arriving at Benares he found himself in the midst of the bustle of preparation for the great hunting-party of which everybody was talking.

"Everybody says I am lucky to get such a chance of seeing sport, and fellows are making all sorts of interest with him [Jung] to be allowed to come too, and I daresay we shall make up a formidable party. The Jung is an immense lion among the native princes here, who all want to go home. He took up his caste (forfeited by his voyage) the day before yesterday, so I missed the ceremony; but it only consisted of all the party who had gone home (i.e., to England), taking a bath in the presence of numbers of spectators. He has three hundred men of the Nepaul army down here

as an escort. There are six hundred elephants waiting
for us at Sagaulee to beat the Terai, and if they don't
get something out of the jungle, it's a pity.   Look for
Sagaulee on the map: it is on the Nepaul frontier,
and we begin our battue from there, going some miles
into the Nepaul country and coming back to it previous to
starting for Khatmandhu."

The account which he gives his mother of the books
he carried with him to occupy his moments of leisure
is added. "I think you will approve of the selection,—
Guizot's 'History of English Revolution,' Bourrienne's
'Memoirs,' Lord Mahon's 'Life of Condé,' a Hindostanee
dialogue—and some of Sir A. Buller's small vols. of
Paul de Kock, which he has lent me." Let us hope
Lady Oliphant believed these last to be theological
treatises.

"The Jung is as civil and kind to me as ever, and
I am beginning to say a word or two to him in Hindostanee now. The house abounds in children, who make
the most desperate noise in Hindostanee without the
slightest control. To-night the Jung reviews his troops
for the benefit of the General, and we are all going to
see it, as they say it is a curious sight. He showed me
his dogs to-day, also his falcons, so you may imagine me
unhooding my bird as in the olden days."

The final scene of the hunting-party was only reached
after various other detentions on the road among friends
who sprang up upon the young man's path everywhere:
old soldiers who had been at school with papa, younger
ones who had got their cadetships from Uncle James,
or who had married somebody's sister in one or other
category, or who knew Perthshire and all the people
there, or who had received the hospitality of Lady
Oliphant at the Cape,—those contingencies which seem
to happen so much more readily in India than anywhere
else. Laurence makes special note of the young ladies,
who were generally pretty, and always lively and de-

lightful, and with whom he felt himself entitled to flirt
with much vehemence, since a single evening was the
limit of his intercourse with them. "I have taken to
making love furiously, as I know I am going away
immediately," is the unprincipled confession he makes;
and he begs his mother not to be afraid of his proceedings in this respect, which would seem to have
been a weakness of hers. It was after a ball, and a
tender leave-taking at two o'clock in the morning, that
the young man flung himself into his palanquin and slept
"far into the following day," while his bearers jogged along,
carrying him to his destination.

"We found the Jung encamped in a picturesque spot.
The scene altogether was very enlivening : four thousand
men, with elephants, horses, camels, bivouacking in a
large mango-grove, with our hut pitched near the Jung's,
who, when we arrived, was out shooting. We soon
joined him on a gorgeously attired elephant provided
for our use, and found him on a still more handsomely
got-up one, his brothers on another. But I must tell
you about his little bride, who was with him, a pretty
little girl of thirteen or fourteen, almost as fair as a
European, and as he calls her 'My beautiful missis.'
She is the daughter of the Coorg Rajah, and was betrothed to Jung in Benares. He seems very fond of
her, and kind to her, and she looks very happy. I
like him more and more. He is so thoroughly European. To give you an instance of it. One day, while
calling on him, the Rajah of Bhurtpore was announced,
so his guard turned out, and the gentleman was received
by Jung, and led to a couch with due honour, when after
a complimentary speech on both sides, Jung said to him,
'Your Highness must excuse me, as I have important
business with these gentlemen,' pointing to us, therewith
coolly leading the Rajah with equal state to the door.
He came back a moment after, laughing and rubbing his
hands, saying, 'That's the way to get over an interview
with one of these natives.' Of course he had no business
whatever with us. He is making his little betrothed shake

hands, and behave otherwise quite like a European lady, and instead of shutting her up, she always goes about with him. We march ten miles a-day, starting out at a quick march with his troops and band, which is a very large one and plays English tunes. The Jung always takes his gun with him, and shoots every cockyolly bird he comes across. You may imagine, therefore, how much I am enjoying myself. The game consists of quails, hares, and partridges. The Jung sends us our dinner, which consists of rice boiled with ghee, and eighteen or twenty other condiments, served in leaves and scented, so that one feels as if one were eating greasy smells. We have consequently come to the determination of accepting Jung's dinner, but of providing ourselves with something edible as well as odoriferous. The chutney smells exactly like the young colonel; it is a very nice smell, but one does not like it to get further than one's nose. I have found out the philosophy of travelling. In travelling you are much more likely to have excitement of one sort or another than leading a humdrum life; but as happiness consists in anticipation, all you have to do is continually to anticipate excitement and you will always be happy, whereas in the other case excitement is so very unlikely that you can't work yourself up to the anticipation of it. Then there is intense enjoyment in eating even ghee and smells when you have gone twenty-four hours without eating anything, also in sleeping when you have been two nights awake— all pleasures to which you are a stranger."

After this there comes a sudden digression, caused by the happy accident of falling into a great picnic party which was spending a few days in tents at no great distance from the " Jung's " encampment—of all the amusements of which young Laurence and his companion were made free, and which suggests the startling question in his next letter, " How would you like a Roman Catholic daughter-in-law ? " I have already said that young ladies were much in the thoughts of this traveller of twenty-one, and he had already intimated with much delight that he alone could " polk " of the assembled party, and therefore had it all his own way. He enlarges for a page of this letter upon the particular lady in question, who was not only very pretty but very sensible, clever, and lady-like, and would not be flirted with at any price, which, adds this experienced youth, " made it so dangerous. I began by trying for fun to cut out two fellows who were rivals, and I succeeded so triumphantly that it became nearly earnest, to the disgust of one, who cut me dead at last; but we made it up when we killed the tiger yesterday. If you knew how much I am envied you would excuse my conceit, which is becoming unbearable." It is perhaps the reaction from this delightful sensation of triumph that makes him a little discontented with his real host, the Jung, when he rejoins the camp.

" The Jung has not behaved well to us in the shooting line, and we are rather cool with him on that account. He makes arrangements for us to go out with him, but being a very jealous sportsman, has contrived twice to give us the slip with his elephants," which leads the young men to the resolution of setting off on horseback by themselves to Khatmandhu and abandoning the party. " Travelling in India," Laurence adds, " is totally different from travelling in any other country. The comfort and pleasure of being made at home in a nice house with nice people, instead of going to an inn, is not to be told. By so doing one is perpetually thrown with new people, who have to be learnt—as is also the knack of making yourself agreeable in the shortest possible time. There are certain hobbies and subjects which every one has in India, and in which I am becoming perfect, having of course no particular opinion on them myself, 'but what master likes.' Then the change of climate and scene puts one in good health and spirits, and the numerous little trials of temper that one undergoes tend to make one a philosopher. I rarely get further than looking a little sulky now and then at a man whose neck I should like to wring slowly. The Nepaulese are excessively stupid, and horribly good-humoured, so I can't do anything else with them; but the Hindostanees are sulky and alive to

ridicule, so I get on very well with bullying them jo-
cosely. . . . The next best thing to having repose of
mind is looking as if you had it, and I often wish I had
a pleasant expression of countenance in my pocket, which
I could fasten on my face when wanted."

This letter—which is tinged with a certain shade of
discontent, with an " I am not so full of the young lady "
at the end—after a few days' interval is however re-
opened in great excitement to narrate "the most magnificent day's sport I ever had in my life."

" We started early this morning elephant-catching, but
did not come up with the herd till two o'clock. I insisted
upon going, much against the Minister's [Jung's] wish,
who said it was impossible for me to do it: however,
saying he was no longer responsible, he gave me an elephant on which was nothing but a sack of straw lashed
firmly on, with a loop of rope to hold by. Taking off cap
and shoes, I was told to stick to this through thick and
thin, throwing myself off the elephant when passing under
branches, and holding on with my hands to swing myself
on him again. Two regiments with a lot of elephants
had been sent to beat the jungle; and when the herd
appeared, about a hundred more, on one of which I was,
started in full pursuit. Besides holding on, I had to
thrash the elephant with a spiked piece of wood: you
may imagine it was no joke, seeing a bough before you
which grazed your hands and arms passing, not six inches
above the elephant's back, the mahout doing likewise. It
was certainly the most violent exertion I ever underwent,
and once the elephant came down a tremendous trip on
his nose, which nearly dislocated every bone in my body.
On we rushed, regardless of everything. A pack of a
hundred elephants in full cry is a curious sight, with two
nearly naked men on each, swaying about like bolsters,
now on one side, now on the other, or slipping down to
the root of the tail and holding on by the crupper. We
got two (wild) elephants separated, and followed them
close, when suddenly I was enveloped in smoke, and very

much astonished by a dozen or more guns let off in my face. The elephants had doubled back, and this was a salvo from a lot of soldiers hidden in the grass, who immediately afterwards threw away their guns and made for the trees. But the elephants were so bewildered by the smoke and hot pursuit, that they kept on until they thought it time to turn and charge, which they did, but took nothing by their motion, our elephants standing like rocks, while the others were belabouring their sides and backs with their trunks. Finding there was no help for it, they tried to bolt; but that was not so easy, each of them, in the meantime, having had two nooses thrown round their necks, which four elephants were all pulling different ways. They were two mothers with two little ones, and the poor little things got dreadfully jostled, and roared vehemently upon being separated from their mothers. I am the only European that has ever attempted to follow, and Sir Henry Lawrence is the only one that has even seen anything of one from a distance, and the Jung says that was nothing to this. He would call me a brick if he had a Nepaulese word for it. You need not be afraid of my going out again; there is not the slightest chance of it, as we leave the elephant country the first thing in the morning."

After this high point of excitement the narrative drops to lower levels. At Khatmandhu, when the travellers reached it at last, things were not so well with the Jung as had been hoped, and Laurence and his companion, though with much reluctance, released him from a promise he had made to allow them to explore the country—a privilege never yet granted to any European, and likely to do the Minister harm if he permitted it. "He finds his position here anything but satisfactory; the Durbar look suspiciously upon him, as being a friend of England, an idea which many little circumstances have tended to confirm; so the Jung's head is not likely to remain long on his shoulders, notwithstanding the cool way he orders everybody about, from the king downwards. This we remarked at Durbar yesterday, when he had his most devoted followers close behind his chair with double-barrelled rifles (loaded), while the men he was afraid of were just in front of him." The excitement of the journey was thus cut short, as well as the young travellers' hopes of exploring an altogether new country, and having really something worth writing about. Nothing remained for it, accordingly, but to push on along the beaten ways, and join Lord Grosvenor's party, which had been circling Laurence's line of voyage for some time without ever coming to an encounter. It is needless to follow him in his detailed journeys, or even in the mixture of diffidence and self-confidence with which he drives up " with a carriage full of luggage " to the house of a stranger to whom he has no tie except a letter of introduction in his pocket, thinking it "an unparalleled piece of impudence," yet consoled by the thought that "it is the custom in India": no need to say that he is always received with open arms.

There are, however, some bits of more serious thought in these letters, and occasionally scraps of self-analysis, called forth evidently by the pious mother's questions anent her boy's spiritual state. It is difficult, he says, to practise habits of self-examination riding upon an elephant, with a companion who is always talking or singing within a few feet ; but it is otherwise in a palkee, which " is certainly a dull means of conveyance," but "forces one into one's self more than anything." The result of Laurence's self-ponderings is, that he discerns his great weakness to be "flexibility of conscience, joined to a power of adapting myself to the society into which I may happen to be thrown."

" It originated, I think, in a wish to be civil to everybody, and a regard for people's feelings, and has degenerated into a selfish habit of being agreeable to them, simply to suit my own convenience. I think I can be firm enough when I have an object to gain, and have not even the excuse of being so easily led as I used to think. I am only led when it is to pay, which is a most sordid motive —in fact, the more I see of my own character, the more despicable it appears, a being so deeply hypocritical that

I can hardly trust myself; hence arose a disinclination ever to speak about myself. How blind one is to one's own interest not to see that, putting it on one's own ground, it would pay much better to be an upright God-fearing man than anything else! Fortunately religion is a thing that one cannot acquire from such a motive, or I am sure I should have done so before this."

No doubt that their son should make such a confession, or any confession breathing of self-dissatisfaction, would be agreeable to the parents—to the Judge, who had spoken naughty words and been so sorry for them, and to the anxious religious mother, always longing after his spiritual advantage. But perhaps Laurence felt that he had been a little hard upon himself. He ends by hoping "there is no humbug in it. It is honest as far as I know, but *don't believe in it implicitly*," he says; while in another letter he shows himself disposed to defend the "flexibility" of which he had just accused his own character and con-science. He is aware of "having Ferentcz's [an uncle] knack of making myself agreeable," but thinks it is to a great extent without any harm in it.

"If an old general likes to hear himself speak, why should you not look interested, however bored you may feel? why should you not take an interest in poor Mrs So-and-so, who has gone wrong, or been beaten by her husband, if Mrs General does? I got a tiffin out of an old couple at Benares simply in that way, and C. says, 'Why, I never saw such a fellow as you, Oliphant; you are a favourite everywhere immediately.' I do not give myself any credit for it, mind; on the contrary, nothing is easier, and I inherit it from your side of the house evi-dently. But the tendency I see to be bad in fact."

One may perhaps be inclined to wish that this tendency, to be agreeable and sympathetic, and to look interested even when you are bored, were a little more general; but it is curious to find that a man, specially distinguished for taking his own independent way in life, and that a most individual, not to say eccentric, one, should have been alarmed by his own early inclination to be all things to all men—a delightful faculty, however, which he retained, in the midst of a life more unfettered by other people's opinions or by any conventional rule than almost any other of his generation, to the very end.

There is nothing more charming in these youthful letters than the cordial and genuine response of this spoiled child to the affection lavished upon him. His mother's advices are not only received well, but asked for with a sincerity that cannot be doubted—a very unusual trait in a young man of twenty-one; and the chance references to his father, still papa to the home-loving young adventurer, are always delightful. Had papa but been there, he and Lowry would have waited for no escort, feared no harm, but set off lightly on foot through the prohibited Nepaul. There is no such travelling companion, the young man says, as papa. The men of his own age are as nice fellows as can be, whom he delights to emulate in every bodily exercise, to win a genial triumph over either in the elephant-hunt or the new polka, making a friendship for life even out of a ball-room rivalry; but, after all, there is nobody like his father for real companionship. Nor is there anybody so acute as the Judge in appreciation of character,—a power of which so many people are destitute, but which Lowry modestly concludes he has himself inherited, as he has inherited the knack of pleasing people from his mother's side of the house. His eagerness to get home, to have post-horses ordered for him on the Kandy road, to lose not a moment in reaching his mother's side, shows how little the adoration of that home had spoiled him. Thus ended the young man's first essay of independent life,—a sufficiently wild flight to be the first, and a most characteristic one. He had been filling the position of private secretary to his father since the return of the family from Europe three years before, at, he somewhere says, the exceedingly liberal salary of £400 a-year. And it was on his savings that he accomplished the rapid and brilliant rush through India which was the beginning both of his life of adventure and of his literary career.

CHAPTER III.

THE BAR—THE EXPEDITION TO RUSSIA.

IT was perhaps scarcely possible that after such a taste of freedom, and of the social life for which he was so admirably constituted, the young man should settle down again at Ceylon to his irregular bar practice and existence of official routine. He had already felt the difficulty of being called upon to plead "before papa," which lessened his sphere, and he was also aware that his knowledge of law was imperfect for one who intended to adopt that profession (which, besides, he hated). Accordingly but a few months elapsed before his mind was finally made up to quit Ceylon, and try his fortune in the greater world. The time was approaching at which Sir Anthony would be able to resign his appointment, and retire from public work, and it was decided that Lady Oliphant should accompany her son home, *en attendant* the happy period fixed for the Judge's retirement; for it was evidently felt to be inexpedient that Laurence should lose any more time in qualifying himself for the more serious work of life. Perhaps some parental, or rather maternal, anxiety about the health of the beloved boy had been alleged to friends as a reason for this step, for I find a letter to Sir Anthony from a friend in Gibraltar who goes out to the steamer to greet the travellers in passing, and who announces that "Lowry looked anything but delicate. I should judge him a great, stout, eleven-stone fellow, able to give me a thoroughly good thrashing on an emergency." Stout, in the sense which the word generally bears, he never was, but well knit, active, and muscular, with that promptitude of eye and observation which are the most admirable of additions to strength and courage. His own letters to his father left behind in Ceylon are admirable, full of playfulness and graphic description, a little more free and less serious than those to his mother, dashed off with a flying pen, and full at first of all the humours of the little sea-society on board ship, which always lend themselves to the remarks of the social critic. The mother and son arrived in England in the end of October 1851, finding the gloomy sea in the Channel "easily recognisable from its John Bull appearance," and already "luxuriating in English fog and damp." Although he knew very little of his own country, London was full of friends, and before he had been more than a month or two in England, he had resumed a hundred old friendships and made as many new ones, among his father's old companions and the men of his own generation. He decided to enter at Lincoln's Inn, where various people assured him he might be called to the Bar very speedily in consideration of his previous studies and practical experience in Ceylon. In those days it was not a matter of strict examination as it is now, and to have read for a year with a barrister was sufficient qualification. Certainly Laurence, with his social tastes and the habit of succeeding without severe preliminary labour, was the last man in the world for the ordeal of examinations, to which probably he would not have submitted, and certainly would not have "crammed" for. There is not much evidence indeed from first to last that he was greatly in earnest about this study. "I think," he says, "if I get up the two or three books necessary for acquiring a proper knowledge of mercantile law, including bills of exchange, together with the law of evidence, pleading and real property may take care of themselves." The beginning of that other most curious but most wonderful branch of legal study, which consists of eating dinners, is however more amusing. He describes it to his father in an early letter, so that it is evident he had lost no time in entering upon this severe portion of his education.

"LONDON, *Nov.* 24, 1851.

"I have eaten some stringy boiled beef at Lincoln's Inn Hall in company with three hundred others, not one soul of whom I had ever seen before; but I unhesitatingly talked to my next neighbour, and soon, by dropping in an unconcerned manner remarks upon a tiger I knocked over here, and a man I defended for murder there, talking learnedly about Ceylon affairs, &c., &c., incited the curiosity of those whose reserve would not otherwise have allowed them to notice me, too much to let them remain silent. Still I felt rather verdant on first entering, and was only saved from sitting down at the table appropriated to barristers by hearing one man remark he was not going to sit there, as So-and-so was his senior; so I concluded that if he was *his* senior he was most certainly mine, and choosing the youngest-looking man I could find, I seated myself next him."

The mother and son began their life in England in a cottage at East Sheen, lent to them by one of their many friends, where they immediately found themselves much at home among a number of agreeable neighbours, including the family of Sir Henry Taylor, the author of 'Philip van Artevelde,' whom Laurence describes as the "idol of the whole neighbourhood, made love to by the entire female portion of the community." But a young man with dinners to eat in Lincoln's Inn, and many other engagements on hand, soon discovered that to be so far out of town was inconvenient, and indeed impossible. It is with great gravity and conviction that he states his preference for England, meaning London, a little later.

"The longer I stay in England, the more I see how necessary a residence here is for a young man, who is utterly unconscious of his own ignorance in a colony, and comforts himself by knowing as much as his neighbours, which is no very difficult matter. It will require no common inducement to make me ever return to Ceylon. Life is not long enough to waste the best part of it by living away from all the advantages which civilisation affords, to break up all the ties one may have formed and which can never be reunited, to be destitute as well of the means of improvement as of common information upon everyday topics."

The record, however, does not long continue in this high tone, and though Laurence always retained a high opinion

of the uses of education obtained in the way of social intercourse, he falls lightly into his natural style as his story
flows from one dinner-party and festive gathering to another. The progress of the young man, as yet wise enough
to listen more than talk, with his lively eyes wide open,
and his mind weighing every novelty and taking in every
information, is delightful to follow. On one occasion he
says: "The conversation, from the beginning of the dinner
to the end (there being sixteen or eighteen people), was
exclusively confined to speculations upon the future Ministers and Lord Derby's policy; indeed I have heard so
much discussion upon politics in general, and the capacities
of various men in particular, that I'll trouble you rather!
and the best thing Lord Derby can do is to recommend
the Queen to send for me if she wants advice."

In spring, as in duty bound, Laurence paid his respects
to her Majesty, whom he found himself so well qualified
to advise. "I have had the honour," he says, "of pressing
my lips upon the fingers of royalty. I went through the
ordeal with considerable fortitude, following Sir George
Pollock. I found nearly everybody was in uniform; the
few who were in civil costume looked like servants of the
royal household. The Queen looked me in the face much
harder than I expected, and I returned the gaze with such
a will that I forgot to kneel, ultimately nearly going down
on both knees, after which, finding the backing-out process
rather irksome, I fairly turned tail and bolted."

It is unnecessary to enter into the politics which he
touches so lightly; nor had he as yet any personal connection with them to justify a plunge into that whirlpool
of which the older reader will remember the agitations.
The period is already too old for contemporary interest,
too recent for history. It was the end of a long period of
peace; so long, that notwithstanding the convulsions of
1848 upon the Continent, many optimists were still capable
of holding the opinion that the reign of war was over, and
that under no circumstances could tranquil England bind
on her disused armour or draw her rusty sword again.
The following note upon the closing of the Great Exhibition of 1851—the first step in the new emulation of arts

and crafts and national intercourse, which was to supplant
and make warfare impossible, as was fondly supposed—
carries us back pleasantly to one of the happier fancies of
the time. The great fairy palace, as it was called, in Hyde
Park, the temple of glass and iron, which took the public
imagination by storm, was still standing, though stripped
of its riches, and there was a great movement in favour of
retaining it where it had been planted. It is to be supposed that public taste has improved since that time, for
the idea of such a construction permanently established
in the midst of the trees of Hyde Park is calculated to
produce a shuddering horror in most minds nowadays;
but that this was by no means the sentiment of the time
is very clear. Laurence, indeed, was no authority then or
ever from an art point of view; but he expressed a feeling
which was very strong in the London of his day when he
pronounced energetically for its preservation. Its aspect,
he thought, even when despoiled of all its previous attractions, ought to be well noted before any proposal was
entertained for its removal. "The miscellaneous crowd—
ragged artisans out of work, with Hyde Park dandies,
Belgrave Square children playing with those from St
Giles', and an orange-woman suckling her child next to a
gorgeous matron who looked like a duchess — would be
more influential than any number of petitions. It is a
mixture of romping, sedateness, and quiet enjoyment."

The mixture of the grave and gay in these delightful
letters cannot be better shown than by the extracts that
follow, which give at the same time an admirable picture
of all the mingled experiences and aspirations of the youth,
half-boy, half-man, at the outset of his life. The first is
all gaiety, the repetition evidently of a familiar subject of
banter between the genial father and son.

Laurence complains, April 23, 1852 :—

"I can't find a single lassie that looks the least as if she
would do for a wife, and the article seems so rare that
when it presents itself I shall feel bound to snap it up at
once for fear of losing it for ever; so beware of hearing
unexpectedly of a daughter-in-law. I have been industri-

ous enough to read law until half-past ten at Charles's [Pollock's—now Baron Pollock] chambers one night, but I should apply myself with much more of a will if I was sure of getting business after being called. If I was to go to the Scotch bar, and you were to be made sheriff of some county, we might shake on very comfortably with a farm to amuse you and a railway near."

A little later there follows a pleasant and amusing account of the manner in which he spends a day, characteristically brought in by way of showing the worthlessness of the excuse of business.which he has just given as his reason for not having written to his father. "Tom," it may be explained, was an old and much beloved friend, Dr Clark, once surgeon in the 72d Highlanders, and throughout his life devoted to them, who shared their rooms with Lady Oliphant and her son.

"My day now is somewhat as follows: I am up at half-past seven to imbue my mother with Foster's sound sense, which I do until half-past eight. At nine we breakfast — viz., Tom and I — my mother maintaining, in spite of a severe system of bullying kept up by Tom, her ground, or rather her room, where she breakfasts. Tom and I talk politics all breakfast-time, our different views affording ample matter for discussion, the idea of a Cobden and Bright Ministry always driving him frantic. I am then in a proper trim for the Debates, which I read while digesting, and then start for chambers, picking up Paul on the way, and talking about boat-building and fast men all the way to chambers, when I begin to read — now on bills of exchange, varying it with abstracting pleadings, for which, being in the Marshalls' chambers, I am particularly handy. At half-past one I go into Groom's and have 'coffee, brown bread and butter,' in a loud nasal twang. Then say, '"Punch" after you, sir,' to any man who has got that or any other paper I may want, pay fivepence, and go back to chambers. Walk home with Charles at half-past four discussing law, theology, or politics.

Then pay a visit or two, now that the evenings are long, and then most probably home to dress and dine out, and go to a party afterwards, or Royal Institution lectures, or debating society, or opera 'according.' Now, I might write to you instead of reading Foster or the Debates, or paying visits; so, as I said, want of time is no excuse."

The Foster above referred to is John Foster the essayist, a Nonconformist writer of considerable ability, whose high reputation has suffered some diminution in the course of time.

The political sentiments of a young man brought up as Laurence Oliphant had been were naturally somewhat vague when, fresh from his little colonial world, he suddenly plunged into London; and his first exposition of his views, as made to his father, are more sentimental than substantial.

"I have become a friend of the people, think that if they are only trusted they will show themselves worthy of the confidence reposed, that nobody has a right to bully them or pull the Crystal Palace down if they wish it to stay up, and that education and kindness, so far from making Chartists, would make loyal subjects."

This sympathetic feeling developed in his youthful breast in attempts to help and serve those lowest classes in London, who call forth so many enthusiasms and generous efforts, with so little apparent result. His benevolent work began by an expedition made into the slums of Westminster in company with Lady Troubridge and a missionary.

"Not altogether pleasant," he says, "addressing a group of thieves in Old Pye Street. Lady T. seemed to think it quite natural, so I could not well help myself, and insinuated to the least brutal-looking of them that a meeting was going to be held in the next street which they might find interesting, upon which he laughed and asked 'Jim' if he heard that; upon which Jim said that he did, and that he had other meetings to attend rather more to his taste than that, he'd be sworn to, 'not reflectin' noways on you, sir.' Whereupon, after a little chaffing among themselves, they decided it warn't the sort of thing that would suit them, 'no offence to you, ye know, sir'; and one man did me the honour to say that he'd no doubt I meant well. So I went unsuccessfully to the meeting, where I found congregated fifty or sixty fellows who had come in from curiosity, none of whom, to all appearance, had ever been in a church in their lives, and who either stared vacantly or chaffed and made jokes, while here and there a little sparring-match went on."

This first attempt, in which the lively youth found perhaps more amusement than was consistent with the desperate character of the enterprise, would not seem to have been very successful. The service, as he reports it, was conducted with difficulty. A hymn was sung, rather to the amazement of the roughs, and the small congregation was addressed by the missionaries; but as this was done not "very judiciously, they soon got tired."

"Some boys began to fight, and had to be lugged out by their legs and arms, creating a great sensation. Some of the men seemed attentive, however, while others made jokes, and the boys who had been turned out began throwing stones against the windows; so that by the time we got to the next hymn there was a considerable row, which increased as we began it, as everybody began to sing at the top of their voices a variety of airs, amid occasional bursts of laughter. When service was over, some promised to come back, while others went away amused; but all through there was no absolute incivility shown, which, considering the men, was a great deal to say."

He had scarcely thus got himself in train, however, laying out his work, his gaieties, and his attempts at missionary exertion in the way specially favoured at the time, when weariness stole upon him, and dissatisfaction. He discovered that the constant dissipation of a London season is absolutely incompatible with any sufficient amount of legal or any other work. "Gallops in the Park," he says, "when too frequent, rather prevent the proper progress of the law"; and his many other engagements and interests could scarcely fail to bear the same tendency. The length of time required for the training necessary for the English Bar also began to discourage him, and the hope of more ready admittance and better prospects in the North seemed to afford an attractive alternative. He thus announces his changed intention in this respect:—

"LONDON, *June* 7, 1852.

"Thinking it nonsense not looking for myself into the prospects of the Scotch Bar, and as it was impossible to do so satisfactorily without going there, I took a run up in the steamer with Aunt Sophy, who happened to be making the move at the time, and remained just thirty-three hours with Anthony Murray, which I employed looking over the courts and into the faces of the barristers, and thought that they did not express the brieflessness of English lawyers—a suspicion that was confirmed upon my conferring with Robert Oliphant, who said the Scotch Bar never afforded such prospects of advancement as at this moment. Anthony Murray said the same, and the result was that I determined to come to the Scotch Bar as speedily as possible—to effect which a Civil Law examination is required; and as attendance of classes is not necessary, I am at this moment cramming Justinian with a view to passing on the 3d of next month, as they said that though a year's study was the usual thing, if I chose to stand the trial and could pass it, they did not care for anything else. I have exactly one month to prepare; but it is worth making the spurt, as it will be such a saving of time. Exactly one year hence I shall pass, I hope, in Scots Law, and be a practising advocate in Edinburgh long before my terms at this hopeless Bar will be com-

pleted. The prizes there do not seem so far out of one's
reach, and I have every intention of going in for everything—which I could never screw up my courage to do
here."

He was, however, at the same time fully resolved to
keep up his terms at the English Bar in spite of his
Scotch practice, and retain the valuable connections he
had formed there.

In the meantime the little book, chiefly composed of
extracts from his diary, about Nepaul, had been put
together and prepared for the press—though nothing is
said about it in the letters until its appearance is recorded. The book was ready in the early spring of 1852,
and confided to "Uncle Tom" for revision. This was Mr
Thomas Oliphant, the youngest brother of Sir Anthony,
well known in connection with music, and the author of
some popular songs. There is no information as to this
gentleman's literary gifts; but in those days no one was
aware, himself least of all, that young Laurence was to be
one of the most popular writers of his time, and his
anxious mother thought it a great matter that the boy's
book should be looked over and licked into shape by a
more experienced hand. "I have handed over your
manuscript to Mr Murray," says the uncle, "after having
carefully gone through it and made such alterations as
will in many cases cause it to read better. The mere
unpremeditated language of a diary won't do for appearing
in print. It gives a flippant character to the style of the
narrative, and is apt to weary the reader. With such
further alterations as I have no doubt Mr Murray's reader
will think it necessary to make, the book will be very
interesting, and likely to do you credit." "I send you the
above," writes Lady Oliphant to her husband in great
satisfaction, "hoping it will please you to see your
brother's opinion of Lowry's book." Whether Lowry
himself was equally pleased with the prospect of being
subjected to the alterations of "Mr Murray's reader" does
not appear; but he shows no such vanity about his first
appearance in print as is general with young authors—

regarding it, so far as can be seen, from a most business-like and practical point of view. He sent out to his father, apparently for the use of Ceylon, fifty copies, and his report of his first venture is made in the most moderate terms, and without any of the usual excitement of young authorship.

"I shall send my book by the Queen of the South," he says. "Two thousand copies have already (ten days) been sold out of the three thousand which formed the first edition, and I have had long and favourable notices in the 'Athenæum,' 'Economist,' 'Examiner,' and 'Literary Gazette,' in which papers look (date about last week in May). It seems to give very general satisfaction, and I hope to have another edition out in a month or two."

This is all that the young writer says about his first performance. It was published in a cheap form, and brought him, I believe, very little profit, though some praise.

In the middle of the summer of 1852 he had taken up his quarters in Edinburgh, and was in full progress of study and equally high spirits, "cramming" for the examination, which was to take place on the 3d of the ensuing month, with great hopes of success. His preliminary steps are amusing.

"I have been introduced to all my examiners, and have buttered them properly, and they look good-natured enough. Robert Oliphant has been overwhelming me with kindness —introducing me right and left, propitiating my examiners, and puffing me splendidly as a colonial lawyer, a young author, and altogether an interesting young personage, that it would be folly to pluck for the want of a little smattering of Latin."

His future companions are described with similar light-hearted satisfaction.

"The more I see of this Bar, the more I prefer it to England—it is so much more snug and sociable; and though there is a considerable sprinkling of snobs, yet there are some gentlemen, and they shine out all the more conspicuously, and indeed get more business on that account. It is evidently the correct thing to be a high

Tory here, so remember I won't pledge myself to any opinions."

The next event in his life was the success of his Civil Law examination.

"The examiners were evidently in a much greater fright of puzzling themselves than anything else, and in the Civil Law they skimmed the surface in very safe questions: decidedly the most trying part was the walking in before seven great fellows sitting round a table in solemn wigs. However, they shook hands with me with great cordiality, welcoming me among them and passing me unanimously, which was nothing more than they ought to have done, seeing I never made a mistake. The whole thing did not last half an hour, and I sent a message down to my mother by electric telegraph, which reached her in half an hour more."

The opinion he had formed of Edinburgh society in those days does not seem to have been a high one, but yet he managed to console himself in many ways.

"I think Edinburgh is such a beautiful town that I am fully compensated for its dulness by its romance, and shall have so many friends near that I can always run over to Keir, Blair Drummond, Abercairney, or Ochtertyre—from all which places I have received invitations—to say nothing of Condie, and Freeland, only two hours from Edinburgh. I think it rather an advantage that Edinburgh offers no attraction in the way of society. Notwithstanding this, I find myself dining out every night, the last place being with old Colonel Phillpott and family. Curiously enough, I met at the station, all in the same carriage, Algernon Egerton, Campbell of Monzie, Sir Alexander Mackenzie, and Hawkins, an Indian judge, all of whom I had known, and none of whom hardly knew one another. . . . Campbell of Monzie, worn out with his week's canvassing, was going for the Sunday to Monzie, and took advantage of his audience to explain his principles, which he did as if he were a Free Kirk minister, thumping the side of the carriage cushion when he grew vehement in his advocacy of Protestant doctrines, and by his explanations of the 'truth as it is in Jesus' seeking to impress upon us the principles as they were in Monzie. He has a smart, amusing way of answering, and told us a story of having canvassed a man who seemed adverse to give him his vote, and was in fact rather grumpy and gruff in his refusal to do so, whereupon Campbell said, 'But if you don't vote for me, who will you vote for?' whereupon the man said he would sooner vote for the devil; on which Campbell answered, 'Well, if your friend should not come forward, perhaps you will give me your vote.' "

In another letter he describes his experiences in the office of his relation Mr Robert Oliphant, a Writer to the Signet in Edinburgh, and gives an account of his day's work, which has a great air of diligence :—

" Everybody overwhelms me with kindness, and I am in great luck to be taken into Robert Oliphant's office on the free-and-easy terms I am; for I am not set down to copy useless papers, but simply to learn the routine. The clerks take a great interest in me, and explain the forms, &c. I go to the Parliament House at nine with the P. H. clerk, and see what is going on, listen to cases I have previously read in the office, and talk to the various counsel, most of whom I know now. Moreover, it is useful to be known and seen often about those purlieus. After an hour or two there I come down to the office, where I remain till four, when I go and attend the Conveyancing class of Professor Menzies. I don't think lectures do one much good. I can get up more in a given time by reading; so I have given up the Scots Law. . . . There are really no clever men at the Bar now coming on, but the juniors are a remarkably nice set of fellows. The Lord Advocate, Inglis, is a very sharp chap and a good speaker, and out and out the cleverest man at the bar. So that there is a great opening, and Robert Oliphant promises he will give me business as soon as I am called, so that it will be my own fault if I do not get on. Everything seems much simpler than in England, and business is carried on in a nice familiar style, of which the following dialogue is a sort of sample :—

" *Mr Mackenzie, loq.*—There is a case just precisely similar to this one, my lord, I might say upon a' fours with it,
which ye'll find in Dunlop, but I'll no' trouble ye with it i'
the noo. . . . Your lordship 'll maybe no' sit to-morrow ?

" *Lord Robertson.*—And why not, Mr Mackenzie ? I
think I'm as well sittin' here as anywhere else ?

" *Mr Mac.*—I was thinking, it being a particular occasion, out of respect for his Grace's interment——

" *Lord Rob.*—I'm no' wantin' in respec' for the Duke;
but I'd sooner be here than at the funeral, and I'll just sit
as usual."

Many readers will remember the jovial and jocular
judge, the

" Lord Peter,
Who feared not God nor man nor metre,"

who is the hero of this story,—one of the last Lords of
Session by whom " braid Scots " was still occasionally
spoken.

Laurence and his mother, who had accompanied him,
occupied during their residence in Edinburgh at this time
rooms in North Castle Street, a locality rendered classical
by the long dwelling in it of Sir Walter Scott. Sir Anthony
Oliphant had all a Scotsman's admiration and half-senti-
mental longing for Edinburgh as a residence, and his son's
exhortation, " Do come home," had doubtless all the more
force as coming from that romantic and beloved city.
" We should all be much more comfortable," the young
man adds; " and," recurring to the old joke, " I could begin to look out for a wife under your auspices. I don't
see any likelihood of finding one for myself."

Shortly after, however, we find him again in London,
whither he went periodically to " eat his terms," and where
he recurs to the " blackguards," his *protégés* in Westminster.
The movement on behalf of reformed or reformable thieves
was then in an *accès* of energy, taken up vigorously under
the patronage of Lord Shaftesbury, with much accompaniment of midnight meetings, and a considerable amount of
excitement. Among other incitements to a life of indus-

try, a number of these men had been set to cutting wood for firewood, and Laurence was much concerned to prove that in patronising this effort the public in general was not incurring the reproach of taking bread out of honest people's mouths.

"If we make a man who has hitherto been dishonest, honest, instead of being a burden to the State, he is a supporter of it, and a cheaper article in that capacity in the long-run, though it may cost something to make him honest. That strange obliquity of moral vision which makes a large portion of the community Tories, prevents them from apprehending this. The problem is evidently 'How is a reformatory not a premium on vice?' We are now experimentally solving it. It seems to me that there should be some place where, when a man is bankrupt in character, he might go and get whitewashed—some probation through which when he passes he should come out registered A 1 in point of respectability. At present if a man sinks below a certain level in this country, unless some one takes him by the hand, no individual efforts on his part will raise him above it."

One of the meetings which followed the industrial experiment is described as follows: "The whole thing was very striking; and I felt, while a whole room full of the worst characters in London were singing 'God save the Queen' or 'I will arise,' that I ought to have wept, and that you certainly would have. It is so difficult to realise the depravity of the men who are so innocently employed, and in whose countenances you can detect the hard lines which a vicious life has imprinted, but which are rapidly becoming softened by their voluntary subjection to a life of restraint and honest industry. It is the most interesting thing I have ever seen."

In the August of 1852 Laurence made use of his first vacation in a Continental tour most happily and fortunately directed, at first designed as a mere expedition in pursuit of sport, but turning afterwards to much more important issues. His companion was Mr Oswald Smith, one of the great banking family of Smith, Payne, & Smith, between whom and the Oliphants there was an old family connection, which had introduced Laurence to the house of a member of the firm, on his first arrival in England. The youth who thus accompanied him in one of his earliest adventures, contributed, nearly half a century after, a brief but interesting memoir of his lifelong friend to one of the Magazines on Laurence's death—and naturally this boyish expedition occupies a large place in it. Mr Smith is perhaps unduly contemptuous of the gifts as a sportsman of one who had ranged the jungles of Ceylon in his boyhood, and hunted elephants with Jung Bahadour; but that the young man, already familiar with such exploits, should look for a fresh and unhackneyed field, something less tame than a moor in Scotland or the banks of a Norwegian fiord, was natural enough; and he was also in search of "something to write about"—a very legitimate object, if seldom so honestly avowed. "The only part of Europe within reach fulfilling the required condition," Laurence himself says in the 'Episodes,' "seemed to me the Russian Lapland: for I heard from an Archangel merchant that the Kem and other rivers in that region swarmed with guileless salmon who had never been offered a fly, and that it would be easy to cross to Spitzbergen to get a shot at some white bears."

As it turned out, this chance project proved of the very highest importance in the young adventurer's life, and set him well afloat upon the career of public service, tempered with personal fancy, in which so many years were to be passed. When the two young men reached St Petersburg they were allowed to go no farther in their equipment as sportsmen—though whether by actual prohibition, or because of the excessive duty demanded on their fishing-gear and equipments, is not quite clear. Mr Smith adds that they were too late in the year to go north with any chance of sport. "It may give some idea," he says, "of Oliphant's sanguine and imaginative character, to record that his plan for future proceedings was to disembark on the right bank of the Volga at Tsaitsin, not far from Astracan, and ride over the Don Cossack steppe, four hun-

dred miles, to Taganrog, on the Azof Sea." They did do
something like this, driving in rude native carriages, and
finally reached the Crimea, then an unknown and unexplored peninsula, and the mysterious city of Sebastopol,
of which many legends, but no definite and clear information, had reached the world. It was known that Russia
was there establishing an arsenal and headquarters of war,
from which she would be able to descend upon Turkey
and overawe Europe; that the entry was forbidden to
strangers, and any attempt to make acquaintance with
the place dangerous; — all excellent reasons why the
young travellers should push their way thither, which
they did after all without much difficulty. Thus the
"something to write about" was most successfully attained.

We find a full account of this journey in the letters to
Lady Oliphant, beginning with the very first steps from
home. At Berlin they paused for a day or two, and
Laurence takes the opportunity to express his satisfaction
with his travelling companion, in a charming and playful
note full of boyish appreciation and fun. "It is a great
thing having with one so handsome a young Engländer,
as all the pretty girls look our way, and I am humble
enough to be quite content with the side-glances I thus
get, he being quite unconscious of his own attractions."
It may be added that Laurence was by no means unqualified "to please a damsel's eye" in his own person, and
was almost certain to be, under any circumstances, the
most entertaining and attractive person in his neighbourhood wherever he was.

"The first thing that astonishes you as you land are
the droskies and their drivers. The former are only
capable generally of holding one person besides the driver,
behind whom the passenger sits cross-legged, somewhat
in that way [a sketch is here given], if you can understand this illustration. The latter are rigged up in caps
like this [with another sketch], and long dressing-gowns,
and longer red beards, and always give you the benefit of
their flavour as you sit behind them. The chief difficulty,

however, consists in maintaining your seat over the pavement, which is execrable. In fact, the only things that are old in the town are the droskies and the pavement—everything else wears an unpleasantly new and fresh appearance; and the builders of the city have fallen into the mistake, though it is one on the right side, of leaving the spaces in front of the public buildings immensely large, so that the stray man or drosky which you see wandering about them gives one the impression of the city only being half full. Still I have never seen anything to equal the *coup d'œil* from the bridge, facing the Izak Church and the Winter Palace, certainly the finest of royal residences in Europe. The Neva is as broad as the Thames, and beautifully clear, and the quays are handsome and substantial: however, Murray's handbook describes the town much better than I can, and unless we have some adventures up country, I shall have nothing to write about."

In spite of this fear, he manages as usual to give a very picturesque account of their evening visit to the Mineral Waters, whither they went in a steamer:—

"Shooting through bridges, the arches of which were so small that you could easily touch the key-stone as you stood on deck, or, leaning over either side, touch the stone buttresses: it required the most beautiful steering; I don't think there was six inches to spare in any direction. Our boat-load consisted of a crowd going up to the Mineral Waters, a place of evening resort during the summer months, and which was as beautifully got up as Vauxhall. However, it was too like it to be interesting: the display of fireworks at the end was grand enough. We went to see a ceremony in the Greek Church the other night, and the prostrations beat those of the most devout and enthusiastic of Mussulmans. It was a very picturesque sight to see the men tossing their long hair and beards about as they flung their heads up and down."

The next day, after driving to a place called Gorilla,

where they slept, they "mounted horses which had been
sent out there for us, and rode eight miles to Krasnoe-
Selo plain, where the Emperor was to manœuvre 80,000
men, a grand sham fight with the whole Russian army,
to close the summer inspections."

"The whole way to the plains the white tents of the
camp extended, and when we reached a rising ground we
had a magnificent view. On a knoll near us was the
Emperor with a brilliant staff, which any Englishman
in uniform might join unasked: unfortunately we were
obliged to keep a respectful distance, but saw none the
worse on that account. 40,000 men under Sidigri advanced, and after some hard cannonading with 40,000
under the Emperor, and a great deal of dashing about of
cavalry and horse-artillery, drove the opposite hosts behind some further trenches. Altogether I never had so
good an idea of a battle before. Sometimes the whole
mass was moving at once, and the position in which we
were enabled us to see everything perfectly. The most
beautiful corps were the Circassian horse, covered with
armour, and the Cossacks, with their long beards and
spears dashing in all directions. We were nearly carried
away by a charge of hussars, and only escaped by shelter-
ing ourselves behind a friendly house."

On the following day Laurence announced the definite
change of their plans, about which they had been uncertain; but "the custom-house has most kindly helped us
out of our dilemma by deliberately and coolly charging us
£15 duty on our rods and guns, which our prudence at
once prevented our thinking of paying." This, however,
he thinks he can avoid, according to the advice of the
Financial Minister, by taking them to Finland, a country
which he has determined to visit, and which is not yet
under the Russian custom laws. "So that we are not
altogether sold; but meantime, as there is no such hurry
now that we have given up the shores of the White Sea,
we are first going to take a run down to the grand fair of
Nijni Novgorod, and spending a couple of days *en retour*

at Moscow." He regards this extra expenditure as justifiable, as he looks upon his journey as " a distinct system of self-education."

" Though I must own that I have not been able to find out much that is really interesting in a country and government which I have always looked upon as likely to afford more information than any other in Europe, further than the palpable hindrance which the policy of the Government offers to anything like advancement or civilisation where it is most needed. I don't think we have anything to fear from Russia: its gigantic proportions render it so unwieldy, and the people are so barbarous, that we shall always have the same advantages which our enlightenment gives us over the Eastern nations. I look upon it as little better than China: the only difference is that usually barbarous nations hold civilised nations in respect, which, to judge from the way they bully you in the custom-house, Russia does not."

The next letter is dated from Moscow, " this most charming of cities."

" If ever there was a town that would bear to be written about it is this, decidedly ranking with Khatmandhu or Cairo in general novelty, while it is far before either in its particular objects of interest. . . . The Kremlin itself is the most unique and picturesque assemblage of churches and palaces of ancient and modern art, and of Eastern and Western architecture, that could be found anywhere collected in so small a compass, and so happily grouped together. The gilded domes and cupolas might be in the Punjaub, while the palace which they adjoin might be in Paris. The church of St Basil is perfectly unlike anything old or new, occidental or oriental, and forms a most striking foreground to one of the views of the Kremlin, which I hope some day to show you."

After this a forty-eight hours' diligence journey brought

the two friends to Nijni Novgorod, where the great fair was going on.

"Your letter reached me in the shop of Aaron, a Jew from Bukharia, who was regaling us with almonds, dried peas, and raisins in his warehouse in the great fair, and displaying the wonders that come from that part of the world. Indeed it would be difficult to think of a part of the world that did not contribute something to this Russian emporium, and I have no doubt that before I have done exploring I shall find a coir-mat and perhaps a Moorman to sell it me. . . . I was rather disappointed in seeing no Chinese, and, in fact, not quite as great a variety of costume as I expected; but the variety of goods disposed for sale compensates in a great measure for this, and though not so striking at first, is as satisfactory when one comes to examine the shops and overhaul their contents."

By some mistake of the steamboat company's agent, Laurence and Smith were detained at Nijni Novgorod two days later than they expected, and consequently outstayed the first freshness of interest. In his next letter he complains—

"It is a great bore, when one wants to do as much as possible in a given time, to be kept in a place after you have seen as much as you want of it. Nor can I make as good use of my time as I might. I am very much left to myself to pick up my information as I best can, and that is only by my eyes, since the merchants are too busy to attend to one, and too stupid to give any valuable information upon matters that from their vocation they ought to know something of. To-day, therefore, having seen every part of the fair, we took to drawing, and found some lovely views. The old town overhangs the Volga most picturesquely, and from the cliffs an extensive view is obtained in all directions, and a very interesting one over the flat on which the fair is situated, quite unlike anything I ever saw before. The view was too difficult

and complicated for me to attempt : the two rivers Oka
and Volga looked alive with human beings, as well as the
peninsula on which 150,000 people are hived like bees.
. . . I would not have missed this fair on any account,
though I would not advise everybody to make the journey from Moscow *exprès* — whereas I should almost say
my father would consider it worth a journey from England alone."

He goes on : " I must tell you what we propose doing,
instead of hovering in a desultory way about the fair,
having already occupied half the day in writing a description of it, which differs so much from that given in
Murray's handbook that I don't think he will approve it
at all. First, then, there being two companies of steamers
lately started on the river for the purpose of towing barges
up and down it, and not of carrying passengers, we are
going to take advantage of them, but must submit to the
inconvenience of going slowly, and of starting on no fixed
day, but when the barges are ready. Still, as the accommodation is most comfortable, and as nobody that I know
except the inhabitants of this part of the world has been
down the Volga, we are going to try it, hoping that it may
pay in the way of interest. The river being low, we shall
not go very fast, and shall probably not get to Zaritzen,
our point of debarkation, under ten or twelve days, during
which time we must amuse ourselves as best we can. I
regret that I did not buy some solid books at Moscow, but
I did not then anticipate wanting one. You will see in
the map that where the Volga takes its last bend towards
the Caspian, the Don approaches within fifty or sixty miles
of it, and trends away to the Sea of Azof. Here we cross,
and embarking in a boat, glide down this river, if we find
it practicable and convenient (there being no steamer) to
Taganrog. At any rate, there is a post-road if we prefer it.
Then a steamer will take us on to Kertch, from which
place we ride through the Crimea to Sevastopol, and then
via Odessa to Vienna and home. . . . The Crimea, at any
rate, I know to be well worth seeing. We should have
liked Astrakhan and the Caspian, and across *via* Tiflis, but
have no time ; and Astrakhan is a mere Russian town, not

half so well worth seeing as one would imagine from its name."

The next letter is written on the Volga, which, in his usual enthusiastic way, he describes as "this most magnificent of rivers." The account of their life on board the steamer is given at length: they were the only passengers.

"We have exclusive possession of the after-part of a ship, having a sumptuous cabin, a nice dining-room on deck, and a good storeroom for our necessaries. It was rather an interesting matter providing for the start; for not having a servant, we were obliged to make our purchases ourselves, and rushed about buying bread and meat and groceries, ultimately attaining a considerable proficiency in making bargains. We fortunately have the use of the captain's cook, but do everything else ourselves, and are expert in laying the table, giving out the necessary stores, and economising our small means. Hardly anything is to be procured at the villages on the banks. This morning we made a tour of inspection of our larder, and found thirty out of fifty hard-boiled eggs had been broken and were bad, and the ham had been put in a damp place and got mouldy: however, we hope to make something of it; but the eggs, alas! are gone for ever. The experience which we have gained in sundry domestic matters, however, will be useful to us hereafter, if we marry unfortunately—as my father did."

This latter little piece of *espièglerie*, as well as the continued and delightful references to his father, are very characteristic of the terms on which the young man stood with both his adoring parents.

After complaining that the speed of the voyage down the Volga was not quite regular, as the barges sometimes drew more water than the steamers and ran aground, when "we lug away for a considerable time to get them off," he goes on :—

"The river is so low that we shall take longer to get to

Zaritzen then I anticipated, and I may as well warn you in time not to expect me home before the 20th October. I shall be anxious to hear at Odessa what news from Ceylon. Our voyage down the Don I look forward to with great pleasure. The whole tour will be a novel one, and I hope it may furnish sufficient incidents and matter to be interesting in some shape or other to the public.

"We are at this moment hard and fast on a *pericarte* or sandbank, and there is no telling how long we may remain where we are. Yesterday we stuck on one for nine hours. When we pass this one, and another one or two, our difficulties will be over, and we shall get rapidly on. We are towing two immense barges, each 320 feet long, and the current is eternally setting them on the shallows, much to our disgust. However, this is not called a passenger steamer, and we were prepared for these delays, so we cannot grumble: besides, except for the temporary annoyance caused by them, we could not be more delightfully comfortable. Our existence approaches to perfection to my mind—gliding quietly along under high wooded banks, past romantic glens and picturesque villages, along the noblest river in Europe; the days beautiful, the climate bracing, the thermometer ranging between 52° in the morning and 72° in the middle of the day; with a walk and a sketch of an afternoon when we stop to take in wood. We have all the elements of a comfortable existence except clean linen. Our larder certainly is not very extensive, and we are most abstemious in the matter of drink, taking nothing but tea and Volga. Still, there is a considerable pleasure in laying one's own tablecloth, and bringing out one's stores, and eating them in contentment.

"I do not remember ever having read an account of this part of the world, or of the country of the Don Cossacks, through which we are going. Many of the villages here are composed purely of Tartars, and they are as unlike Russians as English—in fact, they remind me more of the Bootyas in Nepaul than any other people. Their dress is very curious, and the women wear gold coins in their hair and silver breastplates. The men look just like what

Chinese gipsies would be, if such animals existed, swarthy instead of copper-coloured, with Chinese features."

Sometimes they see "a train of seven or eight barges wind slowly up the river tugged by a huge leading barge containing 150 horses and as many men, the latter employed in laying out anchors ahead, the former in going round a capstan as they would in a threshing-machine, and warping the barges up to the anchors."

"You will be glad to hear," he adds, "that we have at last overcome or undergone all *pericartes*, and that we are getting merrily along, with bright sunshiny days. This afternoon we hope to arrive at Simbirsk, a town which ought to be marked on the map as the capital of a province. I enjoyed my ramble over the old Tartar capital very much, and had a very magnificent view from the Kremlin walls. I hope the waiter to whom I confided my letter posted it, as it contained much information which I cannot now repeat. . . . I shall not write again after leaving Simbirsk until I get to Taganrog. I have got so much to draw and so much journal to write and so little to tell, that I shall do no more now than repeat that I could not be happier or enjoying myself more."

This last threat is not exactly carried out, as we find Laurence writing again from Saratov. He complains, though not angrily, of the frequent delays when detained "by people who do not understand expedition or regularity, and at whose mercy we must be so completely." These vexations were, however, balanced by the amiability of his companion, who never complained, though he had a perfect right to do so, seeing that he came out for a sporting expedition, and had been carried off instead to explore unknown wilds, much more satisfactory to Laurence, whose desire to find "something to write about" was never absent from his mind.

At last, on the 20th of September, the friends arrived at Taganrog, having finished the still more exciting land journey.

" It is with feelings of unmitigated satisfaction that I date my letter from here, after having accomplished in five days and nights one of the most wild, uncouth, and unfrequented journeys that even Russia can boast. I confess that the prospect of a steppe journey through the country of the Don Cossacks was a little appalling to us, not knowing a word of the language, or able to find a single person who had ever been on the road or could give us any information upon it. Our scheme for going down the Don was quite impracticable with our limited time, and so we decided to buy a carriage at Dubofskoi, where we left the steamer, and get across somehow from the banks of the Volga to the shores of the Sea of Azof: there was no alternative between doing this and going on to Astrakhan and then across the Caucasus by Tiflis, which would have taken an indefinite time. Fortunately, even at such an out-of-the-way place as Dubofskoi, we found a carriage, for which we had to pay about £11, and launched ourselves upon the steppe. It was a sort of post-road, and every fifteen or twenty miles was a wooden hut, with a sort of kraal for horses behind. The country was like the sea, with a heavy ground-swell on and calm surface, being covered with a short dry grass. Often for miles not a creature was seen; sometimes bullock-carts passed us, or a wild Cossack galloped by on horseback, and here and there latterly villages came pretty thick, with round houses like the haystacks with which they were always surrounded, and from which you could hardly distinguish them, or ragged-looking cabins like those in an Irish village, from which issued wild independent-looking unshaven creatures. The road was often a mere track across the grass, and the country presented the exact same appearance for so long a time as to become quite wearisome. On arriving at a station, we generally saw no one but a woman or a child or two, one of whom went and called a man, who immediately mounted on one of our last team and galloped across the steppe, bringing back in half an hour or so six or eight horses, which he drove into the kraal at full gallop, selected three, took half an hour or more to harness them, and then went off with us at a full gallop.

Luckily the road was generally smooth, but we occasionally dashed down ugly places, the result of which was that at last one of the wheels was so near coming off that we had to stay a night at a post-station—a rest we were not sorry to take, though it was on a wooden stretcher; but a sheepskin I bought has on sundry occasions made a capital mattress, only it retains the fleas for a long time. Our great stand-by was the *samovar*, or hot-water urn for making tea, with which the poorest peasant is always supplied. Except a little meat at starting, we lived entirely on hard-boiled eggs, rusks, and cheese, comforting ourselves with some capital tea which we bought at Nijni. Not a thing besides hot water was to be procured the whole way, but the people were very civil, though rough and barbarous: they seemed honest, but I saw so few of them I could not judge much about them one way or another. . . . Altogether, though the country was as uninteresting as an Egyptian desert, and we were dead beat and as universally shaken and nearly coming to pieces as our carriage, yet there is some satisfaction in having successfully made so outlandish a journey alone. . . . Luckily our carriage stood it wonderfully, another wheel just coming off as we entered the inn-yard."

At Taganrog the two young men heard to their dismay that instead of two steamers a-week to Kertch there was but one a fortnight, an arrangement which seemed to make the journey so painfully and courageously performed a failure as to its final object. It is almost sulkily, though with the native humour, somewhat angry this time, peeping through, that Laurence complains: "Everything is badly arranged in this country; nobody knows anything, and every piece of information relative to travelling has been invariably quite wrong. I had hoped to see the Crimea quite comfortably, and now doubt whether we shall have time to do it at all; but everybody says it is the thing most well worth seeing in Russia, which will rather reconcile me to missing it, as most probably this is a lie too."

I am sorry to say that here the letters end: and the

reader must be referred for the further course of the journey
and the inspection of Sebastopol which followed—by no
means of such engrossing interest now as it was then—to
the narrative published in the following year.   The purpose
of finding something to write about was most triumphantly
fulfilled, if not the sporting expedition, which was to one
of the travellers, at least, so much less important.   We
can only hope that Mr Smith too was consoled for the big
game he did not shoot, and the salmon he did not catch,
by the humours and wonders of this wild extraordinary
journey.

CHAPTER IV.

AMERICA AND CANADA.

IT is needless to explain how extremely important this
boyish expedition—lightly undertaken indeed, yet not
without that shrewd and clear-sighted apprehension of
coming events which, with all the gaiety and all the daring
love of adventure, love of fun, eager pursuit under all and
through all of new experiences, both in life and thought,
was an inherent part of Oliphant's many-sided nature—
was in the story of his life.   The Crimea was a country
unknown, and Sebastopol a wonder and mystery even
while all the elements were working together to precipi-
tate our troops upon its shores.   " In the middle of this
century," says Mr Kinglake,[1] in the beautiful description
of the Chersonese peninsula with which his history opens,
" the peninsula which divides the Euxine from the Sea of

[1] These lines were written while that accomplished historian and traveller
was still with us, and when the hope of his ever-kind and ready interest
was present with the writer, as his friendship and sympathy had always
been with the subject of this memoir.   There have been many voices to
recall the wonderful force of that unique and elaborate study of modern
warfare which filled his later life, and the airy and sparkling record of
picturesque travel which conferred a blaze of fame upon his youth.   The
gentleness of his age, the tenderness of his sympathy, his ever-indulgent
criticism and delightful praise, are recollections still more intimate and
dear.

Azoff was an almost forgotten land, lying out of the chief paths of merchants and travellers, and far away from all the capital cities of Christendom. Rarely went thither any one from Paris, or Vienna, or Berlin: to reach it from London was a harder task than to cross the Atlantic; and a man of office receiving in this distant province his orders despatched from St Petersburg, was the servant of masters who governed him from a distance of a thousand miles."

This was the distance which the young explorers had traversed; and in the course of the next year their experiences were laid before the public in the book called the 'Russian Shores of the Black Sea,' which was really almost the only work in which the British reader could ascertain what was the country, and what the special difficulties of the war upon the verge of which Great Britain was now trembling. That it was received with extreme interest, and at once secured the general attention, is clear from the fact that on the 4th of March 1854 a fourth edition was called for and in the press. By this time the fact that such a book existed, and that two young men in London had penetrated into these unknown but so important regions, seems to have slowly arrived at the consciousness of the authorities, and on a memorable day Laurence was raised into sudden excitement and a fever of hopes and expectations by a summons to the Horse Guards, to meet the generals who were anxiously employed in the construction of plans for the campaign, in order to give them all the information he could on the subject. He talks in one letter of " Oswald rushing in waving a letter over his head," and on another occasion of "a mounted orderly" who rattled up to his door; dazzling all the lodging-houses in Half-Moon Street, with a mission from these great men. The summons was to the effect that " Lord Raglan wanted to see me at once." He communicates this briefly to his father as follows:—

"I accordingly proceeded to the Ordnance, where I found not Lord Raglan, but Lord de Ros, who questioned me minutely about Sebastopol. I gave him all the information I could, and sent him my sketches, extracts

from my journal, and everything I could think useful.
There were a couple of old Engineer Colonels (one of
them afterwards identified as Sir John Burgoyne), all
three poring over a chart of the Crimea. They are
evidently going to try and take Sebastopol, and I recommended their landing at Balaclava and marching across,
which I think they will do. Lord de Ros was immensely
civil. I think Lord Raglan ought in civility to make me
his civil secretary. It would be great fun. I met Lord
de Ros again this morning, and had a long talk with him.
I did not mention my anxiety to get out. It is very
ticklish saying anything about one's self on such occasions,
and I must just bide my time and qualify myself—be able
to answer the lash, as you always say."

The excitement and eager hope produced by these
interviews may be imagined. It was almost impossible
for the young man to believe that nothing would come of
them. He plunged into the study of Turkish, and read
everything he could lay his hands on to qualify himself
for whatever share might come to him in the tremendous
enterprise, for which the country, so long unused to war,
and with her sword more or less rusty in its scabbard,
was with great general excitement preparing. Laurence
had been, almost from the moment of his arrival in
England, and notwithstanding his law studies and preliminary work in that profession, avowedly seeking his
fortune, with a keen eye upon the horizon for anything
that might turn up. He had already leaped into a
considerable literary connection. Mr John Blackwood,
the editor of the well-known Magazine, a man of remarkable literary perception and insight, had at once divined
an invaluable contributor in the young writer; and he
had also formed a connection with the 'Daily News,' then
a new paper, sparkling with literary life and interest, the
first competitor of the 'Times.' His first arrangement
with this newspaper was that he should contribute
articles at two guineas a column; but when he felt
the wave under him floating him upwards, Laurence, who
had always a most clear and practical business faculty,

thought this remuneration to be inadequate, and in the
same letter which describes his interview with the
generals he informs his father that he had "called at
the 'Daily News' office and said I could not afford to
write at two guineas a column, so they offered to double
it on the spot: terms which I accordingly accepted, and
have knocked off twelve guineas' worth last week. I
cannot always carry on at this rate, however, as I run
dry. As it is, I am obliged to write bosh occasionally,
which I don't like doing; but the public are so gullible,
that it is difficult to resist the temptation."

The new hope, however, carried him away from all his
existing interests. "I hear nothing but the Eastern
question talked of now," he says; "and as I am appealed
to as an authority, although I originally knew nothing
more about it than my neighbours, I have got it up
carefully, in order to answer expectations." He was,
however, by no means idle in respect to charitable and
philanthropic engagements even during this time of
suspense. "On Monday I have to deliver a lecture
to what is anticipated to be a crowded audience upon
reformatory institutions; on Tuesday to make a speech at
a public meeting for the Belgravian Ragged Schools; on
Wednesday to a large soiree to meet the swells who take
an interest in these things. Last Sunday I gave an
address to my blackguards at Westminster." Thus his
hands were full as he stood and waited for fate.

The immediate decision came, as often happens, in an
entirely unexpected way. He had long entertained hopes
of the help and patronage of Lord Elgin, with whose
family, and especially with his sisters Lady Charlotte
Locker and Lady Augusta Bruce (afterwards Stanley),
Lady Oliphant had warm relations of friendship; and it
was in the midst of the excitements of the Crimean
question, when his attention was wholly bent in another
direction, that these hopes suddenly came to fruit. He
was hanging amid alternate hopes and fears, " extremely
anxious to take part in the Crimean campaign in some
capacity or other," and ready to "accept an offer of the
late Mr Delane to go out as 'Times' correspondent, had

not Lord Clarendon kindly held out hopes that he would send me when an opportunity offered," when promotion came in this totally different quarter. "It was while anxiously awaiting this that Lord Elgin proposed that I should accompany him to Washington on special diplomatic service as secretary; and as the mission seemed likely to be of short duration I gladly accepted the offer, in the hope that I might be back in time to find employment in the East before the war was over." His expectation was realised, as will be seen, notwithstanding that the length of his absence exceeded his calculations, and his position latterly was more important than he had expected. Thus after fixing all his thoughts upon the East, he was carried off in an exactly opposite direction, and began his active work with all the interest and excitement of a rapid and special mission, in the New World, with which in after-life he was to have so much and so close connection.

During this period of absence the letters of Lady Oliphant, addressed to her son in America, afford a companion picture to his minute and careful record. The mother's anxious prayers for her only child, her fears for him, her expressions of confidence, her intense longing for his spiritual improvement and growth in grace, reveal as in a mirror the tender woman's pious and sensitive soul, and her absorption in her son's interests and fortunes. Still more interesting and individual, perhaps (for religious longings and counsels are inevitably much alike, to whomsoever addressed), is the cheerful background of the temporary home in Edinburgh, where her husband by this time had joined her, and in which the humour and good spirits of Sir Anthony brightened the whole scene, though he too could think of nothing so much as his absent son. Before he left Ceylon on his final retirement from office, the father had communicated to his wife and son his readiness to follow the fortunes of the beloved boy. "I do not know," he says, "that I have ever clearly expressed myself, but if not, fully understand that I am quite prepared to go to any place in Europe to which Lowry may go, whether as *attaché* or anything else. So long as it pleases

God to spare us, let us all stick together." The parents remained in Edinburgh till Lowry should return from his American mission, waiting to see what Providence might have in store for him, and fully determined to carry out this purpose. One can scarcely help the question, whether the lively and adventurous young man would have been made much happier by their determination, or if the thought of his father and mother following him every-where in his erratic course might not have appeared a little embarrassing as well as ludicrous. The old Judge, however, repeated his intention to some of his friends in Edinburgh in a more humorous way. "The wife is but-toned to Lowry's coat-tails," he said, "and I am tied to her apron-strings. I am just like the last carriage in a train, waggling after them just where they please to lead." They looked forward to some permanent appointment for Lowry, in London perhaps best, with their own house open to all who could serve or please him, and the beloved son coming and going. For Sir Anthony at least this dream of happiness was never to come true.

A full account of Laurence's first experiences in diplo-macy has been written by himself in his ' Episodes in a Life of Adventure,' and it is a very amusing chapter. The object of the mission was to negotiate a commercial treaty between Canada and the United States, and in the execu-tion of a piece of business so serious, and which was sup-posed so unlikely to succeed, Lord Elgin and his staff approached the representatives of the American nation with all the legitimate wiles of accomplished and astute diplomacy. They threw themselves into the society of Washington—which in those days was apparently much more racy and original than it seems to be now, when American statesman have grown dull, correct, and dignified like other men—with the *abandon* and enjoyment of a group of visitors solely intent on pleasure. Lord Elgin's enemies afterwards described the treaty as "floated through on champagne." "Without altogether admitting this, there can be no doubt," Laurence says, "that in the hands of a skilful diplomatist that liquor is not without its value." The ambassador had been informed that if he could overcome the opposition of the Democrats, which party had a majority in the Senate, he would find no difficulty on the part of the Government. But the young secretary, keen as was his intelligence, did not see his way at first through the feasting and the gaiety into which his chief plunged. "At last, after several days of uninterrupted festivity, I began to perceive what we were driving at. To make quite sure, I said one day to my chief, 'I find all my most intimate friends are Democratic senators.' 'So do I,' he replied, drily." This was the young man's first lesson in statecraft. The story of the expedition, as it more immediately concerned himself, was communicated to his parents in a series of long letters, beginning with the approach to Washington :—

"We never went through a tunnel the whole journey, and were therefore well able to see the country. When we came to towns we went slap down the main streets, there being nothing to keep little children from playing upon the rails, except 'Look out for the locomotive' stuck up on boards. When we get to the middle of the town we stop before the principal hotel, and steps are put up for us as if we were a coach changing horses. The houses are shaded by fine old trees, and telegraph wires run overhead in every direction, like bridges from one cocoa-nut tree to another in Ceylon. Niggers become plentiful as we get South, and we have had three experiences of waiters in hotels. At the Clarendon there was not a man at all. We were waited on entirely by rather pretty bare-armed maidens in a becoming and uniform costume; remarkably agreeable I thought it. They used to be very attentive to me at dinner, as they saw I appreciated their charms. There were at least fifty waiting every day. Then at the St Nicholas we had regular civilised waiters —I am afraid to say how many—but everything is done at the same moment, and there is a procession of full and empty dishes which takes about five minutes to complete itself. Then at Philadelphia all the waiters were niggers, and now we are in the land of Æthiopian serenaders. We reached Philadelphia about twelve o'clock. The scenery

E

as we approached became very pretty, the rail passed along the banks of the broad Delaware, fringed with bright foliage to the water's edge, and clothed with islands. The wood is all of comparatively young growth; but the country is often charmingly diversified. Philadelphia is the second city in the Union, and the handsomest. The broad streets lined with trees, the shady squares, the massive white marble houses, all add to its imposing appearance. We only stayed there an hour, and then went to a terminus or depôt, as it is called, at the other end of the town. For day travelling the American cars are very convenient: they are always full of pretty girls, and if the scenery is not pretty you can look at them,—they are always sure to be looking at you. In the same carriage with us we had that notorious Irish "patriot" John Mitchell, another editor of a paper, a very disreputable-looking blackguard, and Routledge the cheap publisher, an intelligent, pushing fellow, who is come over to spy out the nakedness of the land, and is going to set up a shop in the States and Canada, and beat the Yankees on their own ground."

Passing on through Maryland, the first slave State, they spent an hour at Baltimore, which is described as being "more full of niggers and less of trees than the others we had seen": this time was occupied in visiting the Roman Catholic cathedral. They then proceeded by train to Washington, where they arrived late in the evening. After dinner they were "energetic enough to go at once to the Capitol to see the final vote taken on the Nebraska Bill, a measure which has caused more sensation, and is likely to lead to more important results, than any which has ever come before Congress."

" Considering, however, the tone of the papers, there was not so much excitement manifested as I had anticipated. The whole place was crowded, the galleries full of ladies, and when the bill in favour of slavery was carried by 100 to 113, the cheering was considerable. It is likely to lead to totally new combinations of parties, and the candidates at the next election will go to the country upon the question of slavery or abolition. It may possibly," he goes on, " lead to a revolution, so strong is the feeling on both sides. Members have come to Congress every night armed to the teeth, and it is quite an accident that there has not been a row : however, it is all over for the present, and there is a lull, during which we hope to effect our little plans. I was rather disappointed at there not being a row, and only two honourable members were drunk. One was obliged to be carried out, but did not show any sport ; the other asked me what the fools were voting about : considering the row there was at the time, I should not have been surprised at the question even had he been sober."

Laurence found the hotel at Washington uncomfortable, and the aspect of the place depressing, consisting of a wide long avenue, with the Capitol at one end and the President's house at the other. In fact, as he says of it, " it is a town without a population, and exists only by virtue of its being the seat of Government." He found his time also a good deal taken up, not with actual official work, but with much moving about, in constant attendance on Lord Elgin. The Queen's Birthday, however, broke the monotony a little.

" There was a grand flare-up at Crampton's, at which all the beauty and fashion of Washington were assembled. There were numbers of pretty girls, who were delighted at getting hold of Mr Oliphant, ' the traveller,' for by that term I am always introduced, and I found it difficult to be free and easy enough to please them. For instance, one carried me off to a quiet bench in the garden, and because I did not sit down, but stood respectfully talking, she got up, saying, ' Well, if you won't sit down alongside of me, it's no use my sitting here all night.' I need not say that after such an invitation I exerted myself in a way which won her affections ' slick off.' Notwithstanding which, I was rather astonished when, being seduced by her into a waltz, the only one in which I indulged, a fellow came up and took ' a twist with my gal.' I

asked whether that was the custom, and was assured
that I had nothing to complain of. Another girl whom
I took in to supper asked for ice, so I gave her some,
and could only find a fork, which I handed to her, on
which she said, 'Fancy eating ice with a fork!' However, I paid her off by handing her a huge table-knife,
and pointing in justification to a lady who was ladling in
cream in a way frightfully dangerous to behold. Most of
the young ladies I was introduced to asked me to call upon
them. Yesterday we had a great day in the Senate, and
there is to be some serious squabbling there to-day, which
I am going up with Lord E. to hear."

The interesting part of American politics at this time
would appear to have been the "rows"; and diplomatic
work with Lord Elgin could not have been very fatiguing,
since, as he says, they were engaged every night for a
week, and "the serious business of our visit is not yet in
train." Laurence, however, entertained no doubt of his
own diplomatic abilities when they should be called for.

"I have been engaged making arrangements for interviews with Ministers all the morning, and my diplomatic
powers are considerably in request, as they are 'cute
dodgy fellows, and have always got a sinister motive in
the background, which it is sometimes difficult to discover. To-morrow, I suppose, we shall be hard at it: I
shall be delighted. At the same time, this is a most relaxing and depressing place, close muggy air—Kandy temperature exactly—and streets silent and lifeless. The last
place in the world, notwithstanding the pretty girls, that
I should choose as a residence. I am going to join their
riding-parties if I have time, and will get to know them
'to their middle initials,' the height of Yankee intimacy."

The next letter, also from Washington, is dated the 28th
May, and, stimulated by the receipt of a letter from his
mother, is full of grave personal subjects. He finds himself in a difficult position, delighted and grateful for the
expression of her increased confidence in him, and her joy

at the proofs she receives of his changed and improved
character; but at the time tormented by the thought
that while he would not by throwing doubt on these
proofs take away any of her consolation, he could not
persuade himself that, though he was a little the better
for his experience, there was any real cause for self-
gratulation.

"My experience," he says, "has always been very slow
indeed, and while I recognise that an important change
has been going on in my sentiments upon many things,
still I feel as much embarrassed and perplexed as I ever
did. Not that I am rendered in any way so miserable as
I used to be, nor that I ever experience those violent
revulsions of feeling; but wherever there is a struggle
there must be times of depression. It is a merciful thing
that I take very little pleasure in that gaiety in which I
am obliged to mix, and by which formerly I should have
been intoxicated. And perhaps the pleasure of life seems
much diminished by the reflection that one must be in a
dangerous condition if one is not sacrificing some favourite
passion, however much it may be changed by the progress
of time, &c., &c. I heard this morning an admirable
sermon, and one which was peculiarly applicable to me,
in answer to my desire that I should hear something to
stimulate to more vigorous resistance—upon 'one thing
thou lackest.' My difficulty is to realise divine things
sufficiently to encourage me. The strongest incentive I
have to follow my convictions upon such subjects is the
inward peace and comfort which doing so has always
brought to me, and the opposite effect of indulging myself.
Therefore upon the lowest grounds I am disposed to
practise self-denial. In my present capacity I am not
engaged in any work of benevolence or charity by which
I could, as it were, support myself. And though, no
doubt, by my example I might glorify God, it is a much
more difficult matter to do so in a ball-room at the French
ambassador's, surrounded by as unthinking a throng as
ever tripped the light fantastic, than down in Westminster surrounded by M'Gregor, Fowler, & Co. At the

same time, I never saw more clearly the possibility of living in the world and not being of it. At present I am as satisfied that it is my duty to go to balls as to go to the Sunday-school was, provided I go in a right spirit; but it is easy to theorise. Perhaps I shall have an opportunity of testing my resolution in a very simple matter, about which nevertheless you have often expressed yourself—the matter of champagne. In Edinburgh I did not think it worth the sacrifice; but, as is often the case, one is forced into a line of conduct by the additional force of the temptation. It was only this morning that I felt the duty of putting the restraint upon myself of total abstinence, from my yesterday's experience, which was as follows :—

"At two o'clock our whole party went to a grand luncheon at a senator's. Here we had every sort of refreshing luxury, the day being pipingly hot, and dozens of champagne were polished off. Several senators got screwed, and we made good use of the two hours we had to spare before going to the French ambassador's *matinée dansante* at four. Here the same thing went on, with the addition of a lot of pretty girls whom I had before met, and who bullied one to dance, and were disgusted if you did not flirt with them. Everybody drinks champagne here, and there was a bowl on the table in which you might have drowned a baby, of most delicious and insinuating concoction. Then there were gardens, and bouquets, and ices, and strawberries, and bright eyes till six, when we had to rush off and dress for a grand dinner at a governor's. Here we had a magnificent repast. The old story of champagne, besides a most elaborate and highly got up French-cookery dinner, lasting from seven till ten, when we left the table, having been eating and drinking without intermission since two. We then adjourned with a lot of senators to brandy-and-water, champagne, and cigars till twelve, when some of us were quite ready to tumble into bed. Now I have no doubt you are perfectly horrified, and picture to yourself your inebriated son going to bed in a condition you never thought possible; but, on the contrary, yesterday was a most profitable day to me. In the first place, though I did not restrain myself, I did not in the slightest degree exceed. I did not touch anything else *but* champagne, and stopped exactly at the right moment. I felt all through that I was in a position not of my own seeking, and that if it was agreeable to me it was because I myself was at fault. I felt that it was only not positively disgusting because I participated, and that if I had not touched a thing I could not but have been excessively bored. I have therefore resolved never to touch another drop of champagne while in Washington, not because I took too much, but because I see that whether I am doing right or wrong depends entirely upon the spirit in which I participate in these things. It is necessary to the success of our mission that we conciliate everybody, and to refuse their invitations would be considered insulting. Lord Elgin pretends to drink immensely, but I watched him, and I don't believe he drank a glass between two and twelve. He is the most thorough *diplomat* possible, —never loses sight for a moment of his object, and while he is chaffing Yankees and slapping them on the back, he is systematically pursuing that object. The consequence is, he is the most popular Englishman that ever visited the United States. If you have got to deal with hogs, what are you to do? As Canning said of a man, 'He goes the whole hog, and he looks the hog he goes,' which is precisely a description of this respectable race; but I have no occasion even to pretend to drink their wine, and I shall therefore not do it. I was perfectly well this morning, but Sir Cusack Roney and Hincks are both laid up— poor Sir Q., as we call him, fairly knocked up, or rather down, by such unaccustomed proceedings. As I said, I am so far grateful to it all if it is the means of making me form resolutions and sticking to them, which less prominent dissipation, such as that of Edinburgh, would never have done.

" But a far more difficult matter than the champagne is the young ladies. My natural temperament not being amorous but very joyous, I get too boisterous, or rather reckless, in flirting, for simple fun. Therefore, though

there is no absolute command against other than idle
words, which is one none of us can very strictly apply, yet
I feel that I have been talking an amount of nonsense of
which my conscience is ashamed, and the effect of a whole
afternoon spent in the way I have described, which would
formerly be to distract and unsettle me, has been to sober
and solemnise me, and to make me think how I am to
meet the difficulties opposed to me. Under other circumstances, I should keep away from the drinking—this
would be no sacrifice; from the ladies it would be one
that I could easily make. I should call upon the missionaries if I was going to live here, and employ myself as I
did in London; but I am called upon to join in everything, and my conscience would not in the slightest degree
twit me for doing so, provided I was all the time bored
instead of pleased. The test of the thing is whether I like
it, and though I cannot say I do, I very soon would, and
therefore it is I must be especially watchful, while it
would be comparatively easy for me to form and keep
resolutions: and I have enjoyed the quiet of to-day and
the sermon, which was very comforting, though it inculcated a serious lesson. I am glad you spoke about the
tobacco, but at present there is no fear of that; Lord
Elgin hates smoking, and I do not like it in this jovial
soil of parties. I have not smoked half-a-dozen cigars
since leaving England, and every one has been a solitary
one, when I wanted to compose myself and think. I
think it prostitutes tobacco to drink and talk over it.
However, I shall never care really about it, and it is very
seldom that I am in the humour—generally when I am
disgusted with myself; and I am more self-satisfied, or to
speak more truly, have more tranquillity than I used to
have, and do not need soothing. Your letter was worth
all the cigars in the world."

After what he himself termed "this long confession,"
the letter turned to business. He had received much
applause in America on the subject of his book, and had
begun to inquire within himself whether he could write a
book which he felt ought to be written—namely, a phil-

osophical treatise on the American constitution, with the
chief heads of "slavery, federalism, and the great questions
upon which, sooner or later, the Union must fall to pieces."
This, by the way, in 1854, was not a bad prophecy for a
young man, who had not been in the country a month.
"The fallacies of the form of government," he says, "are
only dawning on me, and I should require a long course of
reading and observation before entering upon so serious a
task; but it would be the most interesting topic possible,
and one which, when it does force itself upon public attention, will engross the whole world." Right as he was
in some of his prognostics, he had no time to give to this
work, though he left the subject with a whimsical regret,
"It would be a great thing to have another book out in
the nick of time."

One more letter which followed from Washington was
filled with a sort of chronicle of the days between 31st
May and 5th June. He had at last got to work, though
it was while waiting for Lord Elgin to give him something to do that he took the opportunity of writing his
letter.

"I was occupied the greater part of yesterday in writing
officially. I am afraid I make a bad secretary: my forte
does not lie in business matters. In fact, I should be the
head of the department, not the clerk. It is so fearfully
hot and relaxing that one is not disposed for hard work.
I have not much new to tell. We dine out as usual, and
the dinners last three hours as usual, and I generally get
between two senators, one of whom pours abolitionism in
my ear, the other, the divine origin of slavery. The politics of this country are most complicated, and difficult to
understand; there are so many different parties, rejoicing
in so many different names. There are the Whigs, and
Democrats, and Filibusters, and Hard Shells, and Soft
Shells, and Free-Soilers, and Disunionists, and Federalists,
—all of whom expect you to understand at once their distinctive characteristics. I have not time to 'post myself'
up in all these matters, nor to see sights—in fact, America
would be a great deal more difficult to write about than

Russia, its constitution being so much more complicated, and its practical working so very different from its theory."

This conclusion, however, does not hinder him from indicating his opinion on various points: as, for instance, that whereas the President should be one of the first men in the country, he was in fact, as a rule, a mere cipher in point of intellect; and that bribery and corruption prevailed as universally as in Russia, though in a different way. Many American writers, in days since Laurence's letters were written, have pointed out this tendency and opening to corruption as the great inherent fault in their constitution. To investigate such a serious question, however, so as to find out its real cause, required more time than Laurence could give to it, as "now that Colonel Bruce, and Sir Cusack and Lady Roney have gone, and Hamilton is laid up in New York," he remained the only companion of Lord Elgin, and could go nowhere on his own account; so that he would seem to have given up the idea of writing a book.

"There is a great deal of self-denial involved with the conscientious discharge of my duties, and I am obliged to decline invitations to riding-parties, &c., &c., and take a sober stroll instead—all very good discipline, no doubt. It is a very great advantage to me, being behind the scenes in a matter of this kind, and seeing how an able man like Lord E. manages affairs. I compare him with papa. They have a good many points of similarity in their way of venting their indignation and fuming, and yet 'never acting impulsively. I occasionally take a look in upon Bury, who is living in another hotel: it is pleasant to look upon a kent face. I think it very possible that, now that Colonel Bruce has left Canada, I may act as Lord Elgin's private secretary there. However, that is only a supposition on my part: nothing has been said to me about it, so don't mention it; of course I should be glad to be employed in any way. . . . I am keeping all the accounts, and I think there must be a mistake somewhere, as I have expended and received some hundreds of dollars, and they come right exactly, which is most strange and unexpected.

"The other night I was dining out with rather a singular houseful of people: the master of the house was a senator, a methodist preacher, and a teetotaller; consequently, although it was a party of twenty people, we had nothing to drink but iced water. His wife, who unfortunately was not there, is a spirit medium, and in constant communication with the nether, though she calls it the upper, world. Her daughter, who sat next me at dinner, is a Bloomer, and never wears any other costume; she has an ugly shambling figure, and cuts the most absurd appearance: her husband is an avowed and rampant infidel, so that altogether it was a very odd if not instructive assemblage. I don't know how they all manage to get on together. For the preacher must look upon his son-in-law as a viper, and the son-in-law must look upon his mother as an impostor, and they must all look upon his wife as a fool—while she takes very good care to show the world that she wears the breeches."

Many other amusing notes follow as to the people he meets. On one occasion the gentleman sitting next him volunteered the information that he (the speaker) was a singular man, and related his history; how, left without a farthing at seven years old, he managed to pay for his own education out of his earnings, qualified as a barrister at the age of twenty - one, being then the proud owner of just 2 dollars 50 cents in the world, and owing 500 dollars; how, being not yet thirty, he had already lost wife and child, and was looking out for another bride to go with him on a journey to Europe, to study the politics of other countries before he came back to embark upon a political career in his own. On the morning of the day on which Laurence wrote, his companions were of a still more remarkable kind.

"On one side of me was the governor of the new

Territory of Washington, which lies to the north of Oregon, upon the North Pacific, and is seventy days' journey from this place: on the other side was a senator from Florida, who gave me some curious information about those parts. Then I made great friends with the celebrated Colonel Fremont, who is a splendid fellow, and has been more nearly starved to death, and more often in that predicament, 'than any other man in creation, don't care where you look for him.' Then there was Colonel Benton, who is writing a great work, and is 'quite a fine man'; and Mr Senator Toombs, who is to be president some of these days; and the governor of Wisconsin, whose government has increased in population, within ten years, from 30,000 to 500,000, and who met a man the other day who had travelled over the whole globe, and examined it narrowly with an eye to agricultural capabilities, and who therefore was an authority not to be disputed; and this man said that he had never, in any country, seen fifty square miles to equal that extent in the State of Wisconsin, and therefore it was quite clear that the spot was not contained in creation. As other provincials have informed me that their respective States are each thus singularly gifted, I am beginning to get puzzled as to which really is indisputably the most fertile spot on the face of the habitable globe.

"I have every hope that we shall polish off our treaty to-morrow, in which case we shall retire in the evening, covered with glory. It is a most exciting operation, and for the last few days, as matters have approached a crisis, I have been at it from morning till night, and then dreaming about it. The alternation of hope and fear is most trying, as new difficulties are suggested, and methods of solving them proposed, and new concessions gained, and the old Secretary of State bamboozled. Hincks goes away to-day, and Lord Elgin and I will be left alone. There are so many fellows opposed to the treaty, and so much underworking, that it requires considerable 'cuteness and caution to manage matters; but Lord Elgin is a match for them, and it is a pleasure to see how he works the matter. It would be of advantage to a fool, and of course it is invaluable to a clever cove like me, who is given to appropriating other men's dodges."

While all this serious and exciting business was proceeding, the dinners and *matinées dansantes* seem also to have gone on as continuously as ever, and "the soft balmy evenings in pretty gardens, with fruits and ices, and 'quite a clever piece' for a companion, are enjoyable enough." The next letter is dated the 7th of June, the last having ended on the 5th, and was written at New York, where he had arrived after the successful issue of the negotiations at Washington.

"We are tremendously triumphant; we have signed a stunning treaty. When I say we, it was in the dead of night, in the last five minutes of the 5th of June, and the first five minutes of the 6th day of the month aforesaid, that in a spacious chamber, by the brilliant light of six wax-candles and an argand, four individuals might have been observed seated, their faces expressive of deep and earnest thought, not unmixed with cunning. Their feelings, however, to the acute observer manifested themselves in different ways; and this was but natural, as two were young and two aged,—one, indeed, far gone in years, the other prematurely so. He it is whose measured tones alone break the solemn silence of midnight, except when one of the younger auditors, who are intently poring over voluminous MSS., interrupts him to interpolate 'and' or scratch out 'the.' They are, in fact, checking him; and the aged man listens while he picks his teeth with a pair of scissors, or clears out the wick of the candle with their points and wipes them on his hair. He may occasionally be observed to wink, either from conscious 'cuteness or unconscious drowsiness. Attached to these three MSS. by red ribbon are the heavy seals. Presently the clock strikes twelve, and there is a doubt whether to date it to-day or yesterday. For a moment there is a solemn silence, and he who was reading takes the pen, which has previously been impressively dipped in the ink by the most intelligent

of the young men, who appears to be his secretary, and
who keeps his eye warily upon the other young man, who
is the opposition secretary, and interesting as a specimen
of a Yankee in that capacity. There is something strangely
mysterious in the scratching of that midnight pen, for it is
scratching away the destinies of nations; and then it is
placed in the hands of the venerable file, whose hand does
not shake, though he is very old, and knows he will be
bullied to death by half the members of Congress. The
hand that has used a revolver upon previous similar occasions does not waver with a pen, though the lines he traces
may be an involver of a revolver again. He is now the
Secretary of State; before that, he was a judge of the
Supreme Court; before that, a general in the army; before
that, governor of a State; before that, Secretary at War;
before that, minister in Mexico; before that, a member of
the House of Representatives; before that, an adventurer;
before that, a cabinet-maker. So why should the old man
fear? Has he not survived the changes and chances of
more different sorts of lives than any other man? and is
he afraid of being done by an English lord? So he gives
us his blessing, and we leave the old man and his secretary
with our treaty in our pockets."

This letter was finished at Boston in the middle of the
continued journey. Laurence had been sent on at once to
New York, where he was kept awake all night by a demonstration in favour of a senator in the same hotel, so that
the vigil consequent upon the completion of the treaty was
not his only one. After this he travelled on "through
lovely country, wooded and watered and smiling, up glens
in the railway, which in these countries prefers going up
and down hill to going through tunnels, and going past
lakes embedded in foliage, with pretty villages of white
wooden houses inhabited by prim descendants of the
Pilgrim Fathers—and so on to this city, more like an
English commercial emporium than any other in the
States; and to-morrow we undergo a grand triumphal
reception at Portland, and next day another at Montreal,
and next day another at Quebec, all which I hope to find

time to tell you of in my next. Meanwhile Lord Elgin is rejoicing in the prospect of about six speeches a-day, and I in hopes of amusing myself, which, indeed, I have been doing very fairly all along. We have got Sir Cu. and Lady Roney, and in addition to them a Sir Henry and Lady Caldwell, in our party."

The details of description which he continues to give as he passes along may be less interesting to the sophisticated reader, who since then has heard so much of America; but they are at least brief and graphic. Portland, where the party "arrived under a salute, and went in procession to the house of one of the leading citizens," Laurence described as "lovely." "The situation of Portland is very striking, on a high promontory which overlooks an immense bay, on which upwards of three hundred islands are dotted; while towards the interior a richly wooded and fertile country stretches away to the base of the White Mountains, 6000 feet high. The town is well laid out—every street an avenue of noble trees, and the houses substantially built. It is destined before long to rival Boston, and will form the main outlet for Canadian produce. This treaty will be the making of it; and the inhabitants no doubt felt that they could not sufficiently honour the man who had done more for their town than anybody else."

The festivities here consisted chiefly of a great banquet, at which "Lord Elgin delighted them with his happy speeches"; and "I distinguished myself in responding to a 'sentiment' of a literary character with which my name was coupled." The entrance of the Mission into Canada after this partook of the character of a royal progress, with triumphal arches, cheering crowds, and welcoming speeches at all the stations. But at Montreal, "where the population is somewhat uncertain in its loyalty," their reception was by no means so demonstrative—although the people "behaved very decently" on the whole. From Montreal a special steamer carried the party on to Spencer Wood, the viceregal residence, of which Laurence gives an enthusiastic description. He writes on the verandah into which his rooms open, "enjoying a Mediterranean air and more than a Mediterranean view":—

"SPENCER WOOD, *June* 14, 1854.

"From the verandah extends a lawn studded with noble trees to the edge of a steep wooded bank, and among the trees rise the tapering masts of ships, which look as if they were eccentric branches. They are lying in the St Lawrence, two miles broad, and filled with craft of all sizes. It is at once peaceful and busy, and I prefer it to the sea, as in an epicurean point of view it is disturbing to see anything like commotion; but quiet life is perfect. The opposite bank of the St Lawrence is precipitous and well wooded, with villages at the base, or climbing up valleys or perched upon the edge, and churches prominent and picturesque. When I am tired of looking at the point of view over this lovely scene which my window affords, I stroll down a broad long avenue of magnificent trees; and then, turning through a thick copse by a winding path, I come upon a little wooded gorge, down which a noisy brook tumbles; and I follow that till it gets too impetuous for my sentimental system, or for the proper construction of the path, which there comes out abruptly upon the edge of a precipice where a summer-house is perched, from which you can look up and down the river for miles. In one direction the swelling banks, of the most brilliant green, are dotted with houses, for the whole country is thickly inhabited; on the other, a lofty promontory is crowned with the fortifications of Quebec, standing out into the river as if to guard the beauties that are beyond. The bay formed by the promontory on which I am, and that on which the Fort stands, is filled with wood. It is at once an island of planks and a forest of masts; and as I lie listening to the sound of the busy world, the songs of the sailors and the clang of hammers, the laughter of children and the rushing of the stream, I can enjoy *kief* to perfection; and I am afraid I have insensibly wasted some valuable time in allowing my senses to have the benefit of all these charms. Lord Elgin thinks I am the most romantic of authors, whereas I am rather surprised to find that I can now enjoy what I never before really appreciated, and I rejoice in the discovery of a new faculty of enjoyment and a fitting place to exercise it in. To be sure, I have had more to think about within the last few days than I ever had at any former period of my life—or at any rate, I have thought external circumstances worthy of more consideration than I am in the habit of doing. With one's sense of responsibility grows also the important reflection of its proper exercise, and I look upon moments of quiet as more necessary to fortify one to join in the racket of life, just in proportion as that racket is universal and becomes more distracting. I therefore recognise in the charms of Spencer Wood and the valley of the St Lawrence a legitimate source of comfort and support, intended for my benefit just when I most need it."

These somewhat solemn reflections, by which the young man excuses his love of loitering in a beautiful scene, are amusing enough; but the intimation at the end of his letter of the new position in which he suddenly found himself was enough to warrant the solemnity.

"My book has obtained for me all through our tour considerable notoriety, and I was immensely made of by the citizens of Portland and elsewhere. Here, too, where novelties are rare, I am an object of some curiosity, and am in consequence rather nervous at the prominence of my position—and which was so totally unexpected. I think I had just heard of it as I closed my last letter to you. Know, then, that I am now Superintendent-General of Indian Affairs, having succeeded Colonel Bruce in that office, and having as my subordinates two colonels, two captains (all of militia), and some English gentlemen who have been long in the service, and who must look rather suspiciously at the 'Oriental Traveller's' interposition. However, I hope to get on pretty well, notwithstanding I already contemplate rowing one of the colonels and turning him out if he is not more attentive to his duties."

The appointment of so young a man, not even a member of the Civil Service, and entirely new to Canada and its needs, was evidently by no means a popular one if we may trust the cuttings from Canadian papers which accompany

these letters; and caused great talk of favouritism, and
the sacrifice of the public service to private motives. He
himself, however, was full of great intentions on the
subject, and a determination to do his duty. He writes
in a subsequent letter that he has not been fully employed, and is disgusted by the waste of time.

"SPENCER WOOD, *July* 7.

"However, it is not altogether lost, for I have been
revolving great projects in my brain. One is to remodel
to a great extent the Indian Department, and the whole
system upon which the Indian tribes are at present
managed. However, it must be done with caution and
well matured, as I suspect the Government will not
readily assent to my views, which are a little arbitrary
and despotic. Then I am going to compile information
for a book which I have been planning. It is to be a
sort of treatise on constitutional government, contrasting
this country with the United States, showing the abuses
of the latter and the advantages of responsible government. I have got such great advantages here in the way
of material, that I do not like to let the opportunity slip.
At the same time, it is such a tremendous undertaking,
and I commence it in a condition of such abject ignorance,
that I have not as yet plucked up courage to face it.
Moreover, it is a nervous operation to risk one's reputation upon so grand a theme. However, success will be all
the more glorious, and I shall not be in a hurry, but di-
gest and compile slowly; and then, when the great crash
comes in the States which is inevitable, I will try and
turn out a few notions on the crisis at the nick of time.
If the crisis does not come, I shall put my information
into an anonymous form, rather than publish anything
with my name that is not paramountly interesting. If
Aunt M. and others wish to know whether my appointment is permanent, pray say that I am most thankful it is
not. Nothing can be a greater curse to a young man
wishing to get on than a permanent appointment. It is
certainly not the quickest way to get up a ladder to
establish one's self on the lowest step."

And here is a piece of precocious youthful wisdom, perhaps not quite so wise as that above quoted. It is given with the absolute certainty which members of the human race possess at twenty-five. "No man who has been the editor of a Government paper for twenty years can retain his honesty. You see how the 'Times' has been obliged to go into opposition: they were losing their influence fast. Nothing is more established than the fact that the newspaper which exerts the greatest influence in a country must be in opposition. It is also sure of a larger circulation, because Government supporters are obliged to take it to see what is said, and the opponents take it because they agree with it.

"I confess," adds the young man, going back to questions less abstract, "that I am rather fascinated with the new world. There is such scope for great political chances and changes. Now that we have got reciprocity, there can be no doubt that Canada is best off as she is, in spite of all the nonsense that ass Ellenborough talked. It is a great comfort to feel that if the old world does not pay we can fall back upon the new. There is plenty of room, and great facilities for becoming rich."

Another letter, however, from the paradise of Spencer Wood, where his mind was full of so many projects, both practical and visionary, is of a very different tone. It is like the opening of a door in the secret chamber of the young man's heart and thoughts, at which his mother was continually knocking, anxious above all things to know how his mind stood in respect to the momentous matters of religion, in which, from his earliest childhood, she had desired continual confidences. I do not know what Lady Oliphant's distinctive views were at this time. They were, perhaps, a little open to the influence of the prevailing preacher who interested and instructed her; but they were always full of profound and emotional piety, and her strongest desire was that her son should be like herself, placing sacred subjects in absolute pre-eminence both in his thoughts and life—and that he should tell her so. He writes on a Sunday morning, when "kept back by a wet day from going to church."

"Just now, however, the sun has burst forth from behind the clouds, and makes nature here look more lovely than ever. While enjoying it just now, I was struck with the congenial sentiments expressed in the Psalm to which I was referred in Bogatsky, the 143d: they seemed exactly to explain my feelings. The more sensible one is of the magnificence of the works of creation, the more incompetent one feels to live worthily of the author of them, and a sort of feeling of desolation is induced, which David evidently sympathised with. There is a hopeless longing to be assimilated to the Creator, no doubt increasing in intensity in proportion as one appreciates His works; and in spite of any combinations of external circumstances which, so far as the world is concerned, seem enough to make one perfectly happy and contented, the very fact of one's being capable of a certain degree of enjoyment makes one desire a still higher order. Of nothing am I more certain than of the incompetency of any earthly gratification affording happiness just on the same principle: it is always accompanied with an indefinable longing for something more, just as when one contemplates nature and enjoys it most keenly, the soul begins to thirst after God as a thirsty land, and 'the heart within is desolate.' David evidently looked upon nature as an appointed means of elevating the soul. So many of his aspirations have their origin in this; and in admiring God's works nothing can be more natural than an ardent desire to be imbued as largely as possible with the same spirit that breathes in them. 'Thy spirit is good.' As I think I said in a letter some time ago, we do not half appreciate the influence of the Spirit. I am perhaps inclined to give it too prominent a place, my natural inclination being to overlook the Second Person as the only recognised means of obtaining the Third. But that is just where my faith is most severely tried. Everything around me testifies to the existence of a Being who is all-pervading; but the Son is nowhere visible, and does not, so to speak, force Himself upon the senses. It is a totally different act of the mind which is required

to accept Him as a positive fact. To speak in old
Erskine's phraseology, the subjective Tally is wanting,
which, in the Deity and His Spirit, as manifested in
nature, is so readily found. However, I have rather
wandered from the original idea, which presented itself
forcibly on reading the Psalm; and it is worthy of observation that David had not only the subjective as
regards God in nature but in Christ, and that by an act
of faith infinitely more difficult than ours, as it was pros-
pective. This want on my part is therefore the result,
doubtless, of a small measure of the Spirit, and I have
the most perfect confidence that if I earnestly desire to
be taught and confirmed on this point, the Spirit will
effectually operate. At present, with the small measure
I as yet possess, and the pertinacity with which I grieve
and offend it in spite of its remonstrances, I can scarcely
expect to make any rapid progress; but I think you will
understand from what I have said how the 143d Psalm
should chime in with my feelings, and be comforting in
showing how a man of David's spirituality was occasionally led to lament over his own weakness while meditat-
ing on God's works. You used to say that the more I
was favoured by external circumstances, the more I
grumble and am discontented with myself. I think
even after David was a king he was occasionally affected
in like manner, and were it not so, one would be disposed to think that one was deserted altogether, and left
to one's own evil devices."

While thus, however, opening his heart to his mother
in the way she most eagerly desired, he was very anxious
not to give her too high an idea of his spiritual progress,
or represent himself as better than he felt himself to be;
and in the end of the same letter, continued some days
later, he protests against her too delighted reception of
such spiritual confidences.

"I think you overrate my progress, and give way to
your natural impulses too much in the expression of such
ardent rejoicings. I only hope they will not be turned

into mourning. I am of course very glad of anything that reconciles you to our separation; but at the same time feel my own weakness too much to desire that you should repose too much confidence in my resolutions, or anticipate too great results from what I wrote. This is just one of the reasons which make me hesitate about expressing so very much. It would be far better for you not to form extravagant expectations, than having formed them to be disappointed. However, I do not mean that you should not be grateful with all humility, or that it is not natural, if you feel comforted during my absence, that you should say so; only you must remember that the effects of it might be to produce a spirit of self-satisfaction in me, or a desire to write more of the same comfortable doctrine when I don't feel it, with many other bad effects—to say nothing of the dreadful reaction which is always possible, and which is indeed inevitable when any one emotion is allowed an undue influence. There is a most ungrateful lecture to return to such an affecting outpouring as few sons, I am sure, ever received; but however agreeable it may have been at the time, the danger of going to extremes in these matters struck me too forcibly not to make me feel warranted in telling you, as you always ask me to do so."

The important post to which he had been appointed, and which carried him into untrodden ways, and put the affairs of the Canadian Red men into his youthful keeping, with no experience, and only his native intelligence, shrewdness, and keen perception of human character to guide him, gave him material for an interesting and amusing book, 'Minnesota and the Far West,' published immediately after his return, and for some further recollections published in the 'Episodes in a Life of Adventure,' which make it unnecessary to enter largely into them here. In the carrying out of this work, he had to travel far into the depths of the country, and to meet with many novel experiences. "This duty," he says, "was eminently to my taste. It involved diving into the depths of the backwoods, bark-canoeing on distant and silent lakes or down foaming rivers, where the fishing was splendid, the scenery most romantic, and camp-life at this season of the year, for it was the height of summer, most enjoyable." It was a prolonged picnic, with just enough duty thrown in to deprive it of any character of selfishness. At nearly all the stations there was a school or mission-house of some kind, and here the meeting of the warriors and young braves with their "father" (himself) took place,—"and as I had barely attained the age of twenty-five when these paternal responsibilities were thrust upon me, the incongruity of my relation towards them, I am afraid, presented itself somewhat forcibly to the minds of the veterans on these occasions." The most important result of his work among them seems to have been, as in the case of the work in Washington, the signing of a treaty. Two State negotiations more different than that between Great Britain and the United States, and that by which the poor Indians gave up for a substantial consideration the land previously allotted to them, but which their wandering habits prevented them from making any proper use of, could scarcely be. But the young diplomatist found interest in both.

The latter part of Lord Elgin's viceroyalty was full of stirring Colonial politics, changes of Ministry and much political commotion; and when the young Superintendent of Indian Affairs returned to Quebec from his voyage to the West, it was to resume the duties of his Excellency's private secretary in troubled times—the trouble, however, doing little more than add a zest to the work, and a little excitement to life. "My position here is very agreeable," he writes; "I have pleasant alternatives of excitement and tranquillity, always plenty to occupy me, a climate which agrees with me better than any other I ever was in; and in many ways I think I am gaining much valuable experience.

"I found no less than ten official letters, besides the English mail, awaiting me this morning. I had moreover four appointments of gentlemen wanting interviews, a lot of incidental coves to stave off from his Excellency, which I flatter myself is the part of the business I excel in most. They always leave infinitely better pleased than if they

had had their interview. My life is much like that of
a Cabinet Minister or Parliamentary swell, now that the
House is sitting. I am there every night till the small
hours, taking little relaxations in the shape of evening
visits when a bore gets up. That keeps me in bed till
late, so that breakfast and the drive in (from Spencer
Wood), &c., detain me from the office till near one. Then
I get through business for the next three hours—chiefly
consisting of drafting letters, which in the end I ought to
be a dab at. I have three bell-ropes hanging at my right
hand communicating with my two departments and the
messengers. I also append my valuable signature to a
great deal without knowing in the least why, and run out
to the most notorious gossips to pick up the last bits of
news, political or social, with which to regale his Excellency, who duly rings for me for that purpose when he
has read his letters and had his interviews. Then he walks
out with an A.D.C., and I go to the House. There I take up
my seat on a chair exclusively my own next the Speaker,
and members (I have made it my business to know them
nearly all) come and tell me the news, and I am on chaffing terms with the Opposition, and on confidential with
the Ministerialists. If I see pretty girls in the galleries
who are friends of mine (the galleries are always full), I
go up there and criticise members and draw caricatures
of them, which they throw down into members' laps neatly
folded, who pass them to the original,—by which time I
have regained my seat, and the demure secretary remains
profoundly political and unsuspected. I find nothing so
difficult as keeping up my dignity, and when the Bishop
or a Cabinet Minister calls, I take their apologies for in-
truding as if I was doing them a favour. I am afraid of
hazarding a joke unless I am quite sure it is a good one.
I suppose the dignity of the office was so well sustained
by Bruce, that they are scandalised by a larky young cove
like me."

More serious matters, however, mingled with the fun
with which the gay young secretary diversified his life.
On the day after a great picnic, terminating in an im-

promptu dance which was his suggestion, and which
accordingly he devoted all his faculties to carry out successfully, he describes himself as " fairly done up."

" The Ministers were determined to push through the
answer " (to the Governor's speech from the throne), " in
order that by large majorities they might influence the
election of the new Ministers in Upper Canada; the
Opposition were determined to defeat that object: so it
was a question of who would sit it out. The consequence
was a debate of twenty-two hours. I had dined out and
gone to an evening party, and then went to the House
and remained till half-past four, when Mackenzie the
quondam rebel got up to make a rambling speech which
I hear lasted for four hours; but I left, and when I
returned at one in the afternoon I found the House still
sitting, so you see Parliament is not a mere sham in this
country, and its value is properly appreciated. On Thursday we had a succession of grand doings, beginning at
twelve, accounts of which you will see in the papers.
Lord Elgin made a magnificent oration in French: it is
really a pleasure to be attached to such a man, so stunning in certain respects. It created a great sensation.
The whole thing was novel and exciting: first the reception by a dozen purple episcopates in the Archbishop's
palace, and then the opening of a Roman Catholic college by his Excellency. Your liberality would not quite
come such a stretch as that. There were some thousands
of people assembled. Some of the Protestants here are
highly disgusted, but I highly approve. No sooner was
this proceeding over than we received the dutiful answer
to the address from the Commons, which was an echo of
the Governor's speech, and a great triumph to him after
all the abuse that has been lavished upon him. The answer has been carried through the House by overwhelming
majorities. After that we received a quantity more of
purple ecclesiastics. All this time I had been in full
dress, white tie, &c. Then to the House till dinner, when
I dined with Mr Primrose, Lord Rosebery's brother, who
afterwards had a ball, where I remained till pretty late.

Not the best preparation in the world for our own ball at Spencer Wood to-night; but I shall cut some of that by staying in the House to see the Reciprocity Treaty through. It was read last night for the first time. However, the Governor says the success of the ball depends upon me. I have introduced four new dances into Quebec. What an enviable reputation to have, and how astonished my Edinburgh friends would be! and yet I don't care nearly so much for gaiety as I used to do. Only whatever I undertake I like to carry out with a will; and if we are to leave Canada with a flare-up after eight years of the most successful administration that any Governor ever had, I will do my best."

"Society here is really very agreeable," he adds. "There are no sets or jealousies, but everybody is on excellent terms and very good-natured." As usual, he was specially interested in one portion of society. I do not know if the peculiar institution hereafter described has found a place in any other record: "The girls are for the most part lively and pretty, with a deal of French in them, which prevents their having a taste for solid information, but makes up for it by giving them plenty of small talk and fascinating manners. I go upon the principle of dispensing my favours so liberally that my attentions cannot be said to be particular, though that is not at all the fashion. Every girl has what is called her muffin, —some *devoué*, who never leaves her side, dances with her always when he is not sitting with her in a dark corner, and behaves as if he were engaged. This, however, is not the case, nor is it expected. It is quite an understood thing that he is her muffin and she his, not her future husband, and curiously enough no harm ever comes of it. Sometimes it ends in marriage, but never in anything else."

There is a great deal about these young ladies in the letters, especially as his time draws towards an end; and he becomes full of questions as to his conduct,—whether he has kept up to his own standard, whether it would be possible for him to keep up to it if he stayed longer, and how his young successor, with whom he has had many

confidences on the subject of religion—sometimes feeling
that his advices do the young man good, sometimes that
his inconsistencies do him harm—will be able to withstand the many temptations of society. For Quebec
society, with that delightful mixture of French ease and
lightness, with the charms and frankness of the ladies,
the good - humour and freedom and friendliness of all
around, is sadly against serious thought: and as he half
impels and half is impelled by his chief into the blaze of
entertainment and gaiety which is wanted to make a brilliant conclusion to Lord Elgin's administration, his doubts
and tribulations grow more and more. "Lord E. says he
never knows what I am at, at one moment going to the
extreme of gaiety, at another to that of disgust and de-
spondency. All he wishes is in a good-natured way to
amuse people; and he therefore can hardly sympathise
with my reactions every now and then, which arise from
my being too well amused myself. He sees my twinges
of conscience, and asked me the other day whether I was
going to lay all the sins I seemed so much oppressed
with at his door? At another he said, ' All these comments of yours upon our proceedings distress me very
much. After all, we are only amusing people, and if you
have got anything to repent of, I wish you'd wait and do
it on board ship.'" Then after an outcry, which is not
at all intended to be humorous, " Flesh and blood can't
stand the temptation of such hosts of charming girls!"
the young secretary comments somewhat demurely as
follows :—

" There is a class of sins which are very difficult to
resist, because you cannot put your finger upon the exact
point where they become sins. Now, for instance, a certain degree of intimacy with young ladies is no harm;
and it is difficult to define where flirting begins, or what .
amount even of joking and laughing, though perfectly
innocent, is not expedient, and one gets led imperceptibly
on without feeling the harm that is being done to both
parties until it is too late. As I told you before, I am not
in any degree involved in anything : but I daresay I should

be if I stayed; or as an alternative, become more utterly heartless in those matters than I am already."

These scruples being set to rest, or at least temporarily silenced by being put into words, he gives a most lively description of the setting in of winter, which he had much desired to see before leaving Canada—a wish which was gratified by means of various unforeseen ministerial changes which delayed Lord Elgin's departure. Describing these changes, and lamenting the disappointment to his eagerly expectant parents in consequence, he adds:—

"Meantime I am revelling in the first burst of winter and its attendant novelty. I would not have missed it for the world. My office window looks upon the Place d'Armes, a large square. On the one side is the platform overlooking the river, forming the promenade in summer; on the other the main street, Parliament House, &c., opposite gardens. The day is mild and calm, and the snow half a foot deep. Not a wheeled vehicle is to be seen. Cabstands all sleighs, no two alike in shape. Round the Place sleighs with tandems or pairs, full of ladies muffled up in furs, with buffalo-robes streaming behind, dash about rapidly over the crisp snow, making a merry accompaniment to its crunching with their bells, the occupants looking prettier than ever. Single men dashing about in swell turn-outs, from which I must say Bury with his blood horses bears the palm. They go round and round, cut out and in, and then dash away through the Fort gates into the snow-clad country. With a pleasant companion nothing could be more exhilarating. Some of the faster young ladies are picked up by the most insinuating young men and driven *tête-à-tête*, so snug and confiding. I had a charming muffin yesterday. She is engaged to be married, so don't be alarmed. By changing every day you are quite safe. It does not do to be particular; besides, as you may suppose, the nicest won't go even with their most particular friends unless there is a picnic or a sleighing party, though why it is more correct or less dangerous then, I cannot exactly say.

"From the platform the scene is extraordinary; the river full of floes of floating ice, which collects in the bays, and surges up into fantastic masses. People cross in canoes, and when they get to a floe, the boatmen jump on it and haul the canoe over, the occupants remaining still. I watch them from the platform. The most exciting part of sleighing is turning corners. Unless you know the dodge you are sure to upset, but it is only into the snow, and no harm is done. I have not been upset yet, and always go like the wind."

One of the most pleasant things in these letters is the character—always wholly admired, not always comprehended—the remarkable figure of the chief, his Excellency, who is sometimes called, in puzzled familiarity, "a queer fish," but whose boundless ability, his skill, his command of every resource, his plans never fully expounded, gradually dawning by degrees on the young disciple's brilliant intelligence, his sympathy yet authority, come out before us in a hundred minute touches under the hand of the writer, all unconscious that he is making any such portrait in the letter he dashes off to his mother punctual as the post, before he touches his official work. It is, of course, imperfect, and in a manner accidental; but it is admirably vivid and true. I am not aware if any memoir of the late Lord Elgin has been given to the public; but if not, the letters I have quoted would afford much admirable material to assist in such a memorial.

CHAPTER V.

THE CRIMEA.

LAURENCE returned home early in 1855, to find his parents awaiting him in London. His own prospects, however, were so unsettled—the engagement with Lord Elgin terminating on the withdrawal of the latter from

office, though to be renewed at a later period—that no
definite home was established in London; and the family,
thus reunited, would seem to have contented themselves
in lodgings, now in one street, now in another,—not a very
comfortable mode of life. And it is apparent that the
Chief-Justice of Ceylon, accustomed to so full an existence
and to occupy a very important position in his own sphere,
felt himself considerably out of his element in London,
where at first he had not even the comfort of a club where
he could meet his old friends, these institutions being less
necessities of life in those days than they are now. And
not unnaturally Laurence, after his brief but brilliant
experience of public life, found it difficult to content himself without occupation and with the doubtful prospects
before him. His mind returned with a bound to its
former aspirations in respect to the Crimea, and to the
plan he had conceived of making a diversion in the
Caucasus, and thus drawing away the attention of Russia
to a country which it was of so much importance to her to
overawe and secure. He had declined an offer made to
him to remain in Canada as secretary to Sir Edmund
Head, the successor of Lord Elgin, in the spirit of his own
axiom that a man who means to climb a ladder does not
establish himself on the lowest step. I am told that he
also declined a small governorship in the West Indies,
probably, if this is true, for the same reason; but to
remain inactive, waiting upon fortune, was impossible to
him. The plan which he had reluctantly resigned in order
to accompany Lord Elgin now came back to his mind
with double force; and he soon found an opportunity to
explain and press his views. "I proposed," he says, "to
Lord Clarendon that I should undertake a mission to
Schamyl, for the purpose, if possible, of concocting some
scheme with that chieftain by which combined operations
could be carried on, either with the Turkish contingent,
which was then just organised by General Vivian, or
with the regular Turkish army." He never ceased to
believe that great things could have been done had this
plan been carried out,—that the fall of Kars might have
been averted, and most sensible assistance given in the

carrying out of all the objects of the war. He had scarcely got back to London, plunging again into all the excitement of that momentous time when the Crimea and the struggle going on there was the universal topic, than he flashed forth a pamphlet on this subject, calling the general attention to his project. Perhaps Lord Clarendon, then no doubt harassed with many suggestions, considered it the easiest way at last of getting rid of the eager young man, whose arguments were unanswerable and his perseverance boundless, to send him off to the heart of the diplomatic strife at Constantinople, and thus transfer the trouble of settling the question to other shoulders than his own. "He determined to send me with a letter to Lord Stratford de Redcliffe, authorising him to send me to Daghestan, in the Eastern Caucasus, where Schamyl had his stronghold, for the purpose of making certain overtures to him, at his lordship's own discretion."

It is difficult not to believe that Lord Clarendon's sanction to the journey which Laurence was so eager to undertake was more in the nature of a permission, accompanied by an introduction to Lord Stratford, than anything more authoritative. The young man, however, took it in a weightier sense, and set out in the highest spirits, accompanied by his father, whose delight in escaping from the uncongenial crowd of London, and in the prospect of exciting scenes and experiences, seems to have been even greater than that of his son. A compunction momentarily clouded the mind of Laurence at the thought of the mother left alone behind, with the chief objects of her existence both gone: but he comforted himself with the thought of the visits to kind friends which she was about to pay in the meantime, and the ministrations of a kind and dear Lucy, a favourite niece, who would console her; and also with an immediate effort to keep her amused by the most lively account of the journey, and everything that he and "Papa" said and did. Papa appears in an altogether delightful light in this history. Of course he picks up the greatest snobs on board to be kind to, as Lady Oliphant will understand—he keeps his end of the table full of jokes and mirth, he enjoys everything with the freshness of a boy, and with still more delightful freedom and pleasure in novelty than even his son experiences. Laurence, indeed, becomes for the time middle-aged and serious in presence of his father's *insouciance* and charming boyishness. The pair take the steamer at Marseilles for Constantinople, and find themselves at once drifted into the war atmosphere. With them in the ship is "Captain Speke of the Turkish Contingent, formerly East India Company's service, who was speared in nine places on the coast of Africa, where Burton, with whom he was, was also wounded and their other companions killed. Of course he is dying to go back and try again, but is going to take a turn to Sebastopol first." This is all that Laurence says of the great traveller. It is curious thus to meet undistinguished, before the events that made him famous, passing across our vision for a moment, so well-known a figure. Another of more heroic mould, Gordon, Laurence encountered in the trenches before Sebastopol, but unfortunately there is no record of that meeting.

Lord Stratford was not found at Constantinople, and the travellers accordingly followed him in the blazing August weather, up the Bosphorus to Therapia. The little steamer, which now fusses so noisily yet so peacefully from village to village along the shores of that glorious strait, breathed nothing but gunpowder in those exciting days. "The occupants of the boat were all Crimean officers; none we actually knew, but we found plenty of mutual acquaintance. It was exactly like dining at a mess. Old friends met and talked over their wounds and their dangers—some boys of seventeen who have gone through the whole thing, and were only anxious to get back. One man would come and say, 'How are you, old fellow?' and the old fellow, not remembering him, would add, 'Were you not in the night attack?' and then they would talk over old scenes, not having seen each other since parted by cannon-balls on that eventful night." At the house of the English ambassador at Therapia, Laurence was received with great kindness by

Lord Stratford, who talked to him much about the war, taking the eager young diplomatist into his confidence, and no doubt glad to hear from a new witness so brilliantly observant and free from officialism what was said and thought at home, where already he had been misrepresented. The ambassador ended by inviting his visitor to go with him to the seat of war, whither he was just about to start in his yacht in order to bestow sundry decorations. Amid all his kindness and confidential talk, he would not, however, say anything about the mission to Schamyl, which Lord Clarendon had left "to his lordship's discretion." Disappointed by this, yet pleased and flattered by the place thus offered to him among Lord Stratford's immediate surroundings, Laurence resolved to accept his offer. "On the way," he says, "I shall have plenty of time for imbuing Lord S. with my own notions, and if he does not succumb to my diplomacy in the end, I shall consider myself too stupid to cope with Schamyl, and be consoled."

"As I look out of my bedroom window," he adds, "I see nothing but confusion; the whole quay covered with French troops grouped round their knapsacks, and going off in boats to the steamers, while bullock-waggons containing heavy baggage wheel along the water's edge, and busy steamers of all sizes are passing up and down the Bosphorus in such numbers that people never look at them." The traveller of the present day, who has felt how much the lovely peacefulness of those beautiful shores is enhanced by the stream of vessels of all descriptions that go up and down from the Black Sea to the more peaceful waters of Marmora and the busy port of the Golden Horn, will be able to form some small idea of the commotion and excitement of that moment, when the white sails and peaceful fleets of trade were swept out of the straits, and the transports and ships of war, bound to and fro to replenish the ranks with fresh troops and bring back the wounded and fever-stricken, were all that were visible. Yet even in the midst of this absorbing commotion, the young self-sent envoy, palpitating with eager projects, had time for affectionate and serious thought.

G

"I need not say that you are never absent from my thoughts, in the midst of all my plans more than ever; feeling how deeply you are interested in every one of them, and above all feeling how anxious you must be. I find myself, therefore, referring to you mentally at every moment, and the only thing that gives me anxiety is the fear that you may be so worried and anxious as to interfere with your health. Just in proportion as my present life is one to cause you anxiety do I constantly recur to you. When I was gay and thoughtless in Canada, I did not think half so much about you as now when I have got more weighty matters in hand. I hope you quite see the propriety of not missing such an opportunity of conferring with Lord S. as my voyage with him to the Crimea offers. I have been lying on my back for an hour reading and praying. I think it has done me good and strengthened my faith. I feel ready for anything that God may see fit,—for disappointment, I hope, as well as success."

It is impossible not to feel that now and then his mother's call upon him for spiritual confidences, and a report of all his thoughts, gave the young man a certain impatience, and that he satisfied her desire for information as to the state of his soul, sometimes with utterances which must have startled her, sometimes with attempts, not very successful, to fall into the more ordinary vein of religious musings. And there is always apparent a little relief in getting back to the things of this world, which it was more easy to treat. "I hope to get Sir E. Lyons and General Simpson to see the propriety of a Circassian expedition," he says, carried away from his halting religious revelations to the more eager tide of his hopes, "and if so, shall insist upon being accompanied by a strong military force, which will give a weight to my representations which would be wanting to a solitary agent." It is evident from the uncertainty and anxiety of these utterances that Lord Clarendon's recommendation to Lord Stratford must have been more a favourable one of a remarkable and highly gifted young man, than anything in the shape of official instructions to the ambassador.

His next letter is dated from Kamiesch Bay, and gives a curious sensation of the very atmosphere and breath of war. "Long before we saw land we saw the vivid flashes of the guns, and heard the reports when we got nearer: a heavy cannonade was kept up all night. Very curious," he adds, "to be rigging out in ball costume (to dine in the Royal Albert, the Admiral's ship) to the sound of the booming guns of the bombardment. After dinner we watched the bombardment from the stern of the vessel,— sometimes the flashes rapid and close together, and the noise of the cannonading very great; at others it died away for a time." With their glasses they could see the shells whizzing through the air, falling in the trenches, and the rush of the soldiers in all directions. Few spectacles could be so exciting. In the meantime Laurence had given the ambassador his pamphlet to read, with the opinions of which Lord Stratford expressed his full agreement. "He has done everything but promise to send me to Schamyl," the young man adds; "that he staves off, and says he will think about it, &c. Though he can show no good objections, still he does not take to the scheme kindly." Laurence was not yet experienced enough to understand how different a thing it was to silence a statesman in argument, so that he could "show no good objections," and to get him to take in hand a visionary though hopeful scheme.

Arrived at the camp, Laurence describes to his mother the innumerable lines of tents, some miserable indeed, some comfortable enough, in which he finds as best he can a friend here and there, and snatches an exciting taste of this life of the camp, in which every pulse of existence was at the highest pressure, all the more stormy and strong in their beating from the constant disaster about, and the frequent carrying past of strings of dying and wounded men. The perpetual sound of the guns soon becomes familiar. "Since I have been here there has not elapsed a single minute, either by day or night, in which I have not heard the report of cannon." One of his objects

while he roams among the lines is to find a tent for
"Papa," from whom he has been obliged to separate in
consequence of his invitation to accompany the ambassador,
but who followed him to the camp, and remained a most
interested and excited spectator of the extraordinary life
there, after Laurence himself had hurried on to further
and more wonderful experiences still.

On board the Royal Albert, on the occasion of the dinner-party which took place, while sky and water thrilled
with the extraordinary sensation of shot and shell, Laurence had met the Duke of Newcastle, who had planned
some sort of visit to the Circassian coasts, and who immediately invited the young man to join him. It is curious
to note how, as soon as he appears on the scene, this irresistible young man connects himself with all that is highest and most influential near him. He seems to have kept
the Duke's proposal in reserve as a sort of *pis aller*, not
without a practical consciousness that an invitation from
an ex-Minister and influential political personage was not
one to be neglected, yet more intent upon his own plan
than on any kind of social promotion. At last, scarcely
because convinced by Laurence's reasoning, yet perhaps
yielding a little to the influence of his strong conviction,
Lord Stratford sent Mr Alison, one of his own staff, on a
special mission to Circassia in H.M.S. Cyclops, with instructions to confer with Mr Longworth—the agent in
charge of British interests along the coast-line, where
many forts and villages had been taken from the Russians
—upon the possibilities and advantages of a diversion
such as was proposed; and, as Laurence believed, to consult as to the practicability of his own anxiously desired
mission to Schamyl. As this latter, however, never came
to anything, it may be permitted to the reader to believe
that the ambassador was glad to occupy the eager young
applicant by packing him off in attendance upon this envoy, and thus keeping him amused at a distance while
grave questions were being discussed.

Laurence set out with high hopes, thinking that at last
his somewhat quixotic and adventurous purpose was in a
fair way of being carried out. And for the next three

months he was kept cruising about the coast, now feeling
his object almost within his reach, now further off from it
than ever. He was in the midst of a little group of officials who were by no means sorry to have the help of his
ready wit, and who enjoyed his cheerful company, but
there is no appearance that his plan was ever taken into
serious consideration at all. As time went on, and doubts
on this subject began to cross his mind, he took great
pains to justify himself to his mother for going on with
an adventure which was evidently very pleasing in itself,
though it did not carry out his intentions. "Besides
writing to you," he says, "I have got the 'Times' to write
long letters to. I look upon this as a great duty, because
it brings me in lots of tin, and it is the only way I can
justify my present life. I feel that in no other way could
I be making so much money by my own efforts." This
most excellent reason for continuing in a position so agreeable to him Laurence puts forth, however, with so many
repetitions, that we feel he is not himself quite satisfied
with it, perceiving no doubt that, notwithstanding the
"lots of tin," and the still more consolatory sense that he
was the only Englishman who could give the British public
any real information on the subject which he felt to be so
important a one, he was not at all carrying out the great
plan of public benefit and private ambition with which he
had started.

Amid all the adventures and excitements of this strange
life, however, he always found time to gratify his mother
by that report of his more serious thoughts, and the
progress of his spiritual life, for which she was always
asking.

"I am constantly thinking about these things," he says.
"I am afraid, however, I generalise too much, and am
rather getting into a way of overlooking ceremonies. I
cannot but think that if a man tries to act honestly and
uprightly and singly, the details of the thing are of comparatively little importance; but then I also find that you
need the details as helps. It is a great mistake to attach
the importance we do to the inherent virtue of these de-

tails, and misleads us. Let every man find out which
details help him most, and adhere to them. Looked on in
this light, I think Sunday is a valuable detail. I look
upon your letters as a detail to help me: the day I get
them is much more of a Sunday to me than any other.

"I feel strongly the love of God for me, and thankfulness to Him, and great fear of offending Him. I only do
not always think that I am offending Him, when you and
others would think that I did. The more I think of Him,
the more glorious does His service appear, and I dread
that I might fall into sin, and am sorry that I do not keep
a strict watch on my conversation, and I do not think He
hides Himself from me when I pray."

"When one is knocking about and seeing so much," he
adds in another letter, "one does not always, when the
mail is going out, feel able to write seriously or thought-
fully. Besides, when I am happy, I am sorry to say I am
more contented with myself, and I often think it is difficult to know how much of one's anxiety about the future
depends upon one's troubles in the present: when these
are removed, one is apt to think less of one's soul. Innocent amusement is the most deadening of anything.
Frantic gaiety brings its stings of conscience, but calm
enjoyment produces a permanent *kief* which should be
watched."

It is seldom that so keen a piece of self-observation as
the above comes from the pen of a young man enjoying to
the full, as he was doing, all the delights of a life of adventure. He adds, on another occasion, some remarks on
the subject of the conversion of a friend to Roman Catholic
belief, which throws a light of another kind on after-in-
cidents of his own life. "It is because he has not a strong
will of his own that he wants to be dictated to on points
of faith. Whately says it is the greatest exercise of man's
private judgment to submit it to another. It is only the
exercise of a weak judgment." These are very strange
words to come from one who in after-years put this abne-
gation of judgment to so strong a proof. He describes
himself as always having had "a mania for finding out

what people believe," and holding theological discussions
with many of the people with whom he is thrown into
contact to this end. "He has a creed of his own," he
says of one friend; "but, like most people, has never really
and philosophically considered the Bible." In another he
comments on the "calm Episcopalianism" of a man who
contents himself with externals, and does not trouble himself with thinking,—a state of mind for which the lively
spectator finds a great deal to be said.

Thus he occupied the time of inaction, cruising in the
Cyclops, running errands from one port to another, complaining occasionally of want of occupation, yet in constant activity, picking up every scrap of information that
came in his way, and resolving to learn Circassian, to perfect his studies in Turkish, and generally to qualify himself as the only Englishman thoroughly acquainted with
the subject. At this time he was still certain that Circassia was the key of the position, and that the current of
the war would necessarily flow thither as the best way of
effectually crippling and checking Russian advance. So
far as he himself was concerned, his idea was that, if he
knew the language, and "got up the country thoroughly,"
Government would not be able to do without him, "either
here or in Parliament"; while he always continued to
hold the conviction that, but for the premature conclusion
of the war, Circassia would certainly have been the next
point of operations, and the most effectual.

It gave a little renewed impetus to his thoughts and
plans when, first, Omar Pasha, at the head of a Turkish
force, supplemented by English artillery, appeared on the
scene; and secondly, the Duke of Newcastle, still bent
upon some brief expedition upon Circassian territory.
There were many consultations between the Turkish general and the English officials, in which Laurence took a
part, pleased, as he says, "to have to give my opinion as
an independent swell"; and for a time it seemed possible
that Omar might take the matter into his own hands, and
that the mission to Schamyl, or if not to Schamyl, at least
to Schamyl's brother-in-law, the Naib of the Western
Caucasus, might still come into effect. But Omar changed

his mind at the last moment, when the eager young would-be envoy was actually in the saddle, and the only real result of his schemes was a hunting expedition of a few days with the Duke of Newcastle's party, into the country which Laurence had so hoped to revolutionise. In his account of this he says: "The Circassians are delighted to receive us; but it is not easy to make a duke go ahead enough to please me." And indeed there is something almost ludicrous in the idea of the grave middle-aged statesman, weary with the cares of office and the troubles of life, pricked on by this fiery boy in the full tide of his own young unreasoning ambition and impulses, always endeavouring to push his leader forward, and convert the hunting-party into a political mission.

"Of course, as every step is on ground never before traversed by Europeans, every step was interesting; and the scenery was beautiful, but the roads dreadful,—up almost perpendicular mountains and along the brink of precipices. The weather was heavenly all the time, and I would have given the world to go over the snow mountains, instead of contenting ourselves with getting to the base of them." The party had, however, a *grande chasse* at Prince Michael's, in which they did not kill much, but found it "very good fun." "I live a most vagrant life," he adds; "I just sleep where I happen to be when night comes on,—one night on board the Highflyer (the Duke's ship), the next on board the Cyclops, the next in Prince Michael's palace or shooting-box, the next in a hut." I have been told that during this period, when the eager young man was straining at his leash, eager for fun and occupation, he proposed to the captain of the Cyclops to make a sudden raid into a certain nook in shelter of an island, where he had discovered that a Russian man-of-war had put in secretly for repairs,—replying to the sailor's remonstrance that he would be disobeying his orders by doing so with a "What would that matter? Everything is pardoned to success."

However, dukes and schemes of all kinds passed away, and there remained only Omar Pasha with his army, still holding out the hope of that campaign which Laurence had always looked forward to as the most

effectual step that could be taken. He set out with the
vanguard in great excitement and delight, slightly tempered by compunctions as to his mother's alarms, and fears
lest this should be thought something very different from
the hopes with which he started; yet much consoled by
the letters to the 'Times,' which brought in "lots of tin,"
and kept the country supplied with information which no
other Englishman could give. The Turks proved themselves excellent soldiers, and the scattered Russian forces
left in Circassia fell back before them, only attempting an
engagement on the banks of the Ingour river, in which
Laurence was more actively engaged than he liked at first
to confess. His first account to his mother gives the impression of great caution on his part. He "did not expose
himself at all"—taking refuge in a hut, upon the roof of
which, it is true, the bullets fell like rain, but where he
professes to have been quite safe. The only moment of
risk was "when I got your letter of 11th October, which
was given me on the field by an officer just arrived from
Constantinople, and in which you wonder when and where
I would receive it. There was a pretty brisk shower of
missiles flying about, and I lay down under a bank and
read it. On one side our great guns were blazing away,
on the other the wounded were being carried past. Altogether it was about as odd a place to receive a letter in
as you could have chosen. However, be thankful that I
never was better in my life, barring that I have had nothing to eat for thirty-six hours except your letter (which I
devoured) and a biscuit."

In another letter he is led on to mention "my battery,"
and this elicits the following anecdote:—

"By the by, I never told you I had made a battery.
Skender Pasha, the officer in command, thought I was
an officer from my having a regimental Turkish fez cap
on, and asked me if I knew where a battery was to
be made about which he had orders. It so happened
that I did, because I had been walking over the ground
with Simmons in the morning; so Skender told off a
working party of two hundred men, with two companies

of infantry and two field-pieces, put them under my
command, and sent me off to make the battery. It
was about the middle of a pitch-dark night, slap under
the Russian guns, about two hundred yards from them.
Luckily they never found us out, we worked so quietly.
I had to do everything,—line the wood with sharp-
shooters, put the field-pieces in position, and place the
gabions. Everybody came to me for orders in the
humblest way. In about three hours I had run up
no end of a battery, without having a shot fired at me,
while Simmons,[1] who was throwing up a battery a few
hundred yards lower down, had a man killed. Both
these batteries did good service two days after. The
difficulty was, none of the officers with me could speak
anything but Turkish. Afterwards Skender Pasha was
speaking to Simmons about it, complaining of the want
of interpreters, and instancing the English officer who
made the battery not having an interpreter; so Simmons said, 'Ce n'est pas un officier, ce n'est qu'un
simple gentleman qui voyage,' which rather astonished
old Skender. I think Simmons looks on the 'Times'
correspondent with a more favourable eye since that
experience.

"I assure you it is quite an act of self-denial on
my part leaving the army. I have no doubt I could
get a command if I stayed; but don't be in the least
alarmed. I have not the remotest intention of turning
soldier, and only did that for fun and because of the
consequences; besides, I knew if we worked quietly they
would never find us out. They were rather astonished
at daybreak to see a battery mounting a couple of guns
staring them in the face, and began to pound away
at it with their rifles; but it was too late, and they got
as good as they gave. Simmons had described to me in
the morning exactly where the battery was to be made,
and how to make it. So the whole thing turned out very
fortunately."

In case the mother at home should think that those

---

[1] Now General Sir J. Lintorn Simmons, G.C.M.G.

fortunate and fortuitous accidents which made it happen
that Laurence should know all about the battery, and
be thus able to act upon an emergency, implied any
inclination to risk himself, he hastens to reassure her on
this point. "I hope you give me credit for prudence
now," he says, "and will trust me. I assure you I was
in a horrible fright of getting shot, entirely on your
account, and I don't recommend a man to come to fight
if he has got anybody at home who loves him. I don't
think he can do his duty. If it had not been for you,
I should have taken an active part in the affair. Altogether, though it was in some respects a horrible experience, I am ·glad to have seen it." This was the
only real passage of arms in the whole campaign, and
a long pause ensued at Sugdidi, where Laurence's reports
turn again to less exciting matters, and to his own
thoughts. The external life of the camp is thus graphi-
cally described :—

"I am very jolly here in Sugdidi — such a pretty
place—only we can't plunder. It is a great temptation.
I don't wonder at soldiers going to all lengths. One
does not feel it is a bit wrong. I put a fine cock in
my pocket this morning. I would have given his owner
anything he asked if I could have found him; but if
we don't forage we get nothing but rice and biscuits
to live on. I should not plunder anything but food,
and that I don't call anything. I am not sure," he
adds, "that I am not happier, occupied as my mind
is now. It is when I have time to think much that
doubts arise. When I just say my prayers and read
a text earnestly, and then go and gallop about and am
in hard healthful exercise, I feel much better in mind
and body. I feel my mind much more innocent and
less bothered and perplexed; but I am afraid this is
wrong, and that one's occupations ought to be God's work,
and not what papa calls playing one's self."

I may be permitted to add one more of the common-
sense and reasonable views of religious life, in opposition

at once to the conventionality of many of the so-called
evangelical tenets, and of much of his own after-thoughts,
which are to be found scattered through these letters.
"I wish," he says (a desire in which I am unable to
follow him), "that the whole Bible was like David's
compositions, and that such texts as 'If I pleased men
I should not be the servant of Christ,' were not in it."

"It appears to me that to be a faithful servant of
God, it is not necessary that one should be displeasing
to His creatures; and that, constituted as they are, he
pleases them most who, by an upright, straightforward
conduct, pleases God most. The world does not like
wicked men, and those points in which Christians dis-
please the world are those which are involved in the
peculiarities of the system, so to speak, which do not
really affect a man's moral conduct. . . . There is not
a single thing which my reason tells me I ought to do,
which if I did people would find fault with. I am not
in the least ashamed to say, even in the most dissipated
society, that I believe immorality, which is regarded as
the most venial of all sins, is wrong; but I am ashamed
to say that I think going out shooting on Sunday is
wrong, simply because I cannot understand why it
should be, though I admit that it may be a valuable
exercise of self-denial occasionally, and that Sunday may
be what I said the other day—a very useful detail. I
am afraid you will think from this that I am in an
unsatisfactory state of mind; and so I am — chiefly, I
think, because I do not feel satisfied with holding views
different from many who I think are spiritually enlightened. These, at least, are my camp thoughts, and
you asked me always to write what I was thinking. But
you may imagine mine is not a life now to foster thought;
and if I had never led any other, I daresay I should have
been as good an Episcopalian as Ballard,[1] and perhaps he
is on that account the happier of the two."

[1] Colonel John Archibald Ballard, C.B., commanding the artillery
attached to Omar Pasha's army, with whom much of Oliphant's time was
spent during this period, and for whom he had a high regard.

I think very few writers on religious subjects have recognised the fact that many utterances in the Bible of this description relate to a totally different state of affairs from any existing among ourselves, and that a man who makes it apparent that he serves God truly is in no sense an unpopular man on that account. Indeed in most cases it is quite the reverse, and goodness is the best passport to universal respect. It pays, as Laurence would have said —which is perhaps less acceptable to many minds than the idea that it naturally involves persecution.

Here is another scrap which no doubt made the heart of the mother thrill with grateful pleasure, yet the overpowering sense of danger escaped. He has been describing the shooting of a spy.

"A single execution like this has far more effect upon me than when I see the ground strewn with dead bodies. One then somehow forgets they are men; and when we had a little quiet rifle-shooting on the banks of the Ingour before the battle, I looked at the men opposite as if they had been deer, and adjusted our fellows' sights for them, and watched the effect of the shots without the slightest feeling of compunction. Once, when I was sketching the river, and a fellow took a pot-shot at me, I took a rifle to return it from a man near; but then I remembered my promise to you, and his humanity, and crept away. The fellows Omar sent to sketch the river funked it; so I did a good deal in that line—crawling about on my hands and knees among the bushes, and flattering myself I was not seen. Whenever I was informed of this fact by the whizz of a Minié, I mizzled off to a safer place. I tell you all this instead of at the time, because the fighting is over; and so you have no cause to fear a recurrence of this amusement. But it was very exciting, with the satisfaction, at the same time, of being really of use. It was really sketching under difficulties."

Then the pendulum of thought swings backs again to those subjects of which his home letters are always full. He accuses himself over again of being moved by his present conditions at the moment, to piety or the reverse. When he is in trouble, he is seized with "a sulky fit of devotion." "Because, remember," he continues, "my religion at those times is not of a happy character; but I am gloomy and disgusted when I am trying to go to religion for comfort. Somehow or other something ought to come of it all, for I am always thinking of the subject in some shape or other. My conscience is never satisfied with my conduct, nor my understanding with my belief, so that altogether I live in a state of internal conflict and argumentation; and I would desire nothing more earnestly than to be a devoted Christian. I admit that it involves giving up much that I now cling to; but I think I would not regret giving them up. The best prescription I can think of is to live a month with Ernest Noel; intercourse with him seemed to do me more good than anything else." It is seldom that the conflicting thoughts of a young man are thus clearly, and with so little conventional restraint, laid before another.

The campaign was brought to an end in the first place by the retreat of the Russians, afterwards by the disastrous news of the fall of Kars, which there had still been a hope of recovering; and finally, which was in the eyes of Laurence almost as great a disaster, by the sudden and unsatisfactory peace. And at last he is able to comfort his mother with news of his approaching home-coming, and of his projects for work and patience, and the conviction that an established position of one kind or another must await him. "I do not think that, though my prospects are no more definite than they were, I shall be so miserable and unsettled. I feel more of a philosopher. I have satisfied myself about this question, and intend to be independent. I can write what I know and other people don't. If there is a general election, I shall certainly try hard to get in, but I hate the idea of asking anybody for anything now. I think I can get on in spite of them."

It was the very end of the year before Laurence got home from this brilliant, exciting, and entirely ineffectual journey. He had made many new acquaintances, both in

places and people, and heard a great deal which he expected to be superlatively useful to him, but which, except
in so far as it supplied material for a book, was of scarcely
any utility at all. But he was no nearer a definite mode
of establishing himself in life than he had been when he
set out. He returned after an illness—caught in the wet
and cold of the tents and hardships of the march, which
was in reality a retreat, "not before the enemy but the
weather," and attended by many depressing and wretched
details,—in the last days of 1855 or beginning of 1856.
He came home in the vein I have quoted, determined to
make his own way and ask nothing from anybody, and
with his mind divided between the diplomatic service
and Parliament—a career towards which he had already
directed his thoughts. I think it was during this period
that he first contested the Stirling burghs, though without
success; but of this incident I find no details.

This waiting, however, for something to turn up, Micaw-
ber-like, as he himself describes it, was so little to his
mind, that in the following summer he was again on the
war-path, seeking employment, adventure, or whatever
might befall him. Unfortunately (though perhaps it is
as well for the space at my disposal), I have not succeeded
in obtaining any of the letters of this period, so that it
can only be traced through those recollections which he
thought fit during his life to give to the public. From
these it would appear that, notwithstanding all his philosophical resolutions, his impatience of his own want of
progress soon reached a great height, and that he was
ready for anything that involved movement and activity,
finding himself no doubt at the same time more or less
independent, so long as he had something novel and strange
to tell, by reason of that connection with the 'Times,'
which made the wildest wandering profitable. Accordingly, he left England again in the course of the summer of
1856, at first in company with the well-known Mr Delane
of the 'Times,' to whom "I was able," he says, "to act as
cicerone on our arrival at New York," and whose enjoyment
of the society and ever-abounding hospitality of that capital was no doubt much enhanced by the popularity and

universal acquaintanceship of his young companion, whose previous experiences as Lord Elgin's brilliant secretary were still recent. What the business was in which the young man was engaged, I am not aware; but he speaks of it in a letter to Mr Leveson-Gower as likely to put a thousand pounds in his pocket. When this was accomplished, Laurence went on upon his adventurous way, and, with a keen scent for excitement to come, turned his steps to the Southern States, with the idea, first, of making himself acquainted on the spot with the workings of slavery, as well as with the peculiar social conditions of that section of the American world. "From what I saw and heard," he says, "it was not difficult to predict the cataclysm which took place four years later, though the idea of the South resorting to violence was scouted in the North; and when, upon more than one occasion, I ventured to suggest the possibility to Republicans, I was invariably met by the reply that I had not been long enough in the country to understand the temper of the people, and attached an importance it did not deserve to Southern 'bounce.'" His visit to that old-new world of the plantations—the patriarchal households and primitive innocent communities, bound by a hundred ties to their head, which every picture, even of the most eager Abolitionist character, permits us to see in the slave-holding States, though neutralised by the horrible possibility of a traffic in human flesh and blood—was full of interest to him.

Laurence found his way as usual among "the best people," and his stay at New Orleans was "one of unqualified enjoyment." But it is a practical evidence of his extreme impatience with the as yet undetermined lines of his own life, that he should have been attracted by the idea of an expedition to which the nickname "filibuster," one of the most felicitous coinages of Americanism, was applied—a word of nonsense, aptly expressing with humorous scorn, yet impartiality, the sound and fury, the big intention and pretence, of the modern pirate, half-swagger, half-serious meaning. That Laurence Oliphant, who was still well within the reach of good fortune at twenty-seven, and who was soon to fill a responsible and important place in actual diplomatic service, should have "accepted a free passage to Nicaragua in a ship conveying a reinforcement to Walker's army," and should have carried "strong personal recommendations to that noted filibuster," is one of the most curious events in his career. This strange step was taken chiefly, no doubt, "for fun," as when he made his battery,—but also a little, we can scarcely doubt, from feelings much more serious, and originating in one of those fits of partial despair and disgust with his surroundings, and the lack of advancement, which has been the cause of so many wild enterprises. Walker was requested by his agent, Mr Soulé, in New Orleans, "to explain the political situation to me, in the hope that, on my return to England, I might induce the British Government to regard his operations with a more favourable eye than they had hitherto done. The fact that if I succeeded I was to be allowed to take my pick out of a list of confiscated *haciendas*, or estates, certainly did not influence my decision to go, though it may possibly have acted as a gentle stimulant; but I remember at the time having some doubts on the subject, from a moral point of view. I remember spending Christmas Day in high spirits at the novelty of this adventure upon which I was entering." The Christmas before he had been at Trebizond, just emerging from the hardships of Omar Pasha's campaign. But during all the vicissitudes of his Circassian adventures, he had more or less the prestige of a member of the British diplomatic service. Now, however, in strange contrast to that reflected dignity, he was setting forth on what was distinctly a piratical undertaking, amid a crew of armed adventurers, invaders, bent on conquest. It was a singular change, and one which we can scarcely suppose could sit easily upon his mind in moments of seriousness; but the fun and novelty, with perhaps something of the underlying impatience and disgust of the ordinary which had driven him from London, carried the day.

This adventure, however, was doomed to be but short; and much in the way in which a naughty prince, in a romance, would be arrested and conveyed back to his proper sphere, Laurence was shaken loose from his companions

and carried off to his natural surroundings. When the
filibuster ship came to the mouth of the San Juan river,
its progress was impeded by "a British squadron lying at
anchor to keep the peace," from one of the vessels of which
a boat was soon pulling towards them. " A moment later
Captain Cockburn, of H.M.S. Cossack, was in the captain's
cabin making most indiscreet inquiries as to the kind of
emigrants we were. It did not require long to satisfy
him; and as I incautiously hazarded a remark which
betrayed my nationality, I was incontinently ordered into
his boat as a British subject, being where a British subject
had no right to be. As he further announced that he was
about to move his ship in such a position as would enable
him, should fighting occur in the course of the night,
to fire into both combatants with entire impartiality, I
the less regretted this abrupt parting from my late companions, the more especially as, on asking him who commanded the squadron, I found it was a distant cousin.
This announcement on my part was received with some
incredulity, and I was taken on board the Orion, an 80-
gun ship carrying the flag of Admiral Erskine, to test
its veracity, while Captain Cockburn made his report of
the Texas and her passengers. As soon as the admiral
recovered from his amazement at my appearance, he most
kindly made me his guest, and I spent a very agreeable
time for some days, watching the emigrants disconsolately
pacing the deck."

Thus our young man "fell on his feet" wherever he
went, and instead of suffering at all for his wild and un-
justifiable undertaking, found himself in excellent and
amusing quarters, restored to all the privileges of his rank,
—the admiral's cousin at sea being as good for all purposes
as a king's cousin ashore. The moral of which would
seem to be that, when you have a habit of getting into
risky positions, the best thing in the world is to belong to
a good Scotch family of "kent folk," with relations in
every department of her Majesty's service both at home
and abroad.

He would seem, however, though the letters fail at this
period, to have been in a state of no small depression

about his prospects, and more than usually sick of the un-congenial position of waiting till something should turn up, and besieging his official friends with applications, which is the usual position of a young man seeking advancement—or at least was, before the public services were ruled by examinations as at present. That he should have made such an expedition at all is a proof at once of the extraordinary detachment and independence of mind which afterwards made his life so remarkable, and of great impatience and dissatisfaction with ordinary circum-stances, as well as of the love of adventure, which was always a leading trait in his character. He was so far independent that he had the means of moving about at his pleasure without any absolute necessity to work for daily bread,—a fact which gives wings to impatience, and makes every sudden movement practicable. His hot impulses were, however, stayed by the excellent expedient of legitimate occupation a few months after his return from his filibustering; and in the month of April 1857 he set out with his old friend and chief, Lord Elgin, on his mission to China, occupying the post of private secretary once more.

CHAPTER VI.

THE MISSION TO CHINA.

It is unnecessary here to enter further into the history of the operations in China than is wanted to explain the part which Laurence took in them. He has himself left a history of the mission and all its performances, in a nar-rative published immediately after its termination. Its importance in modern history was much greater than was even anticipated, seeing that it was not only the beginning of legalised and comprehensible dealings with China, but in some degree the means of discovering, diplomatically, and adding to the variety of Nature, the heretofore half fabulous, yet in reality most intelligent, wide-awake, and progressive, empire of Japan. The position of Laurence

was still unofficial. He was not a recognised servant of
the Foreign Office or member of the diplomatic service.
Probably it was part of the disadvantage of his irregular
education, and partly of those independent ways and opinions which had always been characteristic of him, that he
never seems to have made any attempt to constitute himself a regular member of this profession which would seem
to have been so completely congenial to him. But there
was still at that time an accidental character about that
service, and chances for the man who was proved capable,
which were probably much more attractive to him than
the routine of a public functionary.

I have been told by one of the other members of the
expedition, Sir Henry Loch, then an *attaché* serving his
apprenticeship in the service in which he now occupies
so distinguished a position, that the first appearance of
Oliphant among the group of young men in attendance
upon the Minister was somewhat startling to those gilded
youths. He began to talk, as they lounged about the
deck with their cigars, of matters spiritual and mystical,
singularly different from the themes that usually occupy
such groups. They asked each other what strange com-
rade they had here when they talked over the new addition to their party. It would seem to have been the
then quite new development of what, for want of a better
name, people call spiritualism, or more vulgarly, spirit-
rapping, which was the subject of the talk about the
funnel in the soft tropical night. I find, however, no trace
of this in the letters, which give a wonderfully clear view
of what Laurence was thinking, and of the point in his
religious history to which he had now come—which, as
the reader will see, occupied his mind very much even
amid all the excitements of the expedition. He would
seem, during the interval between this and his former
secretaryship in Canada, to have completely burst the
strait bonds of his mother's evangelical views, then holding him but lightly—as it seems inevitable that a lively
young mind awakening to demand a reason for everything
should do: and had now come to something like a tenable
foundation for his personal belief—which differed much

from that in which he had been trained, yet which he was very anxious to prove to be a most real rule of life. Thus the expedition, which was so brilliant and important, and out of the records of which he made a book so readable, interesting, and amusing, is associated in his private history with the rising of religious thoughts and convictions which ripened in the monotony of the many intervals of waiting which came between the exciting episodes of his life. Nothing can be more curious than to see—between the fighting and the exploring, which he enjoys like a schoolboy, always somehow finding himself in the front, always gay, amusing, and amused—the student retired in his cabin, hearing nothing but the monotonous swish of the waves, and pondering the ways of God to man, and especially the mistaken, confusing, and derogatory interpretations given by all human systems of these wonderful ways. Sometimes his own views are very strikingly expressed; but it is not necessary that the reader should agree with him in order to be interested in this curious second side of the versatile, delightful, gay, and adventurous young man, who was ready for everything— the ball-room and the council-chamber and the smoking-room, while still most warmly attracted of all by the book of theology which awaited him all the time in his retirement.

His parents would seem to have been established in the neighbourhood of London—I imagine at Spring Grove, a house within reach of his uncle's house at Wimbledon— when he left England; and to his mother it was always like a rending asunder of soul and body to part with him. He sends her a note from the Indus, the steamer in which he had set out to join the mission at Alexandria, hoping that she is not letting herself be miserable. "There are numbers of partings going now," he writes, "and weeping parents going on shore; so you are not alone." At Alexandria, where the new overland route and the railway across the desert had just been put in operation, he does not enter into any details about the place, which was already familiar both to himself and his correspondent, but makes an amusing note on the subject of the train

coming in from Cairo, "quite a sight." "There was a
harem carriage, and Arabs were clinging like flies to all
parts, crowding the roof, and even perched upon the
buffers.   They jumped off like frogs long before the train
stopped.   I believe a good many are killed monthly ; but
they are cheap here, and certainly take kindly to steam
locomotion."   At Cairo "we go about in grand style,
Lord Elgin in a state carriage, with four grey horses, and
a whole posse of horsemen and running footmen, who at
night carry blazing torches, making the whole procession
very picturesque.   We follow behind in two other of
the Pasha's carriages, accompanied by sundry beys and
swells."   At Galle, where on their arrival the well-known
place brought many recollections to the traveller's mind,
they were met by the news of the breaking out of the
mutiny in India, which, however, does not seem to have
at once disturbed either the secretary or his chief, as after-
records announce.   The mission went on, with a faint fear
that this new contingency might interfere with the public
interest in China, but apparently no graver apprehensions :
until further and worse news met them at Singapore, the
next halting-place in their journey.

Lord Elgin has always received great credit for changing,
on his own responsibility, the destination of the troops who
met him there—the small expeditionary army, without
the support of which his mission could do nothing—and
sending them on to India instead, thus affording the most
valuable aid at an important moment.   The extreme em-
barrassment and difficulty brought upon himself by this
step has, however, received little notice, magnanimity in
such a matter being generally, like virtue, its own reward.
Laurence takes, however, even this credit from his chief,
by an intimation that the troops were ordered to India by
Lord Canning, to the dismay of the plenipotentiary, thus
deprived of his army.   It is difficult to come to the exact
truth even on such a public matter; for I have been assured by another member of the mission, not only that
Lord Elgin took the initiative, but that it was on the
advice of himself, as knowing India, that his lordship did
so !   There is, however, no doubt as to the next step, which

was that Lord Elgin, finding his own position thus diminished, and moved by the tremendous difficulty and
danger of the crisis, himself followed the troops to Calcutta to give Lord Canning his support, and that, still more
effectual, of a naval brigade from the Shannon and Pearl.
That there was some policy in this movement, as well as
a chivalrous postponement of the interests of his own
mission, was perhaps more apparent at the time to the
members of the mission, thus arrested, than it was to the
general public.   Lord Elgin was consoled by a patriotic
address from the merchants of Singapore, whose interests
were much concerned in the success of his expedition, yet
who concurred wisely and sympathetically in the delay.
As these excellent men were not of a literary turn, they
had recourse to Lord Elgin's young secretary, who had
already made himself universally popular in the community, to write their address for them,—a circumstance which
did not in the least detract from its perfectly genuine
character, but which Laurence related with much amusement to his mother at home.

Nothing more self-denying than the step thus taken
could have been.   It involved not only the absence of all
the prestige surrounding a splendid expedition, but the
surrender of the fine ship and comfortable quarters provided for the envoy and his staff, and much miserable
uncertainty, delay, and humiliation.   And though they
were received at Calcutta on their arrival with the greatest enthusiasm, the secretary's letters do not convey the
idea that the magnanimous visitor had any great recompense for his sacrifice.   "He scarcely sees a soul, and leads
a dreary life in that dreary pile," says the young man, who is
for his own part somewhat astonished to see the calm of
Calcutta, the usual show of beauty and fashion on the ordinary promenade, and the usual hospitalities going on—a
thing, no doubt, inevitable, but always jarring upon the
nerves of the spectator.   He himself, however, as a spectator, shared this calm.   There is no appearance in his letters
of excitement, though he was surprised by the ordinary
look of everything around him.   In the same house in which
he was lodged were two ladies lately escaped at the risk of

their lives, and under remarkable circumstances, on the
eve of a massacre; but who drove out with himself and a
friend in their buggies for the evening drive as if nothing
had happened—curious composure of human nature, which
assimilates the most wonderful events, and takes tragedy
itself into the common current of every day!

The Chinese mission, however, were outsiders, and had
nothing to do personally with the Indian crisis. And
when they returned again to the scene of their own duties
humbly in a P. & O. steamer—the Ava—without any of
the pomp of the splendid man-of-war, to kick their heels
in Hong-Kong and wait until a detachment of 1500
soldiers should be sent to them from England, to fill the
place of the 5000 men, soldiers and sailors together, whom
they had parted with to India, it is little wonder if they
were discouraged. The excitement of a great sacrifice is
apt to have a *contre-coup* of vexation and depression. " We
have sunk into such insignificance, and are in such a fix
without an army," Laurence wrote on his return to Hong-
Kong, " nor are the speeches of Sir C. Wood and other
members of the Government very encouraging. How they
expect Lord Elgin to carry out the same policy without
any army which he was instructed to do with one, is not
very clear." He adds, with a little amusing malice, " I
have one consolation, that you will be much more relieved
thinking of me living cooped up in a ship in harbour for
the next three months, where there are neither women
nor Chinese, than if I were doing anything else." It is
apparent throughout that Lady Oliphant largely shared
what is supposed to be a general feeling with mothers,
against the intrusion of love into the hearts of their sons.
She upbraids him sometimes as being heartless, when some
instance of inadvertent fascination on Laurence's part
rouses her pity for the lady whom he has loved and ridden
away. Indeed it would appear to have been the truth
that our young *diplomat*, always addicted to making himself agreeable, was still more so where ladies were concerned; and, whether by means of polkas or theological
discussions, was wont to work considerable havoc upon his
way through the world. His mother is glad to hear that

he is in a place where such intercourse is impracticable; but Laurence himself does not like it. It is to be said for him, however, that he always informs her of his amusements in this way, keeping her, no doubt, in a flutter of alarm which he was apt to enjoy.

Yet with all this, these letters, which are so confidential, so full of the comradeship and equality which is rare between parents and children (there was, as I have said, only some eighteen years' difference in their age), so free in discussion and remark — continue to be filled above everything else with his religious views and feelings: the revelation of what he has come to in the way of conviction after much struggling, and tortures of doubt—and his indignant disapproval of the hackneyed types of Christianity with which he is acquainted. His first letter on this subject is in answer to an expression of much dissatisfaction on her part as to his views.

"Hong-Kong, 4th July [1857].

"All that related to J. pained me much, but so did that which related to myself. I thought you understood that it was no obstinacy on my part which compels me, before adopting a faith, to judge of the merits of its claim by the light God has given me. It is no light thing attributing to the Deity a work containing much that appears derogatory to His dignity. Nor is there any means whatever of knowing whether it is His or not, except by an exercise of the means He has given us. I do not in the least set up my reason against His, but against my fellow-creatures', who tell me to accept a book as from Him upon no better evidence than I myself possess, the chief reason being that it is better than any other, which I am quite ready to admit; but I feel that I should be sinning seriously against Him were I not very jealously to guard against adopting any system which involved what I consider degrading to Him, without overwhelming evidence of its authenticity. Such evidence must of necessity be supernatural, as everything coming through mortal agency is, *prima facie*, from the very nature of things, imperfect. I do not like to dwell on a subject which I know is painful to you, and I

am afraid you will never understand what I mean, or, after
all I have said to you, you would never have used the
old arguments about not exercising my reason on what I
do not understand. I certainly do not understand God's
dealings with man, nor am I so presumptuous as to suppose I ever shall; but if I did not exercise my reason,
there would be nothing to prevent my accepting the Koran
or any other system of theology my fellow-creatures might
assure me was right, and deny me the privilege of judging
for myself. You say you would be glad if I could give up
my career for God's service. I would willingly go into a
dungeon for the rest of my days if I was vouchsafed a
supernatural revelation of a faith; but I should consider
myself positively wicked if upon so momentous a subject
I was content with any assumptions of my erring and imperfect fellow-creatures, when against the light of my own
conscience.

" With regard to prayer, I have lately been asking for
things, because I could not endure, as it were, merely
stating my case, and I felt so strongly what you say
about answers; but it has been, and is, with a strong
feeling of doubt and disquietude that I am dishonouring
Him by supposing I can influence Him in anything.
However, I have too strong a sense of His love to think
it can be displeasing to Him; and the instinct seems
so deeply implanted in one to do so, though I think it
is only the instinct of a low spiritual creature, and
when one gets further advanced one will not need it.
However, it is no pleasure to me to be thus distracted
with doubts and difficulties, and therefore pray do not
think I am doing it from a spirit of pride or opposition.
I am really anxious to know and do what is right,
though the circumstances of my present life are un-
favourable; and, moreover, I do not attach importance
to the infraction of what are really the conventionalities
of the Christian world. I may appear to be irreligious
because my religion does not consist in the same course
of action, and my standard is different. I do not say
that I act up to it, but I think if I did I should shame
the professing Christian. My faith is not strong enough

to bring me up to my standard, but I hope it may be some day.

"I quite agree·in what papa says about the spiritualist's God. I felt it myself. It removed him too far off. But, on the other hand, what papa calls God's invention of Christ does not remove the difficulty: it substitutes another being, whose merit is that you are to think of Him as God. The moment you think of Him as God, He is as far away as ever, besides the dire confusion which such a mixture immediately raises in the mind. I never from my earliest day could get over that difficulty, and always found myself instinctively yearning for the fountainhead, and overleaping all intermediate beings. However, I am glad you wrote, because it stirs me up. I get too distracted sometimes by my mode of life, and do not think so much as I ought. In order to keep up the proper peace of mind, one ought to be constantly thinking, and not contented with a morning and evening ejaculation. I would sooner go to the stake than do violence to what I believe to be the yearnings and whisperings, weak and imperfect no doubt, of my divine nature."

He returns to the subject of prayer on another occasion, quoting a passage from Francis Newman to illustrate his position. "So," he adds, "because I pray I do not feel that I can influence God, but that in expressing my desires I am holding almost the only communion which is open to me, giving Him, as it were, all my confidence, as the most pleasing homage I can do Him, and the fullest recognition I can make of His love and beneficence, and the interest He has in my happiness and welfare." This is little more than a modern expression of the same sentiment which John Knox stated, in far stronger and more eloquent words, when he described prayer as "an earnest and familiar talking with God." Laurence, however, had not, I fear, notwithstanding his many qualities, that preference for the best and highest in literature, either sacred or profane, which we expect to find in a mind so well endowed. Theodore Parker is the fount from which he

chiefly draws in these religious speculations, and he
finds pleasure in Longfellow which Tennyson does not
convey.   It is not necessary to be a critic because a man
is full of native ability and force of mind.   The juxta-
position of these two names in poetry, with a preference
for the former unhesitatingly and strongly expressed, will
make most readers smile : but it would be vain to claim
for him a perfection which he did not possess.   Perhaps
his early association with America, in the first independent opening of his mind, may have had something to do
with it ; perhaps his imperfect education, which fed him
upon " good " books, and shut up to him the highest
sources of poetical imagination.   Some one, I do not
remember who, tells of the excitement and delight
with which he discovered Shakespeare, who had been
unknown to him — coming back and back to tell his
amused friends of some new wonder in the book which
they had recommended to him in the dearth of other
reading.   It is well to know that he was capable of being
thus stirred : he was not capable, it is evident, of judging
the respective magnitudes of the lesser lights.

The subject of religion, however, is far the more important to him, and continually in his thoughts.   His feelings
on this subject are saddened by the consciousness that his
correspondent will not enter into them, but rather blame
him for his views on many matters of faith.   " A transition
state," he says, " such as I am in, is never a favourable
one ; but I do hope that I am getting hold of something.
I have learnt, however, to believe in nothing which I cannot see manifested in life.   The influence of early life,
and the constraints which one set of opinions imposed, are
loosened.   Though another set of opinions may involve
precisely the same restraints, time is required to ripen
their influence.   Of course, a man cannot bring a faith to
bear upon his life and conversation until he has got a
very firm hold of it."

The one point upon which he is assured is that this is
his only test.   He sees all round him men who are very
nice fellows, who would be horrified not to be called
Christians, but in whom religion of any kind is as little

apparent as if they believed nothing. "I am a thorough Christian," he says, "so far as my reverence for and belief in every moral principle Christ has propounded is concerned; but I am utterly opposed to the popular development of Christianity,—indeed I think it quite inconsistent with His teaching. I never felt so deep an interest in any subject, and am thankful for the leisure I have had to read and think of it." The same sentiment appears again and again. "Those who have seen war," he says, "can best appreciate the value of Christ's 'Blessed are the peacemakers.'

"If that was to be the aim of the diplomatist, his would be the noblest of professions. My natural man is intensely warlike, which is just as low a passion as avarice or any other. I went last Sunday to church to hear a parson, with a Crimean medal on his surplice, preach between a lot of 68-pounders on 'Fear not man that can kill the body, but fear Him who can cast both body and soul into hell,' and I wondered what sort of morality you could expect from men whose occupation was the destruction of their fellow-creatures, to the conscientious discharge of which they were to be urged by their fear of an avenging Deity, the Creator of them all. One would think even a sailor would discern the impossibility of elevating his moral nature by the application of two such principles as cruelty and fear."

It is not my part to point out the fallacy as well as the strong *parti pris* of these remarks: they are intended to show the working of the mind, which it is my business to delineate in its weakness as well as in its strength.

"The more I consider my own nature," he adds, "the more I see the tremendous power a creed ought to contain within itself to become a living principle. A flaw here or there does infinite mischief. In order to prevail over the tendency to evil, it must invade with overwhelming force a man's whole nature, obliging him by its purity, and the strength of its appeal to his convictions, to recognise its truth; but if his moral instincts discover the slightest flaw, the whole fabric goes by the board, and he has hard work to make up the leeway, which the absence of the old faith and the struggle for the new involves. I can well understand any man giving up in despair the hope of finding a creed containing elements powerful enough to govern him absolutely. It is a long time before he gets over a sort of repugnance at the very idea of the old one, and recognises again all that is good and beautiful in it. I do think that God satisfies every man's craving in this respect in time, if he keeps on fighting and groping."

It is very seldom that we have the spectacle of a mind thus seething with dissatisfaction and eager desire after a better way, so curiously unphilosophical in his philosophy, and so penetrated in the midst of his revolt by sentiments of reverential and strongly realised faith. Here is a very interesting exposition of his standing ground and its disadvantages :—

" In looking upon my own state and experience, I find to the good that I have made certain advances towards a faith which no doubt influences my life perhaps not more than my life used to be influenced before ; but the difference is that formerly my life depended not upon the sincerity of my moral convictions, or even on my fear of offending God, but entirely on the fear of making you miserable. Had that check ceased to exist, I have no doubt I should have gone to the bad. The old associations and habitual restraints might have held me in for a short time, but very short, and the end would have been utter recklessness or defiance. Now that is all changed, and although, as I say, my present life may not be better than my past, still it is founded on a different basis, and, I trust, will go on improving, irrespective of any mundane event. That, I say, I find to the good. To the bad I have to lament an entire looseness in my moral tone and conversation, for which I can perfectly account, but which I find it most difficult to overcome. It arises from the contempt I feel (but which is wrong) for professors of a creed which has no power over them, but all the dogmas which I am blamed for not subscribing to. When men who keep harems go to church regularly, and blame me for not going with them, I am apt to confound the faith with the individual, and swear at the whole concern. And so, because I do not confess to a good deal that seems to be hollow in the practice of a popular theology, I am put down as being without religion, and so lose any influence which, did I refrain from this, I might have, besides giving a totally wrong impression of my real convictions. But it is a mistake to confound religion with theology. It is the fashion to regard the former as springing from the latter, whereas if you have the former it makes little difference what you profess as the latter.

"But do not think I confound the Christian religion with the practice which its professors follow, in accordance with a theology they have deduced from it. The Bible is a very different thing from the popularly received traditionary interpretation of it which rests on human reason. I quite believe in its inspiration, but in a particular way. I had first thought of an illustration when I found an almost exactly similar one in Morell. He proves, by a very well-argued and elaborate process, that revelation and intuition are the same thing. I had long arrived at that, but did not know how, until he proved it. Theodore Parker has the same; but my notion is this, that supposing a man's whole moral nature was in perfect harmony, and his spiritual intelligence perfect, his mind would be like a perfectly calm lake upon which would be accordingly reflected the mind of God; but the moment the surface is disturbed the image becomes imperfect, the amount of the imperfection depending upon the amount of the disturbance. Now, according to my view, the minds of Christ and of His apostles were in that state of almost perfect spiritual repose. They reflected more accurately than was ever done before or since the mind of God: that is, the apostles caught their repose from the mind of Christ—but you see in them the imperfections of a disturbed moral nature. Peter and Paul quarrel, and attach

importance to things strangled and to circumcision—that
is, the surface was ruffled by old prejudices, undue spiritual enthusiasm, strong passions, &c.—and so fail to
give that perfect image of the mind of God. We may
perceive these imperfections, though very far from having
minds so spiritually enlightened as theirs, just as you can
tell the faults of a picture without being an artist. I feel
sure that as men's minds become more enlightened, and
they begin to receive those revelations which the apostles
did themselves, they will no longer accord their writings
the infallibility which they do not claim (they only claim
inspiration, which, as I say, they certainly had, and which
I trust others may yet have). The goodness of the
inspiration must depend upon the medium. The purest
inspiration may be polluted. If the channel is a sewer,
it does not matter how clear may be the spring; so in
the Old Testament we find all sorts of people chosen as
mediums; but of the value, for instance, of Solomon's
inspiration we must judge for ourselves. It is in accordance with the divine plan always to make use of human
means, with all their imperfections, and I see no reason to
suppose that the Bible is the only thing that ever came
through human instruments that does not partake of their
imperfections, more especially when the internal evidence
that it does so is irresistible to my mind."

He adds, that in the midst of the rising excitement of
an approaching crisis, which in former times would have
occupied him wholly, he feels himself much more interested in metaphysical questions than in the bombardment
of Canton, or anything that can happen. His guides in
these researches seem to have been Theodore Parker, to
whom he constantly refers, and Mr Morell, whose 'History
of Philosophy' had recently made an impression upon the
public attention which has not proved permanent. It is
unfortunate that a mind so active, yet which was never
without a certain confusion in these matters—which, curiously enough, he proclaims at this period as his favourite
study—should not have been under more thorough and
trustworthy guidance. It seems a paradox, yet it is one
of which there are many examples, that when a mind

essentially practical, with a special literary gift of clear narrative, involves itself in metaphysical subjects, this strange confusion is often the result. General Gordon is another example of a heroically keen intelligence in practical effort and dealings with men, which yet became hopelessly clouded and bewildered in theological matters, wandering in a fog of chaotic thought, and substituting subject for object, and *vice versâ*, with a boldness which is also heroic, though sadly perplexing to the reader. Laurence Oliphant's religious theories at this moment, when he pursued them hotly in his cabin, amid all the curious surroundings of an expedition which was at once diplomatic and military, will show how ready his mind was for the influences which afterwards took possession of it,—how superficial in theory, how heroic in determination to follow out his conclusions to whatever end they might lead.

Meantime, as he says, the plot was thickening around, and had it not been for this preoccupation with metaphysics and the religious question, "I ought now to be in an intense state of excitement.

"Wade has gone up the river with a flag of truce and Lord Elgin's ultimatum to Yeh. I volunteered to go; but he was quite right not to send me, not being a Chinese scholar, though I begged hard. The Admiral has drawn a cordon close round Canton, and is to occupy the island of Homan, immediately opposite the town, to-morrow. The French fleet has gone up the river to take part in the blockade. The 59th and artillery go up with the General; in a day or two we shall have upwards of 6000 men as a land force, half red jackets and half blue, including the French. If Yeh does not give in, they will take Canton on Tuesday week, the 22d, probably. I do not anticipate any great difficulty even if he holds out; but the bazaar report here is that he is in a horrid fright, and going to give in and come to terms. I hope he may, for in case of bombardment of a town containing a million of people, the slaughter of innocent women and children and people generally will be dreadful. However, the bishop has appointed a day of humiliation for the Indian business; so we are to humble ourselves to-day, and make up for it next week by sending a few thousands of our fellow-creatures into the next world."

On a similar subject he enlarges at more length in a following letter:—

"I see you have been having a great day of humiliation. I am very strongly opposed to this, as very derogatory to God and reflecting upon His love. He has created a universe with certain laws; all violation of these laws implies misery—a misery which is ordained to teach men to improve themselves. The child trying to walk tumbles and hurts its nose. It was no judgment on the child that it fell: it was a wise law that provided a misery, and its humiliation consisted in keeping its legs straight for the future. It is a mockery to say you are sorry, and go and do the same again; and a sin to think that God acts by fits and starts as we do, with a judgment here and there, as if the whole thing was not obedient to fixed and certain laws. The general notion is that you are appeasing an angry Deity, which is the worst of all."

It is curious that this very *banal* though plausible view of national prayer, the frequent utterance of the superficial thinker, had been already met and answered by himself in the individual point of view a few letters before, as above quoted. After so many details of these opinions as to the demerits of Christians and merit of Christianity, and his own uncomfortable substitution of the one for the other, which is very much what they come to, the reader will be refreshed by his thoughts upon another subject—one, too, of the greatest importance to him in after-life, and of which it is apparent here he already held the germ. His mother's letter had informed him of the death of their friend Dr Clark, which he says gave him at first a painful shock:—

"We have been so accustomed to surround death with

horrors, and to be selfish in our sorrow, that news of the departure from the world of any one we love gives us quite a different feeling from what it ought. No doubt this partly arises from an uncertainty whether we shall ever meet again, and a want of faith in the love of God, who, I feel certain, will never separate people for long who love one another. In the meantime, I have no doubt Tom is often present with us, it is possible exercising some influence for good over our lives; at all events, the loss is only on our side, and that for a short time : so that I cannot talk of poor Tom, or call the news sad—I only feel the very earthly feeling of regret that when I get back I shall not see his dear kind old face, or hear his favourite greeting, into which he used to throw so much love and interest, of ' Well, boy !' The very feeling which will perhaps make the tears come into your eyes as you read this, as they have into mine as I write, only shows what a softening influence love is, and what a beautifying effect it would have on our lives if we could feel more universally for our fellow-creatures what we feel for Tom."

In a similar way he discusses the feeling of thankfulness for his escape from drowning, of which he tells her :—

" As far as you are concerned, I often think if I have a narrow shave that it is perfectly legitimate the feeling should be one of thankfulness. I should feel the same about you, but not about myself. The reason I feel it about you, and you about me, is because we are both selfish in respect to one another; but thankfulness on the part of the individual himself at being saved from death seems to me the most wretched mundane sentiment possible, to say nothing of its being dishonouring to God. If we are always thankful for being kept alive, it is very evident that we must regard His dispensation of death as a hardship to be disgusted with whenever it comes. As if He were not to be trusted to keep us in this world or send us to the next in His own good time ! I am not in the least a fatalist: I should struggle in the water to the last gasp; but when it did come, as I feel now, I should

be perfectly satisfied.   I have the most unbounded confidence in the universal economy of things, and I don't
like implying that God could be guilty of an act of caprice
or injustice by being thankful for His sparing me, when,
if He did not, I should not be entitled to complain."

Nothing can be more interesting than these indications
of the way in which the thoughts of the young man, amid
surroundings so little congenial to any prolonged process
of thinking, were occupied.   It would be vain to pretend
that they were either original or profound ; indeed they
are throughout pervaded by the curious confusion between
Christianity as a religious system and the shortcomings of
its professors,—as if it were incumbent upon a thinking
man to abjure the faith in order to protest against the
faults of those who failed to obey it, which we have
already pointed out.   But they are interesting as showing
how early and how independently the germs which were
so to develop in after-life had gained possession of his
mind.   His views upon that inspiration, which was the
same as intuition, and the consequent subjection of every
actual truth to the feeling and instinct of the believer ;
his determination that every influence should be judged
according to its practical power over himself—even his
views in respect to the parting of death, and the attitude
we ought to hold towards it,—are all germs of the faith
which afterwards led him to so many singular steps.
They are interesting in this respect as well as for themselves,—unusual matter to occupy the mind of a young
man in his circumstances.   He was approaching his
twenty-ninth birthday, and his life hitherto had been one
of almost wild adventure, continual movement, and restless occupation.

On the other hand, however, there was plenty of adventure to record.   He took a share in everything, whatever was going on.   When a flag of truce was sent up the
Canton river with Lord Elgin's ultimatum, he volunteered,
as has been said, for the duty ; and though he agreed that
it was better left in the hands of Wade, who was a Chinese
scholar, than in his own, yet he " begged hard," as he says,

to have the errand. When Captain Sherard Osborn went off in the Furious to Manilla, Laurence got permission to accompany him, to vary the monotony of the long waiting at Hong-Kong; but here a difficulty arose. "Sherard Osborn," he writes, "is the fellow whom I pitched into so furiously at the Geographical about the Sea of Azoff, so I may not get him to take me;" but Captain Osborn was magnanimous, and did not recall this old score. The most amusing thing in the journey is the description of High Mass in the cathedral at Manilla, which "was a most grotesque performance."

"The troops marched into church, filling nearly the whole of it, and six men with swords drawn took up a position on the altar platform to present arms to the priest. The band was immediately below this, and opened proceedings with a very pretty *deux-temps* waltz. They principally played polkas and waltzes, sometimes kneeling, sometimes standing,—the men crossing themselves in quick time, making a sort of polka step on their faces with wonderful rapidity. I tried crossing myself in quick time, but made a mess of it. The whole thing lasted about half an hour, and consisted entirely of music. The officiating priest was a black man, who never said anything, and only occasionally elevated the Host, and turned round to bless the congregation in pantomime."

After long inaction and various attempts at negotiation, the united forces found themselves compelled to proceed to the bombardment of Canton, which was taken with the greatest of ease and the utmost rapidity, scarcely any resistance being made. Laurence and some of the other non-combatants watched the proceedings from an eminence close by, on a hill used as a cemetery, where they found "shelter from the flying balls in a deep little grave." "Unfortunately," he says, "the very imperfection of their modes of defence is the greatest danger in Chinese warfare. If you are alone in the midst of a silent turnip-field, you are as likely to be hit as if you were immediately under the walls with an attacking party, for they have no idea of taking aim, and their rockets go shying about in all conceivable directions." He had seen "a brave young fellow killed by one of these wild projectiles within five or six yards of him," but still it was difficult to believe there was any danger, they were so few and far between.

"This sort of thing went on until half-past eight, when the Braves made an attack on our extreme right, of which we had a capital view; but we were soon diverted from looking at this by the cheers in front, and we saw the scaling-ladders up, and our fellows clustering like bees into a hive. We immediately bolted down to join them, and in five minutes stood upon the city wall, deserted by every vestige of a Chinaman, except those that were lying dead along the parapet. We had a magnificent view of the vast city, with its million of inhabitants, at our feet, not showing a sign of life. Not a living creature was to be seen throughout its whole extent. The streets, to be sure, are so narrow that you can't see far into them; but when you did, you only saw dead or occasionally wounded people. I went down with the General to the other end of the wall, a mile and a half distant, where they were potting at our fellows from the tops of houses, and while I was there poor Bower of the 59th was wounded—I fear mortally. However, it was their last effort. We made this our advanced post in this direction. I wanted to get back with all my news to Lord Elgin. I took advantage of a party going to open up a new communication, got down to the river, and was on board the Furious in time, as you know, to catch the post by about five minutes."

He defends himself some time later, when he has had time to receive letters from home blaming him for thus unnecessarily exposing himself at Canton, in an amusing way. He was wrong, he allows. "But it involves a greater act of self-denial than any I know to refrain from going to see anything approaching to a fight. And though in principle I utterly disapprove of war, when it comes to 'Away there, second cutters!' human nature can't resist jumping in, whatever good resolutions one may have formed to the contrary."

It is unnecessary to follow the course of the expedition, which was still exposed to extraordinary delays, even after this apparently decisive step. Laurence cannot refrain from a temptation still greater than that of warfare—a little abuse of the spirit of revenge, which he found so strongly developed among so-called religious persons. He tells his mother that the missionaries at Shanghai, where the expedition went after reducing Canton to the most prostrate subjection, were revolted by the mildness of Lord Elgin's measures. "Like Lord Shaftesbury, they are truly English, and grumble at our not having murdered Yeh and given Canton over to pillage and slaughter. As a general rule, one thinks that justice ought to be tempered with mercy; but they would have vengeance tempered with justice!" It is well to add, however, that the "parson with a Crimean medal pinned on his surplice," who had made him angry by preaching on hell, turned out "a very nice fellow" when they watched Canton together from among the tombs. But Laurence was little favourable to missionaries in general, and felt with many others that the good incomes, good houses, and worldly comfort of men who were supposed to be sacrificing everything for Christ's work, were jarring circumstances, to say the least. His comparison between the Jesuit schools at Shanghai and those of the Protestant missionaries was perhaps touched with the same prejudice, yet no doubt had truth in it. Of the first, he says :—

"I was struck with the intelligent expression of the youths' countenances, and the apparent affection they had for their teachers. Instead of cramming nothing but texts down their throats, they teach them the Chinese classics, Confucius, &c., so as to enable them to compete in the examinations. The result is, that even if they do not become Christians, they have always gratitude enough to protect those to whom they owed their education, and perhaps consequent rise in life. I also went over a school with the Bishop. The contrast was most striking. Small

boys gabbled the Creed over in what was supposed to be
English; but in one instance Lord Elgin was profoundly
persuaded it was Chinese. They understood probably
about as clearly as they pronounced. Then, instead of
the missionaries living among them and identifying themselves with the boys, they have gorgeous houses, wives,
and families. A missionary here with a wife and four
children gets a house as big as Spring Grove rent free,
and £500 a-year: and that is called giving up all for the
sake of the heathen!"

The difficulties under which the expedition had to be
carried out throw a curious light upon the hindrances,
unsuspected by the general public, to which even the
most important public work is exposed. Thus between
two and three months were lost at Hong-Kong, while the
forces sent out from England to replace those carried off
to India were on the way. And again, at the mouth of
the Peiho the whole mission was arrested for a month by
the blunder or obstinacy of the admirals, who would not
furnish gunboats which could cross the bar and ascend the
river. I may quote one amusing incident of the subjection of the town of Tientsin, in which the private narrative
of the letters is even more picturesque than that afterwards published. The town had capitulated, but was un-
friendly and apt to do or say something disagreeable when
occasion served. Thus two of the captains of the fleet
were insulted on a visit they paid, without escort or alarm,
to some of the shops and streets. A detachment of a hundred marines was sent to punish the offenders, but on
reaching the town found the gates closed against them.
Laurence, generally to be found by some lucky accident
wherever anything was going on, had accompanied them
on horseback.

"Osborn and I, however, discovered a scalable place
where a house was built against the wall; so we took
three blue-jackets, and with Drew got on the roof and
thus scrambled on to the wall, the bricks being decayed
so as to give us something to hold to. Then with bayo-

nets and revolvers drawn we rushed down with a frantic
yell upon the unsuspecting crowd collected at the gate,
thinking they had succeeded in barring us out.   They
took to their heels, struck to a panic by the six barbarians,
and we smashed the bar of the gate and let the warriors
in, with whom we paraded the town, making six prisoners
at the place where the outrage was committed."

The commissioners from the Emperor, obtained after
much difficulty to settle the treaty, which for the first
time admitted foreign traders, as a right, to the Celestial
Empire, met Lord Elgin at this town,—Laurence in the
meanwhile having been much occupied in " collecting from
old treaties and other sources all the points" that could
be employed in the new.   The other special missions upon
which Laurence was himself engaged—such as that to
Soochow, Nankin, and some others—are fully recorded in
his book.   The private narrative adds little, except on the
former occasion an account of his troubles with a vapour-
ing French consul, who was the adviser of his colleague
the French secretary, but exceedingly unpopular as well
as injudicious.   Having achieved the treaty, the expedition went to Japan, returning to Shanghai and Canton for
the final ratification.   In the hurried and brief visit to
Japan there was nothing but pleasurable excitement before
them,—the first discovery, so to speak, of a wonderful new
nation, the wonder and enigma of modern times.   In the
second volume of Laurence's ' Narrative' there will be
found full details of this visit; but in his letters it has
very little space, partly, I think, because, like all the rest
of the mission, he had become very tired of his banishment, and in the hope of a speedy return home put off his
descriptions of the unknown country till he should be able
to give them by word of mouth.   "We were all enchanted
with Japan," he says, writing from Shanghai on their
return.

> "*Sept.* 1, 1858.

"At Sinoden we heard from the American consul that
in consequence of the moral effect of our having forced
the Chinamen into a treaty, he had just been able to

conclude one at Yeddo ; so we proceeded there, and the
Japanese saw for the first time in their lives four foreign
ships anchor off the capital. They were most civil, and
gave us a capital lodging on shore in a temple. Six commissioners were appointed to treat, and I never ceased regretting that you had prevented me from learning Dutch
at the Cape in consideration of my morals, though I daresay I should have forgotten it—as it was the only medium
of communication here, and we had to make use of the
American interpreter. I had a considerable finger in the
pie nevertheless, Lord Elgin very kindly letting me take
as prominent a place as circumstances would permit. The
commissioners were capital fellows, and so different from
the Chinese, so full of animation and life, and very go-
ahead. They are the most good-tempered people I ever
met, and Japan is the only country I was ever in where
there is no poverty and beggars are unknown. Much as
I should hate going to China in any capacity, I would
willingly go to Japan, and I am sure, were I to get the
appointment of Consul-General there, you and papa would
like it. Of course all this has furnished me with plenty
of material for my book."

His mind, it must be added, was at this moment, as the
work of the mission was nearly over, again much occupied
by thoughts of a permanent appointment. One of those
which were spoken of was the appointment of Governor
of the Straits Settlements, to which he was inclined ; but
it is evident that he would gladly have accepted any fitting
post in his anxiety to attain a settled position in life. To
be Secretary of Legation at a foreign capital would have
been in some respects still more congenial. A wife, which
he had for years decided half in jest and half in earnest to
be the first necessity of all, is also spoken of. On the
other hand, " I sometimes think I will throw up all my
present ambitions, try and find some one with three or four
hundred a-year, and settle down in a small way at a European capital to work out' my own problems. After all,"
he adds, " there is no such happiness as living in one's own
world of thought. At present my thoughts run on aniseed,

almonds, beans, *bêche de mer*, and so on through all the tariff. What ennobling and elevating subjects for contemplation!" At the moment when he thus expressed himself, he was discussing point by point with the Chinese Commissioners the details of duties and imports, and very weary of his work.

The snatches of gaiety which broke the routine of tedious life furnish some amusing incidents to the narrative, but very often are weighted with a moral, and many assaults upon the manners of the mercantile communities. At one place the ball came to its conclusion in an effective surprise. "Lord Elgin and I finished with a reel for the edification of the public, took a tender farewell of society, and embarked during the small hours of the morning, so that when the world awoke next day we were no more to be seen." At another place the company was *dévote*, and a different kind of entertainment was necessary.

"The King of Denmark's fiddler has been here, and we had music and singing for Mrs M. and other non-dancing ladies; but when they left we danced till a late hour. Lord Elgin stumped Mrs M. by asking if that were not the time for dancing mentioned by Solomon, and what hour of the day she thought he would approve? She denied that he said there was a time for dancing, but has since found chapter and verse, and has given in, but evidently thinks Solomon was wrong. The Bishop and his wife are becoming dabs at billiards; but the other night when the missionaries were dining he would not allow the billiard-room to be lighted, though he is generally the last to leave it. Woe unto you Evangelists and Puseyites, hypocrites! To abstain from dancing, and love to be seen in fine bonnets at church, and at the head of subscription lists ostentatiously [here follows a long tirade]. . . . There is a sudden explosion for you, which has taken me as much by surprise as you. Poor Bishop! I don't mean to abuse him. I think by the way he buttonholes me, and talks confidential platitudes to me in corners, that he rather likes me. He constantly excuses the missionaries for going into the country against treaty, &c.,

though I carefully refrain from reflecting on them ; so I
suppose it is his own conscience.   I believe he is a good
man.   He confirms to-day a lot of middies who have
been prepared for the ceremony by our convivial parson,
and who, though nice young fellows, are some of them
such scamps that their sponsors must be immensely relieved by the load that will be lifted from their shoulders."

Laurence is never happier than when he sends a flying
shaft thus at the "worldly holy," against whom afterwards,
in ' Piccadilly,' he poured forth his keenest satire.   He
tells his mother afterwards that he had nearly embroiled
himself with the lady mentioned above, for laughing at a
society for Biblical discussion among the ladies, one member of which had distinguished Bishop Heber as a descendant of Heber the Kenite.   "I said that as a lawyer I was
superior to all clergy as an interpreter of texts, and suggested that I should be elected permanent referee to the
ladies—with other foolish nonsense," he writes, repentant,
having made his peace.   But the society of these seaports,
"worse than a colony," as he says, grew more and more
intolerable to him as the days lingered on.   "The men
think of nothing but tea, silk, and opium ; the women are
too apathetic to care even for gaiety and crinoline.   We
are going to make a spasmodic attempt to amuse them
with a ball ; but Fitzroy is in despair, for only eight
ladies have accepted and 120 men !"

Meanwhile his metaphysical thinkings and readings go
on, and he has a mingled disappointment and delight in
finding the metaphysical and religious work he had intended to produce forestalled by Mr William Smith's
'Thorndale,' in which he has been "revelling," and which
"represents my own ideas and condition of mind better
than anything I could myself give."   "Mind you read
every word of it to papa," he repeats, "and think over it
the while, and of me, when you read the chapter called
'Childhood,' as I did of you."

He is afterwards astonished and delighted, "after what
I wrote to you about 'Thorndale,' that just as I should be
making you a present of a copy of it, I should receive one

with your dear handwriting on the title-page!" Another
book which he had read with pleasure was a very different
one, Miss Marsh's 'Hearts and Hands,' an account of her
mission among the navvies. He wonders, not unnaturally,
whether his complicated religious system would have any
influence upon such people; but comforts himself by the
thought that a complicated system need not be less true
than a simpler one, and that those who act by reason are
less likely to be backsliders than those who are moved by
enthusiasm. Their progress may be slow, but it is sure.

" In my own case it is awfully slow; but then consider
the difficulty of having to build away for one's self and
fight against prejudice existing in every form around, and
compare my condition with that of the worldly man who
becomes a 'converted Christian.' He flings himself at
once into the religious world, where he is supported and
taught and cared for, his difficulties explained and his
faith strengthened, and sails smoothly and easily down the
stream. To put it in the form of an equation, he is to me
as is a Roman Catholic to him. He thinks the Roman
Catholic has his religion done for him, I think the Protestant has his religion done for him. So different is religion
in these days from what it was in the days of Christ, that
the worldly man does not persecute the saint, but the
saint persecutes the worldly man. It requires infinitely
more strength of mind and moral courage to come out
from the religious world and to be separate, than to come
out from the worldly one."

This perpetual assault against the religious world may
be explained by the fact that the exterior conventionalities of that world had been more or less always present,
overshadowing his life, until the young man emancipated
himself from them. It would have been perhaps more
wonderful had he lived to perceive nowadays that in
many circles the greatest courage and strength of mind is
required from those who profess any belief at all. He
defends himself once more from the accusation of "setting
up his reason," which his mother had brought against him.

" You must remember that the fact that we believe many things we don't understand does not prove that when we don't understand a thing we should believe it. We have only our reason to decide for us the cases in which it voluntarily allows itself to be suspended.   It preaches faith equally in your case as in mine, only I require stronger grounds to influence me than you do. But I think that it is a mistake to hold on to it too long. I have long since taken refuge in my intuitions."

Reason, tempered by intuition, was thus the rule to which he had attained, alone and without spiritual guidance of any kind.   The reader will perceive that thus the doors of his heart were wide open, so that any interpreter who commended himself, if that were possible, to both, might enter in.

His return home after this, the longest absence from his parents which he had ever undergone, was a very mournful one.   For the dear "Papa," whom he rarely called by any but that tender childish title, died suddenly a short time before the expedition came back.   It was, I think, at one of the ports of Ceylon—a place so associated with him—that Laurence received the news.   Sir Anthony's death was entirely unexpected, and occurred, I believe, at a dinner-party to which he had gone in his usual health.   I have been told that, being at sea at the time, Laurence came on deck one morning and informed his comrades that he had seen his father in the night, and that he was dead—that they endeavoured to laugh him out of the impression, but in vain.   The date was taken down, and on their arrival in England it was found that Sir Anthony Oliphant had indeed died on that night— which would be a remarkable addition, if sufficiently confirmed, to many stories of a similar kind which are well known.   He always appears in his son's letters and in his wife's in the most engaging light—a cheerful and bright spirit interested in everything about him, as curious of novelty and excitement as his own son was, delighting to find himself in the heart of everything that was going on.   The jokes about "the darling," in which he indulged in the earlier Colombo days, half hiding under a humorous pretence at jealousy the delight and pride in the beloved boy, which he felt as warmly as the mother did, and his readiness to follow Lowry wherever his fortunes led him, are as lovable and delightful as is the confidence of Laurence in papa's comprehension and sympathy and the charm of his companionship. The mother and son discuss him indeed sometimes as mothers and children will do, as if he were a big schoolboy, whose pranks are charming, but whose health and comfort has to be looked after by more careful heads than his own; but in his judgment on serious matters his son had always the fullest reliance, and the highest testimony his wife could give to the excellence of the new tenets she adopted in later days was that "our beloved Sir Anthony" would have found comfort in them.

He would not seem, however, to have exercised much guidance, but rather to have allowed himself genially to follow where his boy's erratic steps led—now to the Crimea, now to the Stirling burghs, where papa's electioneering was most lively and active. The only "No" which seems ever recorded of him is when Laurence, young and sanguine, made a demand for money to invest in America —to which Sir Anthony replied with the dry but admirable advice that his son should save anything he could from his official salary and invest that. This advice was so far taken that Laurence became the possessor of "a town lot" in the city of Superior, of which he afterwards made the admirable use of establishing upon it a friend who was under the shadow of severe misfortune, and for whom a refuge was thus obtained. It brought in, however, save in this way, no profit to its proprietor.

Sir Anthony's death made the union between mother and son more close and all-absorbing than ever; but it did not bind the active and restless young man to England, a result for which his spirit of adventure is not alone to be blamed. For he neglected no effort to establish himself in the diplomatic service nearer home, and it is evident that it was the prick of injured feeling, the sickness at heart of continual disappointment, the spurns which patient merit has to accept, if not of the unworthy, at least of the official world, which drove him again and again from England.   It was indeed impatient merit in Oliphant's case.   He would not wait kicking his heels outside the doors of the Colonial or Foreign Office.   It was a necessity with him to be doing, if not one thing then another.   Both his active temperament and the state of his mind in respect to religious and other matters fomented this impatience.   He explains it to his mother by the following excellent reasons, while also apologising to her for not writing of his "interior," which was what she always most desired :—

"So long as I have anything to interest me, I keep myself so fully occupied and usefully employed that time passes pleasantly and profitably, and I do not compromise myself ; but when I have nothing to do except to be consistent in hours of temptation which are constantly recurring, and have no employment to absorb me, I go with the stream, having an utter want of self-denial.   I find the only substitute is occupation, and that I cannot have on circuit, as it must be engrossing, which law is not.   The consequence is, that I am in low spirits unless I am actively engaged."

It is characteristic of his breeding and the perpetual self-examinations to which he had been made to subject himself, modified into a curiously unusual vein by the originality of his own mind, that he should go on from this into a lament over the incongruity of his mental and moral position :—

"I find it impossible to divest my conversation and conduct of that frivolity which marks the worldly mind, and which gives the lie to any sudden outburst of morality I may think it necessary to assume.   Nobody could conceive how deeply I feel the reality and truth of religion from my conduct, considering the force of my convictions and the occasional earnestness of my prayers.   In days when

I was almost insensible to religion of any sort, or had any principle except my love for you, I was infinitely less capable of evil than I am now; but now that I begin to delight in the love of God after the inward man, the law of my members seems moved into activity. As this said law always gets the best of it, you will perceive that I must be harassed in proportion as the struggle is great. However, I could go on theorising for hours; and now that I come to read it over, I daresay it is all humbug from beginning to end, and that is another reason why I don't like writing this sort of stuff. How am I ever to be satisfied, after analysing my feelings, that I am right? It seems to me one of the most fruitless occupations in the world. It does not appear to me that the human mind is endowed with faculties adequate to the task. It instinctively knows its own weakness, but it is not competent to say where that weakness lies or how it may be cured, or else it would be competent to cure it, which it certainly is not. If a divine power is necessary to overcome the depravity of one's human nature, a divine revelation is necessary to enable one to discern wherein that depravity precisely consists. Therefore, as I said before, I may be all wrong, with which consideration you must comfort yourself; also with feeling that I have relieved my mind by writing all this, whether it is nonsense or not."

One cannot but feel a half-amused sympathy for the mother, thus tantalised by revelations in which there was so much which must have satisfied her craving for information respecting her son's innermost thoughts, and so much that must have puzzled and confounded her. How far did the boy mean what he said? and how far was it humbug, as he says? All the pages of theorising which he addressed to her—his bold criticisms of the things she reverenced most, and breakings-off into new paths—never, however, discouraged her; until the time came when they both beheld the new light, as it seemed to them, together, and all qualms on the one side and uncertainties on the other were swept away.

After his two years' service in China, it was natural to

suppose that his hopes of definite and permanent employment would have been realised; but either the Foreign
Office did not think so, or its slowness of operation and
prejudice in favour of those who had entered its service
in the usual way made its authorities impervious to the
claims of the brilliant young interloper, who had, though
so successful and valuable a public servant, leaped into
the service rather by private favour of a friendly plenipotentiary than in the legitimate way. At all events, he
had got tired of waiting by the end of the year, and in the
early beginning of 1860 we find him plunged into a new
excitement. Probably he had remained more or less a
sympathiser with Italy since the time when he took a
delighted share in all the mischief going on, a dozen years
before, when he was a boy travelling with his parents;
but there is no indication to show us what it was which
made him suppose that he could do something to stay
the course of events, when just at the crisis of the fate
of Nice and Savoy he rushed out of London and threw
himself into the excitement of Italian politics in Turin—
where the cession was being reluctantly carried through—
and Nice, where he actually hoped to have reversed the
order of things, and roused the languid population to resistance. It is curious to find him discussing sentimental
methods and quoting the 'Biglow Papers': "I don't
believe in principle, but oh I du in interest!" in respect
to national action, while setting out on the most romantic
piece of knight-errantry in his own person. His journey
to Nice and Turin had, of course, two aspects; and he
scarcely discloses even in his delightful after-narrative,
published when all necessity for secrecy was over, the
daring hope he had of becoming himself an important
agent in the matter, and perhaps saving the provinces
which Italy, not yet consolidated into a great nation, was
compelled to sacrifice to her great and noble aim. To
ordinary eyes it was pure love of adventure, tempered by
the pursuit of " copy " and material for articles, chiefly in
' Blackwood,' which carried him forth; and he is profuse
in his explanations to his mother that the fifty pounds he
would make by two articles was quite justification enough

for the brief crusade, lasting only a month, upon which
he set out in high hopes.

Leaving Paris, Laurence found himself, to his great
annoyance, yet amusement, in the same carriage "with
some frowsy parties enveloped in tobacco - smoke," who
turned out to be the very deputies from Nice, returning
from their interview with the Emperor, whom he was
bent on overcoming; but with whom he became so friendly,
picking their brains of any political secrets to be found
there, that he was taken for one of them by an official
who came to the railway to pay his respects to the dep-
utation. "He made me a low bow, which I returned
with all the dignity becoming a man who has just sold
his country." In Savoy he found enough of patriotic
feeling and smouldering undirected enthusiasm to fill him
with high hopes; and his first resolution, after egging up
these local patriots to resistance, was to write letters to
every member of the Parliament in Turin, urging them to
delay the ratification of the treaty,—a tremendous step
to be taken by a young man on his own responsibility.
His earnestness and conviction that something might
actually be done in this way was not unmingled with
levity. "It is great fun," he writes, "to have another
object than churches and picture-galleries;" but he was
not the less seriously disappointed and humiliated when
he found that things had gone too far, and that all his
eloquence, excitement, and inspiration could not produce
the effects he had desired.

His acquaintance with diplomatic society carried him
at once to the heart of affairs in Turin, and made him
acquainted with all the now historical details of that great
era in Italian history. He met and dined with Cavour,
whom he describes as " a thick-set solid man, with a large
square head and spectacles, an able, mathematical, practical sort of head, without chivalry, principle, or genius,"
—a harsh judgment, which he afterwards saw cause to
alter. But his chief interest was Garibaldi, by whose aid
alone any operation like that of which he dreamed was
practicable. The impatience of the young man, used to
constitutional methods, and conscious of the efficacy of

popular agitation, with the still bewildered patriots, who were quite unable to employ such new tools, is characteristic.

"Why I should take such intense interest in affairs that don't concern me I don't know, except that I cannot stand by and see a good cause ruined, and such blackguards as the Emperor carrying all before him, without wagging a finger. And these people, with all their patriotism, are so childish and unpractical, Garibaldi worst of all. I have got him regularly in tow, but cannot din the only practicable plan for the salvation of his country into his head. He is the most amiable, innocent, honest nature possible, and a first-rate guerilla chief, but in council a child. The worst of him is that he puts his trust in anybody, and unless you stick to him you lose your influence; but he has a name with the people that may be turned to any account."

The zeal of the young self-sent emissary seems to have been able to inspirit the drooping party of disconsolate Nizzards so far as to procure the proposal of a resolution against the annexation, in Parliament, by Garibaldi, Laurence himself drawing it out. But "it is of no use, I feel certain," he says; "they can neither work popular movements nor parliamentary tactics." That the malcontents should never have thought of calling a public meeting at Nice, where the people might have expressed their feelings, fills him with indignant astonishment. Failing these constitutional methods, remained the romantic one of seizing and breaking the ballot-boxes when the votes were collected, so as to make another ballot necessary, and thus gain a little time, which would seem to have been fully planned by the energetic young revolutionary. But this promising plan was abandoned by the distraction of Garibaldi's thoughts toward Sicily, as may be seen in the 'Episodes.' The young man promises to his mother to "keep out of the row"; but we know what such undertakings come to in the case of an individual who had confessed that it was beyond human nature to hear that a

fight was going on, and not rush out to see it. And what
the Foreign Office would have thought of a possible
Secretary of Legation breaking the ballot-boxes at the
head of a party of Garibaldian red-shirts it would not be
difficult to predict. Thus, perhaps, according to his prevailing conviction, it was all for the best that he should
have been compelled to add, in deep disappointment,
"There is not the slightest chance of a row—the people
are like sheep."

"The business here has gone off with the usual flatness.
Still I am glad to have seen it, and to have known the
villanies that have been perpetrated under the pretext of
universal suffrage. The whole thing was a sham of the
most transparent character. A popular leader like Garibaldi ought to have turned the tables. A little more of
Walker in his composition would have settled the matter."
Always philosophical, however, and remembering now that
the affairs of Italy did not really concern him in the least,
Laurence consoled himself by thoughts of the pounds which
would be brought in by two articles in 'Blackwood,' which
were more than his expedition had cost him altogether.

He seems to have travelled much this year, since we
hear of him two or three months later in Montenegro,
where various amusing incidents happened to him, related
in the 'Episodes'; and after that in Naples, where he was
once more received by Garibaldi, by that time victor of
Sicily, and about to round out the new-formed Italian
kingdom by the magnificent present of the ancient Regno,
the only royal state in the peninsula. Laurence relates
that he was accommodated on this occasion in the very
palace and bedchamber of King Bomba himself, "in a bed
so gorgeous with its gold and lace and satin, that I doubted
whether the king himself did not keep it for show. However, it turned out a very good one to sleep in," adds the
light-hearted traveller, whose next night's rest might be in
a brigand's hut or in the close little cabin of a felucca, for
anything he knew or cared.

It was in one more out of the way still, in the paper
chamber of a Japanese temple, that for almost the first
time in all his adventurous career we find him in absolute

peril of his life. Notwithstanding what seems at the first glance the rapid advance and invariable success of his life, Laurence had not been as yet, as I have already had occasion to remark, distinguished by Government patronage. When the appointment as First Secretary of Legation at Japan was offered to him, it was thus a most important step in his career: though possibly, as it was to replace a gentleman murdered barbarously in China, and involved danger to life as well as a very distant exile out of the world, it was not eagerly sought after by the usual candidates. To Laurence, however, whose experiences of Japan in his former brief visit with Lord Elgin—when all was novel and fresh, and the strangers were received with *naïve* enthusiasm before any complications had arisen— were all delightful, the offer, as he says, was "extremely tempting," especially as it was in reality the first really official appointment which he had held. He arrived in Yedo (I adopt his own spelling of the word) in the end of June 1861, the Minister, Sir Rutherford Alcock, then Mr Alcock, being at the time absent, which constituted Laurence for the time being *chargé d'affaires*. His usual correspondence with his mother here unfortunately fails me; but I am permitted to quote from a letter addressed to the Duchess of Somerset, which gives a very vivid representation of the state of affairs, and shows the changed condition of the Japanese mind towards the powerful invaders whom they had previously received with so much cordiality. This letter was written only a few days before the outrage which so completely changed his prospects.

"YEDO, *July* 2 [1861].

"I am at present luxuriating in that feeling of repose which arises from having arrived at one's journey's end, and am agreeably surprised with the aspect of my future abode. Mr Alcock is still away, so that I found myself *locum tenens* immediately on my arrival. The important questions which are pending are of course left over until his return, and things are going on quietly enough, in so far as one's personal safety is concerned. That we shall have ultimately to join issue with the Japanese no one

can doubt who watches for a moment the tone of their
diplomacy; but I shall be able to write to you at more
length upon that subject when I have been here a little
longer. We expect the Admiral in a week or ten days,
and I trust that when he comes he will see the expediency
of keeping a large force in these parts. At present we
have only one despatch gunboat for the whole of Japan.
So far as we are concerned here, with a due amount of
prudence and submission to Government restraint, there
is no reason why any disturbance should arise; but at
Yokohama, only seventeen miles off, there are upwards of
a hundred Europeans, and their patience under the galling
restraints to which they are subjected cannot always be
counted upon.

"I can imagine few places of residence more delightful than this, if that one all-pervading drawback of Government surveillance were removed. In fact, a State
prisoner would consider himself in clover, but a free-
born Briton cannot regard matters in the same light. At
Yokohama these restraints are much mitigated, and people
may ride and walk where they like unattended; but we
here are never for a moment unwatched. The beauty of
our pleasure-grounds, which consist of twenty or thirty
acres of garden, wood, and water, is quite destroyed by
the fact of three hundred guards being posted in them.
If my servant runs after a butterfly, a two-sworded official
runs after him; and one post completely commands my
rooms, so that my every act is noticed. As the whole is
enclosed by a palisade, every gate is guarded. We are
never attended by less than eight when we go out; these
scramble over the country after us, and prohibit our stopping to speak to the people, much more to shop in the town.
Indeed there is no inducement to go into the town after
one is familiar with it, as the streets are crowded and the
chances of collision greater. As a general rule, our guard-
ians exercise their functions with civility. When they are
impertinent, as sometimes happens, one has to submit as
one would to one's jailer. All this is rather trying, and
is a useful exercise of temper.

"It is due to Mr Alcock to say that his retirement to

Kanogan produced a good effect, though it was a bold stroke, as, if the Government had not yielded, there was no escape from the dilemma. Practically one is perfectly safe if one is prudent, submits to discipline, and is respectful in one's bearing when one meets the native grandees or their retainers. For instance, on a narrow path the Englishman, if he desires to avoid a collision, makes way for the grandee's servant. Then there is no occasion to go out after dark, or to resent insulting expressions from intoxicated Yacomins. With entire humility one is in no danger whatever, and a truly sincere Christian who exercised the highest of Christian graces might live here in perfect safety all his life. All my old friends have disappeared from the scene. One, who was an especial favourite of mine when I was here last, ripped himself up a short time ago; and two of the other commissioners are disgraced, and it is supposed have followed his example. This was all on account of their friendship for foreigners. A man told me that he was struck by the subdued expression of my friend's countenance the other day when he went to see him; but he had no suspicion that that high-spirited individual intended to put an end to himself. He had, in fact, already sent out cards of invitation for a 'happy despatch' party, and at the most jovial moment of the banquet he addressed his friends in a few telling words, and vindicated his honour in their presence.

"Every one, down to the lowest interpreter, who has had anything to do with the introduction of the foreigners, has disappeared or been disgraced, and the hostile nobles do not hesitate to say that they are only waiting till they are better drilled and organised to go to war with us. In fact, they pay us the compliment of saying that we are the only nation they can go to war with, as we are the only nation from whom they can learn anything."

This state of affairs was evidently an impossible one to last; but its conclusion, so far as Oliphant was concerned, though most alarming and nearly tragical, was not a public outrage, but one that might have happened in any unsettled country, the work of a handful of unauthorised ruffians;

and the guard, whose inquisition was so intolerable to the
gentlemen cooped up in the lodging which was thus made
into a prison, seem to have defended them faithfully at the
cost of several lives. The attack, which was of the most
highly dramatic character, is perhaps one of the best known
incidents in Oliphant's life. He has described it in the
most vivid manner in his 'Episodes': and the letter in
which he communicated the event to his mother, though
with a few characteristic and individual touches of private
sentiment, differs little from the after-narrative, and bears
marks in its broken sentences and hurried contractions of
the difficulty with which he still wrote. He had been
only about a week in discharge of his functions, and had
just been relieved of his responsibility as chief of the embassy by the arrival of Mr Alcock, when one night, having
sat late to look at a comet, most fortunately, as it happened, Laurence was startled by various sounds, — the
barking of a dog which he had attached to himself by
kindness (which was a way he had with dogs as well as
men), and which slept at his door, the sound of the rattle
used by the Japanese watchmen, and other suspicious
noises. Jumping up in the dark, he could find no weapon
handy but a hunting-crop with a heavily weighted handle,
with which he rushed out into the narrow passage on which
his room opened, calling several members of the legation
as he went.

" Just as I turned the corner I came upon a tall black
figure, with his arms above his head, holding a huge two-
handed sword. As the only light came round the corner
from R.'s room, I could only see indistinctly that the figure
had a mask on, and seemed in armour. Short time for
observation, had to dodge the sword, and get back a step
to get at him with my whip, yelling loudly. It seemed
like a nightmare, meeting a huge black figure coming in
the night into your house to take stealthily your blood,
whom you had never harmed. He made no sound: we
were at it for a minute or two. I could not hope to do
him much harm: my only object was to keep him at bay
until somebody came; nobody did. I soon got a cut in

the right shoulder, and then managed to entangle his sword in the handle of the whip—it has the marks. I could not see his blows, as it was dark; but at length one came down on my left arm, which I instinctively had kept over my head as a guard. At the same moment Morison, who had time to load a pistol, opened his door and fired. The man dropped, but another fellow rushed at Morison and cut him over the head; then both got back round the corner, the man on the ground only floored, the other fatally wounded. Morison and I retired."

This is the first breathless account of the sudden fight in the dark. When the two wounded men fell back on the room in which two or three of their fellows were now gathered after a hurried search for arms, and in which there was a feeble light, an interval of terrible suspense occurred. Bligh, Oliphant's servant, had dashed through the paper partition of his room, to join the party with his double-barrelled gun: all the arms that could be mustered besides were two revolvers and a sword, and with these means of defence, paper walls and screens their only shelter, and two wounded men to hinder any escape, the little group stood listening for the renewed attack. Fortunately, however, the guards outside were faithful, and the assassins were successfully driven back, although fighting went on during the whole course of the anxious night. Next day Laurence, whose wounds had been bound up by Mr Alcock, was conveyed to the gunboat in the harbour, the Ringdove, "escorted by Alcock and whole mission, file of blue-jackets, second of Yacomins, all armed to teeth, a most pic. procession," writes the sufferer, his eyes open under all circumstances. "One's collar-bone sewn up prevents use of right arm yet; other hurts are left arm, two cuts above wrist. Doctors promise better in three weeks." This was scribbled on the 10th of July, four days after the event. On the 11th he goes on: "Better: first three days both arms had to be strapped across chest. Bligh fed me and nursed me in the tenderest manner; but I alone here, captain and men on shore. Sleeping on back, with thermometer at 85°, trussed like a fowl, is difficult, but we are jolly."

After some discussion of the position, the following note is added at the end :—

"My only thought that night was for you : for myself I am glad ; it made me know I could face death, which at one time seemed inevitable. I found my creed or philosophy quite satisfactory. I take everything as in the day's work, and that is why in one sense I do not feel thankful like others. I have such a profound feeling of being in God's hands, and having nothing to do with my own fate, that gratitude even would be presumption. If killed, I have no doubt my first feeling in the other world would be one of relief ; just as my first feeling at not being killed was one of relief too. It seems to me to make no difference : whatever is, is best ; and I feel I could realise this amid considerable pain. Since wounded do not wish to complain ; acquiescence during short stay here no great heroism. I do not know that I should say so always ; but as yet I can, and I see it is the right thing. It must all end ; one has only to hold on, and feel sure that the use and object of it all will be evident. Meantime to do the right thing :

> Live I, so live I
> To my Lord heartily,
> To my Prince faithfully,
> To my neighbour honestly,
> Die I, so die I.

"If God is good, it must all come right in the end. I never doubt Him. I have got 'Thorndale' on board, which is a most comfortable book."

Four days later, he wrote that he was able to move his fingers, and the stitches were taken out of his shoulder ; and describes the cook, who in running away had received two dreadful gashes in the back, and could only lie on his stomach. "Very lucky I did not turn round to bolt," he says ; "if so, must have been cut down from behind. I owe my life to Morison coming up when he did, and R. and L. owe their lives to my stopping the two men who were hurrying along the passage within three yards of their doors." His opinion was that after this assault, which the Japanese elaborately made out to be an expression of private hatred alone, and entirely unconnected with any official, the British Government had but two courses before it—the one a war with Japan, the other withdrawal at once and summarily. " I don't depart from my old theoretical views. The result of our forcing ourselves upon people who never wanted us, has been to place us in the dilemma from which the only escape is one or other of the courses I have proposed. If we are withdrawn, I shall feel very much my tail between my legs ; if we go to war, I shall go in for looting daimios' palaces and feel a blackguard ! "

Laurence discovered afterwards that the unaccountable ineffectiveness of his encounter with the Japanese ruffian was fully explained by the fact that the blows on both sides were rendered comparatively harmless by a great beam, which neither saw in the darkness, immediately over their heads, and on which the sword and hunting-whip respectively had expended their blows. It was discovered to be slashed and dinted with the sword-cuts which ought to have killed the combatant on one side, and the blows which ought to have felled the assailant on the other. But for this it is almost impossible that Oliphant in his night-dress, with his loaded whip-handle, standing against an antagonist in a mail-coat and with a sword, could have escaped with his life. But in the meantime the all-important moments during which he kept back the assassins decided the failure of the attempt. " I believe our escape was mainly owing to the determined manner in which your son kept our assailants at bay for some time, till our guards came up," wrote one of the *attachés* to Lady Oliphant ; and I am tempted to quote entire the letter of Bligh the servant, who was ready to stand by his master to the death, but who chilled the very blood in his veins by his tragic whisper when the little group stood waiting for the rush which they expected every moment, " Do you think, sir, they will torture us before they kill us ? " Half fainting from loss of blood, unable to defend himself further whatever might happen, and with the

certainty in his mind that escape was impossible, Laurence
was lying in a chair, too dizzy and weak to mind what
was happening, when all the blood remaining in his body
was brought to his brain by these words. "This horrible
suggestion brought out a cold perspiration," he says; "and
I trust I may never again experience the sensation of dread
with which it inspired me." Bligh's letter, however, was
more considerate than his speech.

"LADY OLIPHANT,—Believing a letter from me just now
would be acceptable, I take the earliest opportunity. I have
already disobeyed your commands in not writing before,
for which I crave pardon, and can only now say a few words
about the late occurrence. It was a very cowardly assault,
but fortunately without the results intended. You may be
quite comfortable about my master, whatever you hear to
the contrary. He has a slight wound on the shoulder, the
right side, and a cut on the left arm just above the wrist,
which I am very glad to say are doing wonderfully well;
and am very happy to add my master's health is excellent,
which, combined with the care of the kind and attentive
surgeon of the Ringdove, with all due allowance for such
wounds, within three weeks or one month my master will
be himself again. He is very irritable at not having a
more deadly weapon than the hunting-whip, so as to have
floored his opponent. I believe had it not been for my
master stopping the fellows when he did, so gallantly and
quite unsupported, we should have had a different tale to
tell. I may add, three or four of the fellows were killed
and as many taken.

"Hoping this short letter will meet your approbation, I
beg to remain, your ladyship's humble servant,

"SAMUEL BLIGH."

This good fellow had been engaged in helping his master
to form an entomological collection for the British Mu-
seum,—"running after butterflies," as Laurence describes.
They had found a rare beetle, to their pride and joy, a day
or two before; and the tragic, half-seen, black figures, invading the sleeping house in the dark, gave note of their

stealthy coming to Bligh by stumbling over the tray full of sharp pins upon which the insects were impaled—a curious mixture, half comic, as so many tragic occurrences are.

It was considered right that Laurence should return home with the news of the condition of the embassy, and the necessity for taking some decided steps to secure their safety and dignity, or withdrawal—as soon as he was able to travel. He had a curious commission on his way—to find out and warn off a Russian man-of-war, which had stolen into a secluded island-harbour in the face of all treaties, and was then ensconced guiltily in the shelter of the endless windings of the waters, surveying and preparing for anything that might happen in the future. Laurence was so far recovered that he was able to carry out this commission with his usual coolness and success, and caught the Russians, without warning, in this curious secret employment. He returned home within a few months from the time he left London, and he never again returned to the diplomatic service. He had only been about ten days in his post: this was all the actual and formal employment given him directly by the Government, without the intervention of any such powerful and friendly patron as Lord Elgin.

CHAPTER VII.

POLITICAL ADVENTURE—SOCIAL LIFE.

NOTWITHSTANDING the consequences of his wounds, which he felt for some time—indeed he never fully recovered the use of his left hand, several of the fingers of which were permanently disabled—it was not for long that Laurence could persuade himself to keep still and recover his strength in quiet. It is difficult to make out, from any certain information, whether he had some mission of inquiry in hand, either from the Government or the 'Times,' or was merely working on his personal impulse, with that thirst to know all the intricacies of foreign politics which was always strong in him, when he set out again, in the leisure of his sick-leave, on a journey much more serious than the usual wanderings of convalescence. I believe, however, I am right in saying that many, if not all, of his apparently personal travels at this period of his life were in reality charged with a political object, and that his wildest wanderings and farthest afield were in the public service. It was his luck—a kind of good fortune which was constantly befalling him—to encounter at Vienna the Prince of Wales and his suite, then, in the beginning of 1862, on their way to the Holy Land, and to be invited to accompany them for a portion of their way, as far as Corfu. The Prince of Wales was then a very young man, and his character as yet unknown to the nation, which has learnt to know and esteem its fine qualities since then; and it is interesting to read the early estimate of the royal youth formed by so keen an observer:—

" As I had already been to all the places on the Adriatic coast at which we touched, and was able to do cicerone, I spent a most pleasant ten days, at the same time doing a little quiet political observation. I was delighted with the Prince, and thought he was rarely done justice to in public estimation : he is not studious nor highly intellectual, but he is up to the average in this respect, and beyond it in so far as quickness of observation and general intelligence go. Travelling is, therefore, the best sort of education he could have, and I think his development will be far higher than people anticipate. Then his temper and disposition are charming. His defects are rather the inevitable consequences of his position, which never allows him any responsibility, or forces him into action."

From Corfu Laurence crossed over the mainland within the line of those blue mountains of Albania, which rise with so much soft majesty over the sea. The country was then, as perpetually in its history, distracted with wars and tumults, little comprehensible to the rest of the world; but which he was of opinion would one time or another force themselves upon the general con-

sideration,—an opinion which those who are acquainted
with the commotions and revolutions going on in the
out-of-the-way corners of the earth are very apt to
entertain, since it seems incredible that matters so
momentous on the scene of operations should not affect
sooner or later the larger mass of the body politic, the
band of nations which make up what we call the world.
"I was very much struck," he says, "with the popular
ignorance which prevailed in this country in regard to the
revolt in Bosnia and Herzegovina, which finally led to
the Russo-Turkish war. At the outbreak of that movement, the press, so far as I remember without an exception,
assumed that it was a revolt of Christians against Turks,
and I found the same impression existed even among
members of the Cabinet; the fact being that it was an
agrarian rising of Slav Christian peasants against Slav
Moslem landlords, very much analogous in many aspects
to our own landlord and tenant question in Ireland."

He does not, however, tell us on which side were his
own sympathies, though he speaks of being the guest, in
Herzegovina, of one of the landlords thus described.
Whether it was with this rural dignitary, or with some
expedition on the other side, that he himself went out
to taste that whiff of war which he could never resist,
there is no information. "We went out one day to do a
little skirmishing," he says in the letter already quoted;
"but we found the enemy, who had occupied the place in
force the day before, had retired, so we had a 'walk over.'
I found a great deal that was of political interest going on,
or rather germinating, and indited a despatch accordingly.
Nothing can be worse than the present condition of the
Turkish provinces, and when taken in connection with the
row, the prospect looks bad."

He was not then aware how much he would have to do
with the Turkish sway in after-years, nor was he yet
personally acquainted with that exasperation which it
seems capable beyond all other governments (which is
saying a great deal) of raising in the mind. The following
curious anticipation would seem to have referred to some
project of State which was never carried out: "I do not

see how Venice is to be freed except at the price of the Ionian Isles. I know you don't care about that; but I think it is hardly fair that while the Emperor *makes* by freeing Italy, we should lose by the same transaction." Does this, one wonders, refer to some passing project of handing over the islands to Austria as a compensation for the loss of the Veneto: which changed into a determination to give them away to somebody, as often happens when a present is determined upon, and the first proposed recipient fails?

This expedition concluded with several amusing adventures, all set forth in the most charming way in chapter xii. of the 'Episodes.' On his way through the wild region of the Abruzzi, then scarcely known to travellers, and unsafe without a strong escort, he received in one instance an enthusiastic reception as the supposed nephew of Lord Palmerston; and in another came upon a most curious official, in the shape of the wife of the English vice-consul, who had been for some time exercising such small duties as appertained to his office, the husband having deserted her and his post simultaneously. But naturally this strange substitute was unable to act in the political business which Oliphant had in hand. It was here, too, in the little port of Manfredonia, that he received the following invitation: "Miss Thimbleby requests the pleasure of English gentleman's company to tea to-night at nine o'clock. Old English style;" and accepting it, found a quaint little fossil of an Englishwoman, "very old, well on in the nineties," "a little old woman like a witch," with whom he drank tea solemnly, and to whom no doubt he made himself as delightful as if she had been young, beautiful, and a duchess. She was a sister of Mrs Jordan the actress, of all people in the world.

In a prison in one of the little towns which he visited, and where the captured brigands were the chief object of curiosity, Laurence saw "the beautiful wife of a notorious chief of one of the bands, who had been captured dressed in man's clothes, and using her pistol with such effect that she seriously wounded a soldier before she was taken prisoner,"—which incident no doubt suggested to him the

L

extremely amusing story of the "Brigand's Bride," published some time afterwards in 'Blackwood's Magazine,'
and reprinted in a little volume called 'Fashionable Philosophy.' It is not a tale which professes to be authentic;
but the humorous dare-devil of the story has a sufficient
family resemblance to our active explorer—who pushed
his way everywhere, feared nothing, and delighted above
all in strange and novel experiences of humanity — to
make him interesting, even with the fantastic accessories
of the air-gun, and the wondering timorous population,
which is done to the life. It is easy to imagine Laurence
himself seated, like his hero, outside the chemist's door,
the usual gossiping-place of the provincial Italian, with
the notary and doctor and priest and the Sindaco of the
little town, acute but ignorant, hanging upon his lips,
knowing nothing of England but its greatness and the
eccentricity of the Inglese, and Palmerston the fetich of
the age; and receiving all the wonderful stories told them
with a faith tempered by surprise, and the keenness of that
Italian intelligence which understands humour better than
any other Continental nation. The reader would do well
to take in the wild fun and extravagance of this story to
the more sober record, not as fact, but as a must amusing
and vivid illustration of the wanderer's possibilities, and
of that characteristic rural yet urban life. Nowadays the
traveller on his rush to India passes Foggia and the other
little towns of the coast at something as near express speed
as is possible in Italy—and no doubt they must have gone
through certain revolutions in consequence; but the gossips
still sit round the apothecary's door in the soft evenings,
although some smatterings of knowledge may have penetrated, with much politics and the newspaper, into their
antiquated society.

On his return from this expedition it became necessary
for Laurence to decide whether he should or should not
return to his post in Japan. The alternative was to do
this or to retire altogether from the diplomatic service,
and all the hopes involved in it. "It was with great
regret," he says, "that I found myself compelled by family
considerations to adopt the latter alternative, and abandon

a career which had at that time peculiar attractions for me, and in which, considering my age, I had made rapid progress." Had he returned to Japan, it would have been to the highly important position of *chargé d'affaires*, which could not have failed to lead to continuous and profitable employment, and represented indeed the ball at his foot so far as diplomatic service was concerned; but there can be little doubt that the anxieties of his mother, after the dreadful experience she had passed through at the time of his wound and illness, were not to be trifled with, and that it was in consideration for her very natural feelings that he gave up the far-distant and dangerous post.

It was one thing, however, to give up Japan, and another to give up the travel and adventure which were his very life; and accordingly not many months had elapsed before he was afloat again. "In January 1863 the Polish insurrection broke out; and as," he says with frank humour, "I had by this time acquired a habit of fishing in troubled waters, I determined to go and see it." Once more I must refer the reader to the 'Episodes' for the account of this interesting historical event. The evolutions of foreign politics are always difficult to follow, and the difficulty is largely increased when it is the outs and ins of popular feeling and the policy of an insurrection, even when so important as to be called a national movement, that are in question. Laurence penetrated into the councils of the unfortunate Poles, who were playing so tragic a game, and into one of the camps of the insurgents, a stray corps, pathetically small and defenceless, but animated by such a fire of enthusiasm as kindled the very heart of the spectator, open as that was to all generous sympathies. He made this visit at peril of his life, with a perfect consciousness that the Cossacks were very little discriminating, and would not have stopped to inquire what a wandering Englishman had to do *dans cette galère*, or to respect his nationality, had they chanced to come upon the little agitated party who had escorted him to the camp. He must, however, have had that confidence in his own fate which a man who has made a hundred hairbreadth escapes naturally has.

His picture of the camp in the woods, almost within hearing of a Russian army, where every man held his life in his hands, is singularly impressive and interesting. When the whole party united in the Polish national song, the effect was overwhelming.

"When all joined in the grand prayer to God which forms the swelling chorus, and the men, with swords drawn, uplifted their arms in supplication, the tears streamed down the cheeks of the women as they sang, for they remembered their sisters slain on their knees in the churches at Warsaw for doing the same, and bloody memories crowded on them, as, with voices trembling from emotion, they besought, in solemn strains, the mercy of the Most High. The scene was so full of dramatic effect that I scarcely believed in its reality till I remembered the existence of six thousand Russian soldiers in the immediate neighbourhood, who were thirsting for the blood of this little band of men and women. There was something practical in this consideration calculated to captivate a mind too prosaic to be stirred by theatrical representations; for I confess I find it generally more easy to delude myself by believing in the sham of a reality, than in the reality of a sham. However, upon this occasion he must have been a most uncompromising stoic who was not touched and impressed."

I quote the above passage chiefly from the curious little bit of self-disclosure which betrays the Scotch nationality of a man so cosmopolitan. Many Englishmen, and almost every Scot, will sympathise with this suspiciousness in respect to theatrical circumstances and instinctive horror of the sham, which sometimes reacts upon his appreciation of the true. That this keen intuitive criticism should exist in a spirit open to every enthusiasm and full of sympathy, in this particular case, may astonish those who are not familiar with that remarkable and most interesting development; and it all throws a very singular light upon his own after-career.

In the course of the same year, after a brief return to

England, Laurence once more set out for the same distant and little-known region. The portion of his correspondence which refers to this period of his life has not fallen into my hands; but there is no doubt that all these repeated journeys had their distinct political object, and were far from being the mere adventures they seem. Only a short time had elapsed since his previous visit, and yet it was long enough to permit the downfall of the Polish hopes, the imprisonment and death of many of the friends who had then received him, and the all but suppression of the revolt. As it still lived, however, in out-of-the-way corners, and still entertained pathetic hopes, never to be fulfilled, of French or English intervention, the deep interest which Oliphant felt in the brave men who had welcomed him so kindly, impelled him to another visit, though the expedition was full of risk. He was accompanied by a friend, the Hon. Evelyn Ashley, and their object was to penetrate into the Russian provinces of Volhynia, where it was believed that revolution was smouldering, if not yet accompanied by any perceptible blaze. It is curious that he should thus have made his way over ground which, many years after, he was again to traverse in the interests of the Jews—a people who did not in any degree commend themselves to him during this first journey. The attempt to penetrate into the disaffected province was, however, wholly ineffectual; and after some adventures, which are amusing enough in the narrative though far from amusing in the experience, the Englishmen were turned back, and made a masterly retreat to Jassy, where, on the invitation of a nun encountered in a box at the opera—a most remarkable scene for such a meeting—Laurence and his companion made a most amusing and picturesque tour in Moldavia, proceeding from one convent to another, each more piquant and interesting than the one preceding it, in which companies of recluses lived in the most liberal and uncontrolled manner, the nuns, like Flemish Beguines, in little cottages picturesquely grouped together, and both monks and nuns surrounded by blooming gardens, and much that was calculated to make life agreeable. This was perhaps the only detour among many journeys which had no political meaning, though it furnished a most agreeable article for 'Blackwood' and a delightful chapter in the 'Episodes.'

At the end of this pleasant break in his exciting life, he turned his steps northwards in another direction where trouble was brewing, always the greatest attraction, notwithstanding his keen enjoyment of every novelty in human life. This time it was to Schleswig-Holstein, then enveloped in the smoke and fumes of a contention which nobody at least within our four seas understood, that he went to study the disputed succession and all the questions involved. "As confessedly it was one which the British statesmen of the day considered beyond their comprehension, and as the British public never even tried to understand it, it was no wonder that our policy was mistaken throughout. When a question has more than two sides, the popular intelligence fails to grasp it. As most questions of foreign policy have generally three at least, and sometimes more, and as Ministers are compelled to adopt the popular view if they wish to retain office, the foreign policy of England is usually characterised by a charming simplicity, not always conducive to the highest interests of the country."

The question in this case was a triangular one, the little Schleswig-Holstein desiring its own sovereign and a peaceable small independence, while spectators at a distance considered the conflict to be one between the Danes and Prussians for the possession of a coveted morsel of which the nationality was just doubtful enough to give to each a certain claim. In the distant eddies of opinions in those days I remember that the French Government was warmly censured for not taking energetic action on behalf of the Poles, their traditionary allies and *protégés*, while Great Britain was equally blamed for not interfering to defend the rights of the Danes. I recollect overhearing upon the deck of a steamboat on the lake of Como an animated discussion on the subject between some Italian gentlemen, whose energetic denunciation of the British Government as " un governo infame," in consequence of their desertion of Denmark, was loud and vigorous. Laurence, however, held a very different view: his sympathies were with neither of the greater contending parties, but for the Duke of Sonderburg - Augustenburg, whose claims were overlooked on both sides.

This was the last of these purely political adventures in which a thirst for information, the desire of novelty and excitement, and a certain ambition to know thoroughly and make himself an authority upon the most complicated questions of European politics, were the ostensible motives. Though he is always individual and interesting in whatever he writes, the hundred little personal revelations of his private correspondence are wanting in these bustling but unproductive years, in which he seems to have worked off a great deal of superabundant energy, and gradually calmed and settled down into a state of mind adapted to residence at home, and the routine of ordinary English life. He was now, in 1864, when he returned to England from the battle which settled the fate of Schleswig - Holstein, a man of thirty - five, in the height of life and faculty, with an extraordinary knowledge of the world and mankind. The reader may think, perhaps, that such experiences as those of Japan and Circassia were not entirely adapted to form him for the localities of Mayfair and St Stephen's. It must, however, be remembered that between his journeys there had interposed on many occasions a slice of society, usually at its most animated and gayest moment; that he knew everybody at home as well as abroad,—British Ministers as well as Chinese mandarins, literary circles as well as political, and fashionable circles better than either; that he had friends everywhere, among both small and great, and was acquainted with English life to its depths, but especially with the representative classes which we call the "world," —and in which the brightest intelligence and grace, as well as the most perfect frivolity and foolishness, are to be found. He knew these classes, understood their importance and their worth, and scorned their social superiority while esteeming it, in full consciousness of the paradox which existed both in them and in himself. He saw through every social pretence with the keenest glance of

intelligence and humour, and never hesitated to impale
any offender upon his shining spear, or laugh at any
absurdity; yet instinctively held by that world to which,
satirist and revolutionary as he was, he belonged, and felt
himself at home in it, as he never was in less distinguished
but possibly more genuine spheres. This curious distinction was never more clearly evidenced than in Laurence
Oliphant's life. He was not rich: his ancient race had
never been of great pretensions, or with claims beyond the
modest gentlehood of the county to which it belonged:
yet his standing-ground throughout his life was that of
society; and the world of fashion, though he mocked it
continually, and shot a thousand darts at its mannerisms
and follies, was, after all, his natural sphere.

It was in the year 1864 that Laurence returned home
more or less "for good," with the determination of finding,
if possible, settled employment in England, or at least
carving out some occupation for himself which would
permit him to have a settled home there, and relieve and
cheer his mother's loneliness. I think her comfort must
have been his great motive in this determination, and
perhaps, too, a little disgust with the public service in
distant parts of the earth, where the best efforts of one
representative of England were apt to be altogether dis-
credited by the actions of another, or by misadventure, or
by Government neglect, as happened in the case of Lord
Elgin—whose proceedings were subjected to endless anim-
adversion as incomplete and unsatisfactory, as soon as the
next difficulty with China arose. The interval which
elapsed between Oliphant's return from his late wanderings
and his election to Parliament was most actively and fully
taken up, although he held no appointment; and what
between literature, society, lectures—which he seems to
have given in many places, generally with a view to the
future election—and visits, his mind at this time was fully
occupied. He had always, or almost always, a book preparing for the press, always a round of country-houses
attending his leisure, always a hundred engagements in
town. I find a succession of letters recounting the experiences of one autumn, which I at first concluded to

belong to this period, difficult as the chronology is always, for his correspondence as usual is completely destitute of dates, but which in reality belongs to the conclusion of 1859, after his first China expedition. However, it does very well as an example of how his autumns were generally spent, and the reader will, I hope, admit the retrospective glance.

He was coquetting with various constituencies at the time, in a series of experiences, repeated a few years later; hoping to move the heart of Glasgow, but not unwilling to content himself with Greenock, and with a steadfast eye upon the Stirling burghs, as the sober certainty upon which he could always fall back. His letters are full of amusing sketches of the people among whom he moved; from the lively and distinguished visitors in country-houses to the chance companions he picked up in railway carriages, of one of whom, for example, he writes: "Had a delightful journey, my companion being a young man from London in the wholesale woollen and stuff trade, from whom I derived much useful information." This "delightful journey" carried him to Sir James Clarke's house of Birk Hall, where he met "a most learned and delightful party (including Professor Owen, Sir Charles Lyell, and various others of the same calibre), all *savants* of the first water, and consequently most agreeable and entertaining society. I wish I could always live in it." The leap from the young man in the woollen trade to these high potentates is long enough; but they were equally interesting to his always eager and lively intelligence, and nothing could give a better idea of his universal interest in human life and character.

The occasion on which he met this delightful party was a meeting of the British Association at Aberdeen, where he took a considerable share in the proceedings, along with Captain Sherard Osborn, Captain Speke, and other travellers of authority, and read a paper in the Geographical Section upon Japan, which was at the period his special subject. He gave as usual a brief, but lively, description of this to his mother in London:—

"I wish you had cared as little for the ordeal of reading a paper as I did. There was nothing on earth to be nervous about. The hall was crowded to the door, and they listened with great attention for the forty minutes which my paper lasted, and cheered me vociferously when it was over, so I suppose it pleased them. I have promised to lecture at Leeds on the state of our political relations with China. If I can't say what I want in the House of Commons, I must find some other place. I will get it fully reported in the 'Times.'"

Other proposals to the same effect poured upon him. He was asked to Glasgow to discourse: at one time to the merchants in the Chamber of Commerce, "who are coming in a select body to hear me, a regular business lecture," "no ladies admitted," he adds regretfully; at another to the Young Men's Christian Association. "I shall have treated Japan in every variety of way before I have done," he says. He had also lectures to deliver at Dunfermline, at Stirling, at Greenock, and was invited by the Philosophical Institution in Edinburgh to deliver two, all on the same subject of Japan. The last proposal was accompanied by an offer of £20 for the two lectures, which does not seem a large sum, but which he considers "not to be despised." He was also moved by the fact that "only distinguished men lectured there, and the audience is large and important." "I never expected to turn popular lecturer," he says; "I have not sought to be pushed forward in this way, but seeing that I am without any special occupation in London, I think I ought to do what comes to my hand." He had, besides, the strong induce-ment of a desire "to get hold of Glasgow," "which would give me a position in the House of Commons," he says, "above what a young man could expect." And indeed there seem to have been vague negotiations on this subject, invitations to stand from "a Glasgow body," whom he evidently considered without sufficient authority. Laurence desired nothing more than to be asked to stand; but he was wise enough not to commit himself, even on the warrant of his enthusiastic reception, and

the compliments of the Glasgow potentates, while the
fumes of his lecture were still in their heads. At
Greenock he had an amusing experience, which I think
he describes in one of his books, but of which I will
quote all the report to his mother, at first hand. He was
disappointed and half offended on arriving to find no one
in waiting to meet him, and to have to find his way
by himself to the hotel.

" However, the secretary came at last to show me the
way to the Free Kirk where I was to lecture. Dunlop
was not in the chair, having been detained in Edinburgh,
so the sheriff presided instead. I was somewhat dismayed
to find myself mounting the steps of a very high pulpit,
and looking down upon the upturned faces of about twelve
hundred people, who crammed the church to overflowing ;
still more dismayed to hear the minister, who occupied
the precentor's desk beneath me, call upon the congregation to join him in prayer—which was a very long one, a
great part of it personal to myself, and asking a blessing
upon the discourse I was about to enter upon. I began
to think I would try my hand at a sermon, as the lecture
I was going to give was likely to be far too full of jokes to
be appropriate to the occasion. However, I discoursed at
starting on Japan as a field for missionary enterprise, and
then, finding I had a sympathetic audience, I was more
light and airy, until at last I kept them all in a highly
amused condition. I looked over my red pulpit cushion
and saw the old minister giggling immensely. Altogether
I think it was the most successful lecture I have given.
I despise even notes now, and find practice is improving
my delivery. Nor did I feel the least fatigued. Four of
the leading people were profuse in their apologies afterwards for the coolness of my reception, which they
declared was a mistake. I am to go a round of visits
with one of them this morning."

These coquettings with the busy towns and cities of the
west of Scotland did not, however, come to anything ; and
when the decisive moment arrived, it was to Stirling,

where his name itself was a recommendation and his family so well known, that he turned. He had already contested these burghs, unsuccessfully but hopefully, before going to China — an incident of which I find scarcely any record except of the mere fact, and that he had much enjoyed the business of canvassing, in which his father, also greatly amused and excited, as was the character of the family, had helped and accompanied him. His reflections on this subject, on a renewed visit to Stirling, are touching and full of feeling. He gives an account of a brief visit to Stirling on his way to Broomhall, the home of Lord Elgin, and his meeting with his former agents :—

" They declare they can bring me in against Caird next time, if I wish it. The few of my old supporters whom I saw are most enthusiastic. I have a strong body of friends in Stirling. I feel quite melancholy in renewing all these associations, however : they recall papa so vividly to my mind. He has been so warmly mentioned by several persons to me. They got to like him so much. M'Farlane says that the look of him as he walked down the street got me votes."

This pretty and very Scotch touch of affectionate hyperbole is affecting, between the smile and the tear, and was no doubt spoken with water in the eyes of the plain Stirling "writer" so unexpectedly poetical.

As a background to these public appearances, comes a lively and shifting panorama of Scotch country-houses, in which there are many vivid glimpses of individual character and manners. Laurence was not superior to gossip on occasion, as perhaps it is impossible for a man so full of interest in his fellow-creatures to be ; but he had not time or inclination to send to his mother anything more than a rapid *aperçu* here and there of the individualities with which he was brought into contact. There is but one case, I think, in which a private and painful imbroglio of real life is referred to ; and in that case both mother and son were actively employed in smoothing down and clearing up the unfortunate difficulty, in the course of

which the young man gives vent to various judgments
upon the impossibility of Platonic attachments, for instance (afterwards the chief doctrine and belief of his life),
which are very authoritative and decided; but offers himself, as few men would be likely to do, as the agent to
bring "the man," the disturber of domestic happiness, to
reason, and to convince him, not without reference to his
own (Laurence's) private experiences, of the necessity of
absolute withdrawal.

I am happy to say, however, that, in contradistinction
to so many series of correspondence that have been made
open to the world, there is no scandal, no piquant stories,
no indiscretions or betrayals, in these ever lively and
graphic letters. If he sometimes speaks in his books as if
he believed all society to be corrupt, he finds, as a sane
and wholesome man should do, no trace of corruption in
the households that receive him—nothing but points of
character, cheerful indications of identity, something to
like and to please everywhere. As usual, the young ladies
call for a great deal of his attention, and "a walk with the
lassies" in the afternoon, after he has got through his work,
was a very favourite amusement. Indeed there is a little
glamour of easy sentiment in his eyes as he goes from one
circle to another, always ready for a touch of pleasant
emotion, and by no means unwilling to be awakened to
deeper feelings. "I am deeply in love with them all," he
says of a bevy of pretty sisters, which no doubt was consolatory to the mind of the mother, always uneasy on this
point. One lady, whom he had already admired and
speculated a little upon, is more particularly discussed.
Some one has been describing her to him in the highest
terms. "She has a charming disposition, thoroughly unselfish—but muckle hands and feet! What is that, you
will say, to good mental qualities? I don't think she is
the least brilliant, but with very good common-sense. In
fact, she would suit you perfectly. As for myself, I despair of finding any one; probably when I do, she will be
an aversion unto you."

While thus living with his work and his lectures, and
his afternoon walk with the "lassies" of the house, his

reports of himself are exceedingly cheerful: "Whenever I can dispose of my time to my own satisfaction between innocent recreation and profitable employment, I am happy; but, when employment is wanting, the recreation often ceases to be innocent, 'Satan finding some mischief still,' &c. And when the recreation is wanting, as in Edinburgh, I become low-spirited and depressed."

The light-hearted reports of his letters inform us—at second-hand through his mother—of such incidents as his performances at a tenants' ball in a house where he "danced reels violently till 3 A.M., and woke so fresh at seven that I wrote my book till eleven o'clock, when the rest of the knocked-up world at last came to breakfast": how he gravely interviewed a young man in an office who "wants me to put him in the same line of life I have followed myself, as he hates the writer's desk; but I don't know how that is to be done." How he discusses theology everywhere whenever he has a chance, "exchanging 'Thorndale' with Lady A. for two of Maurice's works"; and finding a great *savant* "utterly off the line in secret, and confirmed by recent geological discoveries, but he is afraid to publish. I urged him strongly to go in for truth, *ruat cœlum*. He said, 'Nobody with less than £3000 a-year can afford to hold my views,'" which does not say very much for the philosopher. All this shows the versatility of mind with which he leaped lightly from one subject to another, with a lively interest in all. He was not disposed, I am sorry to say, to church-going, professing "a terrible tendency to ague in the draughts of country churches, but not saying anything about a much greater dread which I have of country parsons." Once at a service of the kind called Puseyite in those days, he declared it to be "like badly got-up Buddhism." He describes a popular clergyman of the time as "a man with the mind of a woman and the voice of a trumpet, very aggravating but amiable." But on the occasion of a visit to Glasgow, he declares with much warmth, "Norman Macleod is a trump. He and Guthrie are the only decent parsons I know." His enjoyment of the life thus described is very clearly set forth in one of his letters, and all its delights, not without a little natural complacence,

while yet he anticipates with philosophy the need for settling down in a more humble way :—

"My life is necessarily (in general) a good deal made up
of excitements and reactions; for instance, just now here
I am scarcely able to turn, for a press both of business and
pleasure. Half-a-dozen lectures to prepare, proofs constantly to correct, and book not yet finished. Charming
women at hand when I am inclined for a cosy chair in the
drawing-room and a touch of the æsthetic. Any amount
of game merely for the trouble of strolling through a few
turnip-fields: A. and I killed twenty-one brace of partridges the day before yesterday. Any number of horses
to ride—all the more to be appreciated after two years of
filth, heat, and absence of social and intellectual enjoyment.
But I hope I shall not be such a goose as to growl at London because I have enjoyed myself here. If I see my way
to being comfortably independent, and am allowed that
amount of personal liberty which, from being so much
my own master, I am accustomed to, I think you will find
me a happy and contented companion in our lodging, even
though occupation and pleasure are both suddenly slack.
I should be more than ungrateful if I were not thankful
for the blessing of having you to share it with me."

That this sentiment was thoroughly sincere, every line
of his letters testifies; but yet there were times when his
mother's continual anxiety to have his "serious thoughts,"
as well as the lighter record of his sayings and doings,
communicated to her, brings a momentary touch of half-
comic irritation. "You must be philosophical as to the
condition of my spiritual being," he says; and while telling
her of one after another of the great ladies, his friends,
who desire to make her acquaintance, and whose somewhat puzzled admiration of the close bond between
mother and son is apparent, he adds an amusing story
told him by one of them, of a certain old Lady Campbell
who had, like Lady Oliphant, one dearly beloved and
perfect son but no more. "One day at prayers, when the
minister was saying, 'For there is no good in us, and we

are every one of us miserable sinners,' she was heard
audibly to protest, 'Oh, no' my Airchy, no' my Airchy!'"
The application was easy.

The year 1865, however, forms a definite era in his life.
His wanderings, his vagaries of mind and thought, even
his impatience with the imperfections of so-called religious persons and desire of finding some better way, had
plunged him during the two or three previous years more
and more, whenever it was within his reach, into the
excitement of society, which was at once an antidote to
the restlessness of thought, and which the attitude he
repeatedly compares to that of Mr Micawber, of waiting
for something to turn up, made a necessity to him. For
where was he to find the patron, the appointment on
which his mind was set, save among the great personages,
holders of power and influence, who were to be met with
there? I do not pretend to be able to give a history
of his social experiences during the intervals when he
reappeared in London, always with the *éclat* of some
new performance or event — the successes of China, the
hairbreadth escape of Japan, the mysterious politics of
mid-Europe — something always fresh and unknown, to
surround him with attraction. Probably it involved episodes of another kind from those of adventure, and in
which his heart was more deeply concerned; and it is by
no means unlikely that, on the eve of a great religious
change, the current of his life may have run more high in
other directions, and the impetus of existence at its fullest
force have carried him further than conscience approved
—thus adding a deeper need to the necessity always felt
of a new foundation, and a sharper point to his prevailing
consciousness of the imperfections in him and about him,
the hollowness of social pretences, and the difficulty of
holding the right way in a society which condoned moral
failure so easily, and was only inexorable to poverty and
social defeat.

In this year, however, these wanderings and waitings
came to an end, and Laurence's election as member for the
Stirling burghs fixed his residence in town, and seemed
to all his friends the beginning of a brilliant and useful

career. That he had every endowment and faculty likely
to make his new position a satisfactory one need scarcely
be said. He was no recluse, likely to be intimidated
by that so - called "august assembly,"—he had full habit
and usage of the world, and was thoroughly acquainted
with the atmosphere of political life. The reasons which
brought about another result, and the disappointment of
many of the hopes conceived by his friends, if not by
himself, will become apparent further on. I cannot doubt
that he was pleased with the new beginning of life, at
least in its first stage. It had been in his mind from the
very commencement of his career as the alternative to the
life of diplomacy, which was what had commended itself
to him most. And he took it up heartily, hoping to play
an important part in the history of his country. He had
contested the Stirling burghs once, if not twice, before,—
the first time while still very young, in his father's lifetime, before the China expedition,—and he had many
humorous stories to tell of the incidents of his canvassing.
One of these, of which a friend tells me, describes how he
was taken to one person of influence after another, the
most important of all being a cobbler, ensconced in a dark
little shop approached by two or three steps leading
downwards below the level of the street. Here he underwent the process of "heckling" with much severity, and
was put through his political catechism so entirely to the
satisfaction of the shoemaker politician, that he smote the
candidate upon the shoulder in the intensity of his satisfaction, exclaiming, "You're the billie for me!"

This event was to all appearance and human likelihood
the beginning of a mature and established life. It was in
reality no such thing, but only a transition period—a
temporary pause and point between the life which he had
lived like other men, and another so unique and extraordinary as to separate him from all his fellows. But
this time of transition was in itself signalised by so much
that was brilliant and remarkable in the development of
his mind and genius, as to form a special and most important chapter in his career. His intellect seemed to
have reached a sudden climax of energy, wit, and power,

M

and his whole nature burst forth in an overflow of gifts
which hitherto had been restrained in channels inappropriate to their full exhibition,—in a kind of riot of fancy,
fun, and satirical brilliancy and insight, of which he had
given scarcely any indication before.

This extraordinary new outburst, in which all the fire
of contending elements long smouldering in him rose into
sudden flame, was preceded by an undertaking, briefly
alluded to in the 'Episodes,' and very unique in its way,
which may be taken more or less as the conclusion of his
entirely mundane career. He had never been one of the
"worldly holies" of his own brilliant classification, nor
was he ever at any time reckoned among those who affect
superiority to the world, and thank God that they are not
as other men; but yet the distinction between the two
portions of his life is very marked, though as paradoxical
as ever. He was never so cynical in expression, so dazzling
in satire, as when his whole life was disorganised by the
new impulse which moved him to live for humanity and
take love for the race of mankind as his only inspiration ;
nor so wild in his apparent vagaries as when he first became conscious of an anchor in the unseen, and a certainty
of conviction and established standing-ground.

It was, however, before he had altogether opened to
this new development that the singular and romantic (if
such a word can be applied in such a sense) little venture
of the 'Owl'—projected in laughter and high spirits, and
carried out as an excellent joke by everybody concerned—
was tossed into the mystified and astonished world. He
explains its first beginning by a few words in respect to
the exceptional position he had made for himself by his
perpetual travels and political adventures. He had friends
everywhere throughout the civilised (and indeed we may
add the half-civilised) world, and in all the quarters which
he had visited and studied, plunging into the troubled
waters whenever he had a chance, and mastering every
political combination he could push his way into; and
from these friends over all the world he was in the habit
of receiving communications on the exciting subjects which
had brought them together. "For instance," he says, "a

conference was at that time sitting in London on the
Schleswig-Holstein question, consisting of plenipotentiaries
of all the European Powers who had been parties to the
Treaty of London, the proceedings at which were kept
absolutely secret; yet a few days after each meeting, I
received from abroad an accurate report of everything that
had transpired at it—and this, I hasten to say, through
no one connected with our own Foreign Office. I felt
bursting with all sorts of valuable knowledge, with no
means of imparting it in a manner which suited me."

It was in these circumstances that "a little dinner" was
given at a little house in Mayfair, the residence of ladies
who were great friends of Oliphant's, and through him
exceedingly hospitable to various other young men of his
immediate intimacy, all in the fullest current of society
and energy of life. I have heard one of them say regretfully that such conversation as that of this little *salon*—
in which every man did his best to shine, and to win the
smile of a hostess full of wit and brilliancy, and capable
herself of a full share in the *bon mots* that flew about, and
the discussions that took place between whiles—it has
seldom been his lot to hear. Amid the brilliant talk on
this particular occasion it was suggested by some one
"that a little paper should be started by way of a skit, in
which the most outrageous *canards* should be given as
serious, and serious news should be disguised in a most
grotesque form." No doubt the merry party began its
composition on the moment, with all the eagerness of a
new amusement, and the *canards* made their first flight
over the bright dinner-table, with an additional touch of
colour laid on to each wing as they flitted from *convive* to
convive. They had the means not only of dazzling and
mystifying a dull public, but also of getting at that public,
which often fails to such amusing projects; for one of the
company was Sir Algernon Borthwick, who "kindly under-
took to print the absurd little sheet."

The gay conspirators watched, with all the gusto which
attends a mystification, to see how the jest took. And it
took like wildfire. The world got note of it while it was
still damp from the press, and soon in all the circles they

frequented, amid affairs of state, and the last great scandal
or discovery of the day, there rose a murmur of inquiries,
of guesses, and discussions about this little droll solemn
invader of society, which knew everything, and had the
secrets of the Foreign Office at its finger-ends, and confounded and tantalised everybody with its extraordinary
acquaintance with life and events.   It was the most excellent joke to the young men.   When they saw carriages
thronging the street in which was the little shabby office
from which the 'Owl' was issued, they stole aside into
corners to laugh till they could laugh no more—and in
the evening eyed each other over the shoulders of the
fashionable mob with twinkling eyes, while all the great
men and all the fine ladies asked each other, What was
the 'Owl'?   Who had communicated to it those startling
secrets?   Where did it get its information?   When the
plotters discovered that they were actually making money
by the jest which they all enjoyed so thoroughly, their
amusement and satisfaction became more piquant still;
but in faithful adherence to their original principle, they
determined to spend their profit gaily,—not putting it
away in any dull banking account, but dedicating it to
a weekly dinner of the most sumptuous description, and
other "larks."   One of the surviving members of this
brilliant band tells me of a great entertainment offered by
the Owls to all the "smart" ladies of their acquaintance,
when jewelled gifts were hung among the flowery ornaments on the table, and all was harmony and splendour,
the whole defrayed by the fun and wisdom of the eccentric
journal, which appeared when it pleased, always affording
society a new surprise.   It is scarcely necessary to say,
however, that Laurence Oliphant did not follow the career
of this wild little bandit of the press for any long continuance.   He was a large contributor to the first numbers,
and continued until the tenth.   Then, or soon after, he
found the other contributors in the mind to adopt a more
business-like arrangement for what was in the beginning
pure sport, and he retired altogether from the undertaking.
It continued its career, I believe, for some years, appearing more regularly, although only during the season, and

falling into more ordinary lines; for, to be sure, neither mystification nor "larks" could continue for ever.

Perhaps it was the success of this venture, so far out of the usual decorous habitudes of the press, which had not then fallen into the evil ways of "Society" papers, which turned the thoughts of Laurence to another use of the remarkable gifts of social satire and criticism, which probably he himself became acquainted with in a sort of surprise as well as his readers. Even in the letters I have quoted, though they are always full of humorous touches, there are perhaps fewer shafts of satirical description than could be extracted from half the confidential letters written from country-houses in any autumnal season. And the books he had hitherto published were entirely descriptive and political, full of information and facts, though handled with so light a hand, and pervaded by such an airy wealth of amused and amusing observation, that they read, as people say, "like a novel." But it was altogether a new beginning when the traveller, the diplomate, the serious spectator of distant countries and political intrigues, suddenly perceived that round about him—within the radius of that mile of streets in which, for a part of the year, there lives and feasts and dances and talks, a community quite unconscious, in the simplicity of its assumption, of any arrogance in calling itself the World— lay boundless material for satire and fancy. The inconsistency of people calling themselves Christians had long been a favourite subject of indignant remark and criticism to Laurence, as has been repeatedly noted already—perhaps too favourite a subject, since to judge a system, and particularly a belief, not on its own merits but on those of the people who profess it, is scarcely either fair or logical. But when or how it first occurred to him, with a flash of sudden inspiration, that he possessed, hitherto unnoticed in his armoury, a sharp-edged weapon of the kind of Ithuriel's spear, upon which he could pick up and exhibit, impaled upon its shining point, not only to the world but to themselves, the masquerades of society, I have been unable to discover, unless the 'Owl' was the instrument of revelation. In his letters to the editor of 'Blackwood's Maga-

zine,' in which the first number of ' Piccadilly,' published
as a serial in that Magazine during the summer of 1865,
appeared, the doubtful character of the entirely new venture—whether it would be successful or not, whether it
might merit success, how the world would receive it—are
discussed with all the uncertainty of a beginner.   It had
occurred to me as quite possible that it was the suggestion
of the able and far-seeing editor referred to, the late Mr
John Blackwood, whose literary perceptions (though he
never touched a pen save to write letters) were singularly
trustworthy, which directed Oliphant to the unthought-
of medium of fiction.   And I find on inquiry that this was
indeed partly the case, Mr Blackwood having mentioned
to him a similar project on the part of J. G. Lockhart, the
son-in-law and biographer of Sir Walter Scott, which probably acted as a spark to the ready fire of Laurence's as yet
undisclosed thoughts.   The first intimation of the work
occurs as follows :—

" LONDON, Jan. 24, 1865.

" I enclose the MS. according to your wish.   I am glad
you think I might succeed in this kind of work.   You will
see from reading it what my idea was, one entirely ' novel,'
and which could only be done in a serial—that is, to write
a novel in the form of a contemporaneous autobiography,
in which I should parody the incidents of the month, make
my hero make speeches on public questions in the House
of Commons, stay in country-houses, flirt, shoot <i>à la</i> Bur-
naby if need be, lecture, argue, &c.   But the difficulty is
the plot : I cannot proportion the importance of the plot
and the opinions.   I am always losing sight of the former,
being extremely full of the latter.   Then they are what
would be called extravagant in many points, and I don't
know that you would like to publish them.   I feel disposed to go in against most of the popular ideas of the
day, and utterly ignore existing prejudices on many serious matters ; therefore the chief aim would be to point a
moral, with a vengeance.   I am afraid of doing it too
seriously, and yet I don't want to bring it into ridicule by
too much burlesque. . . . The whole thing is an experi-

ment, not only in its chronology, but in its other features.
In the first place, it is a caricature, and not intended to be
quite natural or possible. I look·upon it as the highest
form of art to supplant the natural with the imaginative;
but of course it runs the risk of failing by reason of its
extravagance. My difficulty in the present undertaking is
to keep the grotesque element within bounds: it is like a
strong spice, the flavour of which easily overpowers. As a
sort of qualification to this, I have determined on making
Vanecourt more or less mad. In this character he becomes
intensely interesting to draw, and the play of his mind is
a good study. Moreover, it enables his opinions and acts
to be extravagant and inconsistent always, based, nevertheless, upon truth and rectitude, which two principles
are so extremely dry and distasteful that nobody would
care about a novel conveying such an old-fashioned moral
unless it were put in some new-fangled form. Nevertheless, I am quite sure the first parts, at all events, will
mystify the public, and set up everybody's back. I shall
consider it only a success if it is the best abused novel out.
I see some of the reviewers think it is O'Dowd."

That all plans of this kind are much modified in the
progress of the work is very rapidly perceptible. In no
operation is the *solvitur ambulando* so strikingly manifested. "The best laid schemes o' mice and men" go
astray nowhere so completely as in the working out of
fiction. Only a few weeks have elapsed when Laurence
writes again: "I get so interested in writing it that I feel
it difficult to keep it waiting for events, so that the contemporaneous element will perhaps in course of time give
way to the story, but that won't matter." As a matter of·
fact, neither the contemporaneous element (so soon out of
date and forgotten) nor the story are the points that took
all readers by storm in 'Piccadilly.' The startling types
of character—the worldly holy and the wholly worldly:
Lady Broadhem, with her high principles in religion and
her absolute, almost innocent, obtuseness to the first
principles of honesty in speculation; the Stock Exchange
fashionable, Spiffy Goldtip, perhaps the earliest revelation

of that strange nondescript and audacious schemer; the bold yet abject parvenus; the mob of fashion, carried hither and thither as the secret impulse was given— were its greatest attractions.   Even the muscular colonial Bishop, Joseph Caribbee Islands, the curious American (a type very rampant in those days, now obsolete), and the converted Hindoo, though exceedingly amusing, were less heeded, being less tremendous in their exposition of reality and sham, than the other terrible yet airy sketches, so light, so powerful, almost tragical in satire, so true to life.

"The fact is," the author adds, "that the class which would appreciate it are not a magazine - reading class. If it went down at all, it would be entirely among the fashionables, who never read serials or much else, and who would read this because it came home to them.   It would go exactly where the 'Owl' did, to the young ladies and people who never read newspapers.   When it got well talked of by the *beau monde*, the 'middles' would buy it—not because they would understand it, but because it would be the correct thing."   Perhaps he was a little contemptuous here, as not unfrequently happens, of the "middles," among which highly indefinite and widely extended class there are plenty of Lady Broadhems, and the worldly holy flourish largely.   But it was Society which was hit, and in the very centre of the shield.

"As for hurting me in the House, nothing," he says, "can hurt me, provided what I do is from a right motive. My only fear about my motive in this instance is that I may have a lurking vanity in it; but the motive I try to have is to wake people up, and make them either believe or disbelieve, and not go on humbugging with Providence any longer.   If I am single and earnest in this, I defy all efforts to injure me anywhere."   "I do feel that the times are so bad that they require exposure."   These arguments in defence of his book are taken from letters to his pub- lisher, who, it is curious to find, hesitated to republish as a book this extraordinarily brilliant work, to my mind the most powerful of all Oliphant's productions.   "It is a great tax upon your friendship," Laurence says, "to ask you to do what you feel so disagreeable. This has weighed very much with me; but as you . say, ' If you are very much bent upon it, I am willing,' I confess I am." This hesitation, afterwards justified by the fact that ' Piccadilly,' though a great literary success, was scarcely so in a commercial point of view, had its share in keeping back the republication of the book, which — notwithstanding the effect it produced on its appearance in ' Blackwood's Magazine,' even when its daring assault upon the world was broken by the intervals of publication, and it was still possible for the Solomons of the newspapers to " think it was O'Dowd "—was not produced in a permanent form until five years had come and gone, bringing with them many strange revolutions, and none more strange than those which had taken place in the fortune of the author. That extraordinary crisis in the meantime altered every-thing for him, — who was, at the time ' Piccadilly ' was first printed, the man we know, newly elected member of Parliament, one of the first authorities upon foreign politics, the favourite of society, the friend of all that was best and highest in England, a courted guest, a brilliant writer and still more delightful conversationalist, capable almost of any advancement : and who was, at the time of its republication, no more than a visitor in the brilliant circles which had before been his home, with hands hardened by manual toil, a career thrown back into the regions of the accidental, and all advancement, as the word is generally understood, put away from both life and possibility. How such a wonderful change took place has now to be told. The reader who has followed his career so far will be able to foresee that it was at all times a possible thing that this might happen, and that the latent spark of the revolution had been lying for years in his heart, awaiting the hand that should stir it into life.

CHAPTER VIII.

THE NEW LIFE.

THAT hand was now found. I cannot tell with any precision at what time Lady Oliphant and her son [1] were first
attracted by the preaching of an obscure American, who
lectured in Steinway Hall and other such places, to a few
earnest disciples and a number of curious chance hearers,
more or less moved by the unusual character of the man
and his utterances; nor do I know whether it was Laurence or his mother who was the first to be moved. The
probabilities would seem to be that it was Lady Oliphant
who was most likely to betake herself to an out-of-the-
way place, and a teacher who never touched the sphere
of fashion, or became a public celebrity, for spiritual instruction. So far as I know, the public interest was never
roused, as it often is by much less notable appearances,
and the man and all about him remained always shrouded
in a certain mystery—cleverly shrouded, I should say, if
I could believe, what is the general opinion, that he was
from the beginning an impostor, with a scheme concocted
of profit to himself from the empire he acquired over his
followers. I am myself very slow to believe in system-
atic imposture, and think it very unlikely to affect seriously
any man or woman with ordinary capacities of judgment;
and in the present case the persons affected were of more
than ordinary capacity.

From the very beginning this mystery is apparent. The
first mention of Mr Harris occurs in a letter from Italy in
the year 1860, and it is of the vaguest character. "I hope
you will go and see Miss Fawcett," Laurence writes to his
mother. "She may tell you some interesting things about
Harris. I was sure you could not see him now, but I am

---

[1] A curious glimpse of what seemed like real light came in the statement
of a relation, that Harris was a member of the American Legation at Japan
in 1861, and that he then for the first time made his views known to his
future disciple. There certainly was a Harris at Japan at this time, but I
can find no proof that he was the man.

glad you have got a promise for the future." Thus not
only the convictions but the issues of practical life were
held in the balance for these three at least; for the lady
referred to, afterwards Mrs Cuthbert, became one of the
closest companions of the Oliphants in their religious life,
and the sharer of their experiences for good or evil.

This intimation shows that the American evangelist, if
I may so describe him—apostle, prophet of strange things,
as he appeared to them—was already chary of personal
encounter, unwilling to vulgarise his doctrine by communication with chance inquirers, and assuming a much
higher position than is usual to wandering preachers. He
was generally, upon his first appearance, but I understand
erroneously, believed to be a minister of the sect of Sweden-
borgians calling themselves the "New Jerusalem." The
only definite ground upon which the historian can go in
respect to Mr Harris is contained in the shabby little
volumes of sermons and addresses delivered by him in
various localities—chapels in provincial towns, Marylebone
Literary and Scientific Institutions, and suchlike—which
attracted sufficient interest to be taken down by a short-
hand writer and published obscurely for the benefit of
that portion of the community which, in all the quarters
of the country, gets note, by some mesmeric token or intuition, of anything that is new in the shape of religious
doctrines—but never came to the knowledge of the general world.

And yet there was little that was new in the doctrine.
With nothing but prejudice in my mind concerning this
mysterious guide and teacher, I am bound to admit that
these addresses are of a very remarkable character. A
little florid in phraseology, as was perhaps necessary for
the class to which they were addressed, they seem full of
lofty enthusiasm and the warmest Christian feeling. Very
little, if anything, is said that is inconsistent with orthodox
Christianity, slightly tempered by a theory, afterwards
more fully developed, which replaces the Trinity by a
Father and Mother God—a twofold instead of a threefold
Unity — though even that is so little dwelt upon that
it might easily be overlooked, even by a critical hearer;

but not even the most careless could, I think, be unim-
pressed by the fervent and living nobility of faith, the
high spiritual indignation against wrong-doing and against
all that detracts from the divine essence and spirit of
Christianity, with which the dingy pages, badly printed
upon bad paper and in the meanest form, still burn and
glow. The effect, no doubt, must have been greatly
heightened when they were spoken by a man possessing
so much sympathetic power as Mr Harris evidently had,
to an audience already prepared, as the hearers in whom
we are most interested certainly were, for the communication of this sacred fire. The very points that had most
occupied the mind of Laurence Oliphant, as the reader
has already seen—the hollowness and unreality of what
was called religion, the difference between the divine creed
and precepts, and the everyday existence of those who
were their exponents and professed believers—were the
object of Harris's crusade. He taught no novelty, but
only—the greatest novelty of all—that men should put
what they believed into practice, not playing with the
possibilities of a divided allegiance between God and
mammon, but giving an absolute — nay, remorseless —
obedience, at the cost of any or every sacrifice, to the
principles of a perfect life. I presume confidently that,
so far as the disciples could be aware, the prophet himself
at this period was without blame, and maintained his own
high standard. Perhaps, it may be suggested by profane
criticism, the mystery in which he wrapped himself would
be beneficial to the maintenance of this impression upon
their minds. The great novelty in him was that he required no adhesion to any doctrine, and did not demand of
his converts that they should agree with him upon anything but the necessity of living a Christ-like life.

This was precisely what had been the dream and desire
of Laurence since ever he had begun to think for himself:
not a creed—he had been saturated with creeds. From
his earliest childhood, when he had been made (as so
many children in those days were made—perhaps even
some still) to collect texts out of the Bible in proof of
this and that doctrine—till now that he had begun to

sharpen his shaft against the worldly holy, and to feel
his heart sicken in the untruthfulness of fashionable
life, it had been his longing and devout prayer to get
hold of something that was absolutely genuine and true
—something that promised not wrath and condemnation,
but judgment and mercy ; and here at last he had found
it.   The very hardness of the terms which the new prophet required, the severity of the obedience which was
demanded of his disciples, heightened the effect of the
revelation.   Bidden to be natural, to think the best of
others, to do the best he could for himself so as not to
interfere with his advancement, to be content with a
modified standard, and to allow that in so imperfect a
world only a very imperfect goodness was possible—
were the soothing counsels that had been given to him,
when in the intervals of amusement and occupation the
pendulum swung back, and his thoughts returned to rend
him.   It was not in his nature steadfastly to make this
compromise with the possible, as most of us do ; but he
was able, as he has himself so often said, to push the
great question aside altogether, to occupy himself with
his work, his pleasures, the excitement of novel encounters
and experiences, so that there should be no room left, or
as little as possible, in which to ponder upon the problem
of humanity.   The exhortation to come out of the world
and be separate, which had rung in his ears from so
many pulpits, was a farce to him, knowing so well as
he did what it meant ; that it meant Lady Broadhem's
conversazione instead of Lady Veriphast's ball, and the
craft of that worthy Bishop who was the last to leave
the billiard-room on most nights, but would not even
have it lighted up when the missionaries were there.
But when the unknown apostle appeared out of the
Unseen, and, holding out an austere hand, said, " Come !
give up everything : live the life—not with judicious
restraints, so as to keep your place in society and do
the best for yourself ; but absolutely, putting that life
before everything : " then for the first time Laurence
heard the voice which for all his previous life he had
been longing to hear.

But I am unable to dive so far into the secrets of this period of his history as to tell how it worked, or whether it required many struggles to convince him that this was of far greater importance than the fabric of life which he had spent so many years and so much labour in building up, which he had brought now to a kind of climax, if not exactly as he hoped, yet such as few men of his age had attained, and to which almost any advancement he desired might be possible. A man whose opinions and information were so notable that he was sent for to Windsor to explain to the Sovereign an important complication in foreign affairs, was, of all men in the world, the one, we would think, to be least easily tempted to retire from a sphere in which such consultations are possible. But we have no longer the assistance of those confidences which were poured into his mother's bosom at other periods of his career; for she was now with him, fully sharing in all his thoughts, perhaps trembling for the result, even while she rejoiced over her son's capability for such a sacrifice. I am not, for my own part, disposed to believe that it was in any sense a life-and-death struggle with Laurence to make up his mind to the tremendous disruption before him. He would not hesitate, as most of us would do, to enter upon a course which might entail such supreme self-denial. To step back in sight of whither that tide was leading him, would not occur to a mind which had been in search at all times of the absolute. Perhaps prudence moved him so far as to suggest waiting until the result probable to follow upon his parliamentary life was clear. But even this supposition fails us in the after-light thrown by himself on that parliamentary career, when he confides to his future wife that his mouth was shut, in its beginning, by command of the prophet, so that he who had hoped all his life to make a name in the House of Commons became "a parliamentary failure." This of itself proves how long his intercourse with Mr Harris had lasted before the final resolution was taken.

The reader will remember in 'Piccadilly' the sudden appearance of the stranger whose arm is linked in that of the hero as he walks along his favourite pavement expounding the secrets of the better life to an astonished companion, and who finally accompanies him to America, making all doctors or other attendance unnecessary, when he is left half dead with excitement and the strain of feeling at the end of the book. "Ah Piccadilly! hallowed recollections may attach to those stones worn by the feet of the busy idiots in this vast asylum, for one sane man has trodden them, and I listened to the words of wisdom as they dropped from the lips of one so obscure that his name is still unknown in the land, but I doubted not who at that moment was the greatest man in Piccadilly." This is the disciple's estimate of his new master. In another portion of that work he quotes a passage from "the greatest poet of the age, as yet, alas! unknown to fame," being an extract from 'The Great Republic : a Poem of the Sun,' by Thomas Lake Harris. It was in 1865 that 'Piccadilly' was published (in 'Blackwood'), and it was not till 1867 that Laurence took the decisive step; so that it is clear it was no hasty step, but one fully considered and turned over during a couple, at least, of momentous years. "I daresay you will be surprised," he writes to Mr Blackwood, "at the half-serious, half-mysterious tone of the last parts; but after having attacked the religious world so sharply, it is necessary to show that one does not despise religion of a right kind."

It was in the early part of 1867, and in the House of Commons itself, that my own recollections become of any use to me in this record. I had previously made his acquaintance, but only in an accidental way, and it was for the first time on this occasion that we really became known to each other. It was in one of the galleries of the House, then, and probably still, appropriated to ladies, called at the time Lord Charles Russell's gallery, and placed at the other end of the House from the dark oriental bird-cage of the Ladies' Gallery, from which women are permitted to peep at the legislators of the country. I remember very vividly the perspective of the House, brightly lighted, with something of the aspect of a vacant theatre during some dull prefatory piece: its

benches empty save for an obscure figure, watchful of
an opportunity, here and there; an unimportant voice
asking a question; the patient officials in their places
about the most patient Speaker, waiting, business-like and
uninterested, going through their evening's work.   Ladies,
who are only on sufferance in that place, come early to
secure their places, and all the routine of the question-
hour had to be gone through before the debate began.
The occasion was an important one.   It was the evening
on which Mr Disraeli was to bring forward in the form of
resolutions the same Reform Bill on which he had just
succeeded in driving Mr Gladstone out of office ; while
the latter statesman, suddenly turned into Opposition in
respect to his own measure, had to do his best by all
practicable parliamentary wiles to destroy its chances of
success in other hands—one of the most curious manifestations of government by party which has perhaps ever
been seen in England.

   The conversation in the gallery, at that moment so
much more interesting than anything going on below,
began by some questions on my part as to the spiritualism so-called in which I was aware Laurence had many
experiences.   These questions were lightly put, but they
were answered with a gravity for which I was quite un-
prepared.   It was not that his new enlightenment had
taken from him his former faith in the reality of those
communications with the unseen.   The result was quite
contrary to this ; and I listened with the surprise of a
sceptic accustomed to think somewhat contemptuously of
the freaks of table turning and rapping, while he warmly
condemned these manifestations as not only vulgarities
and impertinences, so to speak, but attempts to debase
and lessen a new revelation of life and truth—and dangerous in every way to those who thus opened communications between their own spirits and the most debased
inhabitants of the unseen world.   The gasp of discon-
certed astonishment with which one listened to this
new view, in which the vulgar revelations of the mediums
were recognised as real but denounced as pernicious, in
utter contradiction not only of the trivial explanation with

which the great Faraday had attempted to put these phenomena down — to the very partial satisfaction of the
world, but also of one's own private conviction of their
folly and unimportance — remains in my recollection as
vividly as when, abashed and silenced, I listened, drawing back into myself. It was, he said, no place to enter
into the deeper question ; but he promised on some other
occasion to make me acquainted with a better way.

It was perhaps in some haste to escape from an unlucky
opening, as well as from the confusion of mind consequent
upon having visibly approached with levity a matter of
the deepest importance to my companion, that I put some
question about parliamentary life which drew from him an
equally unexpected reply. Notwithstanding the revelations of ' Piccadilly,' which had excited and startled the
reader, while leaving him still doubtful whether there was
more than an unconscious self-identification of the author
with his strange hero, it was very difficult to realise how
a man so apparently successful in everything he touched
should be possessed with so strong a sense of dissatisfaction, so much impatience and indignation, with his present
mode of life. He declared it was a life unendurable, which
he at least could support no longer ; that truth of purpose
or earnestness was not in it ; that no one, except a few
powerless individuals, cared for the country or the real
benefit of the people, but each party for the triumph it
could win over the other—the opportunity of securing an
advantage, the hope of placing itself first, and pulling
down its opponents. This sudden burst of indignant disgust with the realities of life, so fiery and lofty in tone, so
unexpected from those easy yet eloquent lips, to which
banter and jest seemed more familiar than denunciation,
in face of that slumbrous scene, so tedious yet so full of
expectation, ready in a moment to wake into brilliant conflict, was very remarkable. A natural reluctance to believe
in such a verdict, or accept a general and sweeping censure
of the sort, mingled in the mind of the hearer with regret
and sympathy for the higher aims and disappointed ideal
of the speaker. It was no doubt the very curious transaction then going on, and which soon filled the empty

N

House with eager listeners, and silenced every whisper to hear Mr Disraeli's statement, which had brought to a climax Oliphant's doubts and difficulties.

I add the following report of his own account of this matter, which had a great influence on his mind, from the recollection of another friend. He had come into Parliament as a Liberal and follower of Mr Gladstone, then pledged to introduce a new and widely reaching Reform Bill. Upon this, Mr Gladstone was, as the reader will recollect, and as has been already mentioned, defeated by Mr Disraeli. The new Government had barely begun its functions when Mr Disraeli took up the bill upon which he had defeated his adversaries, and brought it in again, a little changed in form but identical in principle, thus turning the tables completely, and placing the politicians who had formed the project in party opposition to it.

" After Mr Disraeli had intimated his intention of reviving Mr Gladstone's Reform Bill, a great Liberal meeting was held at the Reform Club to consider the state of affairs, when Mr Gladstone made a speech, in which he said that the principle of the bill was good, as it was one for which he was personally responsible, and that of course they must support it; but that its details must be greatly amended. A hole was to be picked here, and another there ; such a clause must be cut out, and such another put in—till Oliphant clearly saw that the real intention was to wreck the bill, if possible, rather than let it count to the opposite party. This utterly silenced him, and convinced him, as he said, 'that there was no honesty on either side,' in a party sense, at least. With the help of a few genuine Liberals who refused to join in the party tactics, he formed a cave, called the Tea-Room Cave or Clique, as it was their habit to meet in the tea-room. The object of this party was to pass the Reform Bill at all hazards. It must be remembered that, while he considered Mr Gladstone's conduct as the most inexcusable, he always thought it dishonourable of Mr Disraeli to take up his adversary's measure. Only, Laurence could not see that this was a reason for opposing a bill that was good in itself. He was quite ready to serve God, though the devil bade him; only it gave him a lower opinion of the devil."

After the conversation above recorded, I waited for some time for the fulfilment of his promise to let me know more fully the terms of his new belief, and eventually wrote to him to remind him of it. His reply I have unfortunately mislaid; but it was to the effect that he had not forgotten, but that he was under great restrictions as to where and when he was permitted to speak, and to whom. He had not, it appeared, received any indication that I was one of those who had the ear to hear. He sent me by the same post one of the volumes of Mr Harris's sermons, to which I have referred. I presume that I must have replied to this, expressing my admiration for the singular fervency and earnestness of the addresses contained in this little book, which indeed struck me as very remarkable. The mystical part of it, in which the writer claimed to have seen and received actual communications by word of mouth, so to speak, from our Lord Himself, was very small—a few sentences here and there—while the appeal made to all to "live the life," and carry the imitation of Christ into every detail of existence, was the chief motive of the whole, and put forth often with great eloquence and most unusual animation and fervour. But I found so little that was not already known, and which I had not understood all my life as the burden of all Gospel teaching (except those few mystical sentences), that I must have asked for further information as to the revelations which were unexplained. I received the following letter in reply:—

"I still prefer, in answer to your note, to speak to you through the words of Mr Harris rather than from myself, and I therefore send you another of his books. I think you will see from it that the important factor in his teaching is not so much that a spirit-sight exists by which, as you say, 'we may penetrate the mists of this world and see into the sacred mystery beyond'—though that is most undoubtedly the case—as that organic changes are taking place whereby men are being brought into closer relations with the unseen world, and are becoming more open to the influences which directly proceed from it; and that thus we are enabled to bring ourselves into closer *rapport* with Him who was once a man, and established a human relationship with us for this express purpose—or with those evil ones who now, as of old, can take possession of, and destroy physically and morally, those who do not resist them. This change of organic conditions is evidenced by manifestations of a character novel to our present experiences, but which existed in past ages of the world. While, on the one hand, the powers of darkness made known their presence by various forms of possession, and the physical phenomena resulting from these multiplying, the breath of Christ, descending directly into the organisms of men to meet the invading force from below, makes known its presence also by physical sensations of a blessed and life-giving character, conveying with irresistible force the consciousness that Christ is actually descending with power and great glory a second time to dwell with us, and so to quicken their faculties and inspire their lives, that those who give themselves up to Him wholly and without reservation of any kind, and are ready, by a process of absolute self-extinction and self-sacrifice, to die as to their old nature, even while on this earth receive a divine influx, which will result in their own active regeneration, and enable them to act with great power on others. The world professes to believe in Christ, and in living Christ's life; but the popular belief in Christ is either a mean concession of opinion or an empty superstition: and the embodiment of His life in ours practically, and I may almost say dynamically, so that we can be conscious of His living in us and living out through us, and by physical sensations (consisting chiefly in changes in the natural respiration) that we should feel His bodily life in ours, would be considered an absurdity, though it is promised from one end of revelation to the other. It is this physical union with Christ which is the deeply solemn subject upon which I felt myself unable to converse with you, from a deficiency of this divine life in me, which would make my utterances still feeble and uncertain, and which has rendered it a matter of considerable doubt and difficulty even to write this much; for every effort to impart this truth is resisted so strongly from below. But it so happens that Mr Harris has recently returned from America to this country. He is not living in London; but if, after you have read these sermons, you would wish to hear more, I will let him know, though the life of suffering which he is called upon to lead, and the almost entire isolation which the great work in which he is engaged imposes upon him, renders it impossible for me to promise whether he can see you. But whether this be so or not, none who are really seeking fail to find, and those who are yearning for the Father's embrace will be led into it by the way specially appointed for them."

The reader may perhaps think that there was a want of courage in not following up this opening, though but a partial one, and endeavouring to see the man whose personal influence was so great and his views so interesting; but I have never pretended to be a conscious student of human nature, and the pretence is one highly objectionable to me,—while at the same time I have so rooted a faith in human sincerity and so little in imposture, that though never very likely at any time to fall under the spell, I was still more incapable of seeing through it. Besides, this strange and mysterious kind of transubstantiation, by which a man could be made not only spiritually but physically one with Christ, affected me with a sort of moral vertigo, which I fear has been the chief effect since of other and fuller expositions of that and further doctrines. It will be perceived that Harris still continued to envelop himself in a remoteness and inaccessibility which made it impossible for his fervid disciple to promise that he would see a new inquirer.

The next commuication I had from Laurence was dated from Liverpool. He was just about to sail for America, having given up everything that had previously tempted him—his position, his prospects, politics, literature, society, every personal possession and hope. A universal cry of consternation followed this disappearance, expressed half in regrets for the deluded one (who was so little like an ordinary victim of delusion), and half in scorn of his prophet, the wretched fanatic, the vulgar mystic, who had got hold of him by what wonderful wiles or for what evil purposes who could say? A man who thus abandons the world for religious motives is almost sure, amid the wide censure that is inevitable, to encounter also a great deal of contempt: yet had he become a monk, either Roman or Anglican, a faint conception of his desire to save his soul might have penetrated the univeral mind; but he did not do anything so comprehensible. He went into no convent, no place of holy traditions, but far away into the wilds, to "live the life," as he himself said, to work with his hands for his daily bread, giving up everything he possessed; in no tragic mood, from no shock of failure or disappointment, but with the cheerfulness and light-heartedness that were characteristic of him, and that sense of the humorous which in living or dying never forsook him. He knew what everybody would say,—the jibes, the witty remarks, the keen shafts of censure, the mocking with which his exit from the world would be received by those whom he left behind. He saw indeed, so to speak, the fun of it in other eyes, even when he felt in his own soul the extreme seriousness of the step he was taking. He disappeared, as if he had gone down for ever in the great sea which he had traversed to reach his new home and new life. The billows closed over him to all appearance as completely; and for three years he was as if he had never been.

I am enabled, by the kindness of a friend, Mrs Hankin, to add here several particulars, drawn from his own lips, of the experiences of the extraordinary new life into which he thus plunged. It was given many years after, when everything was changed; but his account of the manner in which he was led to throw in his fortunes with those of Mr Harris's community, contains no reflections upon the methods used to draw him there. He was indeed, according to this narrative, rather held at arm's-length than cajoled into the tremendous step which severed him from all his past life. Perhaps the apparent reluctance was but a more able way of drawing him on.

The fact that he was forbidden to attempt to seek the parliamentary success on which his heart had been set, proves at once that there were no false ideas conveyed to him of the character of the yoke he was about to take upon his shoulders. This went so far that he was discouraged from making the final sacrifice as one above his strength, and even on landing in America was met by a messenger from Mr Harris to warn him that he should reflect again before coming to Brocton. "At the same time, however, there was forwarded to him such an exact moral diagnosis of his then condition, as to determine him more than ever to join this extraordinary leader." Thus he was held back and attracted irresistibly, at one and the same time.

On his arrival at Brocton, or, as it is formally called, Salem-on-Erie, the home of the community, he was plunged into the severest and rudest elements of life. Coming straight from Mayfair, "he was sent to sleep in a large loft containing only empty orange-boxes and one mattress, and he remembered arranging these articles so as to form some semblance of a room. His earliest work was clearing out a large cattle-shed or stable. He often, he said, recalled in a sort of nightmare the gloomy silent labour for days and days, wheeling barrows of dirt and rubbish in perfect loneliness, for he was not allowed to speak to any one; and even his food was conveyed to him by a silent messenger, to whom he might speak no word. Often, after this rough work was ended, and he came home dead-beat at nine o'clock, he was sent out again to draw water for household purposes till eleven o'clock, till his fingers were almost frost-bitten."

Even this picture, however, is scarcely so gloomy as that which depicts one feature of the spiritual life of this extraordinary place. Many mediums and possessed persons were brought to Harris, that he might cast out the devils by which they were afflicted. "Sometimes 'the infernals,' as they were called, were very active, and in that case the whole community had to watch to save those who were 'infested,' because it was believed that the infernals were more active in sleep. For this reason, in many instances persons were kept almost without sleep for months. One woman, in particular, for weeks was allowed only to sleep from nine o'clock till twelve, all the rest of the twenty-four hours being spent in the hardest work. In casting out or 'holding' against the devils, it was the custom to concentrate the mind firmly on the principle of evil, till it seemed almost to form itself into a definite form, and then to pray with frantic fervour, 'Bind him, Lord!' When the crisis was past, and the man or woman became open to spiritual influence, as betokened by deep sustained breathing, members used to sit up all night to 'bind' the infernals: it being understood that those who were most open to spiritual influence of the highest kind were also most subject to the other."

The wonderful understanding which, by general consent, the extraordinary man who was at the head of this strange community possessed of the characters, moods, and conditions of the minds subject to him, was endued with special powers of spiritual torture by the system which follows.

"He arranged them in groups of three or four persons to assimilate; but if the magnetism of one was found to be injurious to another, Harris was aware of it at once, and instantly separated them. Any strong, merely natural affection was injurious." In such cases, all ties of relationship were broken ruthlessly, and separations made between parents and children, husbands and wives, until "the affection was no longer selfish, but changed into a great spiritual love for the race; so that, instead of acting and reacting on one another, it could be poured out on all the world, or at least on those who were in a condition to receive this pure spiritual love," to the perfection of which the most perfect harmony was necessary, any bickering or jealousy immediately dispelling the influx and "breaking the sphere."

And not only did the head of the community keep incessant watch over all these occult manifestations, but he was at once the director of the domestic life within, where the members of the community worked together at agriculture—and also the head of every operation without, many of his disciples being sent out into business affairs, to conduct commercial operations or other kinds of profitable work, in order that they might bring in money for the community. "All the schemes connected with it, mercantile or agricultural, were in his hands; and he would constantly change the heads of departments if he thought their minds were becoming too much engrossed in business, recall and replace them with others who often knew nothing of their management, and had to learn through mistakes." The life at times was of the most primitive description, deprived of every pretence at physical comfort,—although, until the end of his existence, Laurence never departed from the belief that it was a life calculated to produce the highest development of the spiritual nature.

"The whole system was based on the belief that we are all batteries of some sort of unseen force, which we call influence, which is always uncertain in action, and often injurious. Under conditions of entire self-devotion, of absolute purity of life, and of earnest obedience to the voice of God, it has been found that the nature of man contains another quality of spiritual life, which connects him with a higher order of being, and completes his human nature with a divine complement, which has in it a power to attract and draw others to a higher spiritual plane, and by degrees to bring all who feel it into a divine bond of perfect union, which will at the last bring about a kingdom of God on earth."

It was in 1867 that Laurence disappeared from England. In 1870, as suddenly, he came back. The usual tales had been current, that he had awakened out of his delusion and unveiled his prophet, and returned to his senses, as people said—stories which I for one hoped were not true, feeling what such a disenchantment, after such a sacrifice, must have been for such a man; but nothing of this kind was the case. He came back more assured in his faith than ever—as serious, as humorous, as enter-

taining, as delightful a companion, and as much disposed
to social enjoyment as when he had been one of the most
popular men in London. And as he was one of those
whom Society, always eager to be entertained and amused,
does not forget, he stepped back out of the wilds into his
place again, and became the courted of many circles, as if
he had never missed a day. In the course of the summer
he came one day to see me, and I need not say with what
strong curiosity and interest I followed all that he told
me about his new life. He explained, in the first place,
many of the facts that seemed most hard to understand,
describing how Mr Harris exacted a two-years' probation
from his disciples as a test of their sincerity, that he might
have no fanciful followers coming and going as feeling
or caprice moved, but a band whose truth and endurance
had been fully tested, and who knew their own mind, and
the ground of their allegiance. The test in Laurence
Oliphant's case had been the severe and extraordinary one
of giving up all congenial work, all adventure, novelty,
society, everything he had hitherto lived for, and making
experience, as above related, of the hard existence of the
labouring man. He had worked upon the farm, which
was the headquarters of the community in America, a
teamster, as he told me with a laugh, and a very bad one,
oversetting his cart in the mud, and committing all manner of awkwardnesses. It seemed to my mind to put
a certain reason, satisfactory in its way, into this ordeal,
that it was not a mere fantastic preference of the ruder
life of the fields, but had a real meaning as a proof of
absolute sincerity and truth. While the probation lasted,
the neophyte had stuck at nothing. He had "cadged
strawberries" along the railway line, not as a penitential
self-humiliation, but because it was a thing that had to be
done by somebody, and conveyed to his mind no humiliation at all. He did not enter into any such details as
those I have quoted, but talked much and freely of the
general aim and purpose of the community, and of
individuals who had been drawn into it from the very
mouth of hell, so to speak, with no bond of doctrine or
demanded belief, but only with the charge to "live the

life." For his own part, having fulfilled his probation, his prophet and director, in whom his faith was unbounded, had bidden him return to his own sphere of work, and take up again his accustomed tools. All this seemed perfectly natural and reasonable when once the wisdom and greatness of Mr Harris was taken for granted; and on that point he had no doubt. Laurence had made over all he had to the community—I do not know how much it was—and the community made him an allowance when he returned home, to provide for his necessities until he got remunerative work. With this little provision, and with all his former prospects thrown aside, he came back in the full force of his matured powers — as ready, as witty, as cheerful, as potent a personality as ever—to do whatever Providence might find for him to do.

Lady Oliphant had followed her son to Brocton in 1868, the year following his own arrival there, and had entered upon her own very bitter probation before he had accomplished his. It has been often told that she, a woman always delicate and much regarded and studied by her husband and her son, was made to lay her ladyhood aside and all the habits of her life, and to engage in manual or menial labour, the work of the large household, taking her share of the washing, cooking, and cleaning of the house. I have no doubt that this was the case, any more than I have the least doubt that it was the smallest of matters to her fervent mind and strong faith, probably attended with much less hardship than appears on the surface —even perhaps with a little real good, in the way of strengthened health and a mind freed from many other preoccupations, by the healthy influence of personal exertion. But Mr Harris would have been a less man than he evidently was, had he accepted this as a sufficient ordeal; and accordingly the mother, whose son had been, as the reader knows, all in all to her—her companion, her correspondent, giving up his diplomatic life to calm her fears, opening to her the very depths of his thoughts— was ordained to give up her Lowry, so far as any special possession of him went. They lived, indeed, in the same community, and saw each other as any two members of

the community did; but all the close and confidential
intercourse of their life was made to end, and when the
time came for his return to England, it was without a
word of special leave-taking,—she who had broken her
heart over every parting; and—she who had lived upon
his letters and desired to share every serious thought—
without a line of communication during his absence, to
let her know anything about him, where he was or how
he was. It was bitter, the highest refinement of cruelty;
yet, if any man had the right to exact such a thing, the
most severe proof of sincerity. Laurence went away without even a look of farewell; and he came back—and they
had not a word together: not a moment of communion,—
nothing to tell her where he had been, what he had been
doing, the old friends he had seen, the new objects to
which his life was to be devoted. He told me of this with
the troubled laugh of emotion, and of how it had been
almost too much for her, and had threatened to bring
about an absolute break-down of heart and strength. She
fell ill, and her son had to be sent for lest she should die.
But in the end her faith, her obedience, what she thought
her religious duty, conquered, and she stood out the trial.
I have been told that she was also commanded to go to a
lady whose influence upon and relations with Laurence in
a former part of his life had given her the deepest pain,
to offer her the new light, and to invite her to become
a member of the community and abandon all evil ways.
This, if true, must have been before she left England; but
even such a terrible commission would have been little
beside the tremendous renunciation required of her—which
she made. Thus the prophet put his hand upon the very
sources of life, and controlled them. He must at least
have been a man of extraordinary skill and insight, as
well as of remorseless purpose and determination.

No sound, so far as I am aware, came out of the unknown during these years. I can find no letters of the
period, unless it be one, which I may give here as an exposition, so far as was ever given, of the principles and
practice of the community. It was in answer to an anxious
letter from a very old and dear friend, Mr Louis Liesching,

of the Ceylon Civil Service, who had been a favourite
in the Oliphants' household during their tranquil colonial
life, when Laurence was a boy and the young friend not
much more. The love which both mother and son bore
him had justified this affectionate and sorrowing inquirer
in his anxious claim to know the reason of their withdrawal from the world, and in what Lady Oliphant calls
his "agonised appeal" to them to reconsider their decision.
Mr Liesching's letter was addressed to her; but it was
Laurence, excusing her by the explanation that she was
by no means so good a correspondent as in former days,
who answered the letter, giving his friend an account of
their motives and practices :—

"When I sat down to write I thought it would be possible for me to give you some account which would satisfy
you : the subject is so sacred, so vast, and so mysterious,
that I am unable to enter upon it within the limits of a
letter; but this you must believe, that I have submitted
neither my reason nor my will to any man,—that nothing
but a guidance as directly from God as that which Saul
obeyed when he left his old life for a new one, could have
induced me to abandon a career which, humanly speaking, was full of the brightest promise, and throw up a
social position which it had cost me a lifetime to establish.
That God, after having spoken to the world for thousands
of years directly through the lips of man and through no
other channel, should now, at the moment of its greatest
extremity, utterly abandon it, is not a reasonable supposition. In taking the Bible as your only guide, as I do, you
take what came only through man, and what was decided
by other men, no better judges than you and I, to be inspired. If you ask what our tenets are, they simply con-
dense and crystallise into the uses of our daily life the
teachings of Christ, under direct divine guidance, and we
enjoy evidences both of an external and internal character
which the world would call supernatural, encouraging us
when we are obeying His will, checking us when we are
going astray, and uniting us daily more nearly to Him
and to each other. Thus we believe that Christ is again

appearing in this world, making Himself felt in the very organisms of those who open themselves directly to His influence, and endowing them with wisdom and with power which will enable them to cope successfully with all those social, political, and ecclesiastical inversions which constitute antichrist.

"Before, however, we are in a condition to begin the work of reform without, we have to establish it within,—before we are soldiers fit to enter the lists against the forces of Pandemonium, embodied and intrenched in the institutions of mankind, we have to wrestle not against flesh and blood, but against the spiritual powers which assail us from within,—and we have to undergo a most severe and scorching discipline to prepare us for the struggle upon which we shall enter when we are summoned from our retirement, and called upon to live out literally in the world the life which Christ inculcated. It will be far easier to do this among the heathen than among the Levites and Pharisees, hypocrites, of Christendom. For the devil's stronghold, as you seem to have found out, is now, as it was when Christ came, not among the publicans and harlots, but among the sects.

"We have no dogmas : our fundamental principle is absolute and entire self-sacrifice ; our motive is not the salvation of our souls, but the regeneration of humanity ; our absorbing study is the practical embodiment of that new commandment which those who heard it only partially understood, "that ye love one another," but which is as new, in the sense of never having been up to this time either comprehended or practised, as it was then. The hatreds and shams of Christendom drove me into, and kept me for years in, open infidelity and most reckless dissipation. When I was your son's age, like him I desired to love God and live for divine ends : for God mercifully implants in the hearts of most children the germs of pure and lofty aspiration ; but constituted as the world is, where are they to find development ? Let him join any so-called Christian denomination, and he finds the preachers of religion envious, bigoted, and the best of them unable, if they wished, to live a Christ life. If he goes into the world, he finds the infernal principle of competition, which strikes at the root of all unselfish love, entirely paramount: he can only succeed by taking better care of number one than his neighbours. The most sacred tie of life, marriage, is a lottery; for he has no means of knowing certainly who is the one for whom God destines him, or where to find her. He instinctively yearns for solidarity, which is harmony, and he finds competition, which is natural hatred. It is terrible what a condition society is fallen into, and how sad must be the fate of those growing up with generous divinely sent ambitions, destined to be crushed almost before they have had time to make their presence felt.

"Dear Louis, knowing what I have gone through and where I am, the thought of your son's fate seems to press itself upon me with an irresistible force. I would save him while there is yet time, and bring him under the influence of that calm and peaceful sphere where the presence of Christ broods like a dove over the efforts of those few devoted souls who are striving at all hazards and at all costs to fit themselves to be His absolute and exclusive servants, literally loving neither father nor mother, nor wife nor children, nor brother nor sister, nor even their own lives, as they love their divine Master. You need not fear erroneous or unorthodox teaching in doctrinals: all we claim is a direct consciousness of divine guidance, without the comfort and consolation of which, mercifully vouchsafed to us, it would be impossible to support the trials and spiritual sufferings we are called upon to bear for His sake. Still, I would rather you would read and judge for yourself, if you feel so disposed: at the same time, do not think that I am pressing this, or manifesting any desire to persuade, however difficult it may be for me to resist doing so. It is not we but the Lord who calls, and therefore act only in obedience to your highest impressions, after looking earnestly to Him for help and guidance in the matter. I shall say no more, fearing that I may, unconsciously to myself, allow some wish of my own to creep in. Of this thing I am assured, that however much we may differ here,—

however widely sundered by sentiment, by distance,—if we are all three determined to love and serve Christ, to the exclusion of every other object, we shall all three be hereafter indissolubly united in His divine harmony by the object of our worship, Himself."

Lady Oliphant added to this letter a little note of tender kindness, repeating the assurance that her affection was unbroken either by the great distance, the change of her ways of thinking, or the silence which had fallen between herself and her friends. "One thought," she says, "is constantly with me, and that is, how heartily our beloved Sir Anthony would have embraced this life, how he would have found so many of the perplexities which troubled him solved. I am reminded of him daily, and I am sure we are both doing just as should have made him happy by remaining here. My head," adds this dear lady, "is my weak point, and I am thankful that I am able to be useful in other ways." The reader will feel the pathos of these simple words, remembering in what occupations a delicate woman, whose antecedents had been of so different a kind, was now making herself useful.

Enclosed with this letter was a copy of one addressed by another member of the community to a brother, as little enlightened on the subject and as anxious as Mr Liesching, which Laurence thought, with the unconscious humility of a man absorbed in a great subject, to be a better exposition than his own. He adds that this is written by a Quaker, a man known and reputed for his Christian life —"not come out of the slough, as I am." It may be added that in his account of himself, as given up to reckless dissipation, there is evidently much of that exaggerated penitence which all sudden converts are so apt to fall into. Society abounds with slander, and he was not likely to escape from its too-usual darts; but that he was ever a vicious man I do not for a moment believe. The vortex of London society in the season, although a giddy whirl, and requiring a strong brain (or none at all) to maintain a proper equilibrium, would scarcely represent "reckless dissipation" in the ordinary sense of the word, or in the

phraseology of a man of the world. The Quaker gentleman's letter is as follows :—

"You ask after our daily life here, how we spend our
time. There is a short sentence of G. Fox which will not
inaptly express what we do and propose to do. The words
are, 'All things useful in creation.' That one word ' useful' has a particular charm for the people here. They
are of an intensely practical genius. With us everything
must have a *use* and every one his work. We have none
set apart for the ministry, and we have no salaries to
spare for any clergyman, minus a cure, who chanced to
come our way. Our maxim is, that the more spiritual
we become, the more practical we must become also. We
must meet the world in its own way and on its own terms,
and conquer all uses, arts, sciences, industries for the City
of our God, until the time comes of which it is written
'that the kings of the earth do bring their glory and
honour into her.' Our community here we often call ' *the
Use.*' Every one here must have his or her 'use' or 'uses,'
according to his or her special genius. I said in my former letter that the New Church renewed the body and
mind as well as the soul. Now, the influx of the Spirit,
or internal breathing of which we are sensationally and
organically conscious, natural respiration undergoing a
new change, begets a new ardour, a divine activity for
all work ; and whether we are planting potatoes, cooking
a joint, singing a hymn, or having a picnic in the woods, it
is our ambition (if I may use the word) to do it the *very
best*, as God would do and does His own work. Our pleasures are joy-births from God ; our labour is worship, and
our meals more than Passovers. We have no place here
for those who want to meditate, unless the meditation
ultimates in useful work. There is no Simon Stylites
here—not even a Madame Guyon need come, unless she
would work. Our maxims are the reverse of those of the
world. A Christian manufacturer in Lancashire or New
England employs any men who can work for him, without
reference to the regenerate life : our maxim is, that regeneration makes a man a better worker. The world says,

Every man for himself. I am writing to one who labours for the good of the poor to the best of his ability. Do all your labours touch more than the edge of the festering sore that affects and wastes poor perishing humanity? If all the poor of Leeds were clothed and fed to-morrow, and work found for them, would not the moral malaria that fastens on modern society produce another dreary crop? How is it that, as wealth increases in London, the poor grow poorer and the criminal classes more fiend-like? Political economists wonder how it is.

> ' Reformers fail because they change the letter
>   And not the spirit of the world's design ;
> Tyrant and slave create the scourge and fetter ;
>   As is the worshipper will be the shrine.
> The ideal fails, though perfect were the plan,—
> World-harmony springs through the perfect man.'

Men laugh at Ruskin, but Ruskin is more than half right. The Church of Christ so-called comes, stiff with age, and lame with creed, and pampered with endowment, but it cannot touch the heart of the evil. Christ comes and weeps, and says, 'These are my sheep for whom I died.' If He appeared again as a man among Christians, and attempted to live out His own teaching, they would put Him in a lunatic asylum. There is only one thing can save the world, and that is ' solidarity with holiness '— a oneness of regenerate man. I have in days gone by followed the chimera of universal suffrage ; yet a universal suffrage of unregenerate men cannot materially alter things for the better, if indeed at all. If democracy is the cure for the evils of our time, how is it that the House of Representatives here is more corrupt than the British House of Commons? and this with the many material advantages which America has over England.

"The ancient landmarks are fading, the faith of many grows cold, sects are dividing and redividing. An intense selfishness throughout society is the root of the evils of our times: men of genius point out the failings of their fellows, but they in turn fail to point out the true remedy. Carlyle, Ruskin, Emerson, Tennyson, they can portray all 'the ills that flesh is heir to'; but when we examine their remedies, it is like viewing the remains of some broken glass windows,—very beautiful, but not a perfect picture can be found in all. We point to Christ, His words, His life. 'Ecce Homo,' not the 'Ecce Homo' of Professor Seeley with all his eloquence, but, as Horace Bushnell says, 'Life in Christ, and Christ in Life.'

"You ask how many of us are here. There are between thirty and forty of us. Few, you may think, for such a work—few, indeed, if the work was ours; but we are nothing. Christ is all. We could have many adherents if we relaxed, but we may not unauthorised relax one iota of our faith or life. Those who come here must have no country, no relations or friends, no pursuits but such as are given them of God. They must literally 'forsake all and take up the cross.' Any one coming here must be willing to be anything or nothing,—to be a drudge if the Lord's will can be best served in that way: he must account a martyr death as a very small sacrifice, and a *martyr life* as the great and glorious thing to strive for. The world has come to this, that nothing but a race of heroes can redeem it. Christ was the great Hero-Martyr, and the servant is not above his Lord.

"Death and Hell fight, and will fight, against this Church, as they have fought against every other. It was not a vain boast when Satan said to Christ, 'All the kingdoms of the world will I give Thee, and the glory of them, if Thou wilt worship me.' It was the assertion of a fact, and Satan still possesses the kingdoms of this world and their glory. And he will not give up his hold without a titanic struggle. When this Church rises in the power of its Lord to cope mightily with the evils of the world, it will meet Satan and his myrmidons at every step, as it does already, and a last and direful persecution will be raised against it; and then also it will be known that the sufferings of this present time are not worthy to be compared with the glory which shall afterwards be revealed. But we cannot unauthorised go to preach in the world. Our business at present is to embody heavenly ideas in practical things, to redeem the soil from evil, to consolidate and take deep root. Glimmerings of these truths have found their way into many sects. The Shakers, for instance, have solidarity, but have abolished marriage, which is a divine ordinance; but they are a very pure good people. The Perfectionists have also the co-operative principle; but they have admitted the vile principle of free-love, which is an abomination in the sight of God. The Moravians saw the truth in part, but it could not be carried out until the time appointed of God. We have simply been invited of the Lord, and have come, 'and the Spirit and the Bride say, Come; and whosoever will, let him come.' The world has still to be won, and Christ still says, 'The harvest truly is plenteous, but the labourers are few.' The soldiers in the Lamb's army will have to bear the cross and wear the thorny crown; but these do not conceal the Tree of Life and the crown of glory which fadeth not away."

These sentiments are echoed by Lady Oliphant in another letter to Mr Liesching, who had not been satisfied with the first, but evidently continued his inquiries, with too warm an affection for his friends to be easily contented with their voluntary banishment and exile. She has been warning him not to put any faith in the reports in the American papers, which had already begun the odious system of interviewing:—

"There is no secret, and there is nothing to tell that the world would understand, and the deeper things are too sacred for newspaper columns. That Breath, which is described in the little book entitled 'The Breath of God with Man,'[1] is a physical fact of which all here are conscious, and with many it is sometimes audible. This admits of no doubting nor argument—it is simply a truth: and so of other interior matters which are convincing and satisfactory to us, but which can scarcely be received by those who are satisfied with the religion they already possess. We were not. I beg you not to trouble yourself

---

[1] I have endeavoured in vain to procure this book—one of the publications, I believe, of Mr Harris.

with fears for us, nor for our community being broken up
through some dreadful sin; and certainly it will not be
from the cause you dread, 'forbidding to marry.' It just
proves to me the hopelessness of attempting to explain
these things when the mind is not prepared to receive
them. The foundation of the life here is 'Orderly Marriage,' and the difficulty of bringing Christians to a spiritual perception of this divine relation is the one hindrance
even here to the growth of the Lord's life among us. There
are daily applications from all parts for admission to our
body; but only three have been added to our number during the last year. There have been some who came in a
spirit of self-confidence, who were obliged to leave from
utter failure to understand the process, and submit to it,
of rooting out and crushing out the self-hood. It is a fiery
ordeal; but each one who realises what this life is intended for, feels the need and blessing, being helped in
their struggles to this end."

I can give no details, save these, of the habits of the
community in which Laurence and his mother thus found
perfect peace and contentment. The few relics of it
which strayed after him into Asia, if not into Europe, in
after years, showed little that seemed to indicate an exaltation and superiority so undoubted. Plain and somewhat homely Americans, and more or less eccentric English
—individuals whose absorption in questions of moral and
spiritual interest, and indifference to many other matters
usually held as important, gave them a certain separation
without any marked elevation, either in life or manners—
were all that the ordinary spectator saw. At a later period
the life was certainly without any formal religious observances,—no church-going, no set periods or modes of devotion. The men in their field-work, the women in their
household labours, considered themselves as serving God
more truly than by mere acts of worship, and the inner
life was that which was considered worthy of incessant
cultivation and progress. I have never been able in the
smallest degree to fathom what was meant by the spiritual
respiration by which they believed even their bodily con-

ditions to be changed : nor is it easy to enter into the new
law of marriage, which was already the most distinctive
feature of their economy.   That the relation ought to be
strictly Platonic, to use a comprehensible phrase—a union
as of brother and sister, though distinguished by an
absolute oneness of spirit, peculiar to the "sacred tie,"
"the most sacred of ordinances," in which, as they believed,
the being of the dual Godhead was displayed and imitated
—was, I believe, their strange creed.   That it was not
always consistently carried out was of course inevitable.
What is much more wonderful is that it *was* sometimes
carried out with unflinching. resolution, neither the most
tender affection nor the usual circumstances of confidential intimacy between married persons affecting the self-
imposed rule.   It is not a question which can be entered
into further ; but it may to some readers afford a clue
to the somewhat incomprehensible influence exercised
upon certain minds by the mystic teachings of Laurence
Oliphant's later works,—works which are as chaos to the
majority of readers, but to some direct revelations from
heaven.

I may here quote one amusing episode, to break the
blank of this mysterious retirement, which was told me
by Mrs Rosamond Oliphant (I use this form of nomen-
clature, though it is scarcely English, by way of distin-
guishing the lady, his second wife, who was the faithful
nurse and attendant of his closing life) as having been told
to her by her husband,—an amusing outbreak of the
almost boyish love of fun and hankering after adventure
which never deserted him.   One cannot but feel the
blank of tedium and monotony which wrapped that once
brilliant life, when a man so fond of excitement and
variety, at once a sportsman and a politician, the friend
of insurgents and filibusters, who had scoured every disaffected country in Christendom, and lightly carried his
life in his hands through many a dangerous crisis, could
thus risk it, in pure exuberance of spirits and protest
against the commonplace, in such an escapade.   The story
begins with a brief sketch of the same details of his life at
Brocton, which have been already quoted.

"He slept in a straw bed over a stable, where he also ate his solitary meals on a deal box, no other piece of furniture being in the room. He rose every morning at four—in the winter it was bitterly cold—cleaned and fed the horses, and worked at farm-work till eight o'clock at night. He was quite unaccustomed to manual work, and it wearied him, body and soul. But it was thus only, as he felt, 'that the devil could be thrashed out of him.'

"One bitter winter's night, he was driving back to the stable after his long day's work with a sleigh and a pair of vigorous horses. He had been leading a life of the most tiresome description for many months, and the tedious routine had become almost unbearable to him. Suddenly his horses got frightened at something in the way, and with a quick impulse Laurence threw away the reins, and throwing himself into the bottom of the sleigh, yelled so vociferously as to arouse the villagers, who ran into the street. The horses, mad with fright, and urged on by Laurence kicking and shouting in the bottom of the sleigh, soon left the village far behind, and the sleigh spun over the frozen snow. The barn where they were kept was some distance from the village; and to his surprise, when the horses reached it, they swept through the gate without upsetting the sleigh, and drew up before the barn-door trembling in every limb. Laurence coolly climbed out and led them into the stable. The excited villagers rushed far along the road in search of him, expecting to find him in the bottom of a ditch, crushed by the heavy sleigh. After a vain search, they returned to the barn for a consultation, and found Laurence quietly feeding his horses, very much refreshed by a taste of that excitement which he had so loved in earlier life."

Thus the martyr who had given up everything seized a moment of boyish hilarity, and enjoyed the mystification of the villagers, as if he had never known anything more exciting. The wild momentary dash of the frightened horses, the muddy farm-labourer kicking and bellowing, regardless of life and dignity and gravity, in consideration of the moment of wild fun which made the blood again

course through his veins as of old, make a most characteristic picture.

In all that is said, however, on this subject, and all that
we can penetrate of the utter prose and dulness of the
existence of the community to which Laurence had joined
himself, it must be remembered that we are calculating
without the potent individuality then and for so long after
the head of it, and which was really the connecting link
between the rough American farmer and the accomplished
Englishman. All my attempts to find materials by which
the character and personal power of Mr Harris at this
period could be explained have been ineffectual. He is
described, both by those who find in him an incarnation
of the devil, and those to whom he is nothing less than
angelic—an almost wiser and more imperious Gabriel—in
the same abstract terms, there being neither on one side
nor the other any one capable, it would appear, of making
him visible as a man. From the remarkable picture made
by Laurence Oliphant in 'Masollam,' and which is supposed to be a study more or less from the life, I may
quote the following description of the personal characteristics and commanding influence of the prophet—
adding, however, the explanation that it may not be an
impartial one, having been written after the disenchantment which brought that personage down from the highest
heights of moral supremacy to the position of a mercenary
schemer and false prophet, a diabolical agency for evil, instead of almost the first and best of created beings :—

"There was a remarkable alternation of vivacity and
deliberation about the movements of Mr Masollam. His
voice seemed pitched in two different keys, the effect of
which was, when he changed them, to make one seem a
distant echo of the other—a species of ventriloquistic
phenomenon which was calculated to impart a sudden
and not altogether pleasant shock to the nerves of the
listeners. When he talked with what I may term his
'near' voice, he was generally rapid and vivacious ; when
he exchanged it for his 'far-off' one, he was solemn and
impressive. His hair, which had once been raven black,

was now streaked with grey, but it was still thick, and
fell in a massive wave over his ears, and nearly to his
shoulders, giving him something of a leonine aspect. His
brow was overhanging and bushy, and his eyes were like
revolving lights in two dark caverns, so fitfully did they
seem to emit flashes, and then lose all expression. Like
his voice, they too had a near and a far-off expression,
which could be adjusted to the required focus like a
telescope, growing smaller and smaller as though in an
effort to project the sight beyond the limits of natural
vision. At such times they would be so entirely devoid
of all appreciation of outward objects, as to produce almost
the impression of blindness, when suddenly the focus
would change, the pupil expand, and rays flash from them
like lightning from a thunder-cloud, giving an unexpected and extraordinary brilliancy to a face which seemed
promptly to respond to the summons. The general cast
of countenance, the upper part of which, were it not for
the depth of the eye-sockets, would have been strikingly
handsome, was decidedly Semitic; and in repose the general effect was almost statuesque in its calm fixedness.
The mouth was partially concealed by a heavy moustache
and long iron-grey beard; but the transition from repose
to animation revealed an extraordinary flexibility in those
muscles which had a moment before appeared so rigid,
and the whole character of the countenance was altered
as suddenly as the expression of the eye. It would
perhaps be prying too much into the secrets of nature,
or, at all events, into the secrets of Mr Masollam's nature,
to inquire whether this lightening and darkening of the
countenance was voluntary or not. In a lesser degree,
it is a common phenomenon with us all: the effect of one
class of emotions is, vulgarly speaking, to make a man
look black, and of another to make him look bright. The
peculiarity of Mr Masollam was, that he could look so
much blacker and brighter than most people, and make
the change of expression with such extraordinary rapidity
and intensity, that it seemed a sort of facial legerdemain,
and suggested the suspicion that it might be an acquired
faculty. There was, moreover, another change which he

apparently had the power of working on his countenance, which affects other people involuntarily, and which generally, especially in the case of the fair sex, does so very much against their will. . . . Mr Masollam had the faculty of looking very much older one hour than he did the next. There were moments when a careful study of his wrinkles and of his dull faded-looking eyes would lead you to put him down at eighty if he was a day; and there were others when his flashing glance, expanding nostril, broad smooth brow, and mobile mouth, would make a rejuvenating combination, that would for a moment convince you that you had been at least five-and-twenty years out in your first estimate. . . . These rapid contrasts were calculated to arrest the attention of the most casual observer, and to produce a sensation which was not altogether pleasant when first one made his acquaintance. It was not exactly mistrust,—for both manners were perfectly frank and natural,—so much as perplexity. He seemed to be two opposite characters rolled into one, and to be presenting undesigningly a curious moral and physiological problem for solution, which had a disagreeable sort of attractiveness about it, for you almost immediately felt it to be insoluble, and yet it would not let you rest. He might be the best or the worst of men."

This curious picture, in which the enlightenment of repulsion and indignation had taken the place of the entire faith and submission of earlier days, does yet portray a man of singular interest, and very unlike the common herd anywhere. During the three years of absolute obedience at Brocton which I have tried to describe, he was the chief and most prominent figure, giving importance and harmony to all the rest; for to Laurence he was at that time the one inspired among men, the chief of human masters, in intimate alliance with all the powers of heaven. When he declared, as on a previous page, that "I have submitted neither my reason nor my will to any man," and that it was nothing less than "a guidance from God, as direct as that which Saul obeyed"—his meaning was not that he himself had received any miraculous communication, but that this which was conveyed to him through his leader was the direct inspiration of God. Christ had come a second time: this great event had actually occurred, and Harris had seen and spoken with and received the direct instructions of the Lord. This was the theory which held the Brocton community together. "Come see a man who has told me all that ever I did," were almost the words in which this man was described. "He knew my people at home better than I did, though he had never seen them," was the testimony borne afterwards by another believer.

There were, indeed, always differences of language in the way in which he was spoken of within themselves and to the world. Outside inquirers received the somewhat equivocal answer that will and reason were submitted to no man, with the reservation that it was not Harris's will that was followed, but that of God expressed through him. But within the sacred enclosure there was no such pretence, and the reader will see hereafter that nothing less than absolute obedience was exacted. But he was there, among them, their absolute ruler, a divinely inspired man, full of the extraordinary dramatic attractiveness of a constantly changing aspect, which, even when seen from the darker side, is full of interest of the most exciting kind. And no doubt he was a companion full of interest, if sometimes too overwhelming for human nature's daily food, with his wonderful calm assumption of intercourse with the unseen, with his gifts of natural eloquence, and with the insight of a man evidently born to rule and sway other men. These intuitions of his must have been half miraculous in their way, as such a combination of sympathy, keen perception, and unscrupulous power might be expected to be. It is possible to understand how sometimes, when the other member of the little farming community, who knew life in different aspects from those it bore at Brocton, was assailed by sudden heartrending home-sickness—doubts perhaps as to whether he had sold his birthright for the merest pottage—there would come to him a sudden message, betraying absolute penetration of his thoughts, as clear as if they had been read by light from heaven. Laurence has told me that this had occurred again and again in his experience,

giving him unlooked-for help when he needed it most. Who
can tell how it came about? Perhaps a glance—as the
leader, compelled to have his wits always about him, and
who could only preserve his sway by perpetual watchfulness, passed the disciple, bent under his inappropriate load
—betrayed a wavering, a sickening of heart, a dangerous
recollection of other things, on the part of that disciple, to
which the imagination and skill of the guide responded in
instantaneous enlightenment. At all events, the presence
of that evidently extraordinary intelligence, that keen and
constant observation, that strong imperious will and purpose, goes far to explain how Brocton was made possible to
Laurence. I do not feel it necessary to believe that Harris
was a man of evil purpose or bad motives. Laurence, even
in the sharp revulsion of his after-enlightenment, never
believed that this was the case in these earlier years. At
all events, at the beginning the companionship of this man
was not vulgar magic, but full of human charm and attractiveness, as well as of assumed authority and guidance
from heaven.

CHAPTER IX.

A NEW ERA: ALICE.

IT was in the year 1870, as has been said, that Laurence
Oliphant returned home after his disappearance from the
world. Very few letters had come from him during the
first period of his seclusion. His mother was no longer
at home to be the confidant of all his adventures, and for
two years at least the oracle was altogether silent. In
1869 I find one or two letters to his publisher, Mr Blackwood, chiefly about the republication of 'Piccadilly,' which
had been postponed from time to time, on account among
other things of the delays of Mr Richard Doyle, who had
consented to illustrate the book. But it can scarcely be
supposed that a man labouring on his farm, in the manner
described in the preceding chapter, could have much time
to enter into a literary venture; though nothing can be

more odd and eccentric than the thought that the most
brilliant of contemporary satires, a fiery arrow discharged
into the very heart of the most highly organised and
conventional society, should have come from the hard
hand of a farm-labourer at "Brocton, Chataugua County,"
living the most elementary and primitive life, not much
advanced above the level of the horses of his team.

It is not less curious, however, that this religious recluse
and martyr, who had given up all the promises of worldly
reputation and pleasantness for the sake of what he considered the cause of God and the truth, should, as soon as
he had leisure to cast his eyes around him, and perceive
the novel circumstances of his new location, have burst
into the still more startling satire and pungent criticism
of the strange story called "Dollie and the Two Smiths,"
which was published in 'Blackwood's Magazine' in the
early part of the year 1870, just before his return to England.   How he, who was himself living under the rigour
of spiritual indications, in obedience to suggestions from
the unseen, could treat Mrs Dollie's amazing changes of
sentiment with such daring laughter, is inconceivable to
the looker-on.   Fun had never been so wild in him, nor
satire more bold, nor could anything be supposed more
completely unlike the conventional idea of a man who
had given up everything for the sake of religion, than the
laughable yet subtle sketch of an inconceivable condition
of affairs, too ludicrous to be immoral, which he launched
at his new neighbours with the same laugh which had
bewildered the old.   "Dollie and the Two Smiths" is
however still more trenchant than 'Piccadilly,' especially
as it is pure narrative, and without the faintest intimation
from beginning to end that the narrator found anything
in it to disapprove.

About the time that this wonderful sketch was being
made, he recommenced the more familiar record of life and
thought to his friend Mr Blackwood in Edinburgh:—

"My mother has become wedded to this country, and
has no thought at present of leaving it.   There is much
to write about here; but it is scarcely possible for me to

write it, and quite impossible for you to print what I
should probably write. The country is undergoing a complete change; but the ultimate effect of the forces at work
cannot be judged of by the appearances on the political
horizon. The black cloud may in reality be concealing a
very bright sunrise, and the political features from which
you especially, and I in a less degree, turn with disgust,
may be necessary to the growth of something which will
not turn out such an abortion as it looks now. That this
unseemly infant has only just got through its teething,
and has got measles, whooping-cough, and a host of other
troubles in the shape of civil wars to come through, I have
no doubt; but I believe the highest hopes of humanity
are bound up with its future—and with that of Japan,
widely dissimilar though they be. . . . The revolution
here is not political but moral. That is what I should
have liked to write about, if I dared; but I can only
write now what I feel and know to be true, and that is so
dreadfully different from what the world believes."

The inclination thus stated to discuss the new *régime* in
America, with its many strange developments, sounds very
serious in the letter, and seems to imply the most grave
discussion of existing evils and hopes. It is whimsical in
the extreme to find that what it ends in is the wild fun
and satire of the story of Dollie. The hand that laid down
' Piccadilly ' before the revolution in his own individual
life, picked up the same keen weapon as soon as he was
released, with no diminution of its keen force and daring
trenchant stroke, though indeed the moral purpose is less
visible, and the glittering edge is tempered by no intent of
healing. Thus it is clear that, whatever the first chapter
of the life at Brocton had done for Laurence, by all its
toils and humiliations, it had at least left intact the gleam
of fun and humorous perception that was in his unregenerate eyes.

His first appearance in the home of all his training and
associations, after such a break in his life, was naturally
more trying and notable than any after revisitation. When
I saw him in Windsor during the summer, as has been

related, there was in him a sort of restlessness, as of elation
and pleasurable excitement, which was very striking. It
had been said by many that he was coming home disenchanted, disappointed, returning in the blight of hope and
feeling, which is the natural fate of the enthusiast who
has sold his birthright for something even less than the
mess of pottage; but no one who encountered him was
long left under this delusion. He was in high spirits,
unfeignedly glad to be released from his drudgery and to
return to his native air of intellectual novelty and variety,
after long fasting from all that was exciting or agreeable.
But this natural sentiment did not in the least degree interfere with his faith, which was as profound and unshaken
as ever. The little community, with all its straitness, was
still to him the ideal of society; its undistinguished members his chosen brethren. No one of them, so far as I am
aware, except Mr Harris, has ever been heard of beyond
their own natural and limited circle. Their interests were
few, their occupations of the most engrossing and humble
description; but no doubt had entered the mind of Laurence as to their being the enlightened of the earth. The
convert came back with his head high, and his eyes full of
keen wit and spirit as of old. He told the tale of his own
incompetence as a farm-labourer with the most genial
amusement, and made no secret of his satisfaction in being
permitted once more to work with the tools he had been
familiar with all his life, his probation having been fully
accomplished in the community, and his earnestness and
fidelity having stood all tests; but his heart was with his
brethren still.

He gave me, I remember, details of the manner in which
he was still occupied for the service of the community
in his spare hours, which were so extraordinary in their
humility and devotion, that I fear to add an element
almost of ridicule to the story by describing them. But
notwithstanding the tremendous gap between the past and
the present, his own position was virtually unchanged by
his absence. It happened to him, as it happens to few
men self-exiled from the busy world, to take up his friendships where he had left them, and to find everybody as

glad to see him as ever. Nobody had forgotten him. He
was too piquant in his personality, and amused society too
much, to fall aside out of its favour. Everywhere he was
received with open arms. To be sure, the old paths of
advancement were closed, and to a man who might be
summoned to America at any time at a moment's notice,
diplomatic service or the House of Commons would have
been impossible, even could he have returned to them;
but in every other way he was received and fêted as of
yore. Indeed, if anything, the curiosity about him, his
strange disappearance, and the hundred rumours that were
afloat on the subject, increased the delight in his company
which every intelligent person who came in his way could
not help feeling. Everything that was wonderful was said
about his sect, and the inquiries made of him were sometimes of the most ludicrous character. To these he knew
very well how to respond with a laugh or jest or winged
word, which went through the foolish questioner like an
arrow. To myself he appeared to have a sort of holiday
happiness about him, a delight in talking over the trials
and difficulties he had passed through, such as a man has
who has come triumphantly through a long voyage. "Yes,"
he said, "I cadged the strawberries along the line, it is
quite true: partly because there was nobody else to do it,
and we wanted to sell them; and partly because I would
not have it said that there was anything I objected to do."
These arguments were unanswerable in their good sense,
and made the reasonable hearer feel how foolish were any
objections to such a simple duty.

On more recondite matters he was quite ready to talk
also—but here with much less understanding on my part;
nor did he insist on anything except his old formula of
'Piccadilly,' "Live the life." He told me of some one, an
English gentleman, much fallen and degraded, who had
been picked up in the very worst state of wretchedness
and despair, and redeemed by the charge given him of a
sort of humble inn on the outskirts of Brocton estate,
where there were rough and "rowdy" customers only, to
be subdued and kept in order by some one acquainted
with their ways, and whom the absence of all formulas,

even of church-going, and the simple practical rule of life, had restored to virtue and honour. This was to show how wide were the principles of the community, and how simple its aim. As for the transcendental phenomenon of internal or spiritual respiration, which was at that time the only thing occult and hard to understand, except the boundless influence of Mr Harris, little was said. And I must add that Harris was constantly spoken of as influencing, not as commanding. What he suggested appeared, sometimes instantly, sometimes only after much resistance of mind, but always in the end convincingly, to be the absolute best that could be done, and was obeyed accordingly. Of course there was a certain sophistry in this, as in the corresponding statement that there was no giving up of individual property, but that each member of the community continued to hold his own, contrary to the popular opinion that things were in common among them. But the fact was not concealed that many of the members were poor, and had to be maintained at the general cost, though all gave their labour, as much as it was worth, to the common-weal; and Laurence informed me without any hesitation that he himself had a small, a very small, allowance from the community to pay his expenses in Europe until he should have got something to do, which was to be not only for his own advantage but theirs. The allowance was so small that he had to travel in third-class carriages, and content himself with the most modest and obscure lodging, all which privations were objects of amused satisfaction to him in the happy light-heartedness of his nature. A more cheerful image could not be than that which he presented at this moment, with something of a schoolboy's pleasure and delightful elation in the fulness of recovered life.

The only thing that troubled him was that the 'Times' and other influential papers did not review 'Piccadilly' as he thought they ought to have done; but nevertheless the book had a great success, and was read and commented upon everywhere. The world had been allowed time to forget the first impression made by its serial publication, and it came with a fresh shock of sensation

P

upon those most qualified to understand its brilliant
assault upon society. I do not think that the American
sketch of Dollie was ever appreciated as it seems to me to
deserve, probably because the society of rural America—
at which the critic, disguised in the strange garments of a
farm-labourer, looked out with humorous eyes from the
Brocton settlement—was unknown to the English reader:
or perhaps the subject was too startling for the general.
With the exception of this one extraordinary sketch,
scarcely anything came from the pen which had been
so busy during all the earlier portion of his life, and was
again so industrious in its later part, for nearly ten years.
For some portion of that time, however, he was acting
as 'Times' correspondent, producing daily, and in large
quantities, that kind of literature which is fortunately
well recompensed at the moment, but loses all the advantages of a hereafter, and never ranks as literature at all.

This new beginning was made at the breaking out of
the Franco-German war, in the latter half of the year
1870. Laurence had already written for the 'Times' on
many occasions, but never before permanently and officially as one of its representatives. He had still hoped, it
would appear, for some appointment under Government
even at so late a date; but one way or another, was fully
determined to have his part in the great tumult which
was sweeping over the Continent. The following account
of his start upon the dangerous and exciting mission
confided to him is from a letter addressed to the Duchess
of Somerset, at this period his frequent and most entertaining correspondent.

"TOURS, *Sept.* 25 [1870].

"I left London in such a hurry that I had not time
to write you the line I intended, to tell you why I am
here. I went down and stayed a few days with Lord
Granville at Walmer, but nothing came of it beyond
extreme civility and kindness, and vague promises that
took no definite form; so when I met Delane the day
after my return, and found he wanted a correspondent
to go to Lyons to write letters for the 'Times,' and was

prepared to be generous, I accepted his terms: and here I am on my way to the south of France generally, which would be very agreeable if there were not so much chance of being arrested as a spy. I have just seen Lord Lyons, who sees nothing left for France now but a siege of Paris and a fight to the bitter end, whatever that may be. I have just come off a thirty-six hours' journey along railways encumbered with wounded men, and soldiers hurrying to some army which does not yet exist. The whole country seems to be rising: nothing to be seen but soldiers."

His adventures during the actual campaign of 1870 and 1871 have been so admirably written by himself, that it would be useless to attempt any other description of them. The wanderings from field to field, sometimes in advance of the army, sometimes (but seldom) behind, the terrible scenes of which he was sometimes a witness, the wonderful little vignettes of private life in which he had often some merciful act to perform, always a kindly part to play, are all told with his usual vivid force and lightness of touch. His plan was to drive in the rough country carriage with which he had provided himself at his outset, as near to the point of attack as possible, and then getting out, either to skirmish about on his own account, not fighting, but inspecting everything that was going on, or if possible to reach some coign of vantage, such as the steeple of a village church, from which he could see everything. Sometimes he was carried along in the midst of a charge, sometimes he arrived before the troops, to find himself sole master of an evacuated town or deserted village, set on fire, not by enemies, but by its flying inhabitants. On one such occasion he had stepped forward to receive with a somewhat rash jest the commandant of the regiment which had arrived just too late, and was offered quarters with the staff; " but," he adds, " I had my letter to write and post [he had been on foot all day, and had twice barely escaped with his life in the many chances of active warfare], and this involved a five-mile drive by moonlight to the rear across the most ghastly field which can well be imagined."

" I had some trouble in finding my carriage. I had left
it at a well-defined position on the battle-field of the day
before; but to reach it, I had to walk for more than a
mile over a plain where the carcases of men and horses
were not merely thickly strewn, but frozen into all sorts
of fantastic attitudes. The thermometer had been 16° below the freezing-point the previous night, and men only
slightly wounded, who had not been able to crawl to their
comrades, had been frozen to death. One man was stiff
in a sitting position, with both his arms lifted straight
above his head, as though his last moments had been
spent in an invocation, and it gave one a shudder in the
clear moonlight to approach him. Others were cramped
up in a death-agony, and so frozen. In places many
together, French and German, were mingled—not because
they had been at close quarters, but because the same
ground had first been occupied by one and then by the
other, perhaps at an interval of half a day. I think I was
more comfortable with bullets ringing in my ears than
walking amid the distorted shadows of these dead and
stiffened men; and it was quite a relief to see a haystack
on fire and a regiment warming themselves at it, and
my prudent coachman within comfortable distance of the
ruddy blaze. Then comes the hard part of the correspondent's life—I had still to dine. I had lived since
the morning's coffee on a loaf of bread, which I had been
picking at all day. Then to write my letter—a good two
hours' task; then to see that it was safely posted either
that night or the next morning early, so as to give me
time to get to the field for the third day's battle. And all
this after having been on a strain of exertion and excitement since daylight; and then the gentleman at ease in
London reads it all in his arm-chair after breakfast for a
penny, or at most twopence-halfpenny."

The next night after these adventures he found himself
in a village in which every possible lodging seemed to be
taken up, and wandered about in the dark through the
heavily falling snow, in bitter cold, hunger, and desolation, when he found a hovel in a lane, upon the door of

which no name was chalked, and which had therefore
apparently escaped appropriation. After much knocking,
he was at last faintly answered from within by a woman's
voice timidly inquiring what he wanted. "I said I would
explain as soon as I was let in, and pushing the door open,
I found myself in a room lighted only by the dying embers
of a fire. Striking a lucifer match, I became aware of
the presence of two young women, aged eighteen or twenty,
shivering with terror, one of them weeping bitterly. These
I attempted to reassure by the most dulcet tones and
pacific questions. I explained my forlorn condition, expressed my willingness to sleep under a hedge rather than
cause them one moment's uneasiness, painted in strong
language the dangers which surrounded them in the
absence of any protector, declared my willingness—nay,
my anxiety—to constitute myself their protector, expa-
tiated on my harmless and generally innocent disposition
where the fair sex were concerned, and the length to which
my chivalry was capable of carrying me where they were
in peril; and finally succeeded in extorting an invitation
to become their guest. I declined to force myself upon
them, and would only stay if asked. They said they had
no male protector. One of them was married, but her
husband had left on the approach of the Germans, and
the other was her sister; and they threw themselves upon
my mercy. I asked them if they had any provisions in
the house; but the supply was so small that, after chalk-
ing my designation on the door to prevent the room being
occupied in my absence, I started off to bring my traps
from the carriage and any provender I could lay hands
upon. I came in for a slice of beef while the distribution
was being made to the soldiers, and was soon established
by the side of a roaring fire broiling a steak, and most
eagerly waited upon by my two charming hostesses. I
soon after won their complete confidence by turning off
a rather noisy band of soldiers who came looking for
quarters, and listened sympathetically to the long tale of
sorrows which they poured into my ear. They were very
poor, and there was literally but one room in the house.
This contained two beds, one of which was usually occupied

by the young married couple, while her sister slept in the
other. They were hung with heavy blue curtains, which
entirely enveloped them. The sheets were coarse but
clean, and I had a good supply of my own rugs. When
the cravings of my appetite had been appeased, I suggested in the most delicate manner that I should go to
bed first, pull the curtains together, and put my head
under the bedclothes, while they went to rest in the other
bed. This arrangement suited them perfectly; and I
shortly after received a fresh mark of their confidence by
hearing one of them snore. The weather was so boisterous
on the following day that it was impossible to continue
the march: so I brought enough provisions to the hut for
all three, and paid for my accommodation so liberally
when I left the day after—as I felt it would be an act
of charity which would be highly applauded by the pro-
prietors of the journal I served, and out of whose pockets
it came—that I have every reason to hope that the two
poor girls look back to the days when their village was
occupied by the Germans as among the pleasantest and
most profitable of their lives."

Such were the daily vicissitudes of his life throughout
the campaign, and it would be hard to find more interesting reading than in the pages which record the 'Adventures of a War Correspondent.'

The following letter to the Duchess of Somerset is concerned with the state of mind and temper in the two
armies rather than with personal adventure, and is deeply
interesting as the opinion of a candid observer of both
parties. In some of his prognostications Laurence was
wrong; but that is a very usual occurrence when the keenest student of human nature ventures upon prophecy.

"ALENÇON, 18th January [1871].

"I have often been meaning to write to you, but when
I have finished my letter to the 'Times,' and the business
correspondence which I cannot avoid, my head generally
gives me notice that I have used it enough. Since leaving
Lyons I have been writing from the German armies, and

ever since the Grand-Duke of Mecklenburg has had a
separate command, my letters have been dated from his
headquarters. I have thus had an opportunity of seeing
twelve general or partial engagements, and of forming
some idea of the prospects of the two armies. From the
beginning the French never seemed to have a chance, and
the conviction is at last forcing itself upon the sensible
part of the nation that they have no alternative but to
make peace. The extreme democratic party and the south
of France, which has not suffered, are the exceptions; and
when Paris falls, the question of peace or war will divide
the country and sow the seeds of discussion, which will,
I think, produce a civil war, and may perhaps split the
country geographically, the republican or war party being
in the south, the monarchical or peace party in the north.
Meantime, contact with the German armies has not the
effect of enlisting one's sympathies in their favour. The
official or Junker class detests England with a mortal
hatred, because they instinctively feel that the institutions of England strike at the root of their various class
prejudices and bureaucratic system. The Liberal party in
Germany is only waiting for the war to be over to assert
themselves, and I think a German revolution will follow
very closely upon the heels of the French one, when class
interests may produce combinations between the two
countries in spite of their national antipathies. I have
found it very difficult to get on with the Grand-Duke's
staff: they are so supercilious and arrogant, and cannot
understand how a newspaper correspondent can be a
gentleman.

"The feeling against England among the Germans is
increasing every day, and it is amusing to hear them discuss plans for the invasion of England. They have worked
the whole thing out: Blumenthal told me he had considered it from every point of view, and regarded it as
quite feasible. On the other hand, the French are a danger
to no one any longer. They were a mere bubble at best;
and it seems to me they will never again be powerful
enough to cause alarm to any one. No one was a stronger
Francomaniac than I was, or feared less the German

powers than I did, at the beginning of this war; but I confess I have begun to change. I remember the Duke being of the same opinion, and there is no doubt that France with her large fleet has always been our natural enemy, nor had I any idea of the bitterness which existed against us in Germany. True, the natural enemy of Germany is Russia, and all sensible Germans look upon a war there as inevitable. This is the danger which Bismarck has foreseen, and devoted all his policy to avoid.

"We have had no difficulty in routing Chanzy's army again, as we did near Orleans. He is supposed to be concentrating near Laval, whither we shall probably follow him. Nothing can be more cowardly or miserable than the conduct of the French troops. The Germans pillage terribly; but I am obliged to keep silence on many points, or I should be sent away from the army. I have a great difficulty, as it is, to manage my correspondence so as to tell the truth without giving offence."

This special work was of course ended when the war came to a conclusion. There is a story which was widely circulated at the time, but for which I should not have been disposed to vouch, having merely heard it as everybody did, but for subsequent confirmation,—to the effect that Mr Harris, before permitting his disciple to undertake the work of war correspondent, gave him a sign which was to show him that his term of service was over, and to serve as a recall to America. The sign was to be the entrance of a bullet through the window of the room in which he was—rather an ineffectual token, one would think, to a man about whose head the bullets had been whistling night and day. The sign was accomplished, according to this legend, during the struggle of the Commune, when the prophesied bullet did actually come through a window at which he was eagerly watching the commotion in the street below, — a very likely incident. This story, which in itself sounds somewhat fabulous, has been confirmed by notes (already quoted) taken by a friend from Laurence's lips, at a much later period, where, among other interferences of Harris with his life and cherished wishes, he describes repeated recalls "in the midst of undertakings on which I was engaged for the community, just when I was getting things into working order. I was thus recalled from Paris at a moment's notice, when my departure was most inconvenient, and I was much tempted to disobey orders; but (it was at the time of the Commune) I had turned into a house to avoid a charge of soldiery, and a bullet grazed my hair. I took it for a sign that my protection was removed, and got away as soon as I could manage to do so."

This compulsory visit to America was so short that he was again in Paris, and had assumed the permanent post of 'Times' correspondent there, in the autumn or early winter of 1871. I think, but am not sure, that his mother had returned home about the time of this hasty visit, having gone through the terrible probation of separation from her beloved child with such fortitude as was possible, and being now judged capable of bearing the trial of being happy in his society as of old. At all events, whether she had returned before or came back with him, she was at least settled in Paris in December with her son, when I passed through on my way from the snows and pines of the High Burgundy, where I had been paying a visit. Paris was but a ghost of her bright and careless self in these days. The shining city, clean as a bride in her general aspect as one had always seen her, was almost impassable, like grimy London in a thaw, every corner heaped with slush and mud; and here and there, as the slow cab that conveyed the traveller from the distant Gare de Lyon to the Mirabeau Hotel crept along at a footpace, gaunt ruins rising into the wintry morning light, the Tuileries, the Hôtel de Ville, the Ministry of War, and many others, terrible tokens of what had been. Life and traffic had already begun to recover, since human nature, not only in Paris, loathes the monotony of mourning as much as any other incubus: but the sight of these roofless and windowless piles of building, lifting their charred walls in the very centre of the movement of the great city, was strangely overwhelming and impressive. Lady Oliphant and her son drove me about to see these ruins and the general

aspect of the place; and great as was my interest in themselves, the subjects of the time, the apparent ruin of
France, the chaos of government, the sense that no one
knew what another day might bring forth, occupied our
minds to the exclusion of all personal matters. Laurence,
however, had changed in aspect from the time of his first
reappearance in the world. He was sobered out of his first
elation; and in the return to his natural habits of life, and
recovery of a definite sphere of action—which, if it was
not all that he might once have hoped, was yet worthy of
himself and his training—had recovered his natural tone,
that of a man essentially of Society, and of the *grand jour*
and *plein air*, to use words in which the French have the
advantage of us,—of a large and full existence. He was
no longer displaced from all the common grooves of life, as
when I had last seen him, but had found an outlet for the
activities of his mind and being, and was strenuously and
wholesomely occupied in a manner of work quite suitable
to him. That he had again a home had no doubt also
something to do with this increased composure and tranquillity, notwithstanding that, at the special moment at
which I found them, Lady Oliphant had temporarily left
him to perform the duties of a mother to a family of
children, to whom she was in no way specially linked save
by that bounden duty of "living the life," which made her
hold herself at the service of all who needed help. I
remember that the things which struck me most at this
strange crisis of life, in the larger and lesser circle, were
the forlorn squalor and dirt of that once carefully brushed
and polished Paris in her humiliation — and the little
motherless boy thrusting out his little boot to be buttoned
to the white-haired lady, in whose instant readiness to
respond to his call, though he was none of hers, the child
had perfect trust.

The period of Laurence Oliphant's life spent in Paris
not only led to his marriage, and was thus for ever memorable in his existence, but was, I think, in itself a cheerful
episode, in which his circumstances and work were agreeable to him, and he had the comfort of feeling himself in
a congenial sphere, more or less living among his own

species, after many dangers and discomforts past. But it is indeed vain to speak of a man as living among his own species, however much this may externally have been the case, in face of the fact that in this very sphere, so strangely different from anything they could have known, he was living continually, not only under the influence, but at the command, of the homely and insignificant community at Brocton, and their extraordinary and mysterious head. Externally in most respects his position was a very desirable one. He was in the full tide of that lively intellectual life with which nothing long interferes in the French capital, and at the fountainhead of all that happened, seeing everything, to a certain extent influencing the course of affairs, deeply interested in the great problems that were beginning to work themselves out, and with a daily share in that very process, his good opinion courted on all sides—the very Head of the State, as will be afterwards seen, seeking his support, and opening his mind to so influential an agent as the correspondent of the 'Times'—who was not a mere 'Times' correspondent, but a man already universally known and distinguished in many ways. All these advantages were his, and his wit, his spirit, his prompt and ready judgment, were ready for them all. It was a position much more likely to favour the growth of a certain self-estimation and self-confidence than of humility and submission. It is almost inconceivable to turn from this picture to the image of the prophet, the obscure head of a little sect in America, a preacher and teacher little known, totally unacquainted with the life with which his disciple was surrounded, knowing nothing of its laws or its habits, ignorant of the merest elements of its economy, yet entirely dominating the existence and actions of that brilliant man of the world, and claiming, or at least exercising, absolute authority over him in all the complications of a career of which the despot had neither experience nor knowledge. Yet so it was; and in the next step in Laurence Oliphant's career, which opens up his most private life, and all his personal purposes and motives, we learn, almost with consternation, how unbroken was the bond which existed

between him and not only the Master but the other minor
authorities of the little commonwealth.

For it was in the end of this eventful year that he first
met in Paris the beautiful and delightful companion of
his future life. It is difficult to those who did not know
her to convey an idea of what Alice le Strange was.
" Not a woman at all, an angel ! " cried an enthusiast
who met her in a later portion of her life. It is perhaps
more wise, however, to say with Robert Browning, that
far more than any angelic similitude of which we know
nothing, she was herself—one of the most perfect flowers
of humankind, a young woman of an ancient and long-
established race, with all the advantages of fine and careful training, and that knowledge from her cradle of good
society, good manners, and notable persons, which is an
advantage beyond all estimation to the mind qualified to ·
profit by it. She was the daughter of Henry le Strange
of Hunstanton, in Norfolk, who was not only the representative of a long line of country gentlemen, but a man
of very high artistic tastes and knowledge, and who had
a great deal to do with the revival of ecclesiastical art
forty or fifty years ago: and of his wife, the daughter
of John Stewart of Drumin, Banffshire, an accomplished
woman, of great social distinction and popularity both
in London and Paris. She had also the unusual felicity
of what might be called almost a third parent in her
stepfather, Mr Wynne Finch (Mr le Strange having died
while his children were young), between whom and the
child, so full of brilliant originality, there existed a wonderful bond of mutual sympathy and devotion ; and to
whose constant understanding and care she owed much
of her development, as well as the happiness of a delightful home. Alice was the second daughter, and one of the
most attractive and charming of God's creatures, with
considerable beauty and much talent, full of brightness
and originality, sympathetic, clear-headed, yet an enthusiast, and with that gift of beautiful diction and melo-
dious speech which is one of the most perfect ever given
to man. She was a fine musician as well as a brilliant
conversationalist, and she had been accustomed all her

life to the best of English, or indeed it may be said
European, society, for Paris was as much her home as
London. It very rarely happens that friends, acquaintances, and lookers-on are all of one opinion concerning
any individual; but I have never heard of any diversity
of view in respect to Alice le Strange. I have heard her
spoken of in all kinds of quarters, and from the most fastidious critics in London down to the humble and homely
German colonists in Haifa, there has never been but one
voice. She was so full of "charm," that inexplicable
fascination which is more than beauty, that it was
possible her actual gifts might have been overlooked in
the pleasure of encountering herself, the combination of
them all; so that the beauty, the wit, the sweet vivacity,
the pure and brilliant intelligence, became so many delightful discoveries after the first and greatest, of finding one's self face to face with a being so gracious and
delightful.

It may be said of Miss le Strange, as of Laurence, that
she had fully tasted all the applauses and sweetnesses of
society. She was not a novice, overawed by curious and
entrancing religious experiences on the very threshold of
life, but had known what it was to be admired and wor-
shipped, and learned at once how exciting and how unsatisfactory are the triumphs of society. When she encountered in Paris, in the most natural way, the correspondent
of the 'Times,' so much talked of and so universally known,
she had arrived at the critical moment which in many fine
natures is decisive of all future fate. She was a little
weary even of admiration, tired of unprofitable life, longing for something better and higher than she had as yet
found. The benevolences of country life had not seemed
enough for her, as they do to some women, whom they
enable to hold the balance more or less even between the
dissipations of society and the requirements of serious
existence. She had not felt one side of her nature sufficiently indemnified for its temporary subjection to the other
by any such gentle round of duties. Years before, her
clear spirit had become involved in religious doubt, or
rather in that more general dissatisfaction with all the

remedies and panaceas proposed to her, in which many
young souls make secret shipwreck.   She wanted, like
Edward Irving, something more magnanimous, something
more exacting and authoritative, than the calm and indul-
gent Christianity which she generally met with.   Her
slight shoulders longed for a cross to be laid upon them,
and her impatient heart for some great thing to suffer or
to do.

The first approach to intimacy between the young
creature so prepared and ready for the influence of their
religious views, and the mother and son who were her
neighbours, was brought about, I believe, by an invitation
from Lady Oliphant to Miss le Strange to accompany her
on the long drives which she was in the habit of taking
daily; and Laurence soon had opportunities of meeting
and knowing the beautiful stranger.   It had, I gather
from an intimation in a letter, been conceded by the
supreme authorities in America some time before that an
embargo as to marriage which had been laid upon him
should be taken off—though whether he had been told of
this before he saw Alice le Strange I am unable to tell.
I am glad to say, however, that notwithstanding the
intense preoccupation with the most serious questions,
which is apparent in the letters from which I am about
to quote, and the evident fact that she had been instantly
initiated into the secrets of the new life, and had received
with enthusiasm and faith the lessons of her two ardent
instructors, yet there is every reason to believe that this
pair, so completely suited to each other, so formed and
adapted for union, fell honestly and spontaneously in love
with each other, in the old natural way, without any
arrière pensée.   It was their belief (as they thought, quite
novel and wonderful; but, in fact, the faith of all religious mystics, both Catholic and Puritan), that even in loving
each other, the chief thing to be considered was the service
each could do for God and for the benefit of the world,
and not any selfish happiness of their own.

In the spring of 1872, having had no warning of
the possibility of any such happy event, I received a
letter, written with all the triumph and elation of a for-

tunate lover, announcing the engagement, and the happiness which he said he had never expected should fall to his lot, and enclosing a photograph of the bright and delightful girl who was to share his life. I have mislaid this letter; but I am permitted to quote another of a very similar character, addressed to a much more important correspondent.

"PARIS, *March* 6, 1872.

"My happiness has come at last, one that I am sure you would approve, the sweetest and frankest nature that I ever met, in thorough sympathy with all my vagaries, which she utterly agrees with and understands—with the intellect of a man and the intuitions of a woman; in fact, the one person who, when I was not looking for her, was given to me, so that I could not mistake it. My mother felt from the first that she was the person. But I forget that you have been asking, Who? She is a daughter of the late Mr le Strange of Hunstanton, Norfolk, and a step-daughter of Wynne Finch's, who was in the House of Commons. She is twenty-six, and according to my taste very pretty; but that has nothing to do with it, only it fortunately happens so. I shall be so glad to present her to you some day; but I don't know when the marriage may take place: the same hand that arranged the first part will arrange the second."

He had excellent reason for the doubt which is visible in the last sentence of his letter; for no sooner had the intimation of the engagement been made, than the very depths were stirred against the betrothed pair. The opposition on the part of Miss le Strange's family and friends to her marriage with a man who was disinclined to make any settlements, and who even went so far as to object to her own fortune being settled upon herself, in order not to interfere with her freedom in using it as she pleased (it being no doubt understood that her motive was to dedicate it to the uses of the community at Brocton) was very natural—and their inability to understand his motives in thus risking her comfort in the eventualities of the future is comprehensible enough. But the difficulties put in the way of the lovers by the family were as nothing to the commotion stirred up in the distant community by the news. A fragment of a letter sent by a lady apparently high in the little commonwealth, and I believe addressed to Lady Oliphant, expresses in a way which would be almost ludicrous were it not so solemn, the consternation with which it was received. I may say that the members of Mr Harris's community had special names by which they were known within its bosom, and which I withhold; for it is difficult to restrain an uneasy inclination to smile at the fantastic and somewhat puerile conceit which renders a well-known and distinguished man like Laurence Oliphant unrecognisable amid the little world of nobodies, under a name which might have suited a sentimental schoolboy. It will be enough to use the initial W. in quoting from this letter. "Father," of course, is Mr Harris:—

"When Father left word that W. was no longer to hold himself from seeking a wife, we of course understood that he knew how terrible marriage was, and that unless through weakness or inability to stand alone, while passing through regenerative training, some had to marry, the rapid way to victory and use was through purification first and marriage afterwards, if God so ordered; and he [Harris] never dreamed of his [Laurence's] loving any one till they had been thoroughly tested by the discipline of the life. I am sure he will see this when he is free enough. He has come so near the centre of the Use, that he must, if he holds ground and retains his place, share in its sharpest trials, in its deepest martyrdoms. . . . If this dear girl can give him up utterly to God, and enter upon whatever discipline is before her, to prepare herself for the place and use in God's new kingdom, He will bring them together when and as He will, if they are for each other."

The pair were thus plunged into uncertainties and doubts, which filled the period of their engagement with trouble. The letters from which I am allowed to quote, form perhaps the most extraordinary correspondence that ever passed between a pair of lovers. Unfortunately the replies have not been preserved; but they are reflected more or less in the letters of Laurence, whose love and delight in his chosen bride are thus rudely brought to the question. It does not seem to have once entered into his mind to contest the judgment of the "Father." He implores his beloved to receive it with patience, to believe that it is the best, to trust in the perfect enlightenment of the leader, who cannot do wrong; he entreats her to write, making her own submission, and conciliating that potentate. When there comes an actual order to stop the marriage, he himself would seem to have had no idea of anything but complete obedience; and it is the most extraordinary spectacle to see the passionate lover pausing in all the enthusiasm of his hopes—which are not those of ordinary (or extraordinary) happiness with her, but of the immense advantage to the cause, of her work, and of the redoubled energy and force which her help will bring—to show himself and her what a still more excellent thing it will be to bear the reversal of all these hopes and make up their mind to separation, if their united submission and representations do not change the judgment of the autocrat and his counsellors. It is with this anxious desire that he begs of her to answer the letter above quoted, with a promise to obey its requirements. "Pour out your heart to her as if she were your mother," he says. "Tell her all without reserve. And if you feel you can, call her mother," he adds, wistfully. No more strange exhibition of the strength and weakness involved in such amazing relationships could be: for the faith is one which could move mountains, and the subjection almost too wonderful for words.

The correspondence throughout is, as has been said, a very extraordinary one. The constant struggle to regard their love as an abstract and spiritual passion, and subdue the warm human sentiment which is perpetually bursting forth; his happiness and pride in herself, and the sense that she is his, subdued into a boast of the efficiency of the service she is to be trained to render to the great cause; his eagerness that she should accept the yoke, which yet he has a thousand fears she will find heavy and painful; his anxious descriptions, excuses, deprecations of all criticism in respect to "the dear ones in America," and even the occasional sophistries he is betrayed into, in order that the reputation of these dear ones may be kept intact, —afford, as they reveal themselves, the most curious glimpse into the heart and deepest feelings of the man.

The dates, or rather no dates, are extremely confusing, and it is difficult to attempt any arrangement of the letters; but they were all written in the months of April and May 1872, when Miss le Strange was in London with her mother. The engagement had taken place in March, —too soon, he almost allows; but he had been unable to restrain the avowal of his feelings. Some time before this, however, it is apparent, the eager girl had been admitted into the sanctuary of his religious life, and had felt a new world of sacred joy and a new revelation of active service opened to her, which seems to have answered every longing of her nature, and filled her unsatisfied thoughts with light and love. He speaks to her fondly, as his little one, his nursling, his darling baby, won by him to another and better life, and his, not for time alone, but for eternity; but at the same time as a great instrument in God's hand, a leader of myriads yet to be. To reproduce all his fond instructions, directions, encouragements, and the checks which are if possible still more fond—adjurations to her to be a little dull if she can, to subdue her intellectual powers, and veil her natural brilliancy, and accept the conditions of the work before her—would be impossible; but I may quote a few paragraphs here and there. "What more intense happiness could the world give," he cries, in a sudden outburst of feeling, "than to see my darling overcoming all opposition, and, like some flaming angel, leading on the suffering womanhood of her world to new and unsuspected possibilities of victory?"

"Now that you are one of us, all your gifts belong to those with whom you are spiritually connected, far more

than they do to you. In one sense you efface your own
individuality, while in another the world will find you
more of an individual than ever, and you yourself will
be conscious of increased power and originality. In the
degree in which you can regard your power of pleasing as
belonging to all of us, and as not being in any sense your
own, will it increase, and will the joy which it will bring
you grow ; for you will feel that every one who comes under
the divine spell that you will thus be able to exercise,
comes towards the light, not towards you as an individual.
You will soon get to loathe and hate the idea that it could
ever have mattered to you whether people liked you or
not, considering the importance of what you want them to
like. You will become a divine decoy, luring with angelic
art those round whom the evil ones have woven their toils,
out of them, and getting them upon strong safe ground.
And the notion of taking any credit to yourself for thus
using the talents given you for this express purpose, will
become utterly repulsive to you, and so will be the idea
that the talents themselves are any more yours than mine.
You have thrown them into the common stock, darling,
and they will soon get so mixed up with the other people's,
that you won't know one from another. Besides, now that
you are of us, you will often be conscious of being helped
and upheld, and will therefore have nothing to be vain of.
I have sometimes been conscious that the most successful
things I have done have been owing to the strength I
derived from an internal *rapport* with Mr Harris, who was
fighting down influences opposing me at the time."

His anxiety to lead her to full comprehension of this
bond and willingness to enter into it calls forth many
persuasions and explanations, and anticipatory defences
on behalf of the central figure in the little world into
which Laurence had led his love. He bids her remember
that all the new light which has come to her, and the new
development of life which she has embraced so eagerly,
is owing to one man :—

" It may be that the great life, and knowledge what the

life is, which you are receiving, is to prepare you for the
strain your faith may be put to when you see him, and
have to accept him and the phenomena which surround
him, and which are almost sure to produce upon you a
painful effect. He himself may not be externally sympathetic, his way of communicating things may jar upon
you, and many things may happen which may even appear
faults or incredible. At those times, remember where you
would have been now without him, and that whatever the
mother or D. or I have received or have been able to tell
you, we owe to him."

On another occasion he again takes up the defence of
the prophet, who at this very moment was endeavouring
to postpone or break off the union upon which his heart
was so much set:—

"So far from his wishes being despotic, when we have
got into right relations with him, it becomes our greatest
pleasure and delight to take counsel with him, to draw
from him words of wisdom which we may try to carry
out; because, of course, the very nature of his life and
habits unfit him for the rough contact of the world. He
knows nothing whatever of society and its usages, and
wants the legs and arms and brains accustomed to the
workaday world to carry out and put into practice the
glorious moral truths that he has been the instrument
of imparting. In America, where life is rough, and our
little party are simple and remote from all worldly influences, he has come more out into the direction of the
labours and industries of every day. But here I have
always wondered how it was to be done, and now I am
beginning to hope that it may be done through us, if we
can hold ourselves humble and loving; for he 'senses' the
least coldness towards himself, and it stops everything.
We have each of us to feel more knit into his organism
than into each other. His functions are pivotal, and
we in a sense meet in him; for our breath is in some
mysterious way enfolded in his. All he knows of you
is through the conspiration of your united breaths. It

differs from the afflatus, of which Miss —— speaks so lightly, in certain particulars, which he will explain to you some day. But we all owe under God what we have and feel as the breath to him: the particular quality of it which we enjoy came first to him, and owing to our *rapport* with him we get the same. Nor would it be possible for any one to be in our breath who was not first in closest *rapport* with him and then with each other. It is the sensational bond of our union; it binds us together mysteriously and internally, and with a force which makes us feel so absolutely one that we can oppose to the world, when the time comes, a power before which everything must give way."

The extracts which follow are of a more general character, and I think that some of his expressions, especially about prayer, are very fine, and will find an echo in many hearts. In one instance he has been confiding to her some severe spiritual struggles of his own:—

" Doubtless this is a weakness in my own will, and I ask, Why is not my will stronger? and so get into the interminable circle from which there is no escape except by the very illogical but efficacious means of prayer. And then I always find myself praying about you. It seems as if I was of 'no account,' as the Yankees say, in comparison. It does not occur to me that it would be asking much to give one's soul for those who are chosen by God for His work, much less one's body."

On another occasion, speaking of prayer, and especially of prayer for her, he describes himself as " uplifted with such full breath-pulsations, encouraging me and telling me what to ask for you. In those moments divine suggestions come, the right prayer comes from God as well as goes to Him. It is, in fact, His way of conversing with us."

Once more I can find nothing parallel with this but John Knox's magnificent description of " the earnest and familiar talking with God." One may be quite sure Laurence did not get it from John Knox, with whose ideal he would have imagined himself to have no sympathy whatever, but direct from the understanding of the devout heart. Here is another fine apprehension of that more magnanimous view of Christian work and recompense which was dear to those visionary souls :—

"I was thinking to-day, darling, how it would help us, to realise that all pleasures, joy, and happiness must never be considered except as being the accident of service. The mistake of the popular theology is that it makes people desire their salvation for its own sake, instead of its being the accident of our working for other people. It seems very hard upon God that He cannot invest His service with delight without our having a tendency to drop the service and appropriate the delight. We have thus got into the habit of putting the cart before the horse. . . . We are not forbidden to enjoy intensely the pleasure He attaches to the fulfilment of our highest duties; but the love of those highest duties must be greater than that of the delight which they impart."

He returns again and again to the importance of her mission both to himself and to the world :—

"I felt a little uneasy and sad about something, probably my own evils and the low state from which I am unable to rise into a nearer union with God. It is so hard to keep the interior part of one where it should be, all the time one is in the world; and it often makes me feel very unhappy to think that I am not more spiritual and conscious of divine influences. Then I think, selfishly, if I had you to help me I should rise higher, and get from your strength and support what no one else could give. By degrees you would come to know all my weak points, for my whole desire would be that you should know where I fail, and what my most secret and insidious faults are."

Speaking again of former religious movements, he adds :—

"There is a particular feature in them—the women played no part, or scarcely any at all; and this I believe to be the chief reason of their failure. And this is why, my own darling, I cherish you so for humanity's sake, because I believe that when you come into child-states, and thus become susceptible to the divine influence, which cannot reach you while the old self-hood bars the door, you will become conscious of deep inner truths, not perhaps convertible into language, before at all events they have borne fruit into acts, and these may be the basis of the new feminine part of the religious structure." The battle, he adds, will be made easier for her by the preliminary work of others in America, and "especially when you recognise the fact that you are engaged in a stupendous work of religious and moral reform, which is destined by its irresistible, if slow and painfully developed, influence to penetrate the hardness of the world's selfishness. It will take a long time; we may never live to see it. But I feel as sure as of my own existence that the future of the human race lies in the hands of the members of it; that it is by no apparently miraculous interposition that its regeneration is to be accomplished, but by the steady undermining of the principle of selfish love, which holds everything in an iron grasp now, by the more powerful principle of martyr love; and the whole of what is called the scheme of redemption lies in the hint which Christ's life and death gave us of this great truth."

One cannot but feel a curious sense of the strange misapprehension mingling with so much fine spiritual perception, which could make Laurence think his own struggles to maintain the impossible rule of his creed in respect to marriage, and his bride's conflict with her relations as to the disposal of her money, to be carrying out the "hint" contained in the life and death of the divine example of all martyrdoms. This is the thread of weakness throughout; but it is not without parallel in the reflections of many deeply religious minds, unable to perceive the enormous difference of magnitudes, or to believe how little more than personal at the best, if not purely fantastic,

some of these struggles were. This, however, is to be
taken here only as a parenthesis. He has more to say of
the woman's share in the religious work which he believes
to be before her,—indeed the letters are full of this subject, which recurs again and again :—

" I am feeling more and more the need of your teaching, things that you alone in the world can teach me.
My whole nature is standing still till I can learn through
you what the woman through her ' word ' alone can teach.
I feel this more and more every day. It will not be from
your brain or through your intellect, darling, that those
deeper knowledges which I am thirsting for will come, and
those truths which, when I have assimilated them, will
give me new power for influencing my fellow-creatures.
If in some things you are my child, in others I have got
to become yours ; and this is the moment I am longing
for, when I can drink in and absorb from you the mysteries
of a love which the world knows nothing of yet—when I
can learn from you what I can never find out by myself.
This is why I want you to press on, not because I want
this moment selfishly to come, but because it will enable
us both to come into our uses ; and I feel and know I shall
be so much more powerful for good in the world. Only
believe this to be the case, do not reason about it, take it
for granted for the time, that you have it in your power to
work out these wonders in my organism, almost to change
and renew it, to double all my powers and faculties : and
whether you understand it or not, the thought may be a
stimulus to you, and may prevent you from losing ground
by doubts. I tell you this, darling, in order that you may
feel the additional responsibility as an additional reason
for keeping down the part of your nature that you have
been accustomed to respect and rely upon. It is just the
other part that you have never developed that I respect
and rely upon, and you can only develop this in the degree
in which you keep the other back. The great dual principle of the world is love and wisdom, and the latter can
only be developed through the former. The intellect is
entirely dependent upon the affections. Good comes first,

truth afterwards. Moral truth cannot be discovered by a
bad man, and hence the only way to obtain it is through
developing the emotional and intuitive faculties of our
nature."

Whether Miss le Strange had any difficulty in accepting
the supremacy of the spiritual leader so warmly and tenderly, yet with so many deprecations, pressed upon her,
there is no evidence to show. She did accept the postponement of the marriage with a sweet and humble acquiescence for which he thanks her with enthusiasm; and she
wrote to the autocrat, putting herself in his hands, and
unfolding the secrets of her pure spirit without any signs
of reluctance, as was required from her. What is apparently the *brouillon* of this letter is enclosed with the correspondence from which I have quoted, and I extract from
it a few passages to show how this clear and beautiful
spirit yielded to the yoke:—

" When W. told me yesterday to write to you and ask
you for that help which I have learned to know you will
give me, it was at first difficult for me to tell whether the
hesitation I felt came more from the sense of the impertinence there might be in forcing myself with all my wants
before you, or from the irrevocable and solemn nature of
the plunge I should be making into engagements that I
had felt and professed myself willing to undertake, but
had not till that moment had the courage to invoke. A
few moments showed me that my cowardice on my own
account was greater than my scruple on yours. And you
will, I trust, forgive me for acting upon this conviction, and
trying to tell you why I appeal to you."

Then follows an account of the spiritual difficulties of
many years, which were principally caused by extreme
horror of and pity for the suffering in the world, and
inability to understand how a God of love and goodness
could permit it to be—difficulties which had driven her to
doubts of God's existence, or at least of His benevolence,
had made her for a long time incapable of prayer, and

weighed her down with a miserable sense of impotence in
the face of all those problems of sorrow and pain. She
did, however, she tells Mr Harris, endeavour to do what
she could for others; but always with the intolerable doubt
whether there was any good in it, or if her exertions were
of the least use. She was also hampered by another fact,
which she states with delightful *naïveté* :—

" I could not see my way clear, or feel sure whether I
was doing more harm than good half the time that I
worked for others, and a very great difficulty grew in
me that I hardly knew how to combat rightly; it was,
that the great love that grew up around me among all
the people with whom I came in habitual contact made
it almost impossible to test the purity of my desire to
do right, or to know how far I was independent of this
flow of approbation and affection, that made it seem so
much easier than of old to be working for others."

The beautiful soul, so wrapped round in admiration and
love that she could scarcely believe in her own disinter-
ested charity, is a rare spectacle in this world; and it is
seldom that such a being opens her lips, almost with a soft
complaint of this flattering atmosphere of universal sunshine, and of all the influences that worked together to
raise in her the noble discontent of a new spiritual life.
She goes on :—

" And so I came to know W., and saw for the first time
some one who not only held the highest views I had ever
imagined on the subject of our responsibilities, but had
found it possible to work them out into a life much
purer and more full of use than anything I had thought
compatible with the human nature I had seen around
me. I was beginning to take in the idea of how that
life had become possible to him and to others, when I
began also to know that I was ceasing to feel for him
the mere respect and distant affection with which the
great beauty of his nature had inspired me. I was
horribly disturbed, knowing that to go forward without

feeling ready to fight in the same battle, reckless of consequences, with him, would be doing a wicked wrong to
him; and yet not knowing how I should tell whether or
not the increased willingness I felt to devote my life to
this ceaseless labour was fed by the personal feeling. It
was a different difficulty from any I had dealt with yet,
for love for others, which had guided me before, was this
time bound up with that new vision of a possible happiness to myself; and I was at a loss, in a way I had never
been before, to know what was right and what was wrong,
while this terrible fear hung over me, that I might be
imperilling the happiness of the only man of whom I had
ever felt that I could love him rightly. So I ventured in
this strait to pray for power not to do wrong; and from
that moment the doubt was taken away, and without quite
foreseeing what was going to be, I went about with a calm
and even conviction that all would come right in its own
way, and that I need not be afraid. I was never in all
my life so thankful for anything as for the sense of an
answer to my prayer for knowledge how to do and feel
right. So learning gradually from W. how he had been
taught to serve, I glided into the moment when I pledged
myself to serve side by side with him, and, like him, without counting the cost.

"And now I must make a clean breast to you, as he has
told me to do, of the bad thing in me that I had to fight,
so soon as I realised the completeness of the discipline I
must be willing to undergo. There is no kind or quality
of work that I could ever feel it much of a trial to do; the
sense of possessing property as a thing personal to myself
is one I have never hugged, having lived through so many
times when the power or the ease that people associate
with it were all so impotent to affect me. And I have
gradually for some years been keeping more and more
aloof from prejudices among my friends that had a tendency to hamper my right action, so that I can face,
without any very pressing anxiety, the dislike they may
feel to my working out my life in a way of which the
strangeness will alarm them; while the hope of being
allowed to join in an organised combination of effort for

living in pure goodness and working for others, is so
blessed and unlooked-for a change from the hopelessness
of permanent results in which I have struggled on till
now, that I could not waver for a moment in my desire to
be allowed to make myself fit for joining it. One only
thing has been a terrible pang to me, the giving over of
my own judgment in questions of moral judgment to any
human authority. It is so absolutely new and incomprehensible an idea to me, that any outer test should
supplant, without risk to itself and to me, the inner test
of my actions that my conscience affords, that when
—seeing the impossibility of working successfully with
others without giving practical proof that I can obey
without criticism of the command, I decided to shut my
eyes and leave the seeing to you—I felt as though I were
putting out the one clear light that had been given to me
for my guidance, and that I had been living so many years
to God to purify; as though I had suddenly thrown my
own compass overboard, and was left with my whole life
exposed to the chances of a sea of uncertainty, and with
the grim question asking itself over and over again in
my heart, whether I were not doing wrong? I answered
myself, at first more mechanically than with any conviction, that anyhow one thing in me was assuredly
wrong, the want of humility that added the sting to the
anxiety, and that, in some way I could not quite yet
understand, the only thing by which I could break this
pride in pieces must end in being right. So I am dealing
to the best of my present powers with this mischief, asking
for patience when the wonder at not understanding comes
over me, and settling always to some work to keep my
strength afloat when the danger comes. And I tell you
of it, that you may learn all I can find to say of the
weakness and faults that will want what help you will
give them, and not because you shall ever find in me
any but the most absolute submission both in deed and
will. I hope and believe I shall have bruised even this
inward resistance long before it could run the risk of
throwing upon you or any one else any part of the
suffering which ought to belong only to me.

"So now I ask to put myself and ourselves under your direction in all matters. You will determine what proof we must acquire to ourselves that we hold our happiness in absolute fief to our duty; in what manner, when you think it well, we shall inaugurate the joining of our lives; and the degree in which we can usefully comply with or disregard the prejudices of my family and friends on the subject of performing the marriage ceremony, and disposing of the property belonging to me."

She ends by stating the amount of this last, and that some of it was invested in America, "so that I will, on receiving your instructions, make my part of that easily payable to you for any purpose to which you might see fit to apply it." In accordance with the intention here expressed, I am authorised to say that the whole of her property was placed unreservedly in the hands of Mr Harris, with the result which her family had anticipated.

This extraordinary letter of course disposes of the assertions often afterwards made by both, that their subjection to Harris, and his command of their property and actions, were merely the authority of superior wisdom and love over grateful and affectionate disciples, — the power of suggestion, which, through their sympathy and perfect trust, became acceptable to their own thoughts, and led them to resolve and do, from their own impulse and will, what he had put into their minds in the shape of loving advice. Yet there was enough of truth in it, I imagine, to justify to themselves these assertions; for it was their first endeavour to make the will of this absolute friend their own, and so to bring themselves into subjection to it, that its dictates might in a sense be considered as their own actions, freely inspired and adopted. The sophistry of such statements was either unconscious, or they felt it one of those offices of filial love which devoted children sometimes take up, assuming the responsibility upon their own shoulders, of a step of doubtful policy recommended by their parents, rather than allow them to bear the blame. The following letter from Laurence to his betrothed will show exactly what he thought in this

respect. Their marriage, as has been seen, had been arbi-
trarily delayed, after it had been decided upon, by letters
from America, and they were for some time left in doubt
whether it might not be broken off altogether; notwithstanding which, he warmly approves of her determination
to describe the postponement to her family as arising from
" no outward dictation, but from the results of our own
experiences."

" The more responsibility of this sort we can take off
Father the better. He has only been obliged to appear
dictatorial to those who were unable to act for themselves,
either from weakness or blindness; but he desires nothing
more than that we should decide all these things for ourselves, and it would not surprise me at all for him to say
that we are able to get our life from above without asking
him as to how the next step is to be taken; and it would
be so satisfactory to be able to answer those who accuse
him of tyranny, and us of a blind and servile obedience,
by saying that from first to last we have acted not under
his dictation but according to the promptings of our own
consciences, and independently of any one. Of course,
if in doubt, we might ask his advice; but you see he
explains in his letter there is never any question of
surrendering one's private judgment. It seems to me
self-evident that the man who had hit upon the great idea
not of attempting to apply Christianity in its literal and
practical working to the existing conditions of society, but
fundamentally to change these conditions so as to make
Christianity practicable in society, required a certain
amount of obedience from those who agreed to try the
experiment with him without having his light as to how
it was to be done."

I do not say that this piteous plea of the vassal soul is
a thing to be admired, or even without a little difficulty
excused, in a man so honourable and high-minded as
Laurence Oliphant. It is one of the things so extraordinary as to be incredible if it were not actually and
undeniably true. But the vague sophistry of the argu-

ment, the desperate clinging at all costs to the spiritual
despot, and the pathetic anxiety to justify him and take
all the blame that may follow upon their own shoulders,
is touching as well as intolerable. The ineffable infatua-
tion, folly, or faith which breathes in the peradventure,
"It would not surprise me at all for him to say that we
are able to get our life from above without asking him,"
is far beyond the reach of poetic invention. The most
daring dramatist would scarcely venture to put such an
utterance into a human mouth.

And this almost fatuous veneration and admiration was
called forth by a man who, the speaker well knew, was
like enough to inspire his refined and delicate Alice with
little personal sympathy, and who, even to himself, was
perhaps more love-inspiring at a distance than close at
hand. One of his strongest desires was to persuade Harris
to visit him in Paris; yet of this, though he looked forward
to it as an honour and delight, he spoke as follows:—

"Father's presence is an awful pressure, though it is a
blessed one. Because he feels our states so terribly, the
watchfulness over ourselves has to be unceasing. So it
should be always; but somehow I am so miserably finite,
and I do not realise the divine presence checking me so
much as the human one."

Hence, by that subtle influence of "feeling their states
so terribly," the prophet kept them in awed subjection
while in his presence, as well as absolute obedience out
of it—a sway scarcely comparable to any other tyranny
known to man.

The same sort of sophistry, justified by a reasoning
more or less Jesuitical, yet not absolutely untrue, occurs
in the following letter to Mr Hamon le Strange on the
subject of his sister's fortune, written after the marriage:—

"I observe from your letter to Alice that you are under
an entire misapprehension in regard to my financial position in America. I do not now, and never have belonged
to any company or community in that country in any other

sense than that of living among people I like. There are no
deeds of partnership or written agreements of any sort or
kind existing between us, much less involving any joint liability for debt. So far as property goes, we are neighbours
and nothing more. If I have not held my property in my
own name, it was not because it did not absolutely belong to
me, but because, as a foreigner, I could not hold it; and I
was fortunate enough to have friends I could trust, who
held it for me. . . . The notion that I belong to a society
which has all things in common, or that I approve of the
principle of depriving the owners of property of the privileges, duties, or responsibilities attaching to it, is one of
the many false statements accumulated and believed on
no better foundation than that of common rumour, which
has constructed a fabric of most incredible falsehood and
fiction as to what we do and what we believe, and which
the love of newspaper gossip has spread far and wide.

"At the same time, the views which I hold in regard to the necessity of social and moral reform in the
world, and the possibility of carrying them out—which
Alice, after a thorough and careful investigation, fully
shares — are not commonly entertained, partly because
they are not known or understood, partly because they
are not theoretical but practical, and partly because the
prejudice is very firmly rooted in the world that any
attempt to improve it is Utopian—all attempts hitherto
in that direction having failed. One principle which I
think thoroughly unsound in the law of England is that
which treats women as mere chattels, and deprives them
on marriage of any right to hold property. I could not
agree to Alice dispossessing herself of that faculty which
the law of America recognises, and in respect to which
there was a recent debate in the House of Commons,
which I consider as involving a principle in regard to
women's social status which is the foundation of any
reform of the present social system. . . . You will now,
I hope, understand that any property which, in accordance
with American law, I make over by deed to Alice as her
own separate and distinct possession, is hers now and in
the event of my death, without liability of any kind or

sort; while besides, in accordance with my strongest feelings of what is due to her, I insist upon her remaining
absolute mistress of all she inherited from her father, and
investing it as she pleases. Beyond this, she has a right
to a third of the rest of my property should I die; but
her chance of what this may amount to depends, as in the
case of any other American wife, upon the success of my
financial undertakings. In regard to this, I can only say
that I hold it as the sacred duty of every man to invest
his capital in such a careful way as may give him the
best power to do his duty by his fellow-men."

The most careful way of investing his property so that
he might do his duty by his fellow-men was, in the eyes
of Laurence, to place it under the administration of Mr
Harris in the little domain at Brocton; and the freedom
of Alice to dispose of her money as she thought fit, meant
also, as has been seen, the placing of it in the same hands.
Nevertheless, as it was possible at a later period to reclaim this property, or part of it, it must have been a fact
that Laurence at least retained a claim to the land he had
bought. So that by a bewildering possibility of argument
both things were true—the first, that he had bought land
in America, and held it as his own; and the other fact,
that everything he had was in the hands of Harris. Few
men thus fight for the power of depriving themselves of
their property, yet, by a twist of the Scriptural precept
not to let their right hand know what their left hand does,
conceal the self-sacrifice under a pretence of profitable in-
vestment. But yet one would have preferred that there
should have been no double meaning, and that the spirit
being so, the letter should not have been strained to convey a different impression to uninstructed ears.

I must not omit a curious accidental light thrown by
this correspondence on the attitude of Laurence long
before, at the time of his first connection with Harris,
which has been already referred to. While he is exhort-
ing his betrothed to think less of the intellectual qualities
of her nature and to cultivate quietness, and even the
possibility of being considered dull and stupid (he might

R

as well have said ugly and awkward, both being impossible), "It would do you no harm," he says, "to go through a little course of this"—

"Just as I did during the first two sessions when I went into the House of Commons, and my friends thought I was going to electrify the House and the country—when I was forbidden to open my lips, and finally was set down as a parliamentary failure, it having been the ambition of my life to be a parliamentary success, and I being conscious that I had it in me to be one, if I were only allowed to try."

What enormous responsibility the man took upon himself who ventured to give such commands! and how inconceivable is the submission which a man like Laurence, eager for every kind of distinction, full of capacity, having just attained the position he had looked forward to for years, gave to the obscure Swedenborgian preacher, the uncultured American, who thus assumed over him the authority of God Himself. The act of submission above quoted of a second brilliant and impatient intellect, full of independent sentiment, almost wilful in the previous stages of her development, adds to the wonder with which we contemplate this extraordinary submission. It seems impossible to believe that a mere vulgar impostor could ever have gained such an ascendancy; and more respectful to these two disciples, as well as to the others who submitted to his sway, is the supposition that Harris, at least at this stage, was no impostor at all, but believed in his own mission, as well as that he must have been endowed with extraordinary and imposing gifts of character to give him such power. But the possession of power like this, so much beyond that which should be entrusted to any man, must be more demoralising to the holder of it than to its subjects. They suffered earthly loss, and were subjected to much keen and some contemptuous criticism, but with this compensation, that their extraordinary sacrifices and renunciations gained them a unique position in the world, and surrounded them with interest and sympathy wherever they went; whereas their prophet could do nothing but fall, fall from his high estate into the abyss where broken idols and exploded pretensions must infallibly go.

The objections of Miss le Strange's family were finally set aside, and the marriage took place eventually with no breach of the natural ties of affection, though without any formal approval or sanction from her relations. The objections of the community in America, and specially of its head, were more difficult to overcome; but that too was at last accomplished: and in June 1872 the marriage of Laurence Oliphant and Alice le Strange took place at St George's, Hanover Square. It is impossible to enter into other circumstances of this union, which make it more remarkable still than all that had gone before, but which belong entirely to the privacies of individual life. There were, as the reader will see after, breaches and troubles in it which involved much suffering, through the direct influence of the authority to which both had bound themselves; but the bond was always one of the purest affection and complete sympathy, and it ended as it began, in beautiful and perfect union.

Laurence retained his position as correspondent of the 'Times' for more than a year after this happy event, and I think that the entire period of his residence in Paris was a bright and pleasant chapter in his much-diversified career. His influence was considerable and his popularity great, and his knowledge of everybody who was worth knowing in Parisian society gave him great advantages, both political and social. I understand that it was through his representations that the annoyances of the passport system were finally given up; and he told me himself a curious story of a proposal made to him on the part of M. Thiers, who was anxious to secure the support of the 'Times' at almost any price, to which Laurence responded that the way to secure the support of the 'Times' was to make the Government measures known to its representative, and to secure his approval—which on these conditions he would not fail to express publicly. There was a certain amount of jest in the story as he told it; but there can be no doubt that he was much consulted by M. Thiers, and that the half in jest of such an anecdote is often whole in earnest to those who know.

There is another delightful and characteristic anecdote of this period which must be told, though I am a little uncertain about dates. A revolutionary meeting was about to be held at Lyons, concerning which considerable alarm was entertained, and of which Laurence was anxious to be able to indicate the tendency and real danger or futility. He had apparently thought it of sufficient importance to go down to Lyons, on purpose to see what could be seen. The prefect, to whom he went on his arrival, advised him strongly against attending it, and finally declared that he must take the responsibility on himself, as he, the prefect, could not undertake to guarantee the safety even of his life. But this was no reason against the enterprise for Laurence, to whom at all times "the danger's self was lure alone." He went accordingly, and gained admittance among the crowd; but just as the proceedings were beginning some one got wit of his presence, and rising, warned the assembly that an emissary from that brutal English journal the 'Times' was among them. An immediate tumult arose, and cries of "Cherchons-le! à la mort! à la rivière!" resounded. As may be supposed, Laurence immediately joined himself to the demonstrators, jumping to his feet in overwhelming indignation, and shouting with the best. "Cherchons-le! cherchons-le!" he cried; "moi, je le connais de vue!" He got out safely, it is scarcely needful to say, under cover of this zeal for his own discovery. An acute critic suggests in respect to this story that his accent would at once have betrayed him; but certainly in the excitement of the moment Laurence was not the man to think of such a risk, and perhaps there were Englishmen —or at least foreigners—among the democrats of Lyons, as there are in most places under the sun.

There is also a curious story, which was related to me in much detail by a very competent authority, which tells how Laurence, being present at a *séance* given by a then well-known medium in Paris, was somehow fascinated by the man's looks, supposing he must have met him before, so familiar did his face appear. Though this did not prove to be the case, he got into conversation with the medium, and walking part of the way home with him, was persuaded to go into the rooms of his new acquaintance, where he remained for some time talking over their mutual experiences of the unseen, which always interested him so strongly. At last the medium seemed to recollect something which accounted for the sense of previous acquaintance in both their minds. "Now that I think," he said, "I have surely come across your name in some way not long ago. Let us look if it was among these letters," and he brought out a number of letters, which he laid upon the table at which they were sitting. Laurence, who had long ceased to have any faith in spiritual manifestations of this kind—that is to say, that he believed them to be spiritual phenomena indeed, but produced by the lowest and basest of earth-haunting spirits — turned the letters over with languid curiosity, until startled by finding a letter to himself addressed in the handwriting of his father, who had been dead for nearly twenty years! The story is a thrilling one; but there is no doubt, had such a startling proof of the reality of any medium's pretensions been genuine, the world would have heard it in all details. It is a specimen of the fabulous legends that accumulate around any history in which the occult and unseen are touched, in whatever way.

In 1873, as abruptly as before, and in consequence of a summons from America, the household was broken up, the post abandoned, and the family, consisting of Lady Oliphant, Laurence, and his wife, suddenly departed from Paris, and set out across the Atlantic for the home at Brocton, from whence the guidance of all their actions came.

CHAPTER X.

LABOUR AND SORROW—DISENCHANTMENT.

IT was in the summer of 1873 that Laurence returned to
the settlement at Brocton, to the little community immersed
in farm-work and daily toil, with his mother, who knew
what awaited her there, and his beautiful young wife, who
did not know. Whether the others felt their hearts sink
when they took Alice into that strange sphere, or whether
they were too secure in her faith and enthusiasm to fear
anything, I cannot tell; but one would imagine that the
actual entry into a form of existence so entirely unknown
to her must have been attended — at least to those who
were her guides and leaders, and especially to her husband,
who had first directed her thoughts thither, and held it
before her as the haven and resting-place from all trouble
—with much tremor and searchings of heart. The almost
apologetic explanation which Laurence had already made
of the "rough and simple life," of "Father's" complete
ignorance of the usages of society, &c., show that he
himself was by no means assured of the effect it would
produce upon his wife. Of all this, however, we have no
record.

Neither can I give, nor would it be possible to give if I
could, any further picture of the community and actual
circumstances which awaited the pilgrims. But I may
here quote a letter written by Mr Harris himself, which
has been lent to me, and which gives a description of, at
all events, the exterior circumstances of the community.
It was written in answer to an article upon Brocton which
had appeared in a New York paper. In the beginning of
this letter he protests, as any English gentleman might do,
against the tricks of the newspaper correspondents, who
thrust themselves upon him, and spied upon all his proceedings, which is one point upon which he will have the
reader's full sympathy. But he goes on to give a succinct
account of himself, which is interesting, and in which he
assumes the attitude of a man withdrawn from the world,

yet profoundly sensitive to every prick and touch of vulgar contact. "They are especially painful," he says, "at the present moment, when, having been relieved of my various trusts for others, I have withdrawn into private life." The date is 8th February 1871, so that, whatever the trusts were from which he had been relieved, his position in respect to his own immediate society was still that which we have seen. "As our beloved country," he continues, "sinks daily into deeper profligacy and corruption, and the press becomes more infernal, I shrink more and more from that contact which is caused by publicity. Experience has taught me that this generation is only to be saved by the chastisements and just judgments of God."

"I will only say here for you (but not for the public), that there is here no 'community'; every friend controls his own property and manages his own affairs. Some of the brothers carry on business on their individual account; others in co-operation or partnership. There is no unity other than that which is the result of mutual assistance in seeking to fulfil the requirements of a pure self-denying life. So of creeds and covenants. There is no external bond of religious union; ... the spiritual influences that in earlier times wrought out the cloister and cathedral now work into finance and political economy, with mechanics and agriculture, with whatever promotes the social wellbeing of mankind. Hence I am content, as a reformer and religious teacher, to be merely a business man.

"The Church must become secular if it would be a saving power. When I became convinced that my proceedings and writings, if continued, would result in a new sect, I shrank appalled from the sin and curse of adding a new 'Ism' to the others, and determined that, God helping me, I would simply 'Live the life,' and try to help others to do the same. Beginning on this basis of unselfishness, and filled with the one thought, 'Christianity must be lived as a social life,' friends gathered around me unsought, asking to become members of my family, and interested in my pursuits. Since 1860 I have carried out these ideal principles in their application to a world of practical affairs.

My friends to whom I imparted my thoughts and methods, and the spirit in which they originated, are embodying them here, in Europe, in Asia—preaching not with words but with works. Finally, this phase of my life being ended, I retire from human co-operation with my friends, that they may acquire the power that comes from that independent exercise of gifts. Each of them grasping the enlarged function, goes on to become trained in social use, and so to attract and to impart to others.

"If you should pass this way, you will find, if you need refreshment, that my restaurant at Brocton Junction has a reputation for pure food and drink, and for moderate charges, not surpassed between Chicago and New York. If you stay one night, the Salem-on-Erie hotel, close at hand, will give you, under a modest roof, all the pure kindness and comfort of a home.

"If you step into the nurseries and greenhouses close by, you will see the Gospel in fair vines or multitudinous flowers; while in the neighbouring wine-vaults you can taste from 10,000 gallons of pure wine of last year's vintage, absolutely free from any foreign or deleterious elements. This comprises the bulk of my business at this place. Your old friend B—— resides within half a mile, and you will find him prompt, practical, and kindly as ever, busy with flocks and herds, with grape-vines and a public laundry, which he practically oversees.

"Our genius, in fine, old friend, is domestic, and delights in quiet privacy. We eschew all notoriety. We never proselytise. In this world, nothing in the long-run, nothing tells but work. The homely actual receives and hides the shining ideal, as the splendours and warmth of summer are reborn in humble plants and springing grass. Yet doubtless the ideal will in time transform the actual to its own image. 'For now are we the sons of God, and it doth not yet appear what we shall be.'

"I came in wearied from overseeing my men pressing hay in bales, and seeing the article in the [New York] 'World,' sat down to express my regret at its appearance,"

This modest version of the life of the prophet and his friends is strangely unlike the shadow of the community as seen through the letters of Laurence to his betrothed bride. The autocrat who, across the breadth of the Atlantic, issued his orders to marry or not to marry to his faithful disciple: to whom the new member was impelled and besought to write offering absolute obedience, and placing her property at his disposal; the "Father" whose presence was a "terrible pressure, though a blessed one" —appears in a very different guise from this benevolent patriarch with his flocks and herds, his vintages and his "friends." Yet it must be remarked that Laurence, too, used the same enigmatical and metaphorical expressions when speaking of him, asserting his own independence both in respect to life and money. It is difficult to reconcile the two points of view—it is not, indeed, I fear, possible, except by those principles of mental reservation and equivocal statement which one is grieved to find in the utterances of honourable men. Laurence no doubt considered himself justified by his strong conviction that the commands of Harris were not of himself but from God, and that, in the same way, the money confided to the prophet was directly in the hands of Providence. How Mr Harris justified to himself the discrepancy between the exoteric and esoteric view is another question. It must also be remembered that in the latter case there was some legal safeguard by which afterwards it was possible to reclaim the property,—which is so much in favour of the external claim of independence, if it were not contradicted by every word and thought of the correspondence quoted in the previous chapter.

We might easily form imaginary pictures of the arrival of the party in this practical little community, so entirely occupied with its vines, its corn, its flocks, its hay, and all the matter-of-fact work which was practically its gospel to the world. How helpless must the two ladies have felt, who knew nothing of these things, and especially the young and inexperienced disciple, to whom everything was new, and who brought the glamour of enthusiasm in her eyes to see a use beyond that of all her previous know-

ledge in the homely necessities of existence, the work of
the household, for which alone (and that so badly at first)
she would be qualified. How they must have been in the
way of the busy workers, how little their true gifts and
capabilities could have been wanted, in what elementary
labours they must at first have been employed! I have
heard great indignation expressed over the fact that Lady
Oliphant washed the pocket-handkerchiefs of the settlement
—indignation in which I scarcely feel able to share. For
that being the way of salvation, what better could the poor
lady do? She could not superintend the pressing of hay
into bales, or the cultivation of the vine; and as for Alice,
it is impossible to imagine what she could have been good
for at first, except for offices which any little untrained
housemaid could have done better. They had no time to
hear her talk, or to listen to her music; they knew nothing
of the books, the people, the thoughts which had occupied
her life. Had Laurence married a devout dairymaid, it
would have been far more to the purpose: that he should
have brought so fair a flower of perfect civilisation and
ladyhood among this bustling rustic community must have
been embarrassing on all hands. To be sure, there were
one or two English ladies there before her; but in the case
of each of these, no doubt, as in hers, not only was the
first step a terrible one to themselves, but (to do justice on
all sides) a most troublesome one to the organisers of all
those untrained and unaccustomed candidates for work.

It is, however, quite unnecessary to make fancy pictures of these difficulties. Lady Oliphant herself gives
a simple record of their occupations a little later on;
and in the meantime it would appear from the letters of
Laurence that he and his wife were at first permitted
a period of holiday with little or nothing exacted from
them. I am enabled to trace through his letters to Mr
Blackwood something of the second beginning made by
him of life in Brocton under his new circumstances. It
is, however, a mistake to speak of his life in Brocton, for
though called back there for the service of the community,
he was not allowed to be more than an occasional visitor
in the place where his wife and mother were established.

He would seem to have plunged almost at once into commercial affairs in New York. The farm-labourer phase was over,—not even a divinely inspired autocrat could think of putting him through that discipline again; and financial operations of one kind or other would seem to have been the occupation determined on as most suitable for him — operations which, as the reader will see, did not at all prepossess him in favour of the New York commercial world. The first letter I find is as follows. That it was written not very long after his arrival, is whimsically indicated by the stamp on his paper of " Parkins and Gotto." He had not exhausted, it would appear, the stock brought with him.

"BROCTON, CHAUTAUGUA, 22d Sept. [1873].

" I ought to have written to you before to have thanked you for the cheque you were so good as to send me, but I was in hopes of being able to enclose in my acknowledgment of your liberality another article. Somehow I have not been able to manage it, as my time has been so much cut into. I have been spending three weeks on Long Island, at a lovely spot about thirty miles from New York, and the manners and customs of the natives afforded material, especially as there was a camp-meeting and a revival going on in the immediate neighbourhood, where I saw a young woman perform spiritual gymnastics that would have beaten Marie Alacoque; and indeed, if people are going to make pilgrimages to every place where parties are cutting what appear supernatural capers, they will have their hands full. All this was suggestive of a good deal, but I wanted quiet, as it is a subject which pretty soon lands one out of one's depth. Moreover, I was fishing, boating, bathing, and otherwise putting my wife and myself into robust conditions; added to which, perpetual journeys down the loveliest of island waters into that den of gamesters New York, where I fished up some Wall Street experiences that may also some day be worked up with other phenomena, supernatural, diabolic, &c., of the times. Since I was there, indeed the day I

left, some of the scoundrels began to smash, and I trust
they may continue to do so until not one dollar is left
standing on another. The special occupation which my
destiny leads me for the moment to follow is in the midst
of these ruffians. There I have to make money, and see
if it can be done cleanly. Meantime I have come back
here for a breath of pure air, and I may possibly go hence
to Canada before returning to New York. My mother
and wife are both very well, and desire me to give their
kindest regards to yourself and Mrs Blackwood. The
latter is very happy, and says she finds here at Brocton
all she came for, and enjoys the general novelty and
brightness of American life."

The next letter is entirely occupied with his commercial experiences :—

" The moral side of this financial crisis is most curious.
There is scarcely an instance of a prominent fraudulent
bankrupt who has not made a show of piety the mask
under which he ensnared his victims.   X—— G——, for
instance, has got an island on Lake Erie specially devoted
as a sanatorium to invalid parsons, who are kept there
free of expense on condition that they force his ' wild-cat '
railway bonds down the throats of their congregations,
and so on in every instance. Presidents of Young Men's
Christian Associations, founders of theological seminaries,
Sunday-school teachers, secretaries to charitable associations, and the leading elders of various denominations are
among the principal defaulters. I was thinking of showing it all up in the 'Times,' but have been too busy.
Fortunately, so far I have kept clear of the hypocrites, and
feel comparatively safe among the professional scoundrels.
 " I read Marshall's article on France, and thought it
excellent. I also see his book very well spoken of in the
papers."

We have now a double thread of narrative to follow,
and I may here trace the course of the other, which from
this time was almost completely severed from that of

Laurence, whose errant career led him from one place to another—to New York, to Canada (the only occasion on which his wife accompanied him), and even repeatedly to England, as the claims of business and the orders of the prophet required. On one of these latter occasions he had been seen in London by the daughter of his old friend, Mr Liesching, who apparently wrote to Lady Oliphant in consequence. I quote her reply :—

" She must have been struck, as every one is who sees him, with the change his opinions have effected in Lowry, both spiritually and physically. He is indeed a new creature, and lives only to serve God and humanity, having no desire or aim for self. He looks strong, and is so, and his expression shows the calm and strength within; but all this comes not from faith without works, but after ten years of hard struggle with his evils, and very hard bodily labours, and no small amount of suffering. As for myself, I can say very little, but that I am struggling on to get rid of my selfhood and selfishness, and the rest of that vile tribe of evils, having so much to undo; but I am happy and thankful for the privilege of being in the only place where it is possible for me to be helped, and in due time, if I live, to help others. I am strong, and able for a fair amount of bodily exertion.

" You would be surprised and amused if I could describe to you the ordering of my daily life. Alice (Lowry's wife) has been going through the ordeal, a very hard one, of putting off all the old and much - admired refinement, polish, intellectual charm, &c. Not that these things are wrong,—on the contrary, they are most desirable, but only when coming through a divine source, and used for divine ends, instead of coming from the selfhood, and used for personal ends. She is very brave and true, and fights hard against herself. She and I lived together in a cottage for eight months, quite alone except for the help of a boy to do what was too hard for us, and that only about an hour in the day. It was our own wish: we wanted to realise something of the lives of our hard-working sisters in the world, the cooks, housemaids, &c., and to learn to do things for ourselves. I wish I could explain to you our beautiful system of Christ's religion,—I know it would meet a ready response in your honest loving nature : we cooked, we washed, we ironed, I reared upwards of a hundred chickens, and you may believe we were busy enough; but the internal work was by far the hardest, and I succeed but poorly and slowly. Alice helps me a great deal. Then when winter came on we were directed to come to this sweet home. It is the house Mr Harris occupied; he has gone to California with some of our members : we occupy his own rooms, and are merely boarders; all the housework is done by others of the family. We work in the garden, and help to mend the clothes of the gentlemen of the society. But we gained health of mind and body in our cottage experience. All we aim at is to become Christ-like, to get rid of selfhood in every form, so that He can use us as His instruments in helping to redeem the world, the work He has now come to do—for He has come, and been seen and heard of some, and soon all will feel His presence, for great and startling events are at hand."

It is a puzzle beyond ordinary faculties to make out in what respects Lady Oliphant and her daughter-in-law could be doing more good to the world by performing their household work for themselves in a little cottage in Salem-on-Erie than by living in their natural home, either in England or France ; or how it was fundamentally better for these two accomplished women to live as boarders among the Brocton farmers, working in the garden, and mending the men's clothes, than to occupy their legitimate position. But this is no question for us, seeing that their own convictions on the matter were so absolute.

I cannot but think, however, that the clear intelligence and keen perceptions of Mrs Laurence Oliphant must soon have taken up this point of view, or else that the other circumstances of her life, upon which we have no light, gradually became too much for her. There is no record at first in her case of the ordeal through which both her husband and his mother had to pass at the very beginning of their career at Brocton. To put off her refinement and polish and intellectual charm, though extraordinarily difficult things to do, were not enough to balance the more practical and sensible tests to which the others were put; and it may be perhaps that the ordeal was postponed in her case only to be made more tremendous. Or I think it very possible that Harris himself may have been confused by the two extraordinary captives he had taken all unawares in his net, and foresaw and feared the consequences of leaving them there together to quicken each other's wits and powers of observation, and perhaps to discover with too much clearness of vision what was lacking and what was ludicrous in the economy around them. As iron sharpeneth iron, so were these two likely to act upon each other, perhaps to a consciousness of the wonderful character of their subjection, perhaps to independent plans of their own, both of which would have weakened the master's hold upon them, and made their emancipation merely a question of time.

Which of these varying reasons was the cause of the next step in this strange history it is impossible to tell. It is evident, however, that the separation of the husband and wife virtually took place before the departure of Alice from Brocton. It is comprehensible enough why Laurence should have been kept in perpetual motion, now here, now there, continually on the road. Having once entered into the cares of business, no doubt the exigencies of his new life forced him away from the quiet of the community in which his mother and wife lived in humility and apparent content. And as he was probably the most profitable of all the workers under the orders of the prophet, he was kept very fully occupied, and not encouraged to return too often to that quiet and seclusion. Brocton by this time, as has been seen, was no longer the place of Mr Harris's residence, though still completely under his sway. He had gone to California, and settled himself in a new establishment, Santa Rosa, not far from San Francisco, where he cultivated vines, and swayed the souls who had committed themselves into his hands, with an authority and minute direction as absolute as ever. For what alleged reason

Alice was ordered to proceed to this new settlement I am
unable to tell.   She was so commanded, and with the
unhesitating obedience to which she had pledged herself,
arose and went, to fulfil the objects of the Use in that
distant place.   No part of the career of the Oliphants has
been the cause of more question than this; but it was
in no point more extraordinary, at least in the beginning,
than the rest of their life under the sway of their prophet.
We have already seen that he thought mutual affection,
when merely natural, injurious.   Accordingly he sent out
the husband to work hard for the community in one direction, and called the wife to another sphere altogether out
of her husband's reach except at the cost of a long journey.
The mother, who had so rejoiced in the marriage, and who
had written to her friend in England of her happiness in
the cottage where they lived together, and where in spiritual matters as well as physical " Alice helps me so much,"
was left to wash the pocket-handkerchiefs and mend the
clothes alone.

In the meantime Laurence, after his initiation into
business matters among the bulls and bears of New York,
took a more important piece of business in hand in the
beginning of the year 1874, when he joined the new Cable
Company, then anxiously contriving the means of establishing a new telegraphic service.   He informs Mr Blackwood that he has just returned from Canada, where " we
have been paying a visit to the Dufferins," in company
with his wife—so that it is clear her exile to California
had not as yet taken place.

" I am coaching a bill through the Dominion Legislature,
which has for its object the extinction of the existing
cable monopoly.   My time has been so abundantly occupied
in making preparations for the new cable which is to be
laid this summer, and looking after the interests of the
company, that I have sought in vain for some spare moments to write an article for 'Maga.'   I have not been able
even to fulfil my promise to Delane, and write a few columns for the 'Times,' though I have had material enough;
but I find that when my attention is so fully taken up with

affairs of which I had no previous experience, and which
so completely divert my thoughts from their old wonted
channels, I cannot get suddenly into the literary groove
again. But, though rather late in life, I am learning business in a school which, as they say, requires one to keep
one's 'eyes skinned,' and if you should want any sharp
Wall Street practice exposed or moral detective work
done, I am qualifying myself rapidly for the occupation.
All the mysteries of 'Rings,' the fraudulent manipulation
of stock, &c., are becoming familiar to me. I am at this
moment making four contracts with four separate companies, all managed by—not to put too fine a point upon
it—swindlers; at least according to my former unsophis-
ticated mind I should so have considered them: they are
only called *smart* here. My only weapon is a guileless
innocence, which disconcerts them, as they don't know
whether I am precious deep or precious flat, as Mr Chuck-
ster would say."

The next letter is dated formally from the office of his
new undertaking:—

"THE DIRECT UNITED STATES CABLE COMPANY, LIMITED,
NEW YORK, 16 BROAD STREET,
5th November 1875.

"You will see from the aspect of this sheet what an
entirely new place I have broken out in. The manner in
which I administer the affairs of a Cable Company, and
exercise an autocratic control over an army of clerks and
operators, is the marvel of myself and the admiration of
the swindlers among whom I have the honour to reside.
It is a long time since we have exchanged notes. I gave
up attempting to get 'Piccadilly' republished here, concerning which I wrote to you last. My object in writing
is to tell you that herewith I forward a copy of a New
York paper, which, though mean and contemptible in
aspect, has a circulation of over 200,000, and pays $25
a-column for my humble contributions, one of which the
accompanying contains. As it is a review of that admirable book of Wilson's, 'The Abode of Snow,' I thought

S

you might like to see it. I have to finish this in a hurry,
as an overwhelming rush of business has come in upon me
while I am writing. How did the cheap edition of 'Piccadilly' go off?'"

His occupation with the concerns of the Cable Company lasted for some time. It would be foolish to take
his sweeping condemnation of the financialists of New
York *au pied de la lettre*, though no doubt his indignation
and righteous wrath against the sharp practice to which
he found himself exposed was very warm and genuine.
But he was altogether a pessimist in respect to society,
though the most hopeful of visionaries in other ways. I
have been told an anecdote on this subject by a friend to
whom he himself told it, which is not only very characteristic of him, but throws a gleam of softer light upon
the men among whom he was struggling. One of the
chief persons with whom he had to do was the well-known
Jay Gould, a financier of much greater force than the
new adventurer in such unaccustomed fields, and against
whose overwhelming cleverness Laurence had been warned
by his friends. In the exercise of that "innocence" to
which he refers, which puzzled the gentlemen of Wall
Street, he went direct to this high potentate with the
engaging frankness which is one of the most polished
instruments of diplomacy, being nothing but the bare
truth. "I do not think," he said, "that your interests and
those of my clients are opposed to each other; but it is
needless to say that I am not your equal in the conduct
of affairs, and if you mean to crush me, you can." The
result of this address was that Jay Gould understood and
appreciated the appeal of the honest man, and during the
ensuing negotiations treated his unlikely opponent with
perfect good faith and honour.

These unaccustomed business operations, and the work
and strange company into which they led him, had closed
the mouth of Laurence during the three years which
followed his return to America. Except in the newspaper which looked so shabby, yet paid twenty-five dollars
a-column to its contributors, we hear of nothing from his

pen until in May 1876 we find him in England, writing
from the Athenæum to his publisher at Edinburgh, with
the MS. of an article afterwards published in 'Blackwood's
Magazine' as "The Autobiography of a Joint-Stock Company." This daring and pungent piece of satire, which
portrays the conception, growth, prosperity, and ruin of
one of the many commercial ventures of the age, the
shameless swindling of its promoters, the blind confidence
of its victims, the lesser and competing frauds that gathered
round it, was produced, I have been told, under the stimulus of sudden wrath and indignation consequent on the
discovery of certain proceedings affecting his own immediate object. The story is altogether a perfect romance of
literature.

He had spent the evening in the house of a lady very
closely connected with him, in whom he had perfect confidence, and to whom he recorded in wild excitement the
discovery of fraud which he had made. He talked until
the small hours of the morning, no doubt still further
feeding the fire of his indignation. Next day was Sunday,
and the same lady, on her return from church, called at
his lodgings to know if he was coming to lunch with her.
She found him in his dressing-gown, standing before a
table on which his hat-box answered the purpose of a
desk, the floor all round him strewed with leaves of paper
which he threw down as he finished them. There he
had stood all the morning through, unconscious of the
passage of the hours, pouring forth his fiery indignation
and scathing satire, red-hot, with a lurid energy which
comes only when the pen is inspired with strong feeling.
My informant tells me that the paper completed was
posted that same day. He told her afterwards, laughing,
that the publisher had sent him a cheque for sixty pounds
for the morning's work. Certainly an article more instinct
with righteous wrath and the vivid life of just indignation
was never written. "The facts," he says in an accompanying letter, "were all given me by C., who is certainly a
joint producer; but we neither of us wish our names mentioned." The lady from whom I have this interesting description considers the date to have been later than that

given above, and as I have already said, it is very difficult
to decipher the chronology of a number of letters dated
only by months. Certainly it was at a considerably later
period that the article appeared.

The excitement of the struggles of business life roused
all his faculties, and I have always heard that his capacity
was great in financial matters. No doubt, too, a man so
formed for activity of mental life enjoyed more or less the
keen conflict of wits, more tremendous than any conflict
of literature, in which each man has to keep his eye upon
the other, lest he should be overreached and checkmated.
But I do not think that Laurence entered upon any further
commercial or speculative enterprise on so large a scale as
the Cable Company. His experience in that did not tempt
him to further exertions.

The story of the Joint-Stock Company did not appear
for some time. And it was soon followed to Edinburgh
by the witty and amusing "Recollections of Irene Macgillicuddy," in which, for the first time, the satirist had
his fling at American society, with all the brilliancy and
force of 'Piccadilly' and the freshness of a new scene.
The sketch of Dollie, already referred to, was trenchant
and whimsical enough; but the withers of New York were
unwrung by that dashing stroke at the economy of a lower
and altogether rural region. When, however, the New
York belle appeared for the first time upon an English
canvas, the effect was overwhelming. We have had many
opportunities of making the acquaintance of that wonderful young person since. Her own native illustrator has
taken in hand to expound her many vagaries and charms,
and the manners and habits of the other beings of her
species, which, moreover, have undergone many modifica-
tions, not perhaps wholly unconnected with those efforts
of literature to hold the mirror up to nature. But Irene
was entirely new to the world when Laurence called her
before us. It was the beginning of the American girl's
rage for aristocratic marriages—a taste which has grown
so much since that day; and this curious sketch of
manners, altogether new and wonderful, was made all the
more striking by the introduction of the English young

man of fashion, more or less bewildered by his new surroundings, who had suddenly become the natural prey of the fair American. But Irene needed no languid swell behind her to enhance her originality. In her first revelation, with all her beauty and charm and "go," her suppressed and half-conscious vulgarities, her *naïve* ambitions, her high-handed dealings with her parents, and unbroken conviction that the world was made for her, she was too new to be otherwise than delightful. The highly moral conclusion of the story, in which the disappointed beauty falls in love and marries disinterestedly, to the amazement of all around, is the only part of it which at all palled upon the reader. Even then the young lady was amusing, but in her unregenerate state she was sublime.

If, however, she was received with much jubilation and laughter in England, the effect upon society in New York was more remarkable still. The American reader identified the different characters of the story with that unhesitating certainty on which a local critic plumes himself, and ladies who had received the English satirist into their houses made the welkin ring with their cries. No harm was done, however, nor any special resentment roused. I have been told that one lady was overwhelmed with astonishment by the scene at Niagara where a declaration is made in the midst of the roar of the Falls; and declared indignantly that no one but herself and one other knew of this astonishing scene — to the great amusement of the writer, who had invented it in one of the wildest freaks of his fancy. This amusing production is the subject of Laurence's next letter to his publisher:—

"BROCTON, *March* 25, 1878.

"The story has been republished in various forms in this country. Harpers have republished it in their Half Hour Series, for which they gave me £10; but have not had the grace to send me a copy, though I asked them to do so, intending to send you one. I have not even seen it. It has also been republished in a 15-cent form; but I have not been following its fortunes much, or heard

much of the criticism regarding it, as I have again gone
into my retirement and given up the various occupations
which kept me at New York. I am glad to give up the
society of swindlers for that of sheep for a little. I have
seen no newspapers for a couple of months, and do not
therefore know anything which has been transpiring in
Europe; but my impression is that the Russo - Turkish
treaty will form a bone of contention over which all
Europe will yet quarrel. Perhaps when that time comes
I may pay Europe a visit; in the meantime, I shall remain quietly here."

He adds, " My mother and wife are both well," without
any betrayal of the fact that his wife was far away from
him; but the reader will not fail to perceive the tone of
depression in this letter. He had but just returned from
an expedition to California, the object of which, I believe,
was to bring her back if possible; but in this he was un-
successful, and there is something pathetic in the " society
of sheep," to which he had returned sorely discouraged,
and with many strange thoughts, one may imagine, surg-
ing up in his heart.

An account of the issue of this journey, and of the
events subsequent to it which took place in the same
neighbourhood, which I owe to the courtesy of Mr J. D.
Walker, formerly of San Francisco, one of the most devoted and generous of Laurence Oliphant's friends, opens
up suddenly an entirely new scene. The friendship between Laurence and Mr and Mrs Walker began in a characteristic manner. Mrs Walker, on her way to England
with her children some years previously, travelling alone
and in delicate health, was detained in New York for a short
time by illness before embarking, and met Laurence there
at a friend's house. He himself was also on his way to England, and hearing that the lady he had met was somewhat
faint-hearted about the voyage—the first she had made
without her husband—and generally in need of support
and sympathy, he took his passage in the same ship, delay-
ing his journey, I believe, in order that she might have
the help of a friend on board. Thus he knitted to himself

with hooks of steel, or rather with bonds of kindness, the pair who recompensed this spontaneous act of good feeling with the most faithful friendship and kindness for all the rest of his life. Some time in the beginning of the year 1878, Mr Walker found Laurence in his office in San Francisco waiting for him. He had come to see Mr Harris in his establishment at Santa Rosa; and though he did not inform his friend what was the special object of his visit, he accompanied Mr Walker to his hospitable house at San Rafael to await the issue of his negotiations with the head of the community. There he waited for some weeks, at first cheerful enough, probably unable to believe in the possibility of so rational and natural a demand as that to see his own wife being refused him. It was, however, refused: and he was ordered to return at once to Brocton, which he did in great depression and misery but ever-obedient faith. It may be supposed with what feelings the pair of friends, who did not yet know Alice, looked on and witnessed this inconceivable frustration of all the laws of nature.

Some time after, probably in the autumn of the same year, Laurence wrote to Mr Walker to tell him that his wife had left Santa Rosa, and was in need of friendly succour and help. She had gone out from the prophet's house without money, without introductions or friends, alone, to earn her own bread, whether by his command — sent out, as it was his wont to send forth those members of his community who were capable of earning money, to labour on its behalf—or whether by her own impulse, I cannot tell. It was her wont to attribute this strange step entirely to her own will; but, as has been seen, it was one of the understood duties of members of the community to take upon themselves the entire responsibility of any step which offended public opinion. She had gone to a place called Vallejo, where she was living in a poor lodging and taking such pupils as could be got there—the children of miners and other uneducated persons—in the humblest form of educational effort possible, though what she did teach was chiefly what might be called accomplishments, —music, drawing, &c. She used to say afterwards, when talking, as she did freely, about the experiences of this period, that the confidence of the humblest parents in their own future and fortune—the rudest among them entertaining no doubt that their children would occupy so much better a position than themselves as to make these accomplishments suitable and necessary—was amazing; and that the cost of such lessons was paid ungrudgingly by fathers and mothers who were themselves without the merest rudiments of education. Her reason for the step thus taken she always stated, as Lady Oliphant did the reason for their domestic work—to be her desire not only to share the experiences of other women who work for their living, but to prove to the faint-hearted that work could be found and a living earned without the forfeiture either of self-respect or cheerfulness. In short, that she had gone out, in the purest quixotism, divesting herself of all advantages save those inalienable and belonging to her very being (a most large exception), in order that other women, driven by necessity to the same course, should know that the thing could be done. This was her own explanation always to the world of the mystery of her proceedings. In a world so strange as theirs, it is possible enough that any fantastic reason might suffice for any act of self-devotion, especially if it was the will of the master that such and such things should be done. It is possible also that, though late, this was the ordeal through which every member of the community had to pass to prove their utter sincerity. At all events, it was no breaking away from the rule and obedience of Harris, but done in full allegiance and dependence upon his will.

The friends to whom Laurence appealed to stand by his wife in her solitary and laborious career immediately responded to the call; and Mrs Walker went at once to Vallejo, where she found Alice cheerfully installed, doing everything for herself—such a thing as a maid being, of course, out of the question for a poor teacher among the poor inhabitants of the Californian village. That she was already surrounded by humble friends and warm affection it is almost needless to say, for these sprang up like flowers wherever her foot fell. Far the most touching among the many letters of condolence and sympathy addressed to Laurence after her death came from humble women in this place, with little grammar but loving hearts, to whom her recollection was as that of an angel who had passed among them, leaving life itself more noble and beautiful ever after. The visitor from San Rafael passed a night at Vallejo in this humble lodging, shared the meals cooked by Alice's own hands after her teaching was over, and, it is unnecessary to add, gave her heart at once to the enchantress. Henceforward the exile had a home open to her, full of all luxuries, and especially those of affection and tenderness; and was beguiled to San Rafael for her holidays, and watched over when her delicate strength was breaking down. It was proposed that she should remove thither permanently, so as to be near her friends, and also to have a chance of pupils of a more congenial type; and Mrs Walker remembers looking at various houses in her own neighbourhood with the intention of finding one that would do for a school — a more ambitious undertaking. While considering this plan, Alice went to the house of Mrs Lynch at Benicia, who had a school of a similar character to the one projected, in order to receive information on the subject, and details and advice as to its management. But once again that power of fascination, which she had confessed with so much simplicity to be one of the hindrances to her religious career, came into operation, and the new friends who had kindly undertaken to give her advice as to setting up a school of her own, ended by imploring her, at the end of a very short visit, to stay and work with them. She accepted this offer, and remained there accordingly in a less isolated position during the rest of her stay in California.

But I think her heart was most in the humble solitude of her first outset, alone and independent, in the world. She too loved the sensation of adventure, the launch into the unknown, the primitive manners and thoughts of the uninstructed people among whom she found herself. She loved to speak of them, their curious sparks of refinement amid the rough, their faith in themselves and the future, and the perceptions of higher things that were strongly visible among them. I recollect her saying—a curious and striking piece of observation (I do not know if it has been confirmed by any other intelligent observer)—that a Californian audience enjoyed an opera, that highly sophisticated and recondite work of art, with a sensitive excitement and perception more like those of a Parisian audience than anything she had seen. She remained in the school at Benicia, teaching and shedding sweet influences round her, till she returned to England. And it was on the occasion of one of her visits to Mrs Walker at San Rafael that she painted a portrait of herself — a very real and affecting likeness of her expressive and charming countenance — which was an inexpressible pleasure to her husband in later days, and is the much-prized possession of the friends who added so much brightness to this period of her life, and who cherish and love her memory.

Whether it was that so strong a step as the complete severance of a married pair in this way was found at length to try the faith of the community in general, and to require an equally strong explanation, I am not able to say; but at all events it would seem to have been an idea propounded at this time that the marriage, which the community had at first so strenuously opposed, to which it had reluctantly assented, and which it had done everything in its power to nullify by continual humiliation of the "refinement and intellectual charm" of Alice, and a continuous succession of distant undertakings to Laurence —was not a true marriage of "counterparts" at all, and therefore could have no reality or sacredness. Perhaps this had been the first cause of her departure from Brocton, underlying all the other motives. It was, I think, in the autumn of 1880, when he was for some time in London, where I too was living, and had thus more opportunities of seeing him than usual, that Laurence confided to myself this extraordinary discovery. I remember with great distinctness the humble drawing-room in Victoria Square, that curious little haven of quiet in the midst of the noise of town, where on a wintry afternoon my delightful visitor communicated the strange fact, not only that

his wife was not his counterpart, but that it had been discovered that he had a counterpart "on the other side"—that
is, already passed into the unseen state—of whose communications he had been for some time increasingly conscious,
and who had inspired him with certain revelations in verse
which he asked leave to read to me. To see him produce
these rhymed effusions, and read them with the strangest
boyish pleasure and shyness, astonished at their cleverness,
and pausing from time to time to assure me that of himself
he could not produce a rhyme to save his life, was the most
astonishing experience. If the reader should exclaim, as
many have done, that this was sheer madness, I can only
reply that a more sane person never existed, and that the
verses in question, strange and bald as they were, and most
unlike anything sent from heaven, were nevertheless as lucid
as they were daring, and conveyed a trenchant attack upon
social evils of all kinds, in something more like doggerel
than poetry, but with much method and meaning, though
little beauty. It is a difficult thing at any time for an
unwilling critic to sit in judgment upon the productions
of an author, read by himself; and the wonder with
which one could not but contemplate this brilliant writer,
a master of vigorous English in his own style and person,
smiling and blushing over the inspired rigmarole of verse
which it was his boast was not his, but something far finer
than he could ever have produced by himself, was wellnigh stupefying. I must not avoid the confession of this
strange lapse into foolishness which the extraordinary
strain of faculty and possibility at this exceedingly trying
period of his life betrayed him into. It is the only sign
of mental aberration which I ever saw in him, the sole
evidence I have ever been able to make out of that touch
of questionable sanity which is supposed by many people
to explain the secrets of his life. These things are very
bewildering; but his absolute good faith was unquestionable, and it is almost needless to say that a mind more
capable of discriminating sense from nonsense was not to
be found in England. He was no critic, however, as has
been seen in the earlier records of his life, and had accepted
as divine poetry 'The Great Republic' and other produc-

tions of Mr Harris, so that his admiration of his own
rhymes and wonder at them was less remarkable.

This, however, is an anticipation. In the meantime
Laurence had still some vague years to go through of
which there is little record. He roamed about America,
and made one or two expeditions across the Atlantic,
and was always full of occupation. His sole literary
performances, however, were "Irene," published in 1877,
of which he tells some amusing anecdotes, and "The
Autobiography of a Joint-Stock Company," already referred to. I can scarcely tell whether it was to this
latter production he refers when he says, "'Irene' made
such a row in New York, and they are so sensitive,
that I hardly like to publish it, if I am to mix much
in the society there, as it will make it too hot." "Irene"
was the cause, however, of another amusing incident.

"Dec. 10, 1878.

"When 'Irene' came out and made a sensation in New
York, the authorship puzzled people so much that a man
claimed to be the author, and proceeded to write a continuation as such. Now that the authorship is known,
he is in a fix, as his continuation is coming out. The
claims of J. H. appeared in the American papers this
spring [1878], and were indignantly contradicted by
Hurlbert in the 'World,' who knew the real authorship.
He was replied to by J. H., who insisted, and Hurlbert
threatened to prove the fraud to Carleton & Co., who are
his publishers, and who, knowing the circumstances, continue to be so."

It will be remembered that a similar incident occurred
in respect to the 'Scenes of Clerical Life' of George Eliot,
and that the impostor in that case stood his ground for
some time with extraordinary impudence. It is in the
letter on this subject, above quoted, and which was written
from the familiar ground of the Athenæum, that the first
intimation is given, suddenly and without preface, of a
new and remarkable project which influenced more or less
all the after-portion of Oliphant's life, and which seems at

first to have been taken up as a speculation, with some curious contagion from the atmosphere in which he had been living. He states it first upon this ground, with a somewhat cynical reference to the higher religio-romantic motives, which would give it popularity, he imagined, and secure its pecuniary success.

"My Eastern project is as follows: To obtain a concession from the Turkish Government in the northern and more fertile half of Palestine, which the recent survey of the Palestine Exploration Fund proves to be capable of immense development. Any amount of money can be raised upon it, owing to the belief which people have that they would be fulfilling prophecy and bringing on the end of the world. I don't know why they are so anxious for this latter event, but it makes the commercial speculation easy, as it is a combination of the financial and sentimental elements which will, I think, ensure success. And it will be a good political move for the Government, as it will enable them to carry out reforms in Asiatic Turkey, provide money for the Porte, and by uniting the French in it, and possibly the Italians, be a powerful religious move against the Russians, who are trying to obtain a hold of the country by their pilgrims. It would also secure the Government a large religious support in this country, as even the Radicals would waive their political in favour of their religious crotchets. I also anticipate a very good subscription in America. I shall probably start about the end of the year for Egypt, as I want to look into the working of the mixed jurisdiction, and then go to Cyprus, Syria, Palestine, and Constantinople. I suppose I shall find plenty to write about, but I do not want it all talked of, though I find it difficult to keep it quiet. Both Lord Beaconsfield and Lord Salisbury are very favourable to my scheme."

"I am in close correspondence with Conder,"[1] he adds in another letter, "and have had a talk with him in

[1] Capt. Conder, R.E., one of the latest explorers of the Holy Land.

London. He takes a lively interest in the scheme. He wrote some papers in the 'Jewish Chronicle,' and though there is nothing brilliant in his style, it is simple and straightforward, and conveys a great deal of interesting information about a country which always excites much interest, and of which he is better qualified to speak than almost any one."

The wonderful new project thus begun bears in its first disclosure a whimsical and ludicrous likeness to Laurence's own account of the Joint-Stock Company. He was himself the Promoter, setting out to procure his concession ; feeling all the great possibilities in his scheme, which almost went to his head in the first conception; putting the profit to be secured in the foreground, as if that was what tempted him most, though, as a matter of fact, no single shilling ever came into his pocket from the scheme, which, on the contrary, involved him in many and considerable expenses ; feeling also the innumerable other good things that would come out of it,—the restoration to the uses of humanity of a desert land which was overflowing with fertility and possible wealth, if there were but hands to till and plough ; the opening to a persecuted race of a refuge from their oppressions and troubles ; the help to civilisation and human progress, to good government and justice and peace, that were in it. All these kinds of profit were involved, and made him eloquent. They are repeated over and over again in the continually revised and corrected copies of his prospectus, his petition to the Sultan, his explanations of the same, and a crowd of documents all bearing on this question. He did not pretend that any desire to fulfil prophecy was at the bottom of the scheme, and had not, so far as I am aware, any enthusiasm for the Jews. I cannot indeed trace the first suggestion of the project, or anything of its development until it suddenly leaps forth upon us full blown. But he was at this period, as it is happily described in familiar slang, " at a loose end." He had, I imagine, retired from his previous mercantile ventures in no great mood for entering upon others of a similar description.

He was greatly shaken and nonplussed in his private life,
separated from his wife not only by the arbitrary division
of distance and different work to do, but by the insinuated
belief I have referred to, that they had never been true
spouses, nor partners intended by heaven for each other;
and moved, I can scarcely doubt, by the first difficulties
in his absolute faith, the "little rift within the lute,"
which had hitherto given forth nothing but the harmony
of perfect assent. Disgusted with ordinary business,
shaken in the allegiance which for years had been the
rule of his life, plunged into strange possibilities of
spiritual union with an unknown partner, and the ache
of severance from her whom he had loved and chosen,
there was perhaps no part of his life in which his mind
was less sure and at peace. The scheme about the Jews
gave him at once the liveliest personal interest, the pleasure of a sort of amateur diplomatic negotiation involving
the largest issues, and the mixture of adventure and use,
which was at all times the thing he liked best in life.
He was thoroughly convinced of the large human advantage of his scheme. I am inclined to believe, moreover,
that he had really more interest than he gave himself
credit for even in the religious view of the question.

He left London for the East early in the spring of the
year 1879, and went direct to Beyrout, from which place
he set out on an adventurous journey into the unexplored
wilds, traversing, with a single companion and two or
three attendants, countries much less known and more
dangerous than those which ordinary travellers then ventured upon under charge of a military escort, and with
an elaborate retinue of camp and camp-followers. The
account of this journey will be found in full in the
volume published next year (and first in fragments in
'Blackwood's Magazine'), called 'The Land of Gilead,'—
an exceedingly interesting account of much that was perfectly novel to the English mind. The result of his investigations was the choice of a district east of Jordan,
at the upper end of the Dead Sea, partly lying in the
deep valley of the sacred river, far below the level of the
ocean—the most fertile part of Palestine, and just under

those wonderful blue hills of Moab, which close the horizon with a line of heights more splendid in colour than perhaps any range of mountains in the world. I need not attempt to follow independently the route which Laurence himself has so admirably described. The sudden plunge into travel and adventure, after long cessation and employment among things of more immediate interest than Arab sheikhs and Bedouin encampments, has a curious effect upon the reader, so sudden is it, and unlike the circumstances through which we have just followed him. The great object of the expedition was to discover and select the most suitable ground for the proposed colony, and that was found without difficulty. I may add, however, the description of this wonderful district.

"Perhaps the difference in the luxuriance of the vegetation between Eastern and Western Palestine is brought into the most striking contrast on the Dead Sea itself. Nothing can be more barren or uninviting than the rugged waterless mountains on its western shore, while the wadies opposite teem with an almost tropical vegetation. Here are palms in profusion, and jungles of terebinths, wild almond and fig trees, poplars, willows, hawthorn, and oleanders covering the steep hillsides and fringing the streams of such picturesque ravines as those in which are situated the fountains of Callirrhoe and the wells of Moses. In the spring especially, these glens, adorned with a rich semi-tropical flora, are in their full beauty. There can be little doubt that the celebrated healing qualities of the hot springs of Callirrhoe, and the romantic scenery by which they are surrounded, would render them a popular resort for tourists and health-seekers, if ever this country should be reclaimed, and proper accommodation for travellers and visitors was provided. Included within the territory which I should propose for colonisation would be the Ghor Seisaban, or plains of Shittim, which Canon Tristram describes as 'by far the most extensive and luxuriant of any of the fertile lands bordering on the Dead Sea.' 'This abundantly watered and tree-covered district,' he continues, 'extends

six miles from east to west, and ten or twelve from north
to south. I crossed it myself at its northern extremity,
and rode through an extensive tract of young wheat-fields,
cultivated by the Adwan.' . . .

"Ascending from the fervid subtropical valley of the
Jordan, we gradually, before reaching the plains of Moab
and highlands of Gilead, pass through another zone of
vegetation, until we finally attain an elevation of about
4000 feet above the level of the sea, and more than 5000
feet above the Ghor Seisaban; but the difference in feet
does not really convey an adequate notion of the difference
in climate, owing to the peculiar conditions of the Jordan
valley, which, being depressed below the level of the sea,
produces a contrast in vegetation with the mountains of
Gilead corresponding rather to a difference of 10,000 feet
than of only half that elevation. The consequence is, that
in no part of the world could so great a variety of agricultural produce be obtained compressed within so limited
a space. The valley of the Jordan would act as an enormous hothouse for the new colony. Here might be cultivated palms, cotton, indigo, sugar, rice, sorghum, besides
bananas, pine-apples, yams, sweet potatoes, and other field
and garden produce. Rising a little higher, the country is
adapted to tobacco, maize, castor-oil, millet, flax, sesamum,
melons, gourds, cumin, coriander, anise, ochra, brinjals,
pomegranates, oranges, figs, — and so up to the plains,
where wheat, barley, beans and lentils of various sorts,
with olives and vines, would form the staple products.
Gilead especially is essentially a country of wine and oil;
it is also admirably adapted to silk-culture; while among
its forests, carob or locust-bean, pistachio, jujube, almond,
balsam, kali, and other profitable trees grow wild in great
profusion. All the fruits of Southern Europe, such as
apricots, peaches, and plums, here grow to perfection;
apples, pears, quinces, thrive well on the more extreme
elevation, upon which the fruits and vegetables of England might be cultivated, — while the quick-growing
Eucalyptus could be planted with advantage on the fertile
but treeless plains. Not only does the extraordinary
variety of soil and climate thus compressed into a small

T

area offer exceptional advantages from an agricultural point of view, but the inclusion of the Dead Sea within its limits would furnish a vast source of wealth, by the *exploitation* of its chemical and mineral deposits. The supply of chlorate of potassium, 200,000 tons of which are annually consumed in England, is practically inexhaustible; while petroleum, bitumen, and other lignites can be procured in great quantities upon its shores. There can be little doubt, in fact, that the Dead Sea is a mine of unexplored wealth, which only needs the application of capital and enterprise to make it a most lucrative property."

Whether the Promoter meant to line the shores of the Dead Sea with tall chimneys of chemical works, is a question which will probably make the reader shudder; but the picture he thus gives of untold wealth for the gathering, enhanced by the presence of a peaceful and docile population to act as labourers—for the Jew colonists were rather, it appears, expected to be farmers and overseers than absolute agricultural workmen—was enough to make the mouths of many capitalists water, to say nothing of other motives. When he had thus made sure of his sphere of labour, and reckoned up all its advantages, Laurence returned to Constantinople as a suitor at the Court of the Sultan, to procure the concession which was the first step, —at least he supposed it to be the first step. I have since heard it said by persons well qualified to form an opinion, that had he first secured possession of it by private arrangement, and sought his concession afterwards, he would have been more likely to be successful; but that was not among the methods that commended themselves to his mind. And he was strongly of opinion that nothing could be of more advantage to Turkey than the "development of a single province, however small, under conditions which should increase the revenue of the empire, add to its population and resources, secure protection of life and property, and enlist the sympathy of Europe without in any way affecting the sovereign rights of the Sultan."

At the same time, he had the anxious assent of the Jewish community to his design. From among the Jews in Roumania, and other persecuted districts in which he intended to find his colonists, there was an immediate response. A society was even formed among these suffering people to buy land for themselves, and make their own way in the Land of Promise. "Every one of the members is experienced in the work of cultivating the soil, and it is our intention to journey to Palestine to till the ground and to guard it," they said. Thus armed with all necessary preliminaries—his place chosen, his colonists secured, and furnished in his own person, if not with official warrants, yet with strong letters of recommendation from the Foreign Office—Laurence set about the work of diplomacy. It was the last step, and did not seem at all the most important; and when he first presented himself before the Ministers of the Sultan, it was with every hope of speedy success. The following letter, though without date, must have been written soon after his arrival in Constantinople. He sends to Mr Blackwood a description of several of the articles which were afterwards to form part of 'The Land of Gilead,' and which were chiefly occupied by—

"My explorations to the east of the Jordan, where I have visited parts very little known, and which will give some account of a province for which, I think, there is an immediate and most interesting future in store—that is, if I succeed in what I am about. So far everything has turned out beyond my most sanguine expectations; but I am at this moment at a standstill, not in consequence of any opposition which I have met with on the part of the Government, but because of the dire chaos and confusion which for the last fortnight has reigned in the Cabinet, and which has culminated in the Egyptian question. That, I hope, is now over; but the tenure of the Grand Vizier is so insecure that all arrangements made with him may at any moment be wiped out by his fall. . I am afraid the empire is doomed : it is only a question of time. This last war has given it such a severe shock that it

cannot right itself.   It is like a ship on its beam-ends,
and the rats are beginning to find it out, while traitors
are boring holes in the bottom.   Still, if I can carry my
scheme before it goes, its future success does not depend
upon the present state of things lasting here.

"I do not think of bringing 'The Land of Gilead' out
in the Magazine, as I want it to come out at a particular
moment to chime in with events; but the three articles
which I now propose sending might be added to it, as
they treat more or less of the same country.   I am delightfully established on the shores of the Bosphorus, and
am likely to be detained here for some time."

The next letter is dated from Therapia, the "delightful
establishment on the shores of the Bosphorus" above
referred to—an ideal spot more than half-way up that
glorious strait on the way to the Black Sea, in shelter of
one of the many lovely curves that form the European
shore, and which are lined with shining palaces, villages,
minarets, and towers all the way from Constantinople.
Europe and Asia there smile or frown on each other from
the vast ruins of the old crusading castles at one point, in
the summer-houses of countless princes and potentates on
the other, with the wonderful flood of sea-water, pouring
salt and strong, between—from the dark seas that lead
to mysterious Russian ports, to those which dazzle the
beholder all the way southward to the Ægean, sweeping
on through the Sea of Marmora and the Gates of the
Dardanelles.   At Therapia it is not pashas and effendis,
but ambassadors from all the Courts in Europe, that line
the shore with their delightful houses, and fill the little
bay with their boats, from yachts trim and taut to the
little caique that bobs upon the dancing waves.   Laurence
had spent the summer in this beautiful retreat, in the
midst of the finest society — *attachés* and secretaries of
legation flitting round their former brother in the craft,
and careful ambassadors not scorning to take counsel with
the sage, yet visionary, the man of the world who had
been everywhere and seen most things under the sun, yet
whose heart was all in some inconceivable mystery of
religion, at which these gentlemen did not know whether

to laugh or to frown. They did both; and it did not
matter to him what they did, who was equally ready to
laugh with them, or to fight for the faith that was in him.
His very mission for the sake of the Jews—his curious
design, which sounded at the first hearing as if it had
some reference to the millennium and grand return of
Israel and reign of the saints—would enhance the interest
in him, as he sat looking out, over the wreaths of roses
and overflowing verdure, upon the hurrying tides of the
great strait and the stately vessels that went to and fro
—writing once more the while the story of the country
flowing with milk and honey, yet arrested in the very
wealth of its powers till its ancient people should go
back to till and plough. It would have added much to
the picturesque effectiveness of the scene had Laurence
believed a little more in the fate and fortunes of those
for whom he worked; but if he did not regard them in
the light of enthusiasm, which makes their future as interesting as their past to many, there was yet growing in
him a sort of dedication to the service of the race of Israel
which was not unimpressive. In the next letter which I
shall quote there is still question of the book, which was,
he hoped, to be of service too to the great scheme. This
was in September 1879.

"I am now hard at work on my book, which I hope
will take, as it deals with a part of the world in which so
many are interested. I think I told you I propose to call
it 'The Land of Gilead.' If I had only one or two more
books of reference here, this would be a perfect place to
write in—it is so quiet. Hamley is to leave to-day. I
am sorry I have not seen so much of him as I should
have wished. He lives at Buyukderé, about two miles
off; and as he is a walker and I a lawn-tennis player, we
could not take our exercise together so much as we otherwise should.
"I shall probably be kept here till the end of the year,
and, if I succeed, shall bring out the book at the same
moment that I lay my Palestine scheme before the public:
the two things will help each other. I have not yet

encountered a particle of opposition to it,—quite the contrary. Every Turk, from the Sultan downwards, approves most highly ; but their *vis inertiæ* is so great, and their habits so dilatory, that it requires the greatest patience. I am glad that you are improving in health ; if I succeed, I shall invite you to pay me a visit in the Land of Gilead : it is a lovely climate, and I am sure you would be interested in all there is to see."

It is strange and sad to find this invitation, so lightly given, in the last letter ever addressed to the correspondent of so many years. Mr John Blackwood, the editor of the well-known Magazine and head of the well-known firm, died shortly after its receipt, to the great loss of all who were connected with him—the loss of a friend, adviser, and steady backer-up, if such a word is permissible, in all literary matters, which Laurence, in common with many others, felt deeply. His next letter is addressed to Mr William Blackwood, who had taken his uncle's place in the conduct of affairs—not, happily, a new correspondent or unknown friend to the hereditary supporters and clients of his house. It was accompanied by an article for the Magazine.

"CONSTANTINOPLE, *November* 17 [1879].

" It occurred to me that, under the tremendous pressure that is now being put upon Turkey, the Turkish view by an intelligent Turk might not be amiss. It is not flattering to Christians, but they never really hear the other side of the question. I have thrown into the form of a letter from a Turk opinions which I have heard the most enlightened Turks express. Of course my Effendi is a mythical personage, but his views are those entertained by the most enlightened and independent-minded Turks— men who will have nothing to do with politics, and live in retirement, and who have educated themselves by foreign travel. There are not many such, but there are one or two ; and although a good deal of hostile commentary may be excited by the paper, you are not responsible for the opinions it contains.

"I hope Mrs Blackwood is bearing up under her great loss. You must all feel the blank terribly, and you especially, with your increased responsibilities. I hope you have good assistants to lighten your work."

The next letter of the series is again occupied with the two subjects—'The Land of Gilead' and the great colonisation scheme.

"CONSTANTINOPLE, *April* 9, 1880.

"The introduction is necessarily dry. The subject is one not susceptible of light treatment, nor do I think that the religious public, for whom it has a special interest, will find fault with it on that ground. It gets still worse when we come to the archæological part. But if I succeed in my scheme, I have no doubt it will have a great sale: the success will in a great measure depend on that. I have been kept here from day to day by messages from the Sultan, begging me not to leave until he has had an opportunity of talking with me, and I have another matter on hand which will certainly keep me here for another fortnight. . . . What an extraordinary surprise these elections have been! The Turks are in consternation at the idea of Gladstone Prime Minister, and indeed the situation here is getting so interesting in consequence, that I am not sorry at being kept a little longer." "Gladstone," he adds, a few days later, "is a sort of Moody of politics, and his powers of canting revivalism are unsurpassed. . . . The amount of intrigue I am now encountering at the palace seems likely to beat me: it all seems to hinge on an interview with the Sultan, which Layard does not seem to have influence enough to obtain against the forces brought against him."

Here was virtually the end of this great scheme: the hopes, which at first were so lively, died down by degrees, and finally the project was given up altogether. But though it did not itself succeed, the suggestion was a most fruitful seed, and fell into good soil. Since then a number of Jewish colonies have been settled in Palestine, not

indeed in the chosen spot which Laurence selected with such
care, and for which he foresaw so splendid a future, but in
other parts; and, I believe, with varying success. It is
difficult for a stranger passing through these distant regions,
without command of language or natural opportunities of
intercourse with the inhabitants, to come at anything that
can be depended upon as the truth—which has different
aspects, according to the eyes that look upon it and the
point of view they take. Thus those who dislike the
Jews—and they are many—tell a tale of indolence and
exaction, and relate how the colonists demand everything
from their founders and nothing from their own exertions;
while those on the other side take a much more favourable
view of the strangers brought into their hereditary country.
Perhaps, as generally happens, there is truth in both reports. I confess, however, that the sight of the new cottages, and still more of the half-cleared fields, built round
with what we call in Scotland dry-stone dykes, made of
the stones painfully gathered off the encumbered soil, with
the young corn in its emerald green pushing round the
still remaining boulders, was to myself a very affecting
sight. Not without labour could the long quiescent soil
be cleared of that encumbrance, which makes one feel as
if not alone a martyr here and there but the whole land
had been stoned, for the misdeeds which heaven has been
so long waiting to forgive. I speak with the sentiment
which Laurence Oliphant always disavowed—a great sympathy and reverence in the thought that the most strange
of wandering peoples (I do not say the most lovable or
attractive) may yet be led back, some nucleus and seed of
them, to the country that has never yet been restored to
its fertility by any other hands.

After this failure, which no doubt was a great disappointment to him, Laurence returned to England, and
during the greater part of the year, I think, remained
here. It was in the early winter that I saw him, as I have
already described, and heard those confusing suggestions
about the Counterpart in heaven, and the curious string
of satirical verses which this very mundane angel, too well
acquainted with the devices of society, had, as he thought,

communicated to him. The verses were never printed, so
far as I know, and it was well that this was the case, for
I do not think they would have done the unseen col-
laboratrice any credit. I believe that his little fictitious
liveliness of satisfaction in these apparently quickened
relations with the unknown was in reality the mere endeavour of a sanguine and courageous spirit to indemnify
itself for the clouds and weariness in which life was being
lost. It was a dismal long way from London to the wilds
of California, where, separated from him by more than distance,—by the irksome sway of a false obedience, and the
sophistry of a spiritual guide whose despotism was becoming insupportable,—his Alice was; and his great scheme
had failed; and perhaps the interest which he had hitherto
excited on all hands began to fail a little too, or to be
mingled with other sentiments, as he lingered about with
no longer any scheme in hand, too much perhaps like other
men; and people began to ask where was his wife, and
why was she banished so far away, while he was, as the
vulgar thought, enjoying himself here? The vulgar mind
exists in all degrees of social life, and it was perhaps not
unnatural that lookers-on of this complexion should take
it for granted that the husband was enjoying himself
because he was in England, and his wife injured and
suffering because she was in California, occupied, as their
fashionable friends whispered with bated breath, in the
most menial offices, while he dined with princes. California, however, is not so far from England after all as to be
altogether deaf to what occurs on the other side of the
Atlantic; and when the derogatory rumours and wonder-
ments of society—wonder so easily converted into scandal
—at length reached the ear of Mrs Laurence Oliphant,
her good sense at once convinced her that a summary
answer must be given to the gossip, and the position at
once rectified. The Prophet would also appear to have
been convinced of the necessity of taking from all adversaries such an occasion to blaspheme, for he does not seem
to have interfered to prevent her journey in any way.
Accordingly it became known suddenly in the early winter
of 1880 that at last she was to join her husband in Lon-

don.   There was but one voice of jubilee and congratula-
tion among all who knew them, at this much-desired
reunion: and after her long absence, and wonderful experiences, Alice Oliphant was received everywhere with
something like an ovation, subdued by the impossibility of
saying what had been in everybody's mind, yet expressed
in many a fervent pressure of the hand and outcry of
satisfaction.

It was in a little lodging in Half-Moon Street, just
before Christmas, that I saw her for the first time.   The
fascinating and vivacious beauty of her youth could only,
I think, have been enhanced, in expression at least, by all
the strange vicissitudes she had gone through.   She was
by this time at the full height of life, the *mezzo del cammin*,
and a little worn with delicate health and many labours ;
but so sweet, so bright, so gay in her profound seriousness, so tender in her complete independence, that all the
charms of paradox were added to those of nature.   She
had the gift (which is an inheritance and special endowment of some well-bred Englishwomen) of a certain soft
eloquence and command of perfect words which was delightful to listen to — like music, but better than music
to ears uninstructed in that art.   Her husband was a
brilliant conversationalist, but she was something more.
Her beautiful sentences flowed like the easiest of chatter ;
her sweet speech, in which the most keen critic could not
have found an inappropriate or misplaced word, seemed
simple as the utterances of a child.   She had caught in
America, with her fine musician's ear, a slight accent,
which was amusing and piquant in an Englishwoman,
though perhaps in itself scarcely delightful to English
ears ; and the extraordinary mixture in her of the finest
culture of the Old World and the freedom and strange
experiences of the New — the latter acquired, not in
sophisticated places where New York or Boston holds the
mirror up to London and Paris, but in the Far West, and
in the primitive country districts, where all is individual
and strange—was more fascinating, amusing, and curious
than words can say.   She was in all her beliefs and sentiments a mystic of the mystics, by force of nature as well

as in devotion to the mysterious faith which had held them both in such complete and long subjection; and to which, in spite of all that had come and gone, she was still bound heart and soul. She would talk, in her beautiful way, freely of what that faith and these principles were; but I am bound to admit for myself that, though the talk was delightful, and to listen to the voice of the charmer, so long as she pleased to discourse, a constant fascination, yet I was little more enlightened at the end than at the beginning. But this was at a later period, and hurries the narrative, which here must receive her own explanation of the causes of her long absence, which the reader may think makes the guesses I have offered already unnecessary, or even vain, and which I find in a letter to her mother, Mrs Wynne Finch, dated from the Adelphi Hotel, Liverpool, on her arrival, and which is full of the excitement and buoyant pleasure of the return.

"*1st November* 1880.

"So many thanks for your loving little note, which was delightful to read on the wharf, as a first greeting, after Laurence's, in old England. I am a little more than usually tired with the almost unbroken journey of twenty days, having had an exceedingly rough passage, with much suffering, and having, moreover, taken a cold, which became bronchitis just as I was beginning my preparation for it, in California, so that I have had a weakness and cough working against me ever since.

"It appears that there is a ball at Sandringham on the 12th, and Hamon is naturally anxious that I should be there; which I could do as well as not by taking care of myself up to that time.

"So far as the *on dits* go, I assure you that my presence in this part of the world will soon relieve you of all the difficulties which you have, I know, contended with so bravely. Is it not funny what simple things cause so much astonishment? I tell every one whom I meet the plainest truth about myself and my peculiarities, and in case you have any occasion or any wish to state the circumstances to any one before I meet you, in the same way as I do, I will here reiterate them; otherwise I am in the Old World to answer for myself, and can give all detail of explanation that any one may require when I see my friends. I have always exacted of Laurence that he should leave me free to make my own personal experiments that I may think needful for my usefulness in the world, as also of all my American friends. During this recent period of our separation I have to my own satisfaction, and entirely unknown to Mr Harris (whom I have not, because of his health, been able to see for three years, and who did not know till the other day what I was doing), solved the question to myself of being a producer in the social scheme, unaided by any social connections, besides many other questions related to it, and of great practical value to myself. I return here for a while because I want to see you and my friends, because Laurence needs help that I can render him, and because I need rest—*et tout est dit!* except the thousand things that you will want to ask, and that I shall be delighted to answer.

" It seems unmitigatedly happy to be amongst you."

Thus the simple story was told. It was very simple and true, and explained nothing, which is the best kind of social self-interpretation. Thus from teaching her little music-class in the Californian wilds, among the humble women who afterwards mourned her as an angel departed from among them, she flashed at once to the home of royalty at Sandringham, where all the Norfolk gentry, much occupied in their minds as to what had become of her, and whose fault it might be, could see at once that there she was, both happy and independent—a wife truly united to her husband, a lady just as fit to stand before kings as when she had disappeared from among them. It was in its way a little triumph which, true woman as she was in all things, she enjoyed.

But she came home to find her husband ill, and she was herself still combating the cold caught in California, and greatly worn and exhausted with all she had gone through, and the stormy voyage at the end; and the pair were very

speedily sent off by that habit of English doctors which
sometimes affords a much-desired outlet to the sad and
anxious, and sometimes is so great a burden and vexation.
To the Oliphants it was a very convenient and delightful
way of escape from various embarrassments ; and they set
out for Egypt together with great enjoyment of that fact,
and a return in the mind of Laurence of that healthful
and cheerful impulse " to write something," which happily
was now in full force again.   The record of their journey
is to be found chiefly in the ' Land of Khemi,' which relates
the happy wanderings of the reunited pair among all kinds
of unknown places entirely out of the beaten track, the
fertile district of the Fayoum, and many others where foot
of Englishman had scarcely passed, and which travellers
less happily provided than themselves with official protection and help could scarcely have undertaken, unless at
enormous expense and risk.   I am obliged to add, however,
that this journey, which seems so happy in the narrative,
was vexed by many irritating restrictions on the freedom
of their intercourse, which had been imposed upon them
as the condition of their prophet's permission for the return of Alice.   And another demand was here made on
his part which I believe was whimsically and involuntarily
balked by their residence in Egypt at the time of receiving
the command.   The call which was made upon them, as
upon the other holders of land in the Brocton community,
was that they should formally make over their rights in
that property to their head.   Neither of them, I am told,
had the slightest intention of rebellion or resistance.   But
the Consul-General in Cairo, before whom it would have
been necessary to appear to execute the documents required, was an acquaintance of both, and they shrank from
the inevitable betrayal of their act, and social discussion
of it that would ensue.   This accident, as I am told, saved
as much as could be saved of the property of Laurence :
that of his wife had long been out of her own power.

The Egyptian book was published very soon after their
return to England.   The following letter, addressed to Mr
W. Blackwood on the way home, shows how far the work
had advanced, which must have been chiefly written amid

the perpetual movements of the journey, between December
1880 and March 1881:—

"CAIRO, *April* 19.

"I shall probably leave for America about the 15th of
May; but my wife will remain in England, and she is so
well up in the names, &c., that she will correct the proofs
of the remaining parts. I do not expect my absence to
be long; but as I shall probably have to go to California,
I may not be back before the end of the year. I am
fortunately well enough to travel, but have not got quite
sound." A month later he writes from London: "I have
taken a cottage for my wife at Windsor, not far from
her namesake, so perhaps you will make a trip there and
polish off both the Mrs O.'s. They are great friends."

It was indeed an unusual gratification to have such a
neighbour as Mrs Laurence Oliphant close at hand, and
her delightful company was a pleasure all the greater from
her extreme unlikeness to anything likely to be found on
the homely level of a little country town. She had seen
so much, and of all sorts and conditions of men—her
experiences were so wide-spreading, from Belgravia and
the Faubourg St Germain to the Californian miners and
farmers of Brocton; and she would change in a moment
from discussion of the highest problems to discourse upon
the habits of the cocks and hens which she took pleasure
in feeding and watching; or would rise from the table
where she was making with flying needle a cotton gown
for the summer, to play from memory a movement from
Beethoven or Mozart, all with equal interest and energy
and playful earnestness. There was no weariness where
such an inmate and companion was. To old and young
she was alike delightful—not too wise for the girls, not
too serious for the boys; ready to talk, to laugh, to play
on the piano almost anything they asked her for; to fall
into beautiful discourse one moment upon the love and
service of mankind, to which she felt herself dedicated,
and to break off the next into some homely jest of the
family in which, like the jokes at Farmer Flamborough's,
there might be little wit but much laughter.

I have said that her explanations of the faith she held were bewildering to me. The dual principle carried out in the relations of humanity, but springing from the very Godhead—which was made up of a Father and Mother, the masculine and the feminine in one person—was the heart and soul of this system. I am not able myself to see that this view gives any deeper or more attaching charm of tenderness to the all-embracing love of the Father in heaven: but many good people have felt that it did so; and to many, I believe, the doctrine of the new and close union between the Counterparts of married life, so that the man could be said to dwell in the woman and the woman in the man, each coming forth for their special department of human concerns, and retiring when it was their partner's turn, has been as a revelation from heaven. The additional sacredness thus given to what is already the closest tie on earth, and the conclusion that the deepest interests of the human race were involved in it, and could only be worked out by its universal acceptance, was the chief dogma, if dogma it could be called, of the new faith. It differed only in its intenser feeling from the well-worn doctrine that "they two shall be one flesh," or at least it professed to be the perfect carrying out of that familiar principle, which, like almost all the principles of religion, Laurence Oliphant and his wife considered to have fallen into mere dead words and not living sources of faith. And yet I think I have known many pairs walking by a very sober light, who were indeed and in truth one flesh, or rather one soul. This, however, in the opinion of my friends, was what the world had lost; and to regain the belief in its most superlative carrying out, in that state where each should be the complement, conscious and certain, of the other, and in which the mutual thoughts or breathing together (Sympneumata) of the two were to purify the world and bring in at last the fullest conditions of salvation—not indeed that salvation which the older creeds called saving of the soul, in their idea a purely selfish formula, but the redemption of the race from all its sins, the extinction of evil, the regeneration of the world—was the subject of all their desires and thoughts.

The reader may ask what had been in the meantime the history of the forsaken mother, who, during all these vicissitudes, had been labouring on alone at Brocton, far from the children she loved, in a position which the spectator can scarcely but feel to be cruel, but which she had chosen and accepted with the fullest faith. When Laurence left England in May 1881, it was for the purpose, among other things, of visiting his mother and satisfying himself as to her health, of which disquieting rumours had been heard — not, I believe, from herself, for there had been little if any correspondence permitted between them for years. He had so great a faith in the continuance of her bodily vigour and health, which he believed to be sustained by constant communications of heavenly strength from her Counterpart on "the other side," his father, that he was not, I think, very anxious, but yet felt it necessary to see for himself how things were going. He found her, on his arrival at Brocton, much worse than he had thought, suffering from cancer, completely broken down in strength, and also troubled in heart and faith. I do not know how it had come to her in her long and weary drudgery to begin to doubt the truth of the Master, for so many years a veiled and distant prophet, whose sway had for so long been absolute over her life. Certain rumours about his life in California had reached his distant kingdom at Brocton, and awakened troubles and sorrow there; and this dreadful disenchantment was working in Lady Oliphant's mind as well as the deadly malady in her blood.

Laurence in alarm summoned the best medical aid for his mother, but found little comfort in the opinions of the doctors; and, whether by their advice or with lingering hopes of supernatural restoration, took her away a long and weary journey to California, with the intention of going to a watering-place there, where there were certain springs supposed to be of advantage in her complaint. They went first, however, to Santa Rosa, where in all likelihood he at least had still some lingering hope that the "Father," to whom so much of his life had been devoted, the leader and guide of so many years, would find means of doing something for the faithful servant who had

obeyed and believed in him for so long. I know no details
of this visit, except that the sad pilgrims — the dying
mother and anxious son — were far from graciously received. Their tyrant, who had so sensitive a consciousness of the "states" of his disciples, no doubt felt that
something had come into their feelings towards himself
which was new and strange, and either did not think it
worth his while to conciliate them, or considered it still in
his power to terrify and overbear. I do not know if any
open breach occurred at this time; but such a small incident as the sight of a valuable ring belonging to Lady
Oliphant, which had been given over with all other
treasured things into the keeping of the prophet, upon the
finger of a member of his household, brought a keen gleam
of conviction, both to the one who doubted already and
the other who did not know whether to doubt or, as on
former occasions, to gulp down every indignity and obey.
They remained only a few nights after their long journey,
and were dismissed with, I believe, the scantiest pretence
of hospitality upon the further way.

The invalid however never reached the waters in whose
healing influence her anxious companion had some hopes.
They got as far as a village called Cloverdale (the reader
familiar with that country will pardon my ignorance of
the localities), where there was a woman who possessed
one of those panaceas which are to be found in every
country, decoctions of herbs and faith, curing actually in
some few cases, by what action on body or mind it is
hard to tell, various ailments and diseases. When he
found that his mother could go no further, Laurence wrote
to his friend in need, Mrs Walker, telling her his circumstances. That kindest of friends at once went to their aid.
She found Lady Oliphant very ill, but quite incredulous,
as was Laurence, of the possibility of approaching death—
and attended by the woman with her cure, which, however, was administered without confidence, the rural healer
doubting that the patient had strength to recover. That
any cure should have been sought at all was entirely contrary to the orders and will of Harris, and angry letters
had been received from him denouncing it. On what

proved to be the last night of Lady Oliphant's life, Mrs Walker watched with Laurence in the sick-room: and she has described to me an extraordinary agitation of which she was sensible, in the air, which she could compare to nothing but a storm or battle going on over the bed, which affected even herself, no believer in the mysteries which were so dear to them—with all the sensation of a terrible conflict, during which the patient suffered greatly. And then there came peace and great quiet, and the sufferer looked up, restored to ease, and told her son that she had seen his father, who had poured new strength into her, so that she felt overflowing with vitality, and knew that now she should live and not die.

With these words on her lips, and murmuring something about the angels all around and about, Lady Oliphant died.

She had been greatly deceived in her life, and suffered much. Yet we may be well assured that in the chief point of all, in the divine footsteps she had tried to follow, and the God whom she had always sought, though through mediums of human weakness, she was not deceived. It seems to the spectator a hard fate that this tender mother, so devoted through all his life to her only child, should have been left so long in her failing days, at the end of life, alone in a far distant country, separated from all who belonged to her. But at all events it was with her son's hand in hers, and her Lowry's beloved face bending over her, nearer to her than any angel, that this good woman, much blown about by many winds of doctrine, yet always steadfast to the standard of divine charity, passed into the eternal home, the way to which was never far off from her humble feet.

His mother's deliverance from the bonds of the flesh was a great shock to Laurence, not only in his tenderest affections, but in those hopes which he had entertained that one so supported by the unseen need not die. When they had laid her in her grave, so far away, he returned with Mrs Walker to her home at San Rafael, a sorrowful man shaken loose for the first time from the strong delusions which had held him for so long. He had still

believed, though perhaps with doubts and fears, when he
took his dying mother to Santa Rosa; but their reception
there, and many circumstances connected with it, the unexpected repulse, the evidence of things which he could
not but see, though hearing of them he had not believed,
ripened these doubts into conviction. The revelations
which she had made to him affected him still more powerfully after she was gone; and when, in the silence of his
sorrow, other recollections arose in his heart — recollections of the bitterness he had endured in that same place
when turned away from the doors within which his wife
was, denied even a word with her—and of the manner
in which his life had been foiled and turned aside, his
energies checked, his labours interrupted, and everything
he had and was turned to the profit of another, his heart
burned and his bonds were broken. Ill and sorrowful
and disenchanted, suffering from that most tremendous of
moral convulsions, the throwing off of a long and confirmed allegiance, the destruction of a faith that had
been for many years the chief thing in his life, he passed
through a period of suffering and mental conflict which
had no parallel in his previous life. He had thrown over
the world and all its hopes, his career, his ambitions, and
his pleasures, lightly at the command of what he felt to
be a voice from heaven; but when he had to give up his
faith in that voice and tear himself asunder from the
influence which had cruelly interfered with every detail
of his existence, the effort was not light or easily made.
Mr Walker tells me that, as he discussed the question
over and over again with his friends, great beads of perspiration would come out on Laurence's forehead. The
struggle was one almost of life or death.

Fortunately, however, he was now in the midst of wise
and energetic friends—friends who, as his friends everywhere would have been, were glad to perceive that the
bonds which had been becoming more and more impossible
through all these latter years were broken, and to help
him towards a full emancipation. In this respect there
was a long and difficult struggle to be gone through, which
Laurence would have been totally incapable of conducting

for himself, but which Mr Walker, a man of great standing and importance in the district, was fully able to carry
out, and did carry out, with, I have no doubt, no small
enjoyment in the task.   It is not necessary that I should
enter into the processes by which the land originally
bought by Laurence at Brocton, but which the head of
the community had always administered and virtually
possessed, was dragged back into the hands of its true
owner. The operation took a considerable time, and much
pressure; but as neither the Californian merchant nor
his lawyers were afraid, and their antagonist had by
this time a great deal to lose, and could not afford to risk
all that might arise from exposure and publicity, it was
finally successful. The active agents found the greatest
satisfaction and pleasure in extracting, bit by bit, the
fields of Brocton from the hands which had held them
so long; but the man for whose benefit and in whose
name the struggle was carried on did not enjoy it: he
was torn asunder by the very fact of his escape.   And
I am told that a member of the Brocton community who
was summoned to give an account of the property, a
strong and sturdy young farmer, trembled like a leaf in
presence of the Sorcerer who had thus bent them to his
will, his knees knocking under him, and perspiration
pouring from his brows.   Many, if not all, of the Brocton
people shared the doubts which Lady Oliphant had conceived, and were at the same time delivered from their
long subjection; but I do not know if any were so successful as Laurence, by means of his friends, proved to be, in
the redemption of their land.

There remained, however, a horrible question which
took away all the comfort from these successes.   What
would Alice say in England, whose faith was unbroken,
who had not laid a finger to the pulling down of the idol,
and to whom it might seem the wildest iconoclasm and
blasphemy?   This question was not solved, nor was there
any confidence as to what its solution would be, when
Laurence at length set sail for home.   To escape the
wintry journey he took a roundabout route, which he
has described, I think, in one of his articles, going to

New Orleans, and from thence along the Florida coast
to Havana and St Thomas, and so to England. He writes
from Havana to Mrs Walker, in a letter which throws
some light upon the terrible suspense from which he was
suffering :—

"I ought to be in good spirits so far as my physical
condition is concerned ; but I cannot help feeling anxious
at leaving the enemy so much time to carry on machina-
tions in England possibly during my absence. In spite
of my resolution to forget all the suffering I have passed
through, it keeps coming back like a nightmare, and it
will be some time before my wounds are healed. . . . I
daresay you will have heard from my wife long before
this, and therefore will know more than I do what she
is feeling. It seems so long to be without news from
anywhere."

Alice meanwhile had not been without her share of
suffering. I cannot tell whether, perhaps, had not the
wisdom of him whom Laurence now describes as the
Enemy failed him, it might have been possible that her
strong faith in him might have vanquished her love for
her husband. But fortunately the wisdom of the serpent
sometimes does fail. One day while the struggle was
going on she received a telegram from Santa Rosa, de-
manding the aid of her authority in order to place her
husband in a madhouse, proceedings to which end had
been begun, but could not be completed without the sanction of his nearest relative. It may be imagined what
effect such a message — so fiery, sudden, and imperative
—would have upon a woman trembling between two of
the strongest impulses of humanity. Reluctantly, forced
by an order so inhuman, so treacherous and terrible, the
scales fell from her eyes also ; and when Laurence, still
trembling for the issue, reached Plymouth in the end of
January 1882, he had the happiness to find his wife
waiting for him there, in blessed demonstration of her
fidelity and support in this perhaps most terrible moment
of his life. He sends a hurried intimation of that fact off

at once—and of their pause for a week or two "in a sea-side villa lent us by the Mount Temples," at Babbacombe Cliffe near Torquay—to his friends, with an intensity of relief which may well be imagined.

This strange story of their emancipation from a long tyranny which is more strange still—and strangest of all how it could have endured and affected the whole current of their lives—gives a singularly dramatic conclusion to the wonderful tale. It is strictly and painfully true; but that does not detract from the strange completeness of the construction, for truth, as the most hackneyed of all proverbs says, is always stranger than fiction. Fiction indeed can rarely at any time venture upon combinations and catastrophes which are the daily experience of life.

They remained in London for some time after this, where Laurence occupied himself in preparing for publication the entertaining volume called 'Traits and Travesties,' which consisted chiefly of articles contributed to 'Blackwood's Magazine,' almost all of a high order of merit, and perhaps more welcome to the public than the volumes of travel which one could not but feel might have been done nearly as well by a less gifted hand; whereas nobody but Laurence could have written the stirring adventures of the War Correspondent, the pungent remarks of Turkish Effendi and American Senator, still less the experiences of Irene Macgillicuddy, or the still more astonishing narrative of Dollie, all of which are included in that book.

This was the end of anything that could be called residence in England for the much-travelling pair. Mrs Laurence Oliphant never returned after her brief stay; and he came only for flying visits, sad enough and forlorn. Another, and the last, phase of their united life, in every respect the happiest, but of short duration, was now to begin.

CHAPTER XI.

THE SUNSHINE OF THE EAST.

IT is scarcely necessary for me to enter into the history of the persecution and ill-treatment of the Jews in the provinces of Galicia, Wallachia, &c., which made so many unhappy families homeless, and roused the indignation and sympathy not only of their own people scattered over the world, but of most Christian nations, during the year 1881. It will be well enough remembered that one of those great subscriptions, which show at once the wealth and liberality of the City, and which have done both good and evil under the title of the Mansion House Fund, had been taken in hand for the distressed and persecuted Israelites during the course of the year, and that a large sum of money had been raised which it was of great importance to find trustworthy agents to administer. His previous exertions in respect to Palestine colonisation had called the attention of the heads of the Jewish nation in England, as one who had done a great deal of work in their interest, to Laurence Oliphant, who was, as it happened, at this moment without any serious claim upon his time and thoughts. I have no information as to the preliminaries of his appointment, having only heard suddenly one wintry Saturday evening that they were going off on Monday to the unknown world, and that if I wanted to say good-bye to them, I must go at once. On a Sunday afternoon, accordingly, wet and cold, in one of those London lodgings which look so dreary out of the season, a large dingy drawing-room in Clarges Street, I think, with heavy old furniture adding to the gloom of the London afternoon in its general absence of light, I saw Mrs Laurence for the last time. She was seated by the fire arranging her ornaments in a little jewel-box in preparation for departure, her graceful head relieved against the dull glow of the fire on one side, and the duller light of the afternoon falling upon the slimness of her shadowy figure, the dark hair loosely brushed back from her fine brow, the delicate profile bending over the trinkets, on the other. She was cheerful and pleased with the expedition, the new worlds to conquer and strange sights to see; and presently her husband came in, who told me the story of his mother's death as I have already recorded it, with the invincible cheerfulness natural to a man who looked upon death rather as a means of bringing those he loved nearer to him than of making a dreadful void in his life. They were all packed and ready for their start, not knowing precisely where Providence might lead them before they came back, but facing all the hazards of the future with pleasant confidence — a confidence, no doubt, springing partly from an ever sanguine and buoyant nature, but chiefly from the sense of the great work which they felt to be in their hands, and which they were sure of the guidance of God to enable them to carry out.

It was during this interview that I became aware distinctly, and for the first time, that the guidance of Harris was no longer the rule of their lives. No explanations were entered into, unless it were a brief and unwilling intimation that the point of view on which the disagreement took place was a pecuniary one, and caused by the action of evil counsellors round him. I had remarked a caution in the manner of Alice in referring to him during the latter part of her stay in Windsor, which had prepared me to hear of some change in their relations. And I confess to having felt much sympathy, and even sorrow, for the disenchantment, feeling that it could not but be a great mental shock to be forced to admit that the man who had dominated their lives for so many years was not the prophet, guide, and leader they had believed him to be. The force of indignation with which his later acts had inspired them, however, and the sense of newly regained freedom, and consciousness that no one now could interfere with their union, neutralised the severe blow of discovering his unworthiness. And they were now as people emancipated, safe and secure in being together, and evidently feeling themselves fully equal to the task of guiding and helping

those who should adhere to them.   Free as they had
always been from the usual ties of a settled home, they
were now more free than ever; but with the difference,
that their first aim hereafter was to find an abiding place
and centre for themselves, and that "work" which was
to them the chief end of life, independent of all previous
associations.   What was really meant by that work was
at all times a more difficult matter, and apt to exercise
the minds of those who followed them with ever-increasing
interest and wonder, but limited understanding.

This, then, was their new beginning and independent
set out in life.   No idea of separation crossed their
minds any more; they were more happy in each other's
society than perhaps they had ever been: even in the
first enthusiasm of their marriage there had always been
that chain, sometimes lightly borne, sometimes almost im-
perceptible, but at any moment capable of being tight-
ened by the impulse of an abrupt recall.   They set out
now hand in hand, with the happiness of a boy and girl
going forth upon a new world, which was all before
them where to choose, or at least contained somewhere
a heaven-ordained sphere, where in direct communion
with all they loved, and guidance from on high, they
could work and live.

The preliminary chapter of this new existence carried
them, indeed, into a region of winter and rough weather,
both physically and spiritually, to begin with, in the
midst of the suffering crowds of Jews.   Laurence wrote
to Major Goldsmid, who had at one time intended to
accompany him—from Paris, the first stage of the long
journey, regretting the impossibility of their meeting,
but expressing a hope that " we shall yet be associated
in a far more interesting and lasting work than the
emigration of the Jews from Brody to Canada."

" *9th March* [1882].

" I forwarded to Lord Mount Temple a very important
letter yesterday from Galatz.   There is an immense movement going on in Roumania, and subscriptions amongst

Jews alone there for Palestine colonisation purposes, it is hoped, will amount to fifty thousand francs a-month. I shall visit the local and central committees in Roumania, and report thereupon."

The next letter is from Jassy, Moldavia, and seems to point to a resignation of the immediate Mansion House commission, and return to the always interesting general subject of Jewish colonisation in Palestine. Laurence, however, retained the command of money from charitable sources with which to relieve the poor Jews who crowded about him wherever he went.

"*5th May* 1882.

"I have been so overwhelmed with work and correspondence that it has been quite impossible for me to reply to your letter sooner. I was detained at Lemberg for three weeks through the bungling chiefly of the Mansion House Committee, whose intentions are better than their executive faculty, and, after all, was prevented from accomplishing in that time what would have been a simple operation. However, Montagu and Asher came out at last, and I was able to hand on the responsibility of making arrangements, which are not in the least likely to succeed, to them. They all mean well, and are doing their best. Meantime I am thankful to be independent. On the 3d I attended a meeting of delegates from twenty - eight Palestine colonisation committees. There are forty-nine in the country altogether. It was very interesting and encouraging. My correspondence from all parts of Russia tells me that the movement is universal; but for the moment everything is at a standstill, until I have been to Constantinople to find out the dispositions of the Turkish Government. I hope to arrive in Constantinople next week, and it is impossible to say exactly how long I shall be kept there. Probably I shall go from thence to Beyrout, as I shall also have matters to arrange at Damascus; and it would not be well for you to come out before September or October, which is the pleasantest season, and when something definite will have been settled, and matters regularly *en train*. You would have been immensely interested had you been with me. The poor people are so grateful, that my wife and I are the subjects of a series of ovations. She has just managed to scramble through on the health question, and has had several times to spend a day in bed, sometimes knocked down by the amount of suffering she was called upon to witness, sometimes by the fatigue unavoidable in these long railway journeys. However, I hope the worst is over. I have not had time to write a line to any paper. We leave this to-morrow for Bucharest."

Things, however, looked very black when he proceeded to Constantinople, where, instead of progress, there seemed to be nothing but retrogression since his futile attempt to gain a concession in the previous years. Then it was the vacillation of officials he had blamed; now the motive of delay was more marked, and the hostility declared. The following was written for the information of an American newspaper:—

"It may interest you to know that the Sultan refuses to permit the Russian and Roumanian Jews, who were desirous to emigrate to Palestine in large numbers, to form colonies in that country. Two or three delegations which have already been sent to the Holy Land have selected land, and although the money has been collected and the families are ready to settle, they are unable to do so, as the Turkish consuls at Odessa and Bucharest refuse them the necessary passports. Jewish delegates from various societies are now in Constantinople endeavouring to overcome this difficulty. Meantime two hundred families have arrived there, and are unable to proceed, and their means are rapidly becoming exhausted. Indeed some of them are at the point of starvation, and unless measures are promptly taken, will have no means whatever of subsistence. I have sent letters to be circulated amongst the Russian and Roumanian Jewish communities, impressing upon the numerous colonisation societies the necessity of waiting until existing obstacles shall have been removed. Meanwhile the political difficulties which have arisen in the East, in consequence of the recent action of England and France in regard to Egypt, tend to complicate the situation, and will probably render the Sultan more reluctant than ever to introduce a new element into the Eastern question by opening his Asiatic dominions, and more especially that portion of them with which so strong a religious sentiment is connected, to the immigration of Jews *en masse*. Meanwhile, as the hostility of the Russian peasantry, fostered by the Government, towards the Israelites continues to manifest itself in renewed persecution, the condition of that unhappy people, who find this avenue of escape unexpectedly blocked to them, is truly deplorable.

"The position there, however, is too strained to last. I cannot but think that we are on the eve of an important political crisis, but at this moment I am powerless. The very name of an Englishman is enough to rouse the Sultan's present opposition, and the influence of the British Ambassador is entirely negative—in other words, it would ruin any cause he attempted to advocate. But this is not the present man's fault, but that of the policy he has inherited, and which is imposed upon him from England."

I may also quote here another letter explanatory of the situation in which the scheme of Jewish colonisation stood a month later, which Laurence addressed soon after his arrival in Constantinople to Mrs Wynne Finch, enclosing a communication more formal than a personal letter.

"CONSTANTINOPLE, 20*th June* 1882.

"I have always left correspondence with you to Alice, as I have been so overwhelmed that I have had to go to the extravagance of keeping a secretary, who speaks eleven languages and writes in five, which has resulted in a perfectly ruinous bill for postage every week; but I am thankful this phase is drawing to a close. A certain

Mr Cazalet has, as it were, run across the scent, and drawn the Semitic pack after him, thus giving me some relief; so I am for the present going gracefully to retire from the prominent position into which I have been forced in spite of myself, and wait till the development of events forces me to resume it again. Alice has therefore wished me to explain my situation and that of the question generally to you, and I cannot do this better than by copying a letter I am on the point of sending to the most prominent Jews in Russia, which will be published throughout the Semitic press of Russia, and probably of Europe generally.

" 'The question of Jewish emigration to Syria has become surrounded, as you are aware, by unexpected difficulties, owing to the important political European questions arising out of the European imbroglio, and to the prohibition issued by the Porte against colonisation in Palestine. There is, however, an old emigration law, of which I enclose copy, under which the Turkish Government undertakes to provide all immigrants desirous of becoming Turkish subjects, and possessing a certain limited capital, with suitable tracts for settlement. At the request of Mr Cazalet, an English gentleman, whom I have not the pleasure of knowing except by correspondence, the Turkish Government has under this law indicated, as the region suitable for the Jews, certain tracts in the vilayet of Adana, on the Orontes and in Mesopotamia. So far their assurances upon this subject are merely verbal; but they have also been made to the American Minister, and I have every reason to believe that they will soon be specified in writing, so that I think they may be relied upon. Should you feel warranted in acting upon these facts, I would suggest that you form your central organisation and send delegates to examine the land without delay, and that if on their return to Constantinople they report favourably upon the conditions under which colonisation is to be undertaken, a permanent commission should be established at Constantinople, which should place itself in communication with the Turkish Government, and arrange the details in regard to the settlement of the first

colonies; and that delegates should at the same time be
sent to England to solicit the pecuniary aid in that country
which I am sure would be forthcoming. The lands will
accommodate hundreds of thousands of families, who, according to the explanation given by the Government to
the American Minister, will be planted in villages of from
two hundred to three hundred houses each. It is possible
that even special regulations may be promulgated shortly
by the Turkish Government on the subject, but in the
meantime this is how the matter stands. I regret that I am
obliged shortly to leave Constantinople, but the American
Minister, whose Government takes a benevolent interest
in the subject, has kindly assured me that he will be
happy to render your delegates or local committee any
assistance in his power.

" 'Although it is not possible at the present moment
of public agitation to obtain such special facilities and
advantages as would in my opinion ensure the success of
colonisation in masses, I believe that a more favourable
juncture of circumstances will ere long arise. In the
meantime, I trust that your co-religionists will not allow
themselves to be discouraged by this check, and they may
rest assured that I shall continue to feel a warm sympathy
in their sufferings and their future welfare.'

" The above," he adds, " will appear in the 'Jewish
Chronicle,' but in the meantime it may interest Lady W.
to see it.

" The next [July] 'Blackwood' contains a squib by me,
entitled 'The Great African Mystery,' on the Egyptian
question. It may perhaps seem rather a grim joke now,
but it was printed and despatched to England before we
had heard here of the massacres in Alexandria. I thought
you might like to know of it.

" *P.S.*—Cazalet has a capital of two millions."

The colonies which were begun on this guarantee, and
their success, are too large a subject to be discussed
here. The history of the pair of travellers, whose fortunes
are our immediate concern, goes on through all these
extraneous matters. Before the above exposition of

the existing state of affairs was written, Laurence and his wife were settled on the edge of the Bosphorus, at Therapia, in the midst of the summer society of that interesting place.

"This is a lovely spot," Mrs Laurence writes to her sister, "as indeed almost every place along the shores of the Bosphorus seems to be; and we have chosen rooms in a house that is a little way up the abrupt slope. Our ground-floor is at the height of two or three tall houses above the shore, and we are at the top of it, which enables us to look up and down the Straits from our windows."

"Among the various reports," she adds, in another letter to her mother, "of the prospects of the Jews, you must have been puzzled to know which was likely to indicate the state of affairs. Practically none; for while there is generally some foundation for all the ideas of the correspondents, who catch hold of scraps of information about the various intrigues eternally fastening here upon every public event—how far any intrigue will go it is impossible to predict; still more, how far any frank demand for the redress of grievances will succeed is uncertain till long after it is made, because, as you know, the Government here encourages and smiles amiably on intrigues and open questions alike, and promises for ever but gives nothing, if they can help it, in writing. It has taken most of the time we have spent here for Laurence to get to the bottom of the motives of some half-dozen sets of individuals professedly working for the relief of Jewish persecution by Asiatic colonisation, some of whose schemes seem plausible enough, and combine a good backing of money with sincerity of aim. But, after all, they all turn out to be more of money speculations than anything else, and he finds he cannot work with them on that ground. Among the various ways in which he has found means of approaching the Cabinet without risking a flat refusal of even a hearing, one only has produced a result that may lead to obtaining a definite permission for the colonists for the north of Syria, and that is through the American Minister and Government. But they still delay

the written permission, without which the most certain
probabilities are perfectly useless. So, though there does
seem some chance of soon knowing *où nous en sommes*, still
practically, as every uncertainty here is all uncertainty,
we live on in suspense still. No assertion of permission
obtained that you see in the papers means anything : they
all refer to verbal promises, not documents, alas !"

"It is full swing of summer," she continues, July 5, "of
society and conference now, and this part of the Bosphorus
is as busy as a large town ; but the climate is perfect
enough to reconcile one to almost anything, even to the
torture of Tantalus, which it is to let the ambassadors sit
under one's very nose and be unable to know what they
do. In spite of their mysteriousness, we see enough of
Lord Dufferin, M. de Noailles, and M. Corti (their three
summer embassies being at Therapia) to judge that they
are almost distracted with the agonies of the 'cleft stick'
in which they find themselves. Every other subject than
that of the situation has dropped out of thought here.
Laurence has been sending no advice to Jews the world
over but to wait, for any attempt at a movement would only
bring them into disaster. He thinks upheaval throughout
this empire more imminent than most people do. He
says there can be no question now of our moving ourselves to Syria till the questions pending between the
Governments are defined one way or another ; so we are
making no plans, but stay on here, where we are well,
and well off, for the present, indefinitely. You will see a
very tough article of his, if you have time to read it, in
the next number of the 'Nineteenth Century,' "The Jew
and the Eastern Question," which sums up his view of the
whole prospect.

"We dined last night with the de Noailles. She is
always full of questions about you, and is particularly
affectionate and attentive to me. Laurence likes him,
and all the diplomatists consider him very pleasant.
Count Corti, whom H. and E. will remember at Washington, is a very old friend of Laurence's, and he has completed my comfort here by giving me a key to the door at
the top of the embassy garden, which is just opposite this

house, so that I have his hanging terraces to myself, and a short cut down upon the line of houses where most people live at the water's edge, and to which the scramble down the little street is stony and roundabout. The gardens of the French and English embassies, also climbing the slopes above their palaces, are indescribable for beauty. Periodical garden receptions have begun at both, where all the diplomatic world take tea, and tennis and talk; and one can come and go freely enough not to find it a fatigue to 'see the world.'

"We thought only (August 10) of moving about thirty miles off, and it will not change our address if we do. We have delayed on account of the uncertain appearance of political affairs; but they seem settling into a sort of a groove, so now it depends on our finding a house on Princes Island. If not, we shall stay here another two months. Lady Dufferin has arranged for my bathing with them (in an enclosure with a false bottom, the deep water frightening weak swimmers otherwise), and will send the children's donkey for me, and send me back every day; so I am not absolutely dependent on a change of place for my bathing now. . . . We were greatly amused at another piece of Lady S.'s temper. She is certainly preposterously rude. But Laurence says she would speak just the same before his face, and says she doesn't half mean it! I wish we *had* the benefits our interest in distressed populations is supposed to bring us. With a little more money we could do so much more good. As it happens, though our travelling expenses to Lemberg were given by the Mansion House, incidental matters of charity to them have made us some hundreds of pounds out of pocket this spring; besides that, we had sent between forty and fifty souls of them to Brocton, where all the first year's expenses will have to be borne by our property before their labour can begin to make them independent. Poor things, we get such grateful letters from there. We gave orders to have their Sabbaths and all food and other special observances respected, of course. This experiment interests Laurence particularly, because the great fault and weakness of the Jews is their inability for handy

work ; and he says to train even a few into that, and into
a co-operative manner of life, will be a great gain.   As
soon as they begin to earn their own livelihood, they
will be taught how to share the profits of the land, so
as to have the dignity of part proprietorship.   Meanwhile
Laurence keeps us bravely with his pen ; so we are not
exactly in the reckless enjoyment of moneys obtained for
'Harrisonian' purposes that Lady S. seems to suppose,
though very comfortable and happy, and interested in all
we do.   But it is quite futile to explain, and your quiet
fencing is the only and best way to deal with the class of
people that can never get the right end of the stick in
their hands."

This allusion is to one of the many stories which were
always rife as to the proceedings of two people so little
apt to be "understanded" of the common spectator as
these : it being so much more easy, it appears, to conceive
the idea of a high-minded gentleman living and growing
fat upon money collected for the service of the poor, than
of his adding from his own stores to their relief, and
serving them "all for love and nothing for reward."   I
have myself heard from the same quarter as that which
produced this report the most ludicrous as well as
slanderous version of the original life of Brocton, which I
love little, being, as it was, under the shadow of an un-
justifiable and cruel domination, but which was only too
self-denying and pure.   The body of Jews sent to Brocton,
I believe forty or fifty in number, had a fluctuating fate,
now up, now down, and cost Laurence,—what was for him
a large sum of money,—I am told, about four hundred
pounds altogether; but whether the experiment was a
permanently successful one, I have not been able to
ascertain.   The letter resumes :—

"We have no plans now but to watch, from not too
far, the fate of Islam, which includes the province where
sooner or later we want to make a home.   But how long
the question of any one's going, much less settling in
Syria, will be a castle in Spain, it is impossible to tell.

Probably Cyprus would be a good place to winter in,
because Laurence can make an easier livelihood where
news abounds, and as near the scene of disturbance as
is perfectly safe for me. But he says Constantinople is
very disagreeable in winter, as I see it must be in bad
weather."

A few weeks later Mrs Oliphant writes from Prinkipo,
one of "the Islands" to which at certain seasons all the
higher class of residents at Constantinople resort, and
which rise out of the soft waters of the Sea of Marmora,
within sight of the Golden Horn and all its mingled
masts and minarets, — another variety of beauty, yet
scarcely less attractive than the lovely bays of the Bosphorus.

" Thank you for trying to see Mrs Cuthbert. She had
gone to Broadlands. I am so happy in the possession of
an intimate and understanding friend. Our little household often makes me laugh at its heterogeneity : our three
selves (cosmopo - English), a little Polish Hebrew, and
Hebrew scholar required for the Hebrew and German
and Roumanian correspondence that Laurence has, and a
steady old Greek man-cook, who takes charge of kitchen,
marketing, and table, and does a little housemaiding—the
first excellently, the rest indifferently ; but with a little
charwomaning, we accomplish housekeeping in delightful
simplicity. We are all hard at work like a school of
children. The Hebrew must learn English to fit on to
some other work Laurence will want him for later on, so
I give him a daily lesson through the German. Then
Violet Cuthbert learns German, of which she had a
smattering in her youth, so I have another pupil. She
will want it when we flit to Syria, as it is the modern
language of all Eastern Jews. Then Laurence takes
lessons in the rudiments of Hebrew, besides writing, of
course, more or less all the time ; and what with the *crin-
crin* of education and the ordinary correspondence, with
sprinklings of needlework, sketching, donkey-riding, and
bathing (this probably stopped by the rain, which has

to - day, October 20, brought an autumnal change of
temperature), we constitute a perfect ant-hill of small
activities.   It is only possible because of our complete
absolution here from social duties, but it is very refreshing
to mind and body."

This time of suspense, yet of partial holiday, lasted
some months. They had no pressing cares : the absence
of money, and the need of in many ways shifting for themselves, were to these two, trained by so many experiences
both lofty and homely, *la moindre des choses;* and they
were together, in the midst of the most beautiful scenery
in the world, with as much diversion in the way of society
as they cared for, and a great deal of their own company,
which they liked best of all.   But in the end of the year
Laurence was so far satisfied with the progress made, or
else with the impossibility of making progress, that they
felt themselves free to proceed upon their own business,
and seek the home and settlement upon which they had
set their hearts in Syria.   It was, I believe, more what we
call chance than any deliberate choice that directed them
towards Haifa (or Caiffa, as it is frequently called), a
small bright Syrian town lying on the western edge of the
Bay of Acre, with a beautiful prospect across that bay of
the historic fortress, which has figured in so many wars,
and the noble background behind of the hills of Galilee.
The aspect of the place, lying in almost perpetual sunshine, with a fertile plain sweeping behind to the edge
of the low and swelling slopes of Carmel, charmed the
wanderers, who had no settled ideas on the subject or
attraction to one place more than another.   And when
they landed and found that the little Eastern town, with
its white rounded house-tops and mosque reflected in the
shining water, had—the quaintest of contrasts—a comfortable European settlement behind, with a row of well-
built houses arranged along a sort of rural street with
shady trees and gardens, the additional attraction of this
mixture of comfort and cleanliness, and the kindly faces
of the German colonists ready to help and advise the
strangers, decided them at once.   It is curious to know

that the original aim and inspiration of this German-American community was the same injunction to "live the life" as had given all that was good in it to the community at Brocton; with this addition in the case of the Germans, that their hope, as members of the Society of the Temple, was thus to await in the Holy Land the coming of the Lord.

It happened fortunately that a house remained unappropriated, next to that of the heads of the German community, the kind and friendly Schumachers, German Americans of the most worthy type, their strong nationality scarcely tempered by the atmosphere of the Moslem world about, with which both the Oliphants were so familiar. Nothing, indeed, can be more quaint than the homely village Germanism, which shows so strongly amid the habits and languages of the East; and its addition of solid, honest, and practical dealing was an unexpected and delightful addition to the possibilities of life. They decided accordingly to settle here. It was on the highroad to all the projected settlements of the Jews, and close to some of these still undetermined colonies, as will be seen from the following letter addressed to Major Goldsmid, one of the most energetic and persevering of the Jewish organisers.

"HAIFA, 1st December 1882.

"I was very glad to think that there is a prospect of my having a visit from you here. I have just taken a house for a year in this charming spot, and my wife and I are busy furnishing and installing ourselves—not a very easy matter, with such limited resources as the country affords; so that if you come in March you will find us, and by that time the Jewish colonies will be in a more interesting condition than they are now. I have not written to the 'Jewish Chronicle' about them, as so far there is nothing favourable to report. The Roumanians are the most active. The Russians, having taken my advice, are waiting for a more propitious moment. The former are trying to colonise against the wish of the Government, trusting to backsheesh to overcome opposition.

One colony, the land for which has been purchased about twenty miles from here for 40,000 francs, is still waiting for its settlers, not one of whom has yet been placed upon it; and the expenses so far, besides the purchase-money, have been over 20,000 francs, all which has been contributed by poor Roumanians. I am afraid there is a good deal of misappropriation of funds, but I am keeping clear of it, as they refuse to be advised. I have visited the property. Meanwhile there are about thirty families living in Haifa, waiting for Government permission to go on the land. I hear that the Shaftesbury colony at Latakia has not yet got upon the land. There is another colony near Safed, which I understand is doing better. The climate here at this time of year is simply heavenly."

Several other letters on this subject give a view of the gradual settlement of these Jewish colonies, and the very anxious care and supervision exercised over them. The question is one into which it is unnecessary to enter, and I have not sufficient information on the subject to be able to offer any account of this work. Its success—if it succeeds, which I believe in some instances it is doing—owes everything to Oliphant's initiative, though his original scheme failed, and he took no positive part in carrying his own suggestions out. There are various notes, however, in some of these letters to show the offices of mercy and kindness which he did execute personally towards the weaklings of the flocks:—

"I gave B. W., about whom you wrote, money enough to take him back to Roumania: he was a poor, weak, good creature, quite useless here. There is a man, H., who is poor and deserving, and whom I help on the sly, but I have got him taken on as a colonist at Rochepina. It is difficult to help the poor and deserving, as I do not want to interfere with Rothschild's arrangement; and as a general rule, it is very fair and just, but here and there are cases of hardship. There are two who are not agriculturists who are being dismissed from Summarni. They are offered their passages back to Roumania, but they don't want to go, and say they are willing to work here; so I am going to have them employed by the German colony on general works for the colony, and as they are not worth wages to the colonists, I will pay them. In this way I will test their sincerity as being willing to work as day-labourers, and have them learn agriculture."

In the meantime, both before leaving Constantinople and after his settlement at Haifa, Laurence was " support-ing us bravely by his pen," as his brave wife, generously scornful of all the false reports of the ignorant and ill-natured, said. Article after article poured from that lively and rapid pen—from brilliant *aperçus* of the political sit-uation to the amusing little drawing-room comedy of " Adolphus," a trifle dashed off in fun and haste; and he had nearly completed, while about those golden shores and islands, the novel of ' Altiora Peto,' of which he writes to his editor in 1882. Mr Blackwood had evidently bidden him " Let sleeping dogs lie," in accordance with the prov-erb, in respect to some of the satirical assaults contained in his new book.

" Something must have happened since the ' Turkish Effendi ' and the ' Reconstruction of the Sheepfolds ' to make you fear the ' sleeping dogs.' It is just the sleeping dogs that I am determined to poke up. They have no business to be asleep: but I can quite understand that you should not want to poke them up with the Magazine. The novel is in the ' Piccadilly ' style, but ventilates theo-logical opinions that are not old-fashioned, and goes in largely for attacking the views of modern society."

This book, accordingly, was not published in "the Magazine " (a fond and familiar arrogance of title adopted by all her contributors to distinguish the *doyenne* of all existing magazines, the ever fresh and living ' Maga '), but was brought out independently during the next year in numbers, as the works of George Eliot had been—an ex-periment only capable of being tried with a very well-known and popular writer. I believe it was altogether

the most highly popular and successful of all Laurence
Oliphant's works, and excited great interest both among
those who enjoyed the satire and those who were moved
by the more serious interest. The title of the work and
the name of the heroine were taken from his family
motto — "Altiora Peto" ("I seek for higher things"),
being the distinctive sentiment, among various Oliphant
mottoes, of the house of Condie. There was much appro-
priateness, and some humour, in the adaptation. I fear,
however, that the blaze of wit and social satire which
gave the tremendous sensation of the plot an air of inten-
tional extravagance, were more thought of by the general
reader than the superlative love and high philosophical
mission of Altiora and her visionary lover. It was the
first time that Laurence had mingled his English and
American experiences of the world, and to many persons
the conjunction added much to the piquancy of the work.
Old Hannah, who is the most original of the characters,
may probably bear an ideal resemblance to some of the
mothers of the community at Brocton, in her mixture of
the quaint rural American woman with the prophetess and
seer. So might the woman have spoken who mourned
over the sweet face of the bride to whom, the community
were so much alarmed to hear, Laurence had pledged
himself. "I see great suffering before her whichever
way she turns, for with her feeling is life." One can
scarcely doubt that he was thinking of some such personage when he placed this angular, tender - hearted,
queer-spoken mystic, the illuminated person, yet village
seamstress, upon his canvas.

And then there ensued a peaceful moment, an idyl of
peace and tranquil life, coming late and lasting little, yet
full of a harmony and chastened happiness which was to
this pair, tried by long separation and struggles, like Paradise after Purgatory. They were free from the bond that
had become intolerable to them. No one could part them
more or dictate to them where to go, or how long to stay,
or exact from them any senseless sacrifice. They were
matured in their religious views, and gradually growing
more and more ready to give forth the truth that was in

them according to their own conception of it. Harris
was swept away from their lives, yet he had been one of
the stepping-stones to their present clear perception of
what they thought the highest truth; and as it was their
greatest happiness, so was it one of the deepest tenets of
their belief, that only by their life together, and their
united impulse, the "breathing together" of their work,
could they produce to the world what they felt to be the
best that was in them, and believed to be a new message
of wonder and blessing. In the radiant clearness of the
Eastern air, on the edge of the dazzling sea, with the
homely kindly Germans round them, the wandering poor
Jews, landing forlorn on their way to colonies only half
organised, to succour and help, and a little floating circle
of friends and disciples circling about them,—their life
was very simple but very full. There was no formal
attempt to form a community like that at Brocton; but
their house was hospitable and ever open, and one of their
dearest aims, or rather hopes, was, as Alice told me, to be
able to offer a shelter from the winter to such of the
"dear people at Brocton" as were delicate in health, or
weary with their laborious life. I imagine that after the
establishment of Harris in California, Laurence had become a sort of head of affairs at Brocton, by right probably of being the largest landowner among those remaining there; for the connection with this place was never
broken, notwithstanding the complete severance from its
founder. The accounts of the life at Haifa are modified
according to the reporters, one visitor representing the
ménage as consisting of a number of nobodies hanging on
to and living upon the master and mistress of the house;
while another laments that the disciples saw the truth
only through the eyes of Laurence and Alice, in a spiritual
dependence even more complete than the physical. But
everything that I have heard of the strangely constituted
household gives it an aspect of simple cheerfulness and
pleasant routine, which is soothing and agreeable. It had
the unusual aspect of a household solely held together and
actuated by religious unison, yet without religious observances or united worship of any kind. The fact that the

whole soul of the two to whom the house belonged was
bent upon leavening the world with a knowledge of the
love of God, and of working together with Him to purify
and elevate it, and that their main object was to live a
life like that of Christ in the world, is enough to show
that in their omission of all those links of common
doctrine which bind Christian communities together there
was neither profanity nor neglect, but that in this, as in
other things, they acted upon principle and conviction.
What Laurence has said of prayer fully shows his own
profound understanding of that closest communication of
which we are capable with the Father of Spirits. I do
not know upon what ground they rejected all public
service,—probably from a sense of the temptation to make
a mere show and fiction of religious feeling, a conventional
necessity, if not a falsehood altogether, of every general
form. But it was their idea also that work was a thing
sacred, not as a mere means towards an end, but indeed
an end in itself, one of the methods of the perfect life.

> " A servant for this cause,
>   Makes drudgery divine;
> Who sweeps a room but by Thy laws
>   Makes that and th' action fine."

They divided among the different members of the family,
having but limited help in the way of servants, the domestic
and other duties, one having the charge of the house, another
of the garden, another of the horses—very few in number
the latter, for their establishment was not extensive in any
way. And it was in thus serving each the other by daily
offices of love and practical kindness—the " Use " of their
original foundation—that they considered themselves most
appropriately and continually to worship God. There will
be many who will no doubt be inclined to say, with the
highest of all authorities, This might they have done, yet
not have left the other undone. But this is not the place
for criticism of their beautiful and blameless lives.

Haifa was delightful during the winter, and full of simple
pleasures as well as work. There was no society, it is true,
but plenty of friendly people, all the more original that
they knew nothing of society, nor of what we call conven-

tional life—forgetting that every nation and class has its
own immovable conventions, stricter often than any known
in Mayfair. They had a natural ride laid out for them,
far better than any Rotten Row—ten miles of fine and
shining sands between their village and the little town of
Acre : they had sea - bathing at their doors. They had
visitors, now and then a passing cavalcade of travellers,
something more than tourists, bringing a whiff of home
and all its naughty ways. It would be curious to count
the number of known persons above the common, led to
make that detour out of sympathy and interest, if not
friendship, who thus glided across their horizon, and
brought back reports and descriptions of that strange and
distant home. A row of white gleaming tents on a natural
terrace, within a stone's-throw of the village street, so
cheerful and comfortable, and unlike the domed and
minareted town on the other hand, gave thus an occasional
change and variety to the scene ; and the wistful and
ragged Jew, homeless and faltering upon the edge of a
new life, for which nobody could yet tell how much or
how little he was adapted, made the exercise of pity and
succour to the destitute an almost daily necessity. The
American visitor from Brocton, shrewd yet visionary, filled
up the curious tale of company, along with the Roumanian
Hebrew, and the quick-witted Syrian of the plain, and the
Druses from Carmel, and the travellers from Belgravia.
The two central figures in this curious jumble of nationalities and conditions were equally at home with every
one of them, and delightful and friendly to all.

The Druses from Carmel make soon a very marked
figure among their surroundings. Haifa, notwithstanding
the sea-breezes, proved too hot for comfort in summer, and
an expedition was made to the hills in quest of a refuge
from the hot weather. The low range of Carmel lies behind
Haifa to the westward—a long line of green slopes, folding
over one another, but with no mountain-head towering
over them to give them character and importance, as is
the case with the range of Hermon. Carmel, indeed, is
gloomy in its woods and dark greenness, from the narrow
edge of plain that lies between it and the sea ; and it is

only on ascending the steep and rocky way that leads through a picturesque gorge brilliant with flowers, to the wide opening and fertile undulations of the summit, that the traveller realises its beauty and wealth. It is no steep and rugged mountain, as we are apt to suppose, but rather a district of rich land scarcely needing to be terraced, not more steep than many well - cultivated districts both in England and France, but raised upon the shoulders of these slopes, as if to separate this fertile and flowery land from the common level of the world below. The road from Haifa leads along the shore of the beautiful bay for four or five miles to the wonderful and gigantic ruins of Athlit, the stronghold from which the beaten Crusaders took their final departure from Palestine—ruins that in their utter desolation still look like the work of Titans, and which Laurence has admirably described in one of the short letters that compose the book called 'Haifa; or, Life in Modern Palestine.' The road from this point turns inland; and after crossing the level for a mile or so, begins the ascent, which is no longer practicable to anything on wheels. Truth to tell, the waggons of the German colonists, which are the only wheeled vehicles in this part of Palestine, are as little suggestive of comfort as any conveyance can possibly be, though they are a wonderful resource to that portion of the population, less numerous in Syria than among ourselves, which is not happy on horseback, or able to spend long days of slow progress in the saddle.

Nothing could be imagined more beautiful than the wild and formless track up the hillside through the tangled copse and flowery shrubs of the Carmel slopes. Not to speak of anemones and cyclamen, and a host of smaller flowers, the dazzling spears of the wild hollyhock, and of a kind of glorified willow herb, the great bushes of cistus, which some botanists take to be the rose of Sharon, the sheaves of iris, and a hundred more to which it is difficult to give a name, make the path a continual delight. But the delight is modified to the rider inexperienced in such paths, who has to prick his way up rocky steps, pushing through the flowery scrub, and unable to go beyond a foot-

pace; and still more to the unfortunate traveller who has
to be carried upon the shoulders of half-a-dozen wild
Druses up the prolonged and difficult ascent. My own
progress in this way (if I may make a momentary personal
digression) was amusing, if a little nervous work. Starting dignified, but somewhat dreary, with two bearers who
carried my chair at a low level, with straps attached to the
shafts over their shoulders, the advance was very slow and
the slim Druses easily exhausted. It was at length proposed by some one that the straps should be done away
with, and the shafts themselves elevated to the shoulders
of the bearers, thus admitting of four men to carry the unexpected weight. When this change was effected, the work
became but too easy, the four men being continually replaced by another four, who thrust their volunteer shoulders under the shafts and ousted the previous carriers with
what was evidently excellent sport to them, but a little
alarming to me. Among them was one wild man from the
Hauran, with coal-black hair and beard and a dark-coloured
kuffieyeh (the picturesque kerchief with which they cover
their heads, held on by a sort of fillet of thick black woollen cords), with cheeks slightly tinged with rouge or some
corresponding colour, and eyes brightened by *kohl*—these
enhancements of beauty being general among Druse men.
The others were chosen from among the best men of the
village, and all wore the red-and-white striped coat which
is peculiar to the Druse. As we went along, one began to
play upon the Arab pipe, the most lugubrious of instruments; and as we approached the village, where the stony
track was replaced by the curves of a half-made road,
several of the men burst forth into a chant in which the
same words, unfortunately unintelligible to me, were repeated over and over again; and as the music was accompanied by much "daffing," laughter, and talk among themselves, and the continual pantomimic feat of substituting
one set of bearers for another, I have no doubt the appearance of the procession must have been somewhat baccha-
nalian. Descending on the other side of Carmel, after a
most dreadful experience of precipitous and almost impossible paths, one of the shafts of the much-jolted chair at

last—but fortunately not until we had reached the flowery plain of Esdraelon — broke, and pitched me from the shoulders of my astonished bearers on to the grassy though stony soil below. Happily there was no harm done ; but the childlike dismay and penitence of my poor men, their humble and not very effectual, but most sincere and compunctious, attempts to be of use, were amusing enough. They had really nothing to be remorseful about, for their light-hearted fun had nothing to do with what a few hundred feet higher up might have been a serious catastrophe.

This is entirely a personal digression, but it shows something of the manner in which the Oliphants had to make their summer flittings to the top of the hill. In the chapter called "A Summer Camp on Carmel," Laurence has recounted his first exploration of these heights, where he found ruined towns and villages on every slope—architectural remains very different from the mud houses of the Druses, who are now the sole inhabitants. The description of the wonderful prospect from the summit I may quote from his narrative. It is taken from Esfia, their first camp.

" On the north-west, distant six miles, curves the Bay of Acre, with the town itself glistening white in the distance; and on the south-west, distant seven miles, the Mediterranean breaks upon the beach that bounds the plain of Sharon, and with a good glass I can make out the outline of the ruins of the old fort of Cæsarea. Southward are the confused hills known as the mountains of Samaria; beyond them, in the blue haze, I can indistinctly see the highlands of Gilead; while nearer still, Mount Gilboa, Mount Tabor, the Nazareth range, with a house or two of that town visible, and Mount Hermon rising behind the high ranges of northern Galilee, are all comprised in a prospect unrivalled in its panoramic extent, and in the interest attached to the localities upon which the eye rests in every direction."

The spot in which they finally settled was the village of Dalieh, where they built a little house, very small and primitive at first, though various additions have been made since then. At a later period the discovery was made of a great vault excavated by some previous inhabitants hundreds of years before, close to the little house, in which, in the heart of the blazing summer, such visitors as had no fear of snakes and scorpions sometimes took refuge. But the house above, though so small, had yet some way of expanding to take in a guest or two, like the hearts of its inhabitants. And here, I repeat, between these two houses—Haifa in the winter, Dalieh in the summer—they spent the happiest portion of their lives. Sometimes they explored the endless groups of ruins about, from splendid Athlit, with its remains, which look like those of the palace and castle of a race of giants, to the caves of the shepherds and labourers, and little hill-villages of a previous yet not antiquated age,—for the houses of the East do not change in fashion. And Alice Oliphant, with all her intellectual powers, her beautiful *parole ornate*, and all her gifts, was as happy winning the hearts of the Druse women, teaching them where it proved practicable a little Western lore in the shape of domestic comforts, ministering to them in their sickness — as any queen — time-honoured parallel, but false enough; for what queen, with royal cares upon her head, could be so happy as this beautiful soul in her little kingdom, in the daily occupations of the "Use" which made household work a religious exercise, and with all those primitive untrained creatures about her, following her every movement with admiration, growing a little nearer to her by the link of love between them? It is enough to see their great lustrous eyes light up at the name of the Sidi Alice, to divine what her living presence among them must have been. Laurence, I believe, interfered with even more immediate efficacy in their affairs, taking upon himself the responsibility in respect to the exactions of the Turkish Government, which kept the village from ruin, and opened to him every sanctuary and every heart.

I may now turn to the little store of letters which throw the clearest light upon the first settlement at Haifa, but which in the first place seem almost to contradict what I have said as to the fact of their being no community in the usual sense of the word. They are from Mrs Oliphant, and addressed to her mother, Mrs Wynne Finch.

" *March* 18, 1883.

"You can have no idea what a busy struggle Mrs Cuthbert and I have been having. Just after Laurence left us, nearly four weeks ago, for Cairo, we found that of our Brocton friends three had not only accepted our invitation to come here, but were starting at once. I was delighted, but have since that moment had to be every hour at the back of masons, carpenters, joiners, and upholsterers, such as this simple colony of Germans provides, besides manœuvring the preparation of daily requirements, which requires trouble, as Guy will tell you, in an Eastern country. We now expect them by the Alexandria boat hourly, and have managed to make such preparations as enable us to pack old Mr Buckner and Mrs Fowler into the house, while J. F., son of the latter, will sleep at the hotel at first. To Mr Buckner, who was once a parson, but who has been for twenty-five years meekly serving his Maker, as he believes, in the preferable labours of farm and field, this pilgimage is an unexpected realisation of a life-long dream ; and it is touching to think of the long and painful journey, the first of his life, that he makes for it at nearly seventy years of age. Both he and Mrs Fowler, a most comfortable and responsible assistant to me in household matters, are heart and soul devoted to the effort we ourselves are making to establish a rational and humane manner of life on a basis wider than that of personal, national, or sectarian interests ; and they are anxious to help us to test the advantages of this country over others for pursuing the experiment, seeing with us that it unites many elements of interest, health, and freedom that it is good and unusual to find combined. J. F. comes to see us rather as his mother's guest than as an actual associate, being of a charming active nature, delighted to attempt any kind of pioneering of a material character, but neither given to moral cares nor to speculations as to the hidden issues of the age. . . . Mr Buckner will relieve us of all our account-keeping anxieties at once, and will also take the responsibility of the farming of the little property that belongs to the house, off Laurence.

"It was so good of you to think of offering me pretty things, dear mamma. You could not possibly go wrong in bestowing anything of beauty, from a picture to a frying-pan, on me, if you did not miss it; for we have to be very careful just now to confine our outlay to barest necessities, and those of the roughest sort, so that every scrap which adds a little grace to our surroundings, or a little ease to our work, is of infinite consolation. We have just been arranging our own two portraits (mine by Madame de Rechten), as at present our principal sitting-room ornaments, with our little Paris *étagère* of marqueterie, and a set of four book-shelves along one wall; and you don't know how wonderfully civilised that, with our own plate and linen, makes us feel, in spite of horrid common crockery and other discrepancies. In about a year I shall hope to be able to send for respectable crockery, and I should prefer, at this distance from a matching-place, to keep entirely, when I can afford it, to the pure solid French china. English stone china is villanous when chipped, and not good enough looking unless coloured, in which case there would be endless worry in re-matching after breakages.

"Our building prevents us this year from managing either a piano or carriage; but we shall have all such little extra pleasures by the time Guy brings you to see us. I am very happy, indeed, at beginning to gather round me here some of those collaborateurs of my inner life who are so inexpressibly dear to my heart. It is really the scheme of a railway from here through the Hauran (the grain region), and later to Damascus, and the putting it into English financial control, that has taken Laurence to Egypt; but he keeps it quiet at present, not to excite opposition. It would open up this part of the coast to a great commercial future if he succeeded."

It is scarcely needful to say that this scheme, which seems to commend itself to all who are interested in the country, and which would interfere with none of those hallowed memories which make us shrink from the idea of a railway to Jerusalem, has not yet gone any further. The road to Damascus, made under French auspices in 1860, is an admirable one, and has made that wonderful and beautiful place accessible to many; but a railway would be, I am told on all hands, new life to a country teeming with productions which it would open out to the world.

The two portraits above mentioned as adorning the sitting-room hang there still, forlorn in the unoccupied place, one of them a fine manly portrait of Laurence in a gown of dark velvet like a Venetian noble, by Henry Phillips; the other a charming youthful picture of Alice. Almost all else has disappeared, the inmates every one, the heads of the house into far-separated graves. Even the pretty furniture that made the room look "wonderfully civilised" is gone too; but still these two images of the departed hang on the wall, sorrowful reminders of a joint existence swept away into the still levels of the past.

Another letter contains further accounts of their settlement. The strangers had arrived, and were "delighted with climate and surroundings."

"The general sense of homeness increases with the improvement of the garden, the purchase of a horse, cow, pigs, &c., even with the adoption of a little dog, and the advent into the kitchen wood-box of 'home-made' kittens; while a pleasant incursion was made yesterday by the Wynfords, who found us sitting down to breakfast, and took it with us while their ship was un-˙ and re-loaded, *en route* between Beyrout and Port Said. She will give you more satisfactory and detailed descriptions in her graphic way than I can write. And I am principally pleased with this visit on account of the facility it will enable you to have of picturing us and our friends in this pleasant place.

"I forgot to answer your question about our hours in my last letter. We observe the same intervals as English people at home for meals, only we *devancer* them by two hours. 7.30, breakfast; 12, lunch; 3, tea; 6, dinner; 8, tea. Half-past six is the latest hour when people come out of their rooms, old Mr Buckner setting forth with his hoe among the Indian corn and potatoes at half-past six; and the mornings are now so delicious that I shall get up earlier myself, I foresee, and rest in the afternoon to make it possible. Mrs Fowler and Mrs Cuthbert and I have divided up responsibilities as follows: Mrs F., super-intendence of housemaid, linen, mending clothes for all; Mrs C., ditto, ditto, laundry, chickens, flower department (only embryo as yet) of garden; Alice, as you will guess, *food*. By about 10 I have made the *menu*, prepared the bread (every second day), done the more delicate prepara-tions, as of croquettes, pies, puddings; and have cut up and distributed the different parts of the fresh meat to the soup-pot, roasting-pan, dripping-pot (the household econ-omy depending more upon this process than upon any other), and am then able to hand over baking of bread and finishing of lunch and dinner to my German girl, and have the rest of the morning for writing or other work.

"Now the general arrangements of a life to organise use it up very much. After lunch we manage for ourselves the washing of actual plates and dishes, the 'girl' having gone home to her own dinner after washing saucepans and leaving the kitchen clean. This and setting away the food from the table takes at most about twenty or thirty minutes, and then we generally rest completely till three. After tea I give just now a German lesson to all the others to start them in the language. And about four we scatter about—Laurence and J. F. for walks or rides; I ride some-times, trot up or down the village street, do some little business, or a sick visit, or 'play a tune' upon the village schoolroom piano. We shall soon hire a little trap of some kind, to give us a little more change of air as the warm weather advances. After dinner Laurence reads to us, or we read to ourselves. If I am pretty fresh, I con-sider the aspect of the larder-shelves awhile, or a quiet neighbour looks in for an hour's chat. I consider myself entitled to slip off to bed any time after eight o'clock tea, and Laurence, who is the latest, is rarely later than ten."

The reader may perhaps again feel inclined to wonder a little how the employment of Alice Oliphant—a woman so brilliant and eloquent, so made to fascinate and impress society (where avowedly there is so much need of every improving influence)—in washing dishes could be to the advantage of the world; but there seems a sort of impertinence in the question in the face of her own strong and happy conviction, and of the sunshine of that life at Haifa, where also what she believed to be the highest outcome of her life was soon to come.

In August I find an account of the journey to Esfia, the Druse village on Carmel where they spent their summer encamped in tents, though they afterwards left this place for Dalieh. Mrs Oliphant gives a pretty account of the journey which she made, being ill, in the chair which I have already described; and of the setting up of the encampment, with the vault adjacent, which they made their reception-room and meeting-place, and the big black Bedouin tent, which they adapted and augmented with bright-coloured mats to make a dining-room. Here is a notice, however, which the reader would be sorry to miss :—

"Various acquaintances from the colony will come for a day or two at a time and pay us a visit. General Gordon (of China and Soudan celebrity), who passed a day or two at Haifa to see us, is coming to pitch his own tent near us. We were very much taken with him, and he and L., though they had not met since Laurence was a young man in China, seem to feel like two old friends. They say it must be because they are each considered 'one of the craziest fellows alive'!"

One would have liked to hear more of this meeting. It took place immediately after that strange holiday in his fighting life, when Gordon went to Jerusalem to make mystic measurements and theories, and indulge for once the dreamy side of his valiant soul. To have heard those two crazy fellows talking, as they wandered by the edge of the sunlit sea, would have been something to remember. They might not agree in their talk,—did not, indeed, as we shall see, for Laurence cared little about Jerusalem, and his mystic dreams had no connection with holy events or sacred places. But in their hearts they agreed upon the greater questions—the world that lay in wickedness, and the hopes of new revelation and better things; the dawning of great light, which seemed already to have touched their own heads, as the first rays of the sunrising touch the hills. I do not know that Gordon was ever able to fulfil that prospect, and pitch his tent upon Carmel; but his footstep is among the traces of those other feet on the sands, and by the village paths of Haifa, where they walked, and talked of all things impossible—the great revolution to be accomplished from falsehood to truth, from hatred to love, the turning of all the earth from evil to the love of God and His service,—impossible, yet by His grace one day to be most true.

"Gordon Pasha," Laurence wrote shortly after, 17th February (1884), "started from here for Brussels, and we had many.talks over Soudan matters. I fail to see how he is to escape the fate of poor Palmer and Gill; and he goes because he is ordered as a soldier, not because he believes in his mission. I heard from him not long before he left England. He is a man after my own heart." One other allusion to a name of so much interest was made by Alice two months later: "We had a nice, long, very hopeful letter," she says, "of the 1st April, from General Gordon from Khartoum. He thinks a war by the slaves will in a year or two break out, and solve that question of slave-trade in a manner entirely unexpected by the world."

I may add one other letter, addressed to Mrs Walker, descriptive of the Haifa household, before this simple record ends.

"HAIFA, *January* 2, 1885.

"It hardly seems a minute since I left you all; and a word from either of you brings me instantly amid all the happiness which you made for me in the delightful atmosphere of your home. This winter think of us as being composed again of a pleasant little party—viz., our two selves; my youngest brother, Guy le Strange, an ardent

Arabic scholar, who sleeps and works in two quiet rooms
he has taken in the little German hotel opposite, and
spends all the rest of his time with us; Mrs Fowler, a dear,
meek, old Brocton body, who assumes as her special function the mending; my dear friend Mrs Cuthbert, of whom
you know, who is head-gardener and chicken-keeper, and
universal sister of charity to the sick and weak; old Dr
and Mrs Martin,[1] whom we have just called from their
post at Brocton, and who will, we trust, not leave us or
our neighbourhood here again; and a young, cheery, little
Mrs Casey, who came out to nurse Mrs Martin on the
way, and will return to New York in the spring, after seeing
this country. Ernest Buckner returns by this boat, after
a year's visit, pleasant to him and to us, to resume charge
of all that belongs to us at Brocton. The Government's
fear of Mr Oliphant being charged with some political
mission from England makes it almost impossible for us
to buy much land here at present, so we are still holding
a good deal at Brocton, enough to need young and vigorous
administration; otherwise, we had rather hoped to transfer
Ernest's field of operations here.

"Our days pass very uniformly and very busily. . . .
The principal variations to our simple programme occur
in the shape of business talks or trips to the little town,
longer rides or drives for exploratory purposes, and visits
from people passing through, who bring us messages from
friends far afield."

There are other pleasant details about the summer life
among the hills—"three whole months in a tent on a
breezy hill-top" among the primitive people, "the little
nation or sect" of the Druses, "which is very much attached to the very name of everything English, and has
also everywhere a special character for honesty, so that
they make good neighbours and protectors for us;" where

---

[1] The reader may be interested to know that two survivors of this united
party, Mrs Cuthbert and Dr Martin—the last remnant of Brocton, and of
many hopes that seem to have fallen to the ground for ever—still live in
the old house of the Oliphants at Dalieh, in the mountain village of the
Druses, exercising an affectionate guardianship still over those simple and
tender-hearted people on the Carmel slopes.

they "explored in many directions, entirely escaping all suffering from summer heat;" and where there was time even for a little tough study, as well as many beautiful thoughts. "Tell Guy I am beginning to master Prof. Palmer's hard grammar a little, and really like the precision and noble scale of formation of Arabic. But what a far higher mental calibre must have been possessed by the people who constructed the language than any mass of Orientals own to-day!" Further arrivals from Brocton are announced in the same letter—one gentleman coming "who is the principal agent for our property there, and has certain shares in it," and who is "the best practical farmer in our little co-operative organisation. We want his opinion about the agricultural prospect here, and advice how far to push that branch of industry;" while another comes to "take a rest after many years of hard business work in New York, but will keep his eyes open about mercantile operations, which we think can even be opened up between this place and the United States in course of time." I do not know that much was made of any of these schemes, except, perhaps, at Dalieh, where in subsequent years improvements of cultivation were introduced into the vineyards, and new kinds of agricultural produce. Amid all their schemes there was, however, one which had been like seed in a good soil. "Never mind about what looks like the failure of the Palestine scheme," Mrs Laurence writes; "it is in reality making sure progress." It had come to no joint-stock company, and no grand concession had been obtained; but over all the country Jew settlements were springing up, the future action and influence of which it may take many years still to decide. The scheme had been like the grain in the fields, dying only to come up in varied life.

"Have you seen," Mrs Oliphant continues, recurring to less practical subjects, "Sinnett's book, 'Esoteric Buddhism'? I don't know how widely it is either admired or criticised, but numbers of people write to Laurence about the contents in both senses. His skit on it, which should be, he thinks, in the January 'Blackwood,' is called "The Sisters of Thibet," and will interest you, if the book had done so in any way. I could not read it through; but other people seem to be quite fascinated by its occultism." "The Sisters of Thibet," I may add, was published, not in .' Blackwood' but in the ' Nineteenth Century,' and afterwards formed part of the little volume called ' Fashionable Philosophy.'

I may here quote one of Laurence's letters upon the book above-mentioned, which will bring us back to the other side of the life which was so pleasant and cheerful in its external aspect. It would be giving a false impression of that life if it were allowed to be supposed that the household work and arrangements, the agriculture, the colonies, the dash of Eastern politics, occupied all their thoughts. The very reverse was the case, as indeed the most wonderful proof of that mystic union and oneness of inspiration which was their most characteristic belief— and of the office of the woman in reaching the mysteries of religious truth, which Laurence had so pressed upon the consciousness of his betrothed bride in the months before their marriage, was now about to come. I open the other side of that fair and bright life, having now made the reader acquainted with its happy exterior, in the following exposition of another mystic but never vulgar faith, contained in the following letter, which was addressed to Miss Hamilton, a relative of his own, in reply to certain questions:—

"HAIFA, SYRIA, 15th October.

" You are not the only one of my friends who has been fascinated by ' Esoteric Buddhism,'—indeed one of them is going out to India to become a Mahatma himself if he can. When the Theosophical Society was first founded by Madame Blavatsky and Colonel Olcott, both of whom I know, and others, I was asked to become a member of it; but I had reasons at the time, which I have since found to be sound, which prevented me from identifying myself with it in any way. I believe the whole thing to be a delusion and a snare. Mr Sinnett himself, in the 10th page of his book, describes why it is so. What he says of the 'cultivated devotees' of India is true of the Thibet

Brothers as well. The founders of the system, long before Christ, built up 'a conception of nature, the universe, and God, entirely on a metaphysical basis, and have evolved their systems by sheer force of transcendent thinking': passing into the other world, they retained these delusions, with which they continued to impregnate their disciples in this. As time went on, the Spiritual Society increased, forming a sort of heaven or Devachan, and in a higher degree a Nirvana of their own,—conditions which have no real existence except in the brains of those who retain in after-life the absorbed and contemplative mental attitude they acquired in this, and which they call subjective. Though how, if, as they do, one admits that everything in nature is material, you can separate objectivity from subjectivity is difficult to imagine. Practically the cultivation of what they call the 'sixth sense' means losing the control of the other five. Thus a preliminary for entering into the mysteries is that the neophyte goes into trance conditions. In other words, his five senses are magnetised, and he becomes the sport of any delusions in this condition which may be projected upon his hypnotised consciousness by the invisibles; and as these form a compact society, the images which are produced and the impressions that are conveyed are similar in character: just as a bigoted Swedenborgian in a trance condition would be certain to have all his religious impressions confirmed by an·intromission into scenes such as those described by Swedenborg. I have been for seventeen years in intimate association with those who sought to derive knowledge from such sources, and have some personal experience of my own in the matter, and have come to the conclusion that nothing is reliable which is received while the organism is in an abnormal condition.

"Although Mr Sinnett gives an explanation of spiritual mediumship which is right in some respects, and plausible where it is wrong, the Mahatmas and Rishis are nothing more or less than mediums; and where they are mistaken is, in thinking that the beings in the other world are unconscious of what happens to people in this, while in fact they are constantly engaged in consciously projecting their influence upon them, either for good or for bad. While a Buddhist occultism is infinitely higher than any form of spiritualism, or rather spiritism, that is known, it is nothing more than the highest development of it; but in order to avoid this imputation, it pretends to describe the phenomena of modern spiritism, not touching, however, those phases of it which Mr Sinnett's explanations would altogether fail to account for. The radical vice of the system, however, is that by concentrating universal effort on subjectivity, it is utterly useless as a moral agent in this world. A religion which says that because our objective existence is as 1 to 80 to our subjective existence, therefore all man's moral and physical needs here are unworthy of notice, is itself to my mind unworthy of notice. The foundation of it is egotism, the teaching the Nirvanic condition.

" What we are seeking for is a force which shall enable us to embody in daily life such simple ethics as those of Christ, which were based on altruism, and which no one after 1800 years of effort has succeeded in doing, for want of adequate spiritual potency. If some of us, myself included, have come into an abnormal physical condition, it was not with a view of finding out occult mysteries about the cosmogony of the world, but of seeking to discover a force which one could bring down and apply to the physical needs of this one. It was in this effort I found that trance and abnormal physical conditions were unreliable, though I am far from saying that the experiences gained through them may not be turned to good account, or that certain truths even may not be acquired ; but unless these truths are afterwards susceptible of verification while in full possession of all our natural faculties, they should not be received or acted upon as truths. Nor is it possible to engage in the search for such truths (with no other motive but that of benefiting humanity, regardless of what may happen to one's self) without becoming conscious of an overruling and guiding intelligence — an idea entirely foreign to the Pantheistic system, upon which the Buddhist Esoteric science (which should not be confounded with pure Buddhism) is based, and which makes the Deity a sort of universal grinding-machine with no independent faculty of action or volition. However, this subject is too long and complicated to be treated in a letter; but I am glad it has been the means of procuring me a letter from you, and of giving me the opportunity of saying how much pleasure it would give, both to my wife and myself, if either you or your brother, or both together, could pay us a visit in our home in Palestine, when we could talk over those deeply interesting subjects, and I could read you the results of our many years' efforts and experience, which are now being written, though I am not able to say when or under what conditions they will be published."

The following curious exposition of their life and doctrine, in the visionary and abstract terms always employed, which they were in the habit of communicating freely to all inquirers, and they were many, who came to them—may, and probably will, interest many readers. Repeated examples of the same kind of answers to other questions, like these in categorical form, long letters full of similar discourses (I scarcely know what word to use: I cannot say information, nor would it be possible to use the word doctrine) in reply to vague inquiries—are preserved among their papers. I give the following only as a specimen of much of the same description which remains behind.

ANSWERS TO QUESTIONS.

1. *What are the first steps to be taken towards a more perfect life of love and knowledge and power?*

That love, knowledge, and power, which belong by nature to the human being, will most rapidly evolve in him, as he holds himself most free to discern in himself and put forth in humanity that individual spiritual emotion which in all ages has constituted the real motive power of great souls, and which in the present time holds possession of the breasts of men, because of the maturing period in which we live. Love, knowledge, and power, if they do not appear in every man, are within him stifled; and the phenomena of the social, intellectual, and religious life of the nineteenth century are for the most part to be referred to the struggles of this advanced type of manhood to escape out of those methods of living, thinking, and aspiring which have served their time in other generations, but have now become anachronisms. We need take no other steps towards a perfect life of love, knowledge, and power than these : simply to note the love, knowledge, and power that is spontaneous in us, and convert it into living—that is, action,—which action is at all times to be determined by the needs of our fellow-creatures, in order that we may work at the great body of humanity, to effect more equal distribution of the pure vital current throughout its form.

2. *Is it well to investigate with free unprejudiced mind all the paths that seem to lead to solutions of spiritual mysteries ?*

All unprejudiced investigation is likely to be valuable, provided only two conditions are observed. First, that truth be sought for the betterment of the whole world, and not for any individual satisfaction or consolation ; secondly, that the investigator allows no fact suggested or revealed to influence him, unless the opinion he deduces from it receives the strong intuitive sanction of his own purest emotion.

The first condition arises imperatively out of the simple fact that each man is by his feeling, his joy, his sorrow, his desire, an indissoluble fragment of the vast human universe, and that there is no law of human nature by which it could be possible for him as an individual, and to the exclusion of others, to be truly possessed of a perfect method of life. When happiness is temporarily experienced by the gratification of higher or lower egotistical instincts along the whole range of them, from highest spiritual ecstasy to lowest physical sensualism, that happiness is merely maintained because the gratification acts as an opiate, numbing the greater number of the man's faculties and stunting his true full growth. Later in this life, or after the dissolution of his earthly wrappages, the growth thus arrested must be resumed ; for the universal human being must evolve, and then the agony of starving the faculties which have developed into monstrosities, till the neglected dormant altruistic faculties reattain development, is great in proportion to the meanness of that which was illegitimately fostered.

The second condition is imperative, because each man, while he claims nothing but a method of making the universal good, may not safely receive anything into his mind from the outside —that is to say, from other men—without submitting it to his spiritual part. If the subject-matter which he touches by investigations pursued for unselfish ends be of a quality to assist his spiritual progress, he is keenly and clearly conscious of his spirit's recognition of that fact; for it glows within him at the contact of truth like that which it produces, and urges him to let that increase of truth in him flow forth in action to his fellow-creatures. If the facts reached by research offend his own intuitions, they are, whether true or false, unfit for the time being for his contemplation; they create profitless wear and tear in his fine internal organism, and draw his unready energies into channels where they waste. Or if, in a third case, the subject-matter of the investigation, exciting in him neither attraction nor repulsion, gives rise only to distress, because he neither loves nor hates the possible truth, and therefore cannot know by private judgment whether it be true, this is a sign that there is nothing in the pursuit in question which really feeds a present need of his spirit; this is a sign that that spirit is seeking to make other promptings for other class of work, and that he is wasting time.

3. *Are vegetarian diet and temperance essential in order to purify the body for high spiritual impressions and communications?*

The prejudice in favour of vegetarian diet and abstinence from alcoholic drink, though harmless in its effect as practised on certain constitutions, produces in the case of others very dangerous diminution of the vital powers, creating openings in the deplete organism for access of spirits from intermediate states, who feed on the nervous elements of men. To impose it, or even urge it, implies as from man to man the taking of a very grave responsibility, though it has doubtless served in the hands of the deeply experienced at difficult junctures as a spiritual medicine. The shield of safety against mistakes lies, in reference to this practice as to every other, only in that attitude of mind in which the experiment is made — namely, if its object is the service of all others, and it is attempted with a profound sense of man's incapacity for correct opinion. At the start of universal development to which this century is rapidly ripening mankind, the equable balance of all the forces that play throughout the human organisation, expanding from the deep interior spirit to the outmost frame, will be best maintained, and it will be found that man's strength to think for and act for the world, for whose progress he shares the responsibility, will be best preserved if he utilises wisely all the means present in that world for invigorating the outer body which connects him with its surfaces. Of these things the One of incomparable wisdom said, 'Not that which goeth into the mouth defileth the man.'

4. *What is the immediate destiny of a soul just left this earth, loving and beloved?*

The craving to ascertain the nature of future experiences after accomplishment of earth service is, like many other cravings, not incidental to healthy normal human nature, and only accompanies a one-sided development of faculty. In practice many people at the present day do, without craving or seeking, see and communicate with those who have left this earth externally, but whose hearts are indissolubly welded into theirs, and learn that, except for the film of flesh that overlaid each particle of the vital form, life continues at first without extraordinary sense in each individual of any change, but in conditions which are obviously not accurately nor clearly definable to the minds of those on earth ; but to seek this information by a private act of will is in the last degree prejudicial to a true receiving of it, offering the readiest of all means of access to the outer organism by importunate spirits. Those natures who, by outworking of the divinest thing that they can find within themselves to follow and obey, hold within them such a well-spring of perennial happiness that there remains no power to wonder or crave,—they know that in due time they will know all, and know that knowledge that withholds itself would impair the equilibrium of their present constitution : they feel themselves in eternity, and are not in haste.

5. *Are there any spiritualistic communications to be relied upon?*

No information received by human experience, whether spiritualistic or materialistic, is to be relied on as conveying *finality* of truth ; none is to be dreaded if acquired in the true mental attitude. That people do see, feel, and communicate with spirits of all degrees of elevation and degradation is unquestionable to any one who has incurred, even without will-act, such experience, as fever is an unquestionable fact to those who have been struck down by it.

I may add here a few sentences of a similar purport from one of Alice's letters. The subject is much more universally interesting than any metaphysical inquiries :—

" As you say, it is impossible not to yearn sometimes for the day when the partings will cease. They so lacerate and tear one's very core. Yet except at weak moments I realise more and more that these pains belong only to the impatience of our outer natures, not to our essential part, which remains joined to all that it has ever bound to itself with the magnet power of love. And I also realise as the true sentiment of my being, the unfluctuating and the deep, the love of doing what God wants done for the people in the world—so of course I know that to have a formulated wish about living or dying, having others live or die, having sickness or health or sorrow or delight, would be nonsense, and a mere concession to the superficial impulse. My increasing sense is certainly that we are all put and held, or clearly directed to, the place where we can serve most some fragments of the world's great need, and certainly the love-power of our darlings who are withdrawn from their husking is an immense addition to our power in this life, for I can feel the love for the world that they pour through us has the magnitude as well as the sweetness of its purified condition. I can therefore understand much better than formerly *why* they are required for the grand force combination that can work with us on 'the other side,' even though it may seem they were wanted on this side too. They are joined to the army of high intelligences that work with and through us for the universal progress."

In the minute and laborious way of which I have given an example did Laurence put himself at the command of those who resorted to him. Whether these communications were dictated by his wife or were his own work alone, I am unable to say. I quote them as characteristic of the answers they gave together to many inquiries.

It must have been early in their stay at Haifa that the mystic volume, most curious and least intelligible of all his productions, yet by dint of these very qualities most impressive to the audience to which it addressed itself, 'Sympneumata' was produced. Laurence told me himself, on his next return to England, the story of its origin.

He had felt himself, he said, in a sort of restless excitation, full of the idea of writing something, but quite unable when he took his pen in his hand to gather together or express his ideas, and unable to give any reason for this mingled desire and incapacity, when his wife suddenly called him, and told him that there was something in her mind to which she desired to give expression, if he would put it down for her. They then began together, she dictating, but he so entirely in accord that he would sometimes finish the sentence she had begun. It was, however, so much her work that, after a chapter or two had been completed, he suggested to her that she should go on with it alone, which she attempted to do, but soon found herself, as he had been before, incapable of expressing the ideas of which her mind was full. He then resumed the pen, both of them feeling that it was intended to be their joint work; and thus the book was written. I wish I could feel any enthusiasm about this book, or even could say that I understood it. The strange story of its origin is very attractive to the imagination, and they were a pair from whom one would gladly have accepted teaching; and a number of people did so, I am told: indeed I am acquainted with some to whom this strange work came like a veritable voice from heaven. There is something in its confused and tortuous phraseology so unlike the incisive clearness of Laurence's ordinary style, so very different from the wonderful beauty of his wife's personal speech, that a perplexing sense of the toppling over, if one may use such an expression, of overstrained human faculty from the heights which it was vainly endeavouring to reach beyond, is in the mind of the reader—vainly endeavouring to understand, as they were to express, something beyond the range of flesh and blood. When sublimity is not attained in such an effort, one knows the melancholy alternative; and there has seldom been a work which has more exercised the general mind accustomed to receive with delight everything that bore Laurence Oliphant's name—more disappointed friends, or more satisfied those critics who dismissed him as one of the craziest fellows alive, and his faith and hope as the aberrations of a mind, on these points, hopelessly astray.

From their own point, however, this work was the fulfilment both of their theories and hopes: a something revealed to the woman, communicated to the world by the man, mystic truth only to be established in that way, only so to be taught with full efficacy to the world, which was at once the justification of their union and the reward of their self-denial. This was how they themselves thought of it, in a kind of ecstasy of accomplished work and tremulous humble satisfaction. It was the method in which they had always hoped and expected that the great things they had to do for the world were to be done. Advice to others, spiritual counsel, direction in the right way, could only be perfectly given by him, the husband and public expositor, when he held actually if possible, if not at least metaphorically, his wife's hand; but they had not hoped, so far as I can make out, that they were to be permitted thus to reveal in writing their new light to the world. It came to them as a heavenly surprise, the last complete and perfect proof of that counterpartal union which for a time they had doubted—a doubt which plunged them, as the reader has seen, into the darkest uncertainty for a time, the very valley of the shadow. But after that joint work at Haifa and Dalieh, that work which neither could accomplish alone, grand proof at once and outcome of the spiritual marriage, doubt could exist no longer. Happily it had departed before, along with the tyranny that probably suggested it. Now the facts were proved, verified, and brought to such manifestation as no one had hoped. And it seemed to both that they had found at last between them, in the way which they had already concluded was the only way that help could come, the lever that was to move the world. They felt themselves to have taken up, and to be completing by a new and special means, the work of Christ; yet not presumptuously, as making themselves His equals, but as His instruments in the work which He had begun. To be able to believe this, which they did most sincerely and with the full force of their being, strengthened by all the circumstances of their mutual labour, might well uplift into a rapture of spiritual elation and joy the wedded souls to whom this great acknowledgment of God's use for them and favour had come.

The book was sent to the publisher, with a letter describing its origin and the manner in which the authors wished it presented to the world.

z

"I am sending you by book-post the manuscript of a book which I want published, but which I doubt whether you will care to undertake—indeed I do not want it published in the ordinary way, as it is not an ordinary book. It is the result of the efforts of the last twenty years of my life, and contains what so many of my critics have been anxious I should tell them,—what I really believe, what I have been at all this time, what the result of all this 'mysticism,' as they call it, amounts to. In fact, it is a confession of faith, and certainly deals with a novel class of subjects [the letter here is unfortunately torn] . . . I have been the amanuensis, and so far as it could never have been written without me or through any other hand, I am the joint author. At all events, I assume the responsibility of its contents, and have written the Preface, as editor, to say so. Now as to the publication, I should like it to be published for me. I should like to know what it would cost to print a thousand copies, for which I would pay the full expense—and whether you would print it for me. I should not wish it advertised in the usual way, nor have any copies sent to reviews. . . . The class which will read it is a comparatively small though growing one, and I should like it to make its own way quietly and probably slowly. I believe, if published in the usual way, it would make something of a sensation, and bring down showers of criticism and ridicule: this, though I am not afraid of it, I don't court, though it would sell the book,—but that is not my object."

The following letter, written by Laurence in reply to a lady who had written to him with sympathy and understanding, though without having "personal use for the whole thought of 'Sympneumata' as we have felt obliged and charged to lay it before the world," will give an idea of his own feeling about the revelation while yet the thrill of its production was fresh in his mind.

" The experiences were so long and so extraordinary, yet many of them of a nature that could not at once become universal nor consistent with the present constitution of man, because of the excessive strain entailed by them, which confirmed the apprehension of the biune character of our being — that I know it must at best appear as a hypothetical idea for many people for a long while, or rest as a vague basis of life-theories in their minds. And I believe that whatever the clearness of my perception of the subject, nothing could have made it possible to launch it with the frail and imperfect vehicle of printed words to carry it upon the social mind, but the instinct that arose as the result of work among the weakest and most tempted of human beings, to whose salvation at this date I know no other doctrine than this could serve. It seems very hard to have to remember always in striving to call down God's fire of purity, that it streams as an atmosphere into a vacuum, towards all that is most foul and grievous in social ills. But who are we that we should be fastidious, and dread to see and know the laws of life-operations? What are we that we should dare to be satisfied with sur- face-decency, when we ought, like the light of God, to probe the darkness of caverns wherever they be? Yet, with our natural cowardice and superficiality, we dislike to remember always those very things in human earth-life that inspira- tions and progressions come to eradicate.

" This holding of sad facts before the mind it is that makes the martyrdom to be accepted daily, even while the glory of the heavens opens daily upon us—nay, be- cause that glory opens! Not to rest upon the sight of heavenliness, not to linger in regions of poetic sweetness, only to learn the lesson of it all, and carry it on to the dark depths of morbid life on earth, has been the hard strain of many years, which yields as the result to all men that the sex question must and can be met and solved in the generations that begin: that in the con- cealed nucleus of social living and propagation, even there it is holy and pure love that will cleanse alone and only. But to say it, is wellnigh impossible: it has to be veiled and covered over, not to make it too distressing for all those who have not seen the glory, and only know the grievous perversion of life-facts. Sometimes it seems impossible to go on being apostles of such teachings, just because of the bearing they have upon the very roots of social disorder—that is, sin on earth; yet how unreasonable one is to fear, or feel too weak, and to be puzzled about the ways and means by which the truths or glimmerings of truths one sees shall be propounded."

Other letters of this description might be repeated almost to any extent. It may perhaps be well to show how he replied to some who were not in sympathy with his views or work. He had, it need scarcely be said, many protests and remonstrances, as well as much encouragement, after the publication of the singular book in which, as he believed, the problem of humanity was for almost the first time treated as it ought to be. The letter which I now quote was in reply to a very long, serious, and interesting letter, in which his book was elaborately discussed.

"Your letter of September 23 reached me yesterday, and I have not ceased since it came into my hands to consider whether I know of any answer to the appeal contained in it that could relieve the anxiety you express. I think I do not. This anxiety on the part of a large number of the best, highest, and most earnest people of the refined intellectual type has constituted the greatest difficulty in uttering the message that I am set upon the world (so far as I can understand God's will) to utter. This anxiety will be the most formidable obstacle to the completion of the utterance. All that you say and more has stood before me for years as the protest against my almost solitary duty which it has most hurt me to withstand. Word for word nearly all that you say rises as the long familiar wail of the good, the pure, and the aspiring, who do not feel that they are made to notice the regions of hell-like moral humanity that I must serve.

"I do think that you, or thousands who will show in various forms your thought, should think differently; for I believe that the elements held in suspense by such natures form a wholly indispensable protection to the operation of the doctrine which I dare not refuse to enunciate, but which must not be received too fast. I could name to you many persons whose sympathy with us was close, and who since the publishing of 'Sympneumata' have silently stepped out of spiritual and mental intercourse with us, some in fear of our thought, some in disgust of it. And they are right—at least I have no knowledge that they are not—by thus leaving work that is not theirs for work that is. Their choice is a sacred matter between themselves and God. I wholly disagree with the view you take (while I believe it to be a safe and necessary view for many people to hold) that the divine life in us 'transforms corruption into combustion.' I believe that it transforms corruption into higher types. I do not think the mission of the World-Saviour is to 'smite down evil,' but to bring order among that confusion of faculties which constitutes evil, and raise its victims up without destruction of anything pertaining to human life. I feel that certain servants of God are bidden—that I am bidden—to stir up and dwell upon every part of human thinking and feeling and doing, in order to discover and trace in them all the central vitality which is divine and eternal, and which must be wrested out of the filth in which it wallows. But I dare not say who else can do so. It may be that the whole system of belief, of which 'Sympneumata' is but an introduction, will be scarcely acceptable to any one in this generation. But I am afraid to go on living without saying that I know that God steps down through men and is the vital essence of all their forces, and wills to leave none unredeemed."

He adds that he was at one time moved to answer the letter of objection point by point, but decided otherwise, for the following reasons:—

"I am not aware that I am bidden to scatter vital force in any game of thoughts and words; and if unexpectedly it were more than a game, and I could change a view in any one, I should be afraid I had gone wrong. I think that if to redeem men from sin is the only object of our lives, we are divinely permitted each of us to hold the form of thought by the aid of which we can for that purpose best utilise our special nature in the special era of our residence on earth."

I have been intrusted by a lady, Mrs Hankin, who saw much of Laurence Oliphant during the last years of his life, with a MS. account of her intercourse with him, and with his wife by letters, which contains many interesting details of this period. This lady had been attracted by a phrase in 'Altiora Peto,' and being troubled and disturbed in her mind, had written to the unknown author with that impulse of seeking instruction and consolation which attracts the perplexed mind with so much more confidence towards a stranger than towards the most intimate friend. She received a reply of the most cordial kind, and very soon after an invitation to visit the Oliphants at their summer house in Carmel during her vacations (for she was engaged in the charge and supervision of a school), so frank and kind, and at the same time so surprising, for they knew nothing of her but her letters, that her heart went out towards them with an impulse of responsive affection, though she could not accept the invitation, nor ever came to any mortal meeting with Alice at least, her unknown friend in the East. The account of this strange and warm intercourse is all the more remarkable from the evident fact that Mrs H. found more perplexity than enlightenment in the mystic counsels sent to her by husband and wife together, and even in the 'Sympneumata,' which she received with almost devout interest, yet found herself but little capable of understanding. After the completion of that book, however, she received the following letter from Alice, which turned her wondering interest and sympathy into a warm personal feeling.

"HAIFA, *June* 10, 1884.

"I suppose you'll be taking rest of some kind, will you not, about this time? I am taking it in the straightening out of the household details that I have had to a certain extent to neglect for some months, while helping in the little book we have been about together. Jams and saltings do give great rest of spirit when you must do them yourself, as in Palestine, or let your people go without! I may therefore luxuriate in such forms of rest with a clear conscience; and I am often thankful for the ridiculous weakness of my body, which makes such play thoroughly legitimate by making it at times the highest form of effort in which I may safely indulge. Mr Oliphant has been taking long rides of days about this country of late, with friends who wanted to inspect it for historical or agricultural purposes, and that has been great rest to him."

Emboldened by such communications, and with the pleasant shock of finding in the mystic and ethereal oracle of Carmel so recognisable a woman, involved in cares so homely-sweet, and taking her relaxation in a way so becoming the cheerful mistress of a kindly house— Mrs Hankin ventured to ask whether the mysterious utterances of 'Sympneumata' were "trance writings," which she ventures to allow she had found in other cases feeble. This lady, though afterwards drawn deeply into the circle of feeling, if not of belief, produced by that work, avows throughout an honest inability to follow the sense of its mystical teaching. The reply to her letter was as follows:—

"27*th April* 1885.

"As it happened, I did dictate 'Sympneumata,' though we did not think of my doing it at the start. I went on, fancying it would return to Mr Oliphant, but it did not. I never knew from day to day what would come; and it always flashed like lightning for a short time on my mind, and always left me strangely exhausted, as one is after strong emotion. And I never dared to think of it between times somehow, nor to look up the subjects except for names and dates, where there are references to history or literature; so that it all had to run into what little deposited information I had retained when illustrations of outer things were needed. I did not like to put my name at first, partly because an unknown woman's name would certainly lessen its chance of making an impression, and partly because, in fact, I felt as though it really all came from Mr Oliphant as much as from me. I could never say a word of it except when he had the pen in his hand, nor think any thought when he was not in the room; so he has to take the brunt of opinions. We get various ones, written and printed, of course; but already it begins to comfort a few, which is more than we have any right to hope."

Another letter follows, this time from Laurence, thanking Mrs Hankin for sending him a letter of high appreciation, not from herself, but from a relative, to whom 'Sympneumata' had been a revelation :—

"HAIFA, 8th June 1885.

"Many thanks for sending me ——'s letter. It was an additional evidence of the opposite points from which the book strikes different minds, and is encouraging, as showing that it need not always startle the orthodox. General Gordon, then on his way to Khartoum, who spent some days with me here, took the same view. He only saw the manuscript, and wished it written from the more Biblical point of view, as, though he said that it contained nothing that was not to be found in the Bible, yet few would recognise it, and it would frighten the majority, which it would not if it appealed more to the Bible as authority, and its agreement with it was made clearer. Mrs Oliphant was not allowed, however, to alter the form, and indeed found herself rather prevented from thinking about the Bible, from which we gather, as we told Gordon, that such references as he desired would frighten away those who did not believe in the Bible, and were looking for light. It is not written for those who feel they have all

the light they need, but for those who feel that the old
religious landmarks have disappeared. In regard to what
you suggest about some account by myself of the experiences through which I have passed, it will of course depend
upon other circumstances than my own whether I feel
myself impelled to write them or not. In the meantime I
am engaged on a novel which turns upon such experiences,
and which, though I don't think it will be popular or
amusing so far as the majority of readers are concerned,
may reach the few for whom it is intended."

The novel here referred to is 'Masollam,' believed, and
rightly believed, to convey Laurence's matured opinion of
the prophet—or wizard, magician, as it seems more fit to
call him in the light of that tremendous indictment—who
had been for so many years something like his God. The
book is full of strange things, and its machinery as a novel
is solely constructed to bear the burden of philosophies
and revelations much too great and full of meaning for
such a vehicle. I do not suppose it ever was popular,
though it produced a certain sensation, as everything he
wrote, especially upon these mysterious subjects, was likely
to do. I confess, for my own part, that I would much
rather it had not been written. A fallen idol is a sad
thing: it ought to be quietly, compunctiously put away,
the fragments gathered up, the downfall reverently covered
with a decent mantle, like the weakness of the patriarch.
No doubt, from his own experience, a warning might be
necessary for those who believe too much in prophets, and
who are always liable to deception thereby; but this general lesson was not his aim. He had a hundred things to
teach as well as one deceiver to expose.   •

Nothing can be more curious and interesting than the
fact that it was while in the full tide of these mystical
works, absorbed and exhausted by the effort, whether alone
or in concert with his wife, to give vent to the most complicated spiritual teachings—that he wrote in short chapters, full of humour and fancy, the record of his own
adventures and strange and varied fortunes, which was
published in 'Blackwood's Magazine' under the title of

"Moss from a Rolling Stone," and afterwards collected in the volume entitled 'Episodes in a Life of Adventure.' There could be no better instance of the double nature of the man,—at one moment absorbed in meditations which seem to touch the line between reason and unreason, in his effort to fathom beyond all possible depths the mysteries of man's nature and the cure for his ills: in the next, careering along the path of joyous life, with the free heart and ever-vivacious observation of youth, thinking of no mysteries save those whimsical originalities of the race—those amusing paradoxes and odd situations which give so great a range to the good-humoured satirist and delight the easy-minded reader. This was not the only occasion on which his double being thus expressed itself, but it was perhaps the most notable.

There was now approaching, however, a terrible crisis in his life, more dreadful than the downfall of any prophet. For about a year longer this mingled thread ran on for both: for in the life of Alice also, as the reader is aware, the sweet and soothing service of the household alternated with the high mystic outflowings of truth revealed, furnishing the same double aspect of character as in her husband: and the pair at one moment secluded in responsive rapture of soaring thought, and eager hope that now at last the talisman that was to reconvey celestial love to every breast had been found, descended anon from their mountain-top to the world, all friendly and warm with human interest, opening the doors of both house and heart to every passer-by in need. But now the clouds began to gather over the sky that was so bright. These rising clouds appeared at first in the form of added happiness and pleasantness. Mrs Oliphant's only surviving sister, Mrs Waller, with her husband and child, arrived at Haifa in November 1885; and partly on their account, and partly on her own, there were excursions planned to Galilee and the holy places there, of short duration at first, till it should be proved that the strength of Alice was equal to the strain. By this time the Haifa household had become possessed of a carriage, in which they were able to begin at least their excursions. And they were full of happy projects of all kinds, and hopes of pleasure to come. The letter of Alice to her mother, announcing her sister's temporary settlement beside her, contained a promise of a visit on her own part to England in the ensuing summer, and a wish to find rooms within reach of her mother's house, within walking distance,— "that I may go out and in" for "the four or five weeks of season" in which Laurence and she proposed to indulge; as well as anticipations of an ensuing visit to Scotland, and many other pleasant prospects. And in the meantime there was Galilee to explore, with all the holy places, as yet unvisited. New openings of life after their long seclusion seemed to be rising before the pair.

About a month later Alice wrote, this time to her elder brother, Mr le Strange of Hunstanton, the present head of the family, with affectionate thanks to him for the "noble roll of photographs" he had sent her of the old ancestral home—a long descriptive letter, full of details of the excursion to Galilee which had been so much looked forward to:—

"Dec. 20, 1885.

" We have just returned from a trip which frightened us a little in the prospect on account of my headaches, but which I managed with only one and a half, and so little loss of strength, and on the whole enjoyed very much. The important particulars you will see, three or four months hence doubtless, in the 'English Illustrated Magazine,' where Laurence will have three articles on it, so I will only give you the more intimate story rapidly.

" We started on Thursday, November 26, L. and I, our Druse man for horses, a German of this colony to manage tents, &c., a camel-driver with his two beasts, and the little son of our cook, an Egyptian, to keep him out of mischief, as his mother cannot manage him, and to have a little waiter and runner. L. and I drove to Nazareth, leaving horses and driver, and sending back our carriage next day, as Nazareth does not contain a single roof under which it could be left safely, in case of our returning that way; and being an open American waggon, it could not be left with chance of rain in the khan. That rough long drive knocked me up, and I spent the next day in bed in the Nazareth convent. Fortunately it caused no loss of time, for it rained, and the camels could not have gone on, for they are almost useless on mud.

"D. and K. had ridden after the carriage, and were with us at Nazareth, which they ' did ' conscientiously.

" *3d day.*—The Wallers started early for Tiberias, too long a ride for me ; so we went quietly on in the afternoon, I being still rather limp, to Cana, an hour and a half from Nazareth. St Helena thought it was *the* Cana and built a church there, and the Dominicans have just built a convent on the foundations ; but L. O. and the Palestine Exploration think the wedding in the Bible was at Cana-y-Jallêl, further north — though mind, I was very glad Helena did it, because we did not have to unpack our tents that night, as there was room in the empty convent 'parlour' for us to set up our beds, and they let us cook in the half-finished corridors, and let our people sleep there. We were now one more, having taken from Nazareth a certain Shtawy, well known to Guy, to protect us among the Bedouins, and to forage where there were no markets.

" *4th day.*—Had a cup of tea, and rode off with our own man, and made coffee, and boiled eggs comfortably, after we had ridden an hour and a half. This was my first day's long ride, and we did it very well, reaching Tiberias at one o'clock. The Wallers had ordered lunch for us at the convent there, but as soon as our tents arrived we pitched them and slept in them.

" *5th day.*—In Tiberias buying food for the tour round the lake, sketching and photographing. I took my little photo apparatus on my saddle always, and though very clumsy with it still from want of a master, eked out my sketching in a way that practically made the drawings a possibility, which they would hardly be with only sketching.

" *6th day.*—Rode, Wallers and all, north along the lake to Magdala, a few Arab huts now ; turned next up the Wady Hamman, lunched, sketched, and photo'd, under a fastness cut in the mountain rock where the soldiers were let down in cages to dislodge the Jews by Herod; and so back to the lake and on to Tabjah, at its north-west bend. [Here follow several wet days, during which their progress was arrested.]

"9th.—Rode early to plain at north-east of lake, crossing Jordan and visiting the possible Capernaum (Tell Hum) on the way. In the afternoon rode up some valleys in search of ruins, and came back cold and hungry, to see our tent blow flat down when it was nearly dark. Very hungry!!! It blew a hurricane, and there was only loose sand for the tent-pegs. A providential wheat-magazine belonging to a rich Damascene pacha was there, and they let us sleep in the wheat and cook in the entrance.

"10th.—L. O. excursed, A. O. headache and fever; still in the wheat-vault; marshes all round.

"11th.—Better after quinine; rode off early to get away from the marshes (buffaloes in them); pitched tent in the heart of a great Bedouin camp, at the entrance of Wady Semack, east side of lake.

"12th.—From Wady Semack along the lake past Gamala, which visited; left lake at southern bend, and went to hot sulphur-baths of Hammeh. Roman ruins.

"13th.—Rode in four hours to Tiberias, crossing Jordan at its exit from the lake.

"17th day.—Home.

"Thus it is established that I can manage such work if the moves do not entail more than four or five and a half hours in the saddle; so we may later make such journeys again. It was quite fine except the three or four days I mentioned."

It is pathetic to read this promise of travel and pleasure to come. It was, I believe, the last letter ever written by her hand. These fatal nights in the marshes had breathed death into her delicate frame. She returned to Haifa, however, to all appearance in good health, and continued so for nearly a fortnight, during which time she went up to Dalieh with her husband, to look after necessary business there. But she had scarcely reached her mountain home when the germs of insidious disease began to show

themselves. It was thought at first, however, that there was
no danger, until suddenly with an awful certainty it became
clear that she was about to die. The following narrative
of her last days was sent by Laurence to her mother :—

"Feb. 10, 1886.

"Our trip to Tiberias was simply the happiest fortnight
of my life. It was so rare for us to be quite alone, still
rarer to be both enjoying such interesting scenes, leading
a life in tents, in itself so free from care and enjoyable,
sharing all its little adventures and incidents and pleasures,
a prolonged picnic <i>à deux</i>, with sketching, fishing, photographing, &c., to amuse us. We spent two days at a large
building on the north shore of the lake. I had at first
determined not to camp there, for it was flat, and I was
afraid it might be feverish. On my mentioning this to
Guy's friend, Shtawy, who went with us the whole trip,
he assured me that my fears were entirely groundless,—
that though at certain seasons it was feverish, there was
not the slightest risk then; and this was confirmed by
the Vakeel or man in charge of the estate of the rich
proprietor, who was living there, and who assured me I
might spend the night there with perfect safety. After
the first night, when we slept inside the building to escape
a gale of wind, we both felt a little headache, but this was
attributed to some charcoal-fumes from our cooking-stove.
The morning following the second night she started feeling
quite well, but during our day's ride she felt a little feverish
and took some medicine. It then passed off, and we thought
no more of it. I never knew her stronger and better than
during the next thirteen days. She seemed to have got
into training, would ride the four hours without fatigue,
and quite astonished me by riding up to Dalieh, and at
once setting to work to get the house in order for the three
days' stay we intended making there. Next morning—it
was our fourteenth after the night on the flat, she got up
quite well, and went out to lay out some flower-beds in
the garden. It was unusually cold, and I feared she might
catch a chill; but she seemed all right until the afternoon,
when she complained of a chill. She did not go to bed,

however, till after dinner, and after a restless night told
me she thought she had a slight attack of rheumatic fever.
Ina sent you a diary of the course of the malady after that.
It was not for some days that I connected her fever with
the fatal night on Lake Tiberias fourteen days before. I
also had a slight attack.

"Dr Martin, who was with us, treated her homœopathi-
cally, and she sometimes seemed so strong, and to have
shaken it off so completely, that I did not realise how
serious it was. On Christmas she ate well, dictated a long
piece of writing to me, and passed several hours of the
afternoon in the arm-chair, occasionally getting up and
walking up and down the room for exercise; but in the
night she got delirious again, only to wake feeling free
from fever and better in the morning. It was on the
following Friday, exactly one week from Christmas, that
I had my last talk with her. She woke free from delirium.
'I feel quite well now,' she said; 'the fever has quite left
me: my body is free from all disease, and I only require
to recover my strength. There is no longer any cause for
anxiety.' Seeing that I looked anxious notwithstanding,
she repeated, 'Indeed there is no cause for anxiety. I
am only suffering now from a fearful spiritual pressure.'
I asked her if there was anything I could do to relieve it.
She said, 'No; but sometimes the burden seems greater
than I can bear.' I then tried to amuse her by talking
about our plans for the garden, &c. I also said that I
had sent for Dr Schmidt to consult with Dr Martin, and
she said, 'I am glad of that, but don't be anxious'—and
soon after she fell asleep. The doctors, however, considered the crisis past. The fever had left her for thirty-six
hours, and they attributed the delirium to the quinine
and laudanum they had been compelled to give her: as
soon as she recovered from that, they said, it will only remain for her to get back her strength. At seven o'clock
on Saturday evening I asked them how she was getting
on. As well as we could possibly hope, they said; by
midnight she will have recovered from the effect of the
medicine. I was never more hopeful than when I was
called into the room hurriedly an hour and a half later,

just in time to see the last quick breath drawn. The
doctors called the cause of death ' cerebral irritation.' But
I know from what she murmured during her delirium that
she gave it the right name when she said it was spiritual
pressure. She had overstrained the machine, and when
it was taxed by an illness which I don't think would
otherwise have proved fatal, it gave way."

And thus this beautiful and beloved woman departed
out of the midst not of a family only, but of an entire
people who did not know how to reconcile themselves
to the blow or to bear the loss. The Druses above, the
Syrians and Germans below, all who had seen her coming and going for these five bright years, always full of
succour, beaming with smiles and kindness, stood round
her death-bed with aching hearts, unable to believe that
it could be true.

I am permitted to quote here, from the letter of Mrs
Oliphant's only surviving sister to her mother, the circumstances of her death and burial. The anxious nurse,
better acquainted with every symptom of the illness, had
not taken so hopeful a view as the husband; but even
to her the end came with unthought-of suddenness.

"At half-past eight, Saturday evening, January 2d, as
I was rubbing her foot and watching her face, she suddenly stopped breathing. We called Laurence in. It
was only like holding a breath,—no struggle, no movement. She drew one more breath, and her sweet spirit
had fled to God who gave it. Poor Laurence was just
stunned, and really wanted nursing and attending to,
but I could not be with him at first. Dr Schmidt [1]
gave me all the help I required, doing all I asked of
him in such a really tender and reverent manner that
I am deeply grateful to him. I could not do all for
her so well as I would, for stranded up there on the
mountain there were few necessities to my hand; but
I was able to place her so that she looked at last quite
beautiful, calm, and with a smiling restful expression on

_____
[1] The German doctor at Haifa.

her face, all distress and suffering banished. We placed some pretty mountain daisies in her crossed hands; and when Laurence saw her on Sunday, his first exclamation was, 'Oh, but you did not tell me!—she is quite beautiful!' I was so glad to think he could have such a last recollection of her dear face.

" Dr Schmidt kindly left us as soon as I could release him, and rode down all through the night with a lantern to Haifa (no slight undertaking, as Guy knows, over those steep mountain tracts), and went immediately to A., who, together with him, made every arrangement, and saved Laurence in every way they could. Though Sunday, every German in the colony came forward with offers of help. Loving hands worked both at carpentering and sewing, and in the incredibly short space of five hours everything was ready and despatched to Dalieh. There at 8 P.M. I received all at Phai's hands [a German servant, one of the colonists], and he and Dr Martin and I laid her in the coffin : no one else touched her. The grief among the Druses was intense. As one of them quaintly puts it, 'If five of our best sheikhs die, village not so sorry.' We asked for eight men amongst them to carry her down as far as the plain, where carriages could meet us,—a longer road, but an easier one than the ordinary way over the mountains. Instead of eight, fifty offered themselves, and these men simply vied with one another who should have the honour of lifting her. It was a strange scene that early morning journey. It all seemed to me like a dream. In front rode the principal sheikhs of the village of Dalieh, then the Druse bier on which we had placed her, borne on the shoulders of eight men at a time, and surrounded by the others. Then came Laurence, myself, Katherine, and Dr Martin (all on horseback), in single file. Good Phai ran on foot the whole four miles, so as to be handy in case of any accident. All the women of the village, who had loved her, and to whom she had so often ministered in their various troubles, stood round us (as they set out), and kissed my hand, all weeping. The bearers kept up an even pace without any shaking the whole way down beyond 'Aui Haud (three miles from the sea, at the foot of the hills), going as fast as our horses could walk, and never once paused to rest.

" Here we laid her in the carriage that Souz had brought [one of the colonists, who habitually drove her before they had a carriage of their own], and after a quarter of an hour's rest, of which we all stood in need, we remounted, Laurence and I now following the carriage closely, and Katherine and the doctor behind us. When we were more than an hour's ride from the point of Carmel, we were met by Mr Keller, the German consul, and his dragoman, in a carriage, kindly brought for me and Katherine ; but I could not bear the shaking, and preferred to ride. Then on reaching the point, at two miles from the colony, Adolphus met us ; and a few yards on, a large group of Germans, all the principal men of the colony, and all the foreign consuls and their dragomen and cavasses (guards). They all uncovered as the *cortége* passed, and then silently followed,—only the cavass of the English consul going in front on foot. At the entrance of the colony, and quite up to the door of Laurence's house, we passed through a lane of people,—almost every man, woman, and child in the colony, and many Arabs from the town, and a guard of honour sent by the (Moslem) Governor of Haifa. Had she been a queen she could not have been received with more respectful homage, and it was all spontaneous expression of love—personal love for her. Laurence felt it very much, for we had expected nothing of the kind ; and I think so much sympathy really helped him to go through the hard task.

" A little rest being absolutely necessary for us all (we had been five hours on horseback), we laid her in one of the outer rooms, and covered her with a violet pall, with dull-red cross from end to end, which had been hurriedly made, and which I was glad to find pleased Laurence very much ; but it was soon hidden under the numbers of wreaths and flowers provided from nearly every cottage in the place. A guard of Germans established themselves to watch over her—Schumacher, Lange, Dück, Kreisg—and after them in turn all the head men of the colony. At four o'clock we started for the German cemetery. Nothing could have exceeded the kindness and true feeling with which everything was made easy to us, everything put at our disposal : permission to lay her there, permission for Adolphus to read the service (this, too, by Laurence's wish),—everything, in fact, that they could do was done. Laurence was so much knocked up—indeed he was hardly fit to sit his horse, never having properly recovered from his own attack of fever on the mountain—that we all persuaded him not to go to the funeral; also it was raining hard, and in every way unfit for him. We found the grave lovingly lined with leaves. An immense concourse of people accompanied us, of all ranks and classes and religions ; and when the last words were spoken, the grave was nearly filled by the heaps of flowers, wreaths, and garlands that were laid upon her. So we laid her to her rest, in view of Mount Carmel, and the Sea and the hills of Galilee ; and poor and rough as the other surroundings may be, still rich in the grateful love of the poor people she had so much benefited."

An after-incident proves in a very affecting way the permanency of this deep and tender feeling. When the time came to mark the place where they had laid her dear remains, there was no one far or near to cut her name upon the stone, till the present head of the German colony, the American Vice - Consul, Herr Schumacher, the most respected and honoured among the Europeans, stepped forth. He had not touched a chisel for many years, but long ago, in his youth in America, had learned the mason's trade. And he it was who inscribed her name upon her grave. The blue sea murmurs close by upon the shining strand ; on the other side green Carmel rises, with the mother convent, the head of all the Carmelite communities, upon its nearest slope, over the narrow border of cultivated land. Thus between her home on the hill and that by the sea she lies, the nothing of her that could fade.

I will not allow the reader to suppose that in the heart of the survivor this was an end. He too was stricken with the fever which had killed her, but not enough to give him

the happy fate of going with her to the eternal shores.
The terrible blank which we have all to bear fell upon
Laurence for a few brief but awful days. He lost her
from his side, her helping hand from his, her inspiring
voice. But only for a few days. One night when he lay
sick and sorrowful upon his bed in the desolate house at
Haifa, a sudden rush of renewed health and vigour and
joy came upon the mourner. The moment of complete
union had come at last: his Alice had returned to him,
into his very bosom, into his heart and soul, bringing
with her all the fulness of a new life, and chasing away
the clouds of sorrow like the morning vapours before the
rising sun.

CHAPTER XII.

THE POSTSCRIPT OF LIFE.

THE life which I have tried to trace through all its adventures by flood and field, its spiritual gropings and difficulties, the convulsions by which it was rent asunder,
the strange experiences which it worked through, and the
period of absolute and peaceful happiness in its penulti-
mate chapter, had now come to its last stage. Laurence
was left, when his wife died, more than a widowed husband,—a being forsaken, deprived not only of the consolation but the inspiration of his life. He dwelt but little,
in the after-sense of spiritual reunion attained, upon the
short but terrible interval of desolation. There is, however, a very full revelation of the history of this dreadful
crisis in his life, in a letter to Mrs Wynne Finch, the
mother of his lost love, from which I have already quoted
the description of her death. But this sad narrative is
accompanied by many touching details of his own bereaved
thoughts, and of the wonderful light which had come to
him in the darkness :—

    " I know you will have understood my silence thus far,

and how for long I shrunk, as it were, from turning the dagger in the wound which, when it first came, I longed might prove fatal. It seemed so absolutely impossible that I could go on living without her; and indeed I do not think I could if things had gone on as they did the first week, when I seemed surrounded by an impenetrable gloom of desolation and despair. Suddenly one night the light seemed to burst through, and she came to me so radiant, and at the same time so sad at seeing me unhappy, that my own grief seemed to be lifted by the effort she made to dispel it. She seemed literally to be rolling some great burden off my soul, and I felt that my first duty to her was to be cheerful, and to fight against the morbid condition that was creeping over me. From that time I have continued to feel her more and more, and to be regaining my own health and spirits. She seems sensationally to invade my frame, thrilling my nerves when the sad fit is coming on, and shaking me out of it—flooding my brain occasionally with her thoughts, so that I can feel her thinking in me and inspiring me. There is no analogy with mediumship or spiritualism, for I am never more conscious of her than when all my faculties are on the alert. Nor am I alone in this. Mrs Cuthbert, who has, ever since Alice first went to America, been her devoted friend, and who has been our guest for three and a half years, is in some respects more conscious of her than I am, for she is more sensitive organically to such influences: and we are thus continually able to have the consolation of her presence, which has really robbed death of all its bitterest sting. Of course I miss her sweet companionship every moment, for these last years have been of unalloyed bliss, and every moment I spent away from her loved presence I grudged. And her loss seemed the more irreparable because the work to which we had given our lives, and the common object for which we laboured, and which formed a tie transcending any which could arise from natural marriage, seemed suddenly and hopelessly checked. I felt like a ship on a voyage of discovery, pregnant with the most important results to the world, fatally stranded and wrecked. But now all that is passed.

She has shown how the work can be carried on more effectually with her aiding and guiding than it ever could have been with our former limited powers. And I feel once again afloat, with a different compass to guide me than I ever had before. Henceforward I live in her, as she will, if I am faithful to my own highest aspirations, in me: we are indissolubly bound to all eternity—more firmly wedded now than we could ever be below; and my great desire will be to let her love flow through me in the channel in which she wills it to flow, and which will assuredly be to those she loved so dearly on earth. As my great happiness in life is to know what she wants me to do, and to do it, and as God has providentially assured a means of communication between us by which I can discover this, I can walk no longer blindly. I believe in some way our darling will make our present loss our great gain, and that we may be spared together to a deeper knowledge of those mysteries which she has now fathomed, by which we may rise to greater powers of use."

The letter which follows, addressed to Mrs Hankin, the lady already frequently mentioned, in whom both the Oliphants felt the deepest interest, gives further proof of the strong conviction of Laurence that his wife's affection and solicitude for those she loved was felt and expressed with more warmth than ever from beyond the grave :—

"I know you will excuse a very brief note, for I am only just recovering from the nervous attack which resulted from a shock so unexpected, and am still weak from many sleepless nights accompanied by fever. We both seem to have been attacked by malaria while camping on Lake Tiberias, which only developed a fortnight later up at Dalieh, where my beloved one succumbed to it, after a fortnight's illness. I cannot write about it yet, but you must not suppose I am discouraged. For a week the gloom was terrible, and it seemed as if all was lost—the light and inspiration gone from my life, and nothing left me but to follow. Then she was able to come to me, and roll away the great burden of my despair. And now she never leaves

me, and has explained to me why she had to go, and what
I have to do, and why I can do it better with her on the
other side than on this. And I would not have her back,
though only those who have known her can imagine what
a blank there is—a blank which the whole community,
Moslem, Druse, and Christian alike, feel, and their sense
of which they have manifested in a remarkable way. Even
the German colonists say they feel her among them more
now than when she was visible to them. But I shall hope
to see you before very long, and to tell you what it is impossible to write, and about her whose angelic character it
is impossible to describe. She has been very urgent in
her desire that I should write to you even before my own
and her relatives, and from where she is she knows well
why. I hope to be in England in May, and will write
and let you know when I arrive. She says I must send
you the enclosed lock of her hair, with her love, and she
seems to think that she may be able to be of some special
use to you."

He gave the same account to me personally, in June of
the same year, when he was in England, both of the death
of his wife and the after restoration to him. He carried
out faithfully the programme of what should have been
their joint visit to England and Scotland together. She
should have been doing everything with him, alas! as we
say. But he did not say so. Why should he? She *was*
there with him, a part of his being, taking her share in
everything he did, guiding him in all he had to do. So he
believed. And to hear him tell that bewildering tale, and
to remain unaffected by his entire and happy certainty of
its truth, was, to me at least, impossible. What do we
know of the mysteries of life and death? Such strong
consolations do not come to us, for whom, perhaps, the
long endurance, the aching void, the blank of separation,
may be needful. But so far as his own consciousness
went, his experience was certainly true.

These were the sentiments with which Laurence Oliphant took up from the brink of the grave what remained
to him of life. It was but a brief chapter, and the reader

may think there were incidents in it which seemed, in some sort, to belie its constancy and conviction; but it was only in seeming that the contradiction existed. He says some time after, " I do pity poor Madame de R., who can't get nearer to her lost one than Père la Chaise. The one place I avoid here is the cemetery."

The short visit he paid me was on his return from Cumberland Lodge, the residence of the Princess Christian, always his most kind and sympathetic friend, where he had spent some days, having been seized there by a violent attack of fever. He remained subject to such attacks, which came on without warning and with great violence, for some time. His appearance was changed, but the change was one rather of sentiment than of fact. There was about him the affecting cheerful languor of a life worn out, and from which its chief object was taken, yet which held head against sorrow and weariness with a smile, vowing to bate no jot of heart or hope. How sad the smile can be, and how heartrending the cheerfulness, in such circumstances, it is needless to say. Perhaps the shadow of the wearing illness from which he had scarcely recovered still hung about him, enhancing that effect. His movements, the swaying of his figure, which seemed longer and sparer than ever it had been—a something for-lorn in the smiling look with which he met all kind and sympathetic faces—were so many tokens of the blow that had been struck at his life. Yet he was no less brilliant in conversation than of old, and when other members of the household appeared, turned at once from his personal story to the life of everyday, brightening every topic he touched with all the recollections and experiences and endless illus-trations of which his mind was full, as in his best days. The following letter was written on his arrival in London, in answer to a letter from Mrs Hankin, informing him of a serious illness from which she was recovering :—

                                         " *May* 20 [1886].

" If I were writing to you in conventional language, I should say I was sorry to hear you had been ill, and hoped that you would get better; but we feel that illness has its lesson, and death its use—have learned to take things as they come, and to believe that if we have no other desire but to be used as God's instruments, He will answer that desire by keeping us in this world or removing us to another as His service may require. Of this you may be sure, that if you do go hence, you will find her who has left me waiting for you. What you say about the book ['Sympneumata'] helping people, encourages me: for all nearly of my friends who have read it, or tried to read it, tell me they find it quite incomprehensible; but there are most comforting exceptions, to whom it seems to supply all they need."

The letter concludes with anxious arrangements for meeting the correspondent whom Alice had loved without knowing her. I may add here this lady's account of the first meeting, which led to a very close friendship and much communion:—

"I saw before me not the cheerful, brisk, hopeful man of the world, but a sad, weary-looking mystic, who looked larger than his height and older than his years, with thin, scattered iron-grey hair, a worn, sensitive face, and tired eyes. He silently shook hands, and lay down on a sofa at a little distance from me. As I looked and wondered, his whole frame shook with a convulsive, vibratory motion —a strange shuddering ran through all his limbs. 'She is very busy with you,' his friend said.

"'She wants Mrs Hankin to sit by me: she is so glad we have met,' he said at last; and they exchanged some words about 'strong influence' which I did not understand.

"I sat and held his hand, and he talked to me in a gentle, pathetic way of his loss; of how 'She' had brought about our meeting, for reasons we did not know at present, but must look for with great watchfulness. By degrees the convulsive ripple in his limbs, and the strong agitation moving him almost to tears, subsided, and we strolled out, all three together, into the scented garden, and became very happy. He talked continually of his Alice till I felt as if she were really making a fourth with us, and became full of joy and exultation, as one might feel just enlisted in a glorious, dangerous service in which one was content to die.

"Then came the evening, the house now full of family life, and the talk general and on ordinary subjects; and then it was that I recognised the Laurence Oliphant of my photograph as, to a certain degree, still living in the tired, pale mystic of the afternoon. He told us anecdote after anecdote, as only he could tell, of his past life at home and abroad, or of his literary contemporaries and their modes of thought and action; and throughout proved himself the very perfection of a *raconteur*, absolutely free from egotism, vanity, or ill-nature.

"It was quite early in the following mornnig when my kind friend woke me, and asked if I would dress at once and come with her to Mr Oliphant. I may as well say that where everything had been so strange and unexpected, I found nothing to astonish me in this. I assumed that the 'Alice' of whom they spoke with such assurance wanted to help me in some way, and I was not only ready but eager to be helped. Mr Oliphant, looking less worn and sad than he had done on the previous afternoon, questioned me about the nature of my illness, which was a weakness of the heart, and implied that he thought he might do me good, though, as he was careful to explain, his work was not in a general way that of a healer of bodily maladies.

"I sat by his side and held his hand for some time, finding that a strong current poured through him, shaking my hand and arm with a powerful vibration,—a motion like that produced by the current from a galvanic battery, though the sensation was not similar; indeed I only felt at first a warm and pleasant tingling in my arm and shoulder, and afterwards a great exhilaration and exaltation of spirits.

"After about half an hour's pleasant talk my friend advised me to lie down for a short time in my room before the family breakfast: this I did, but the vibratory motion in my arm continued to be powerfully felt during the whole of that time.

"After breakfast, Mr Oliphant left for town. We had no more conversation, and made no arrangements for future meetings. He said 'Alice would see to that,' and I was quite contented that it should be so. The mental and spiritual exaltation was upon me for two days, and for a considerable time the faintness and other discomforts connected with my ailments were greatly ameliorated."

This will show, better than anything else could do, how tremendous a change had come upon Laurence Oliphant's life. His strange doctrines, his wonderful faith, the beliefs for which he had sacrificed everything, had up to the time of his wife's death led to many proceedings which were unlike those of ordinary men; but whatever these were, they had left his personal dignity untouched, nay, heightened by the natural nobility attaching everywhere to a man who gives to the world the last proof of sincerity and steadfastness. But now the foot so apt to wander into untrodden paths had got detached altogether from the solid earth. The thrill of strange agitation, the convulsive movements, the "strong influx," are strange and painful indications of the changed conditions. To believe that it was Alice—the harmonious and beautiful being, whose office in life had certainly not been to produce any convulsion, but rather order and serenity, and the grace of a trained and disciplined spirit—who now in her perfect state produced effects like these, seems little more respectful to the dead than was the vulgar belief which represented the departed spirit as communicating with its nearest and dearest through the legs of a table. Had it been possible, I would fain have drawn a veil over this portion of the development,—not of Laurence Oliphant, but of the wild belief which now burned with strong desire for palpable and evident signs. But it would not be sincere to leave out of his story these concluding scenes. The man or woman—perhaps the latter most—who has been cut adrift at a stroke from all he or she possessed in life, will be able to understand, with an ache of sympathy and compassion, how the strained body toiling after the eager soul,

which was ever longing to convince itself of the reality of
its sensations of reunion, should have fallen into agitations
like these, triumphantly received as outward tokens of all
the mind most desired to believe.

It would be presumptuous to pronounce judgment even
upon these thaumaturgic movements. There are too many
mysteries of the spirit unknown, to permit us to come to
light and arbitrary conclusions upon such a matter. Still
the reasonable mind recoils from such scenes, and they
cannot but be felt to detract from the hitherto unimpair-
ed personal dignity of the man whom we have followed
through so many wonderful episodes without ever finding
him to fail.

This curious interview took place a few weeks earlier
than the occasion already recorded, in which he spent a
few hours at my own house, without the slightest sign of
any such development. Others of his friends saw him in
the few years that followed under the influence here described: but I, who had but brief and accidental occasions
of seeing him, never had any such experience, and a great
number of his friends were in the same condition. It is
almost incredible, yet it is true that, while he was seen on
one side of his being in this extraordinary aspect, he was
at the same time on the other side the same brilliant
talker, with the same humour and animation, and power
of fascinating all who had the good fortune to find themselves in his company, as ever. In literature, between
'Sympneumata,' which was published in 1885, and the
volume of 'Scientific Religion,' which he was already beginning to turn over in his mind, he had no serious work
in hand; but he was still engaged upon the lively and
delightful papers in 'Blackwood' called "Moss from a
Rolling Stone," afterwards published under the title of
'Episodes of a Life of Adventure.' The rolling stone was
not now bounding from hillock to hillock as in the youthful days, so full of strange and cheerful experiences: but
still this "worn mystic," this man whose life was hid in a
mysterious union with the dead, recalled and recorded
them with the evident pleasure and relish of one to whom
life was still dear and full of natural interest. The union

of the two is more marvellous almost than anything I remember in biography.

He paid a series of visits during the autumn, one among others to the Prince of Wales at Abergeldie, whom he had met at Homburg in August and September, when he spent a month there. While at Abergeldie he was honoured with an invitation to dine at Balmoral, and gave to the Queen, always so graciously disposed to listen to the facts of personal life, some account of his own wonderful ways of thinking and equally remarkable history. The Royal Family in general had indeed always taken a strong interest in him, manifested during many years past. Among other visits of a less splendid but more intimate character was one which he paid to Mr and Mrs Walker, when he saw for the first time the portrait which his Alice had painted of herself during her brief residence with them at San Rafael. He had not been aware, I think, of its existence and it was a wonderful delight to him. These kind friends, ever more thoughtful of him than themselves, allowed him to take the portrait with him ; and it was the greatest consolation and happiness to him during the next chapter of his lonely life.

In the beginning of October I met Laurence again quite unexpectedly in Edinburgh at the house of Miss Blackwood, where he was dining, and where his always delightful talk was as animated, varied, and brilliant as ever. His conversation was of the kind most delightful to the hearer, though perhaps not so well adapted to the purposes of a biography as if he had been one of the monologists whose discoursings keep the listeners dumb. He, on the contrary, was the soul of the conversation, making others talk as well as himself, so that some of his own brightness overflowed upon his interlocutors, who sometimes, to their great astonishment, found themselves shining too, in a light half borrowed, half elicited by the sympathetic contact of a mind so fresh, so ready to respond, so full of original impulses. He talked out of the fulness that was in him about everything, with some novel illustration, some individual view, at the least some witty story to tell *apropos* of every theme. There was no

confining him to one subject or another. His mind knew
no divisions, had apparently no crotchets, and certainly
no assumptions or pretension. Always humorous, always
easy, talking not for talking's sake or with the faintest
idea of producing himself, but from the abundance of
an active and lively mind, to which almost everything
was interesting, and that extraordinary acquaintance with
every kind and condition of man which he had acquired
by means of this very interest in everything he saw,
he was the most spontaneous of conversationalists, never
overbearing a timid remark, never omitting to notice a
shy interlocutor. He brought out of his treasury things
old and new, without the least apparent consciousness
that he was doing anything more than all the rest of the
company could have done had they pleased. To think
of such a man as he appeared at that dinner - table in
Charlotte Square, Edinburgh, fresh from the society of
royal personages, and conscious as he was of a position
more strange and unique in the world of mind and intelligence than any contemporary—and to imagine in him the
convulsions and tremors of an occult visionary, was too
bewildering to be possible. The mere idea of such a conjunction makes the brain go round. The last man in
the world for such experiences the most acute observer,
knowing nothing of his history, would have said.

His publications at this period, which he was busily
at work arranging during the last months of the year
while he remained in England, were many, and of an
equally varied kind. The little volume called 'Fashionable Philosophy,' the lightest of satire; the book called
'Haifa,' which he intended and hoped would be the
authority, or one of the authorities, upon the localities
and modern life of Palestine; the 'Episodes,' one of his
most brilliant and popular publications, a sort of easy
autobiography; and a proposed new edition of that amazing onslaught upon his ancient gods, 'Masollam,'—were
all getting ready for the press during these busy months;
and he himself arranging, advising, discussing sales, &c.,
with all the keenness of a man of business. He was
particularly concerned during all his literary career about

the number of his books that were sold, and the facilities afforded to the public for obtaining them, and reported continually to his publisher the complaints of friends who were unable to procure them—telling of some who had besieged Mudie for weeks to procure a copy in vain, that great authority having professed to the publisher that the book was not sufficiently in request to justify him in taking more than so many copies; and of some who, equally unsuccessfully, searched the bookstands for the volume. "Of course," he cries, with humorous rage, "if that beast Smith does not expose my book it can't sell, and he is not fit to be leader of the House of Commons! A question ought to be asked about it in the House, or something done to get justice."

While all this cheerful bustle was going on in his outer life — occupations which seem continual, cares of the robustest practical kind — the other went on by its side visionary, sometimes with beautiful gleams of thought, sometimes so absorbed in regions beyond mortal ken as to bewilder the faculties of those who strained after him, trying to follow and understand. In the following letter it will be seen there is a mixture of both.

"*October* 17, 1886.

"I am so glad you have been feeling what you have described about the functions of Christ, and the attitude which we who are struggling for the bridegroom life should hold towards Him. If, as you say, a being like Alice can exercise so much power through us, how much more can He, if we open ourselves to Him? It is only since her death that I have been feeling this very strongly,—it was one of the first new sentiments with which she began powerfully to infuse me; and it is clear she is doing the same to you, which is a great source of happiness to me, as it proves how she is operating upon us both. Every time I feel her descent, I am beginning more clearly now to realise Him in her: for it is the function of the woman to get life from Him direct, and to transmit it to man; and I begin to realise the process of her drawing it from

Him and passing it on to me, and this brings me nearer
to Him.   But you can reach Him direct, and hence can
radiate more powerfully than I can; and from all women
who can do this I can gain the kind of strength I need
for my more external and executive work, which is different from theirs.   Hence I seem to crave this feminine
element in the degree in which burdens press and work
increases,—and what is more curious, the life I thus get
through women I can give out unconsciously, and draw
other women by it.   I constantly feel a sort of magnet
among them, and those who have aspirations feel drawn
to give me their confidence, and seek my advice and help,
so that I have become a sort of father confessor to some
who were comparative strangers, and who have told me
that they felt irresistibly impelled, from the first moment
they saw me, thus to approach and absolutely to trust me.
This is a great compensation for much suffering, and I feel
this power is increasing, just in proportion as I magnify
Christ's function, and strain up to Him through Alice.   He
is the connecting link between us and the great Unknow-
able, and for this cause He came into the world, that He
might unite us sensationally to His Father and our Father."

One of the most remarkable incidents in Oliphant's
history during this autumn was his sudden penetration
into the heart and difficulties of a clergyman of the
Church of England—the same who afterwards added an
appendix under that title to ' Scientific Religion,' and who,
having arrived at a crisis in life which demanded action,
threw himself on very small knowledge upon the friendship and advice of his visitor, and thereupon formed the
heroic resolution of forsaking everything and going out to
Haifa with this new guide.   " Imagine," says Laurence in
one of his letters to Mrs Hankin—" imagine my having
read the lessons in a white surplice ! " in the village
church which the gentleman above mentioned found it his
duty to resign.   I may add that they continued together
in very close friendship until the end of Laurence's life,
his new convert being in many ways his faithful hench-
man, and in all his trusted coadjutor and friend.

I may quote once more from the recollections of Mrs Hankin an interesting scene which took place before he left England in the end of 1886, when she met him to take leave, "in a quiet country vicarage." A previous meeting, when the whole party who were bound for Haifa were present, and their plans and preparations for the journey were naturally in the ascendant, and spiritual intercourse scarcely possible, had been a disappointment to this lady; but very different was the effect now produced. She describes the frost-bound country outside, the falling snow, the desolation of the landscape.

"But once within, the sense of spiritual companionship filled us all with a great peace, and once more that internal tranquillity, in which Alice could bring her full power to bear on Mr Oliphant, seemed to reign. I specially remember the afternoon hours which we spent in the room of our hostess, a confirmed invalid, often during the winter confined for days to her room.

"Thick flakes of snow were falling on the garden beds outside, and all nature wore an aspect of intense sadness; but we—that is, the invalid, her young daughter, and myself—listened for hours entranced while Mr Oliphant talked to us. I remember the exquisite tenderness with which he comforted and reassured the invalid, and how her tired face grew restful and placid as he held her thin hand, and, with the strong magnetism pouring from his own, talked to her of that other world of which the inhabitants were still moving round us in love and pity. There was no necessity for explanation or for breaking new ground, for my friends had read and appreciated 'Sympneumata,' while I was still stumbling among its involved sentences and difficulties of expression. When we had talked long on spiritual things, he told us much of his life."

I have already used in previous chapters the descriptions given of his life in Brocton to these sympathetic inquirers. Mrs Hankin adds that in all he said of Harris there was not a word about the downfall of that idol, or the causes that led to it:—

2 B

" In fact, the whole time seemed full of so intense a
peace that all memory of past jars, and all thought of
present difficulties or future dangers, seemed to have faded
out.   He said several times, ' How strong the influx is
here ! ' and again and again the curious rippling vibration
ran over his breast and shoulders, and he would say, with
a half-tearful smile, ' There is Alice ! ' "

This meeting was his farewell for the moment to these
sympathetic friends.   In the end of January 1887 he left
England, and his next communications are from Paris,
where he paused to visit Mrs Wynne Finch for a time on
his way to Haifa.   Here he writes to his correspondent,
bidding her not to pity him, as she did with natural feeling, on account of his return to Haifa for the first time
since his wife's death.   " We have no call," he says, " to
feel compassion for any one who is being so tenderly and
lovingly dealt with by God as I am, or in regard to any
experiences we may be called upon to go through in the
divine service.   In the meantime his pause in Paris
brought him acquainted with some of the occult yet professional, and, as we in England are inclined to think,
partly theatrical researches into the phenomena of hyp-
notism, which to him appeared in a very serious light
as playing with dangerous forces as yet unknown to
the operators.   " I am going," he says, " to see Charcot's
hypnotic experiments some day soon.   There is an immense movement in this direction here, and a ' Revue
Hypnotique ' is published.   They will find they have got
hold of a force they little understand."

" I spent two hours yesterday at the Salpêtrière hospital,
and witnessed the most extraordinary experiments I ever
saw.   It was amusing to see the most able physicians of
Paris perfectly dumbfoundered with their own experiments, unable to account for them.   They have got to the
length of feeling that a law must be passed prohibiting
people from magnetising one another, in consequence of
the number of patients who arrive mentally injured by
amateurs amusing themselves in this direction.   They

will soon discover that they are amateurs themselves, and must injure people unless they probe more deeply, and admit the existence of influences they still try to ignore. The priests, at all events, have the courage of their convictions, and boldly say it is the devil."

He reached Haifa in the end of February, and thus describes to Mrs Hankin his arrival in a place which all his friends had feared he would find so solitary and desolate :—

"2d *March* [1887].

"I was most enthusiastically greeted by the German colony and my own little household, where I found everything running most smoothly. I feel more and more how Alice is really the directing spirit. It was like getting into Paradise to come here out of the turmoil of the world—everything so calm and peaceful and lovely; and the presence of my darling seems brooding over all, and fills me with an ineffable joy and peace, so that the associations with which I am surrounded are a positive pleasure, instead of being a pain. I seem to have got back to her again, where she can get so much nearer to me than she could in the world. My head is now getting full of the book you have been wanting, and the pressure to write what it would not have been possible for me to write in England is upon me; but I doubt very much whether it will be what you desire, or be suited for your babes: but there are others to be thought of besides them.

"I am busy writing," he adds a little later, "two pamphlets—one for the Moslems with quotations from the Koran, which is being translated into Arabic; and another for the Jews with quotations from the Old Testament, which is being translated into Hebrew. It is perfectly wonderful how the light keeps breaking, and the quotations come in support of the thesis. It will be called the 'Star in the East,' and is in five short chapters: the first, the secrets of the world's malady; the second, the origin of religions; the third, the mission of the Messiah;

the fifth, the triumph of the Messiah. I shall probably be engaged during the summer in amplifying them for the Christians. Then possibly it may be adapted later to the Hindoos and Buddhists, with quotations from their sacred books, for they all contain the same truth in their hidden meaning."

This pamphlet I have in English, the original, which I believe was translated into Arabic, but not, so far as I have ever heard, into Hebrew. It produces a curious effect upon the English reader by its many citations from the Koran, and the perfect equality upon which that book is placed with the Gospels. This, of course, was what has been called "economical," as specially adapted to those under the Mohammedan "dispensation"; and as Laurence was of opinion not only that the sacred books of every religion were, in their hidden meaning, equally inspired, he also considered as inspired all the men who have largely influenced the human race, whether Moses, Mohammed, or Buddha; although our Lord always held with him the highest place, as a being of a different and more perfect kind from any of these great men. It was perhaps also in compliance with the "economy" under which the primitive peoples whom he addressed were living, that his statement of certain of his more peculiar tenets is more exact and clear in this singular tract than it had ever been before. His belief in the original creation of man in a semi-spiritual body, a being containing both sexes in one, and in the change of nature produced at the Fall, when the two were divided, made into distinct beings, and for the first time clothed in flesh—is stated with curious exactitude. Our Lord he describes as having been by His miraculous birth restored to this double being, and thus made capable of communicating the divine breath to the world, which was the true and only bond of union, and by which gradually the original nature was to be restored. "And this combined force has been slowly growing in men's powers ever since, so that now many men begin to feel that they have the female half inclosed within them, and many women begin

to feel that they have the male half inclosed within them."
But this physical transformation was not to be attained
but by much suffering and many struggles, both within
and without.

"It is by the active and conscientious performance of
daily duties, by the cultivation of pure love, humility, and
upright dealing, and purity, that the frame can be prepared
for the conscious presence of the other half, and for the
descent of Christ as the comforter and bridegroom. When
the body has, after long trials, been thus prepared, the next
stage can be entered upon, concerning which it is not permitted to write yet. Enough has been said to show how
Christ is making a descent even now into the very bodies
of those who love Him; how this descent is the fulfilment
of the promise made in all the existing religions, of the
advent of the Messiah in the last days; and how this
advent will prove the cure for the world's malady."

This extraordinary statement is nowhere, I think, so
strongly and simply put. It was translated into Arabic by
the one Arab convert made, I think, to its doctrines—a
man not, unfortunately, of much credit to his leaders. "If
it were printed or came to the knowledge of Government, it
would mean my expulsion from the country," Laurence says;
"so it can only be communicated secretly to such of the
Arabs, Moslems, or Christians as would be likely to receive
it." I do not know whether any further result followed.
"I feel bursting with what I have to say to Christians,"
he adds, "but my directions seem to indicate that it must
be written from beginning to end at Dalieh, where I shall
go probably in about a month. It was quite wonderful the
accession of Alice's influence which I felt when I was up
there."
Curiously, into the midst of the account of all these
mystical productions comes a description of an entertainment which Laurence gave to his neighbours—Germans,
Arabs, and Moslems — on the occasion of the Queen's
Jubilee. Even this was not without religious meaning,
for it was specially designed to open a way to dealing

with the women, who were all invited—an event unprece-
dented in the country.

"I was asked to assign for the women a place apart, but
this was refused on the ground that I could make no distinction between Arab Christian women and European
Christian women, of whom there would be plenty coming.
It ended by all the Arab Christian women coming, and
very few Moslems; but this was only because it was
Ramadan, when they can't eat or drink before sunset. I
had considerably over 300 people. I counted twenty-three
different nationalities, and thirteen religions or sects. Such
a jumble was never known here before. Indeed, nothing
of the kind has ever been attempted. I had two tents up,
flags flying, the German band playing, plenty of chorus-
singing, speechifying, &c. The Arabs gave two addresses
complimentary to the Queen, and there were others in
German and French. The Arab women all huddled
together, but they giggled immensely at the novelty of
their position, and absorbed any amount of refreshment.
Of course, no woman would speak to a man, and that I
did not expect; but it was an uncommon step that they
did not wear veils, which Christian women are only beginning to abandon."

I pause before continuing and completing the record of
his literary life by his own account of the composition of
his last work, 'Scientific Religion,' to note the traces which
I find among his papers of his interest and benevolent operations in respect to the Jew colonists. A number of petitions and representations of urgent cases, both individual
and public, in Hebrew (with translations), in German,
and, most curious of all, in phonetic English, prove that
to the end of his life he was appealed to by these poor
people, and acted in some sort as an intermediary between
them and the benevolent-rich of their nation, who were
not less puzzled how to treat, and how to understand, the
colonies which it was their strong desire to plant in Palestine, than are the rest of the world. Much incapacity on
the part of the poor Jews, suddenly plunged into a new

world, some dishonesty, some idleness, a great deal of misery, appear in these records; but Laurence by no means seems to have given up his belief in the plan, or to have decided at any time, after many opportunities of observation, that it was bound to fail, as others less informed have summarily done.

He seems to have regarded with particular interest the Beth Yehuda colony, composed of Jews from Safed—the "city set upon a hill" of our Lord's simile, which still sits high upon the hills of Galilee, and is one of the last strongholds of the native Jewish race. The community there is chiefly supported, I believe, as are the Jews in Jerusalem, by contributions from the wealthy Jews of Europe; and the impulse which prompted a portion of them to settle themselves in the plains, and attempt farming there, was highly applauded by Laurence, as an honest effort after independence. "I think you understand its peculiar character," he says, in a letter to Major Goldsmid, "and the advantages of colonising Safed Jews, and turning into agriculturists natives of the country who have hitherto lived on the Haluka. With the present Government, the only colony which has a fair chance is one composed of natives of whom the authorities are not jealous, as they are of foreign immigrants. I hope, therefore, that the Anglo-Jewish Association will give this one a helping hand." He speaks of it in an after letter as "the best experiment of the kind which exists in Palestine,"—a "really deserving colony," with "more chance of success than any strangers could have." One hopes that these poor colonists throve, if only for the delightful English in which the following formal report of their circumstances is written:—

REPORT OF THE NEW SETELMENT COLONIE OF JULAM OF SOCTIE BENEI-JEHUDA.

1. In wich place?	From Tel-el-Fares, Sout east, tow hours; from Tel-abu-Nida, Nord west, tow hours.
2. Woth was the name before?	At present colled Chirbet-belled el Romsanie; in Olden times colled Romy.

3. Omeny Dullam in clods in wolle ?	About 15,000. About 5000 prary ; 2000 for planting Treas and wine gardens ; 1000 for Wegitation, wolle foul of Wather ; 7000 for crope.
4. Omeny springs ? . . .	3 Springs largeoons ; 13 Sometimes flood in difret directions.
5. Ofar to a city ?	To city of Kometre, 2 hauhors ; to Damaskus, 14 ; to the rever Jorden, 3 ; to Acka, 13 hauhors.
6. Wath kind of catel ? . .	Wolle kind. Kaus, 8 ; Oksens, 10 ; Orshes, 4 ; Donkes, 2 ; Gouts, 30.
7. Plouing Tooles ? . . .	Komen Arabien plous, 5.
8. Omeny buildings ?. . .	One big Bilding, 38 jards long, 18 wide ; 6 stables for catel ; plenti of stons wolle redy to beld from the pondations.
9. In wich state ?	In the state of Damaskus, coantry of Kometre.
10. The name of the niborgs tribes.	The are called Benei Merat, Mochamedins, Arabians.

11. The land is divided between the Familes in dinomte of Fadans.   Every fadan incloodes 160 Dullam, some ocupaing 2 Fadan.

A long list of names follows, in which the heads of the families are described as "Worcingman, Shoumacer, Fien Smith, Budcear" (butcher), &c.; with the number of the "childerin, boyes and gerls," to each.   There is a pathetic air of reality about the document.   The following is what is described as a free translation from the Hebrew original of petition enclosed with it, from a smaller and less important colony :—

"To the honourable and benevolent Sir Oliphant, unceasing in his good deeds, we come to-day before he sets out on his intended journey.   We do bless him with all our hearts, and pray that he may arrive at his destination safely, and that God may protect him and be with him to the end of his journey.   Up to the present time we have done all in our power not to become the objects of charity, and we are truly grateful to his honour for the former many kindnesses which he has voluntarily shown us.   And his past kindness makes us bold enough to ask him to afford us some relief in this time of our great need.

"The honourable Abraham Magal was nominated to act as our superintendent, to afford us protection, and to inspire us with courage and strengthen us in our weak-

ness. But to our sorrow and trouble he died ; for God
took his soul under His wings, and thus we are left without help and protection.   We are now thirty-two souls,
reduced to the lowest extremity, so that our situation has
become unendurable, and so that we are compelled to
send the brave Fishel Solomon as our representative to
lay our matter before you, to whom we call God as our
Redeemer."

I resume the record of his life, by the following account
of his projects and consolations a little while after his
return to Haifa, in a letter to Mrs Walker :—

"HAIFA, 29*th* *March* 1887.

" I am sorry, too, that we had not more opportunity of
quiet conversation than was possible in London, because
so much has been developing in my mind and experience
since Alice left me ; but no doubt there was some good
reason for it, and I think before long you may have an
opportunity of reading a good deal of it, for I think I
shall shortly begin a book dealing with the whole subject
in a way that he that runs may read, which was not the
case with 'Sympneumata.' . . . So far from feeling saddened by the surroundings which recall Alice at every
moment, I am now feeling a happiness and joy which I
thought when I left this I never could feel again.   I
can walk in the garden with her, and seem to feel her
suggesting what ought to be done.   Then I like to feel
living in the midst of a community who all knew and
loved her.   There is scarcely a German cottage in which
her photograph is not hanging up framed.   The Druses
in the mountains treat the monument I have put up to
her with the greatest veneration.   It is a sacred spot to
them, for they say that, although she was not conscious
of it, she was a Druse all the time, and is one now.
Your picture is a great pleasure to me: it is in my bedroom, and my own fancy suggests that the expression of
it seems to change, but of course that is only the effect
of one's own imagination—though it is none the less

strange that one's imagination (whatever that may be)
should have such power."

As the summer of 1887 advanced, the usual move to
Dalieh was made, and from that place Laurence wrote
to Mrs Hankin, intimating that his great work had been
begun :—

"DALIEH, *July* 5 [1887].

"I can only write you a short letter this time, for a
reason that I know you will rejoice in—viz., that I am
hard at work writing the book you have been so long
urging. I have already written what amounts to a third
of 'Sympneumata,' and feel there is a great deal more.
The influx began to press powerfully into me, as soon as
I felt myself in the absolute solitude of the mountain,
with its still and tranquil beauty. I have fitted up the
little room in which my Alice left me as a sanctum, in
more senses of the word than one, hung it round with
curtains, and carpeted it, and put up the oil-painting of
her, and here she visits me while I write, and I feel her
thoughts impregnating mine, and forcing themselves into
expression, and unfolding wonderful things to me so
simply that I hope all who run may read and understand.
This was why she did not want me to write when you
were urging me to do so in London. It was impossible
in that polluted magnetic atmosphere for her to come to
me as she can here, where her spirit lingered to the last
moment."

"I am so absorbed in my work," he writes a month
later, "that I grudge every moment taken from it. Alice
is doing wonders, and developing ideas in me of which I
had no conception. It is therefore as interesting to write
as a novel, for I never know what is coming next. I have
already written an amount equal to 'Sympneumata,' and
it seems developing. It seems necessary that I should
go with it to England when it is finished, so I hope it
may not be long before I see you again. I don't suppose
I shall stay long in England, as I have work to do both

in America and Japan, so I suppose I shall return hither by that route. My life here is extremely calm and un-eventful. . . . The book is the great thing: it states the whole spiritual situation, and if people want to know what I believe, they will find there, I hope, an intelligible account of it. My whole mornings seem spent with Alice, and I think she has used the time to put new strength into me."

Another letter to Mrs Walker announces the completion of the work:—

"HAIFA, 25th September 1887.

"I have just finished a book which has quite absorbed me during my stay on the mountain. It is the final conclusion at which I have arrived after twenty-three years' struggle, and I feel Alice inspiring every word of it. It was written in the room where she died, with your picture on an easel by the side of my writing-table. It seemed to help to bring her. It stands before me now, and I sometimes fancy I can detect changes in the expression. The book came with remarkable clearness and force, and most of what it contains is new to me; but it solves and explains so much, that I hope it may be a help to many. When I had finished it, I could not help ejaculating, 'Lord, now lettest Thou Thy servant depart in peace.' It seemed such an ample compensation for all I have suffered and gone through—such a consolation to think that one's life has not been wasted. But whether Blackwood will publish it, or what the public will say to it, is a very different question."

His letters to his publisher at this period are also full of the book which was his prevailing occupation. "It will be altogether an extraordinary book," he says, evidently without the least idea of an author's vanity, regarding it as something apart from himself. "I can't help thinking I will explode rather noisily on the sleeping consciences of the public." Later he desires that nothing may be printed beyond the tenth chapter, as "new lights

flash upon me containing ideas which have to be inter-
polated."

"In fact, I never know when the book is really finished.
I have never written anything which seemed to descend
into my brain with such an irresistible force and demand
to be put into words, and I am as much surprised at what
I write as any of my readers are likely to be. I never
enjoyed such a period of delicious rest and peace as I felt
while writing this. . . . I think you will find the last part
of my book much more easy to understand than the first.
I shall call it, I think, 'The Divine Feminine.'"

This title, however, was not adopted, probably from the
alarm with which it would be received by all friends; but
it was not till some time after that the title—not a very
successful one—by which it was finally published was at
last decided upon. Nothing could exceed his satisfaction
in having accomplished this work.

The last time I ever saw him was in the early summer
of 1887 in Mr Blackwood's rooms in London. The impression he made upon me on this occasion was that he
was much more entirely absorbed in his religious views than
I had ever seen him, and cared less for any intercourse
which was not upon that subject. A carelessness, almost
impatience, of other topics and persons than those occupied
like himself with one all-engrossing inquiry, which I had
never remarked before, seemed to possess him. "I have
laid my egg," he said, with a laugh of excitement and half-
defiance, as if forestalling any criticism.

The much more intimate understanding and sympathy
of his mother-in-law, Mrs Wynne Finch, to whom since
his wife's death he had shown a special attachment and
devotion, perceived the same change on his appearance
in her house in Paris immediately before coming to London. She found him weak and worn out in frame, which
indeed was partly to be accounted for by the fact that
during his long mystical retirement in Dalieh he had lived
entirely on rice, while wound up to the utmost possible
spiritual excitement and strain of physical work.

I may be pardoned for adding here, that so little did I find his promise of greater intelligibility carried out in his new work, that, taking the book away with me in sheets, for the purpose of reviewing it in a newspaper to which I happened to have access at the moment, I turned my proposed review, in despair, into a rapid sketch of the circumstances and promise with which the book was about to come into the world, the remarkable character of the author, and the certainty that such a man, writing upon a subject which had occupied him for so many years, must, in the nature of things, merit the most respectful hearing, and have much that was interesting and important to say. I have, however, found it an excellent argument for humility to discover since, that many people worthy of all respect have found in it the power and instruction its author so fervently believed in, but which, for my own part, I was unable to see.

With the publication of this book Laurence Oliphant may, I think, be said to disappear from that place in the world which he had hitherto held. He was lost among a crowd of inquirers, of sympathisers, of people anxious to be convinced of his supernatural experiences and to share his faith in them. I discover with surprise, yet with a certain satisfaction which I have no doubt many spectators of the last acts of his life will share, that by this time, in the opinion of some of his anxious friends, the first warmth of inspiration breathed into him by the spirit of his wife had begun to fail, and that he was no longer so strongly moved by the "influx" as he had been when he came to England straight from her deathbed. It could scarcely be expected that he himself, so fully convinced as he was of the "great work" which remained to be done, would readily accept this as a sign that it would be better for him to retire a little and be silent, or to acknowledge himself at all deserted by what had been his guiding star. Another expedient was thought of to bring back the force of inspiration, and keep him in full strength for that work. At this point the impressions of his friend Mrs Hankin come in to instruct us as to the state of his mind and wishes :—

"As soon as we met I perceived that the singular spiritual force, which to my consciousness differentiated Mr Oliphant from all other men whom I had ever met, was no longer, as before, almost of the nature of a persistent attribute allied to his own original character. The sense of great spiritual power no longer accompanied his mere presence. It was only when the sudden spiritual visitation came objectively upon him in a strange rippling vibration that I recognised the influx of his Alice, and the sense of spiritual uplifting and exhilaration which I had formerly experienced. I soon found that his whole heart was set upon a period of usefulness in England; but to support the chain of magnetic life which he poured out on others, it was essential that he should be helped by the magnetism of some woman who sympathised with his aims and understood his views. As I happened to be at hand, he asked me to help him."

This lady, always full of sense and a moderate though strongly believing view of the new faith, and who had before now opposed her instinctive consciousness of what was and what was not practicable, in the way of its propagation and development, to his more eager desires, hesitated for some time before becoming his "colleague," according to his own phraseology; but eventually did so, I believe, for a short time, though always reluctantly, and became—in a way as mysterious as was the former manifestation, if not more so — the medium by which that "strange vibration" and "rippling" of nerves and frame, which, indicating the coming in of the "influx" into his soul, was communicated to him, the spirit pouring its influence through her hands as it had done at first through his own. These are mysteries with which only a mind entirely in sympathy should attempt to meddle. And one cannot but feel that while it was sufficiently hurtful to his individuality and personal dignity, as well as to the balance of his mind, to be always on the strain of expectation for communications from the unseen, it must have been still more so when these communications had to be procured through the ministrations of another.

Very few indications from himself come out of the mystical world which enclosed him after this point. He appears for a moment now and then in a passing visit, in a glimpse, and then disappears again—but the indications are vague. He went to America in the spring of 1888, and returned early in August. During this short time, however, an important event occurred, which I cannot describe better than in his own words. The following letter to Mrs Wynne Finch is the first, as far as I am aware, received from him after his return. He had gone straight, on landing, to the house of Mrs Hankin at Malvern :—

" MALVERN, *August* 4, 1888.

"I am so sorry that I missed seeing you, but events have proved too strong for me, and I shall not be in London for a fortnight. I landed at Plymouth, and came over here, to carry out a purpose which forced itself upon me somewhat suddenly during my passage. I am afraid you will think it somewhat strange, and I wish I could have explained it to you by word of mouth instead of by letter ; but still I think you will understand it better than most people. I was induced by a curious combination of circumstances to make a pilgrimage 1100 miles from New York to see a lady of whom I had only heard, but who I found to be a most remarkable person. She had reached all my results—nothing in 'Scientific Religion' was new to her ; but she had never read anything either Alice or I had written, and scarcely knew of me. Her faculty of internal insight is far more intense than that of any one I ever met, and we felt after an hour's interview that we must combine our forces, as my work with women is too difficult and compromising for me to carry on alone. Still the thought of marriage never entered our heads, as she is a strong-minded person, but she decided to come to Haifa with me. But on the passage she was brought into very close relations with Alice, and at the same time felt that Alice wanted me to give her the protection of my name. So I decided to come here to have a civil ceremony performed. She realises Alice most intensely, and brings her closer to me than I ever felt her, so that instead of in any way separating me from her, it unites me more closely, while she can work through us combined more powerfully than through me alone. The lady's name is Rosamond Dale Owen. She is the daughter of Robert Dale Owen, and granddaughter of Robert Owen—both men who were celebrated in their day, the former especially so. I am sure you would like her if you knew her. I am obliged to stay here for the fortnight's residence that is required by law, and shall then probably be a fortnight or three weeks more between London and Paris, reaching Haifa, I hope, somewhere about the end of September."

This prospect was never to be realised. The marriage took place, to the great astonishment of many friends who only heard it when it was announced by the papers, and to whom naturally the reasons for this step were unknown. And he had not been married more than a day or two when he was seized with the painful illness of which he died, so that the lady, who thus forsook her country and her home to help in his sacred mission, as he understood it, found herself almost from the moment of her marriage confined to the functions of a nurse, perhaps not less sacred, and which she discharged with the utmost devotion. In a second letter to Mrs Wynne Finch, before this event, in which Laurence expressed a grateful appreciation of her kind and affectionate reception of a piece of intelligence which could scarcely be agreeable to her, and understanding of his motives—he insists still further upon the peculiar circumstances under which he acted :—

"Your letter was a great comfort to me, for it showed me that you understood my motives. It is very difficult for people to realise that my marriage can actually draw me closer and cement more firmly my spiritual tie with Alice than ever ; but we are discovering so many mysteries unknown to the world. I should have been myself the last person to think it possible a year ago. I am sorry I shall not have an opportunity of explaining it in a way that is impossible in a letter, but of this you may be quite

sure, that the only difference it will make in our relations
to each other will be to increase the warmth of my love
for you. It will be very kind of you to tell [here various
friends are mentioned by name], and try and explain that
this does not imply any want of faithfulness to Alice's
memory, but is, in fact, only carrying out her wishes. It is
a duty imposed upon me by the necessities of the situation.
As the number of people, especially women, increases with
whom I have to deal, it has become absolutely necessary for
her to have a human assistant of her own sex. She gets so
exhausted with the amount of work she has to do, that I
feel her fatigue. It is a great mistake to suppose that
beings in the invisible have an unlimited supply of nervous
magnetism : they get tired just as we do."

Explanations almost identical with the above were made
to Mrs Walker and to various other friends.

The marriage took place at Malvern on the 16th August
1888, and the above letter is the last I have from his own
hand. A few days after their marriage Laurence and his
new wife went to Surbiton to pay a visit to the always
kind friends of a former period of life, Mr and Mrs Walker,
who had so tenderly befriended Alice Oliphant in California, and whose constant friendship had followed Laurence
through every vicissitude. They had scarcely arrived
there when he was attacked by illness so violent as to put
his life in immediate danger. And in future all the correspondence that concerned him consists of a series of
bulletins, the first of which is dated from Mr Walker's
house at Surbiton. "My husband had a most dangerous
crisis yesterday and the night before," Mrs Rosamond
Oliphant wrote, on the 29th August. "The attack has
been malignant pleurisy : the doctors gave us almost no
hope, and are astonished at the turn for the better, but
I feel assured that the unseen powers guarding my
dear husband have lifted him up." From this time till
the end of October he, his wife, and his Bulgarian servant Yani, remained in the house of these invaluable
and devoted friends, who, though with sickness and
trouble of their own in their family, afforded every alle-

viation that kindness and friendship could give to the
sufferer. Such friends few men secure for themselves.
Nor was it even made easier to Mr and Mrs Walker by
kindred beliefs or discipleship. The bond between them
was one of human affection alone, and unceasing bounty and
goodness on their part to him who still lived and suffered,
as to her whom they had loved and sheltered in her Californian exile. The record of such a good deed, continuous
through months of helplessness, is almost a unique one.

Better and better as the time went on were the sanguine accounts that were given of him week after week
by the strong faith of the wife whose confidence in "the
unseen powers" was so undoubting; but she was yet
obliged to allow from time to time that his progress was
slow. In the beginning of November, a change of air
being considered desirable, he was removed to York
House, Twickenham, the interesting historical mansion
inhabited by other kind friends, Sir Mountstuart and
Lady Grant Duff, to which Laurence had a cordial invitation, and where the sad yet still sanguine party were
housed in a suite of beautiful and spacious rooms, with
one of the most charming of English landscapes—the
softly flowing Thames on one side, the great trees and
velvet lawns on the other—under their windows. Their
hostess gave up her own sitting-room to the comfort of
the invalid, then able to be up for some hours every day,
and again the hopes of the anxious group surrounding him
rose high. He had been condemned by all the doctors
consulted, who considered his case hopeless from the first;
but the hopes of the sufferer, and those immediately about
him, were fixed on other help than those of medicine.
While he was at York House, Mr Haskett Smith, one
of the gentlemen who had been associated with him for
some years at Haifa—his right hand and most trusted
helper there—was summoned to his sick-bed, and it was
hoped for a time that the power in him, combined with
that of Mrs Oliphant, might still suffice to work the mir-
acle they looked for. It did so, they flattered themselves,
at least to the extent of keeping the patient free to a
great degree from pain. The physician who attended him

is reported to have said that "he had never known a case before in which the patient had not suffered weeks of agony, yet so far as this part of his disease went, he suffered almost no pain."

All the signs, however, which buoyed his attendants up, his own cheerful and patient confidence, and the determined faith which would not acknowledge any possible failing, had at last to give way to the certainty which could not be ignored. Throughout his long illness Laurence had been to a considerable extent brought back, out of the close circle of believers and mystical experimentalists who had surrounded him on his return from Haifa in the beginning of the year — to the friends of his life, from many of whom he received visits while he lay, slowly dying as everybody believed, but as full of humour, of interest in life, of genial talk as ever, making that chamber of sickness the brightest of reception-rooms, and leaving the most characteristic impression of his own always engaging and brilliant individuality upon his visitors. This had never altogether ceased to be the case at any time, but it revived in the most affecting and beautiful way in this last chapter of his life, in which not only his intellectual gifts and perceptions, but the delightful light-heartedness and fun, to use a familiar but most expressive word, which had made intercourse with him a continual exhilaration, came back to him with all their original freshness. Even his wife, who would naturally be little disposed to dwell upon that side of his character, speaks of herself in the midst of the long watches of these weary nights as " more amused with his wit " than she had ever been with any one before. As the conclusion drew nearer, the brightness of his outlook did but increase. It had been for some time a heavy thought to him that he might linger for years as a hopeless invalid confined to his bed: but even that feeling disappeared a few weeks before the end in the cheerful conviction that " I can carry on Christ's work on a sick-bed, if He so wishes it, as if I were well."

That dear and sacred name was ever on his tongue. There had been times in his life when he had spoken it with an accent of perhaps less reverence than was con-

genial to listeners probably less devout than he, but holding a more absolute view of our Lord's position and work
—as there had been times when he had called himself not
a Christian, in the ordinary meaning of the word.   But no
one could doubt now of his entire and loving reception of
that name as his own highest hope as well as that of all
the world. A day or two before his death he called his
faithful nurse early in the morning, probably in that rising
of the energies which comes with the brightness of the day,
and told her that he was "unspeakably happy."   "Christ
has touched me.   He has held me in His arms.   I am
changed—He has changed me.   Never again can I be the
same, for His power has cleansed me; I am a new man."
"Then he looked at me yearningly," she adds, "and said,
'Do you understand?'"   As he lay there dozing, smiling,
with the look of this exultation never leaving his face
through the long last hours that followed, he was heard to
hum and sing in snatches the hymn, "Safe in the arms of
Jesus."   Who knows where he had learnt it?—perhaps
at some American "revival" or camp meeting, where the
keen observer would catch up unawares and with a smile
at himself the homely strain, which thus floated back to
the memory of the dying the hymn of the humblest believer, the simplest certainty of a faith unencumbered with
any new lights.

Lady Grant Duff has told me that when he lay in the
last weakness, in the wintry noon of his dying day, his
last words were for "more light": one wonders whether
because the darkness was really gaining on him, or because of some wandering recollection in the confused
musings of a mind shut up from all immediate influences,
of the other great intelligence which is recorded in history
to have made that piteous appeal.   "His last conscious
moment on Sunday," adds his wife, "was one of hope and
effort lifewards."   The actual end was complete and perfect peace.   "He passed away as into a tranquil sleep,
and woke four hours after in another world, or rather
under another form, without having tasted death either
physically or spiritually."   Thus this extraordinary, varied,
and noble life came to an end.

Sufficient time has now elapsed since then to permit a summary which it would have been difficult to make at the moment of one of the most interesting men of his time,—an embodiment in many ways at once of its eager movement, curiosities, and enthusiasm, and of its impatience with the conditions in which the social life of an almost extreme civilisation is cast. The central fact of his life, his renunciation of all that the world could give at a moment when everything seemed possible to him, in order that he might "live the life," and do something towards the bringing in of a higher state and purified ideal, will always remain the fact most interesting in it. Few are the men at any portion of the world's history who have been able to make such a sacrifice ; and it does not detract from it that he was, at the moment of making it, filled with that disgust of the imperfections and falsehoods of society to which the idealist is prone : for he loved society while he hated it, and in every inclination and desire belonged to that world in which all that is most brilliant and beautiful is included with so much that is contemptible and base. He had no ascetic tendency, and esteemed honour and social elevation as much as any man, yet was ready, without a moment's hesitation, to throw them all from him for the sake of what seemed to him a better way. He loved variety, change, movement, the excitement of the new and unknown, yet accepted the monotony of dreary labour, the society of a narrow handful of undistinguished people, the obliteration of every hope, in a high ambition and fervent desire to ameliorate and purify the world. His teaching may not come to much among the many wandering voices which have echoed in the wilderness ; but he himself is more than many books, or a world of sermons : and is perhaps in himself the lesson—at once of greatness and insufficiency, of the noble wisdom of the heart, and the limitations of human reason and power—which he had to teach to the world.

He gave up for what he believed to be the work of God everything that he had formerly thought most worth having in the world—renouncing all, not sadly or painfully, but with all the joyousness and cordial warmth of a nature ful of sunshine. No idea of penance or voluntary humiliation was in his thoughts, as nothing more unlike an ascetic could be imagined than his life. He loved life, and enjoyed it, and was amused and interested by every detail of it, as much when he was following his mud-cart in the American wilds as when he was dining with princes or comparing experiences with statesmen. But to him it was the most simple and natural of impulses to throw aside whatever stood in the way of the work to which he believed God called him, and that without even a passing thought of merit in the renunciation. His sacrifices did not weigh upon his mind as they did upon ours. To us they seem unparalleled self-abnegation, to him the simplest necessity. Words are not sufficient to mark the singular contrast. The priests and martyrs of the old ages had even too much conscience of what they were doing, and never made light of the sacrifice; but the nineteenth century has this advantage over its predecessors which we call the ages of faith. It is all for materialism, for profit, for personal advantage—the most self-interested, the least ideal of ages. But when, here and there, a generous spirit, emancipated from these bonds, rises above the age, his sacrifice is no longer marked with gloom, or made into an operation of pain; it is a willing offering,—more than willing, unconsidered, lavish, gay, the joyous giving up, without a backward look or thought, of everything for the love of God—except the love of man, warmed and mellowed by the divine flame which, with no cloud of smoke or odour of burnt-offering, ascends clear and brilliant as light itself to the realms above.

Of such were both Laurence and Alice Oliphant—she, if possible, more fearless, less considerate of accessories and worldly consequences, than he, with that absolutism and superiority to restraining possibilities which belong to a woman. And yet, I think, complete as their self-sacrifice was, that they never lost a wholesome hold of life and its common laws until the supreme moment when they ascended into their mountain solitude, entered their chamber, and shut to their door, and attained to what they felt to be the climax of their existence, the final proof of all their theories and carrying out of their hopes, the strange mutual ecstasy of inspiration and composition which produced 'Sympneumata,'—that book so unlike either of them, so involved in diction, so wild and wandering in thought, as if two crystal springs had united to form a turbid and overshadowed pool. But neither of this does it become an outside and wondering spectator to speak. For this mystic work so strangely produced—the only child, as it were, of these two clear and elevated souls —has been a breathing of light and comfort to many, and carried to some aching hearts a consciousness of, and belief in, the world unseen, which other teachings have not sufficed to give. Such evidence in its favour is more than all the confused intellect, vainly trying to bring it to a human standard of reason, can say against it.

They lie separated by land and sea,—she in the little Friedhof at Haifa, among the friendly German folk, who still give a kind of worship to her dear and gracious name; he in the cemetery at Twickenham, on the edge of that greater world which so soon forgets, and makes so few pilgrimages. But the generation, not only of his contemporaries but of their children, must be exhausted indeed before the name of Laurence Oliphant will cease to conjure up memories of all that was most brilliant in intellect, most tender in heart, most trenchant in attack, most eager to succour in life. There has been no such bold satirist, no such cynic philosopher, no such devoted enthusiast, no adventurer so daring and gay, no religious teacher so absolute and visionary, in this Victorian age, now beginning to round towards its end, and which holds in its long and brilliant roll no more attractive and interesting name.

INDEX.

PRINTED BY WILLIAM BLACKWOOD AND SONS, EDINBURGH.